continued . . .

"A great, fun romance, an offbeat mix of old-fashioned rural magics, contemporary life (complete with Wal-Mart and comic book shops), and magical sword-wielding warriors."   —*Locus*

"The character development is flawless, the plot inventive, and the pace defies readers to put the book down . . . This one is a winner and shows there is still plenty of room for surprises in a genre riddled with tired replays."   —*Monsters and Critics*

"A wildly entertaining world."   —*Darque Reviews*

Praise for the Kate Daniels novels

MAGIC BLEEDS

"Ilona Andrews is one of the few authors whose books just keep getting better. A series can sometimes stagnate . . . Ilona, though, has no such trouble."   —*Romance Reviews Today*

"Ilona Andrews does it again . . . *Magic Bleeds* delivers on the promise of 'one hell of a good read.' You will not be disappointed!"
                —ParaNormal Romance.org

MAGIC STRIKES

"Andrews's crisp dialogue and layered characterization make the gut-wrenching action of this first-person thrill ride all the more intense . . . mesmerizing."   —*Romantic Times* (★★★★✦)

"Andrews blends action-packed fantasy with myth and legend, keeping readers enthralled."   —*Darque Reviews*

"Ilona Andrews's best novel to date, cranking up the action, danger, and magic . . . Gritty, sword-clashing action and flawless characterizations will bewitch fans old and new alike."
                —*Sacramento Book Review*

"Write faster . . . I absolutely love the relationship between Curran and Kate—I laugh out loud [at] the witty sarcasm and one-liners, and the sexual tension building between the couples drives me to my knees knowing I'll have to wait for another book."   —*SFRevu*

MAGIC BURNS

"Fans of Carrie Vaughn and Patricia Briggs will appreciate this fast-paced, action-packed urban fantasy full of magic, vampires, werebeasties, and things that go bump in the night."
—*Monsters and Critics*

"With all her problems, secrets, and prowess both martial and magical, Kate is a great kick-ass heroine, a tough girl with a heart, and her adventures . . . are definitely worth checking out."
—*Locus*

"[*Magic Burns*] hooked me completely. With a fascinating, compelling plot, a witty, intelligent heroine, a demonic villain, and clever, wry humor throughout, this story has it all."
—*Fresh Fiction*

"The sexual tension Kate emits has me gritting my teeth."
—*SFRevu*

"If you enjoy Laurell K. Hamilton's early Anita Blake or the works of Patricia Briggs and Kim Harrison, you need to add Ilona Andrews to your reading list."
—*LoveVampires*

MAGIC BITES

"Treat yourself to a splendid new urban fantasy . . . I am looking forward to the next book in the series or anything else Ilona Andrews writes."
—Patricia Briggs, #1 *New York Times* bestselling author of *River Marked*

"Andrews's edgy series stands apart from similar fantasies . . . owing to its complex world-building and skilled characterizations."
—*Library Journal*

"Fans of urban fantasy will delight in Ilona Andrews's alternate-universe Atlanta."
—*Fresh Fiction*

"A unique world laced with a thick plot full of strife, betrayal, and mystery."
—*Romance Junkies*

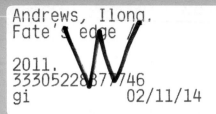

FATE'S
EDGE

ILONA ANDREWS

ACE BOOKS, NEW YORK

THE BERKLEY PUBLISHING GROUP
Published by the Penguin Group
Penguin Group (USA) Inc.
375 Hudson Street, New York, New York 10014, USA

Penguin Group (Canada), 90 Eglinton Avenue East, Suite 700, Toronto, Ontario M4P 2Y3, Canada
(a division of Pearson Penguin Canada Inc.)
Penguin Books Ltd., 80 Strand, London WC2R 0RL, England
Penguin Group Ireland, 25 St. Stephen's Green, Dublin 2, Ireland (a division of Penguin Books Ltd.)
Penguin Group (Australia), 250 Camberwell Road, Camberwell, Victoria 3124, Australia
(a division of Pearson Australia Group Pty. Ltd.)
Penguin Books India Pvt. Ltd., 11 Community Centre, Panchsheel Park, New Delhi—110 017, India
Penguin Group (NZ), 67 Apollo Drive, Rosedale, Auckland 0632, New Zealand
(a division of Pearson New Zealand Ltd.)
Penguin Books (South Africa) (Pty.) Ltd., 24 Sturdee Avenue, Rosebank, Johannesburg 2196,
South Africa

Penguin Books Ltd., Registered Offices: 80 Strand, London WC2R 0RL, England

This is a work of fiction. Names, characters, places, and incidents either are the product of the authors'
imaginations or are used fictitiously, and any resemblance to actual persons, living or dead, business
establishments, events, or locales is entirely coincidental. The publisher does not have any control
over and does not assume any responsibility for author or third-party websites or their content.

FATE'S EDGE

An Ace Book / published by arrangement with Ilona Andrews, Inc.

PRINTING HISTORY
Ace mass-market edition / December 2011

ISBN: 978-0-441-02086-7

ACE
Ace Books are published by The Berkley Publishing Group,
a division of Penguin Group (USA) Inc.,
375 Hudson Street, New York, New York 10014.
ACE and the "A" design are trademarks of Penguin Group (USA) Inc.

PRINTED IN THE UNITED STATES OF AMERICA

10 9 8 7 6 5 4 3 2

To Anastasia and Helen

Acknowledgments

Fate's Edge was a fun book to write, but even the fun books take a lot of work. We're grateful to Anne Sowards for continuing to edit us and to Nancy Yost, our agent, for continuing to represent us despite our best efforts to drive them both to an insane asylum.

We'd like to thank the following people for making the book a reality: production editor Michelle Kasper and assistant production editor Andromeda Macri for bringing it all together, editorial assistant Kat Sherbo for heroically dealing with our ornery e-mails and keeping us on schedule, artist Victoria Vebell and cover designer Annette Fiore DeFex for creating a gorgeous cover, interior designer Kristin del Rosario for making the book look beautiful between the covers, copy editors Sara and Bob Schwager for making sure the narrative was consistent, and publicists Rosanne Romanello and Brady McReynolds for tirelessly promoting the book.

Special thanks go out to Deric Gant for his knowledge of scripture and charismatic preachers. We'd also like to thank Jill Myles, Meljean Brook, and Jeaniene Frost for many hours of e-mail and phone therapy. We'd also like to thank Jessie Mihalik for helping us move to Texas and find this awesome house, where most of the book was written. We'd like to thank each other for being very patient and avoiding divorce despite the AC breaking three times in triple-digit summer heat.

Finally, we'd like to thank our readers for following our stories.

PROLOGUE

IF she had only one word to describe Dominic Milano, it would be "unflappable," Audrey Callahan reflected. Stocky, hard, balding—he looked like he had just walked out of central casting after successfully landing the role of "bulldog-jawed older detective." He owned Milano Investigations, and under his supervision, the firm ran like clockwork. No emergency rattled Dominic. He never raised his voice. Nothing knocked him off his stride. Before moving to the Pacific Northwest, he'd retired from the Miami Police Department with more than a thousand homicide cases under his belt. He'd been there and done that, so nothing surprised him.

That was why watching his furry eyebrows creep up on his forehead was so satisfying.

Dominic plucked the top photograph from the stack on his desk. In it, Spenser "Spense" Bailey jogged down the street. The next shot showed Spense bending over. The next one caught him in a classic baseball-pitch pose, right leg raised, leaning back, a tennis ball in his fingers. Which would be fine and dandy, except that according to his doctor, Spense suffered from a herniated disk in his spine. He was restocking a warehouse when a walk-behind forklift got away from him, and the accident caused him constant, excruciating pain. He could frequently be seen limping around the neighborhood with a cane or a walker. He needed help to get into a car, and he couldn't drive because the injured disk pinched the nerve in his right leg.

Dominic glanced at Audrey. "These are great. We've

been following this guy for weeks, and nothing. How did you get these?"

"A very short tennis skirt. He hobbles past a tennis court every Tuesday and Thursday on the way to his physical-therapy sessions." The hardest part was hitting the ball so it would fly over the tall fence. A loud gasp and a run with an extra bounce in her step, and she had him. "Keep looking. It gets better."

Dominic flipped through the stack. The next photo showed Spense with a goofy grin on his face carrying two cups of coffee, maneuvering between tables at Starbucks with the grace of a deer.

"You bought him coffee?" Dominic's eyebrows crawled a little higher.

"Of course not. He bought me coffee. And a fruit salad." Audrey grinned.

"You really enjoy doing this, don't you?" Dominic reflected.

She nodded. "He's a liar and a cheat, who's been out of work for months on the company's dime." And he thought he was so smart. He was practically begging to be cut down to size, and she had just the right pruning shears. Chop-chop.

Dominic moved the coffee picture aside and stopped. "Is this what I think this is?"

The next image showed Spense grasping a man in a warm-up suit from behind and tossing him backward over his head onto a mat.

"That would be Spense demonstrating a German suplex for me." Audrey gave him a bright smile. "Apparently he's an amateur MMA fighter. He goes to do his physical therapy on the first floor, and, after the session is over, he walks up the stairs to spar."

Dominic put his hands together and sighed.

Something was wrong. She leaned back. "Suddenly you don't seem happy."

Dominic grimaced. "I look at you, and I'm confused. People who do the best in our line of work are unremarkable. They look just like anyone else, and they're easily forgettable, so suspects don't pay attention to them. They have some law-enforcement experience, usually at least some college. You're too pretty, your hair is too red, your eyes are too big, you laugh too loud, and, according to your transcripts, you barely graduated from high school."

Warning sirens wailed in her head. Dominic required proof of high-school graduation before employment, so she brought him both her diploma and her senior-year transcript. For some reason, he had bothered to pull her file and review the contents. Her driver's license was first-rate because it was real. Her birth certificate and her high-school record would pass a cursory inspection, but if he dug any deeper, he'd find smoke. And if he took her fingerprints, he would find criminal records in two states.

Audrey kept the smile firmly in place. "I can't help having big eyes."

Dominic sighed again. "Here's the deal: I hire freelancers to save money. My full-time guys are experienced and educated, which means I have to pay them a decent wage for their time. Unless there is serious money involved, I can't afford for them to sit on a tough suspect for months, waiting for him to slip up. They get four weeks to crack a case. After that, I have to outsource this kind of stuff to freelancers like you because I can pay you per job. An average freelancer might close one case every couple of months. It's a good part-time gig for most people."

He was telling her things she already knew. Nothing to do but nod.

"You've been freelancing for me for five months. You closed fourteen cases. That's a case every two weeks. You made twenty grand." Dominic fixed her with his unblinking stare. "I can't afford to keep you on as a freelancer."

What? "I made you money!"

He held up his hand. "You're too expensive, Audrey. The only way this professional relationship is going to survive is if you come to work for me full-time."

She blinked.

"I'll start you off at thirty grand a year with benefits.

Here's the paperwork." Dominic handed her a manila envelope. "If you decide to take me up on it, I'll see you Monday."

"I'll think about it."

"You do that."

Audrey swiped the file. Her grifter instincts said, "Play it cool," but then, she didn't have to con people anymore. Not those who hired her, anyway. "Thank you. Thank you so much. This means the world to me."

"Everybody needs a chance, Audrey. You earned yours. We'd be glad to have you." Dominic extended his hand over the desk. She shook it and left the office.

A real job. With benefits. Holy crap.

She took the stairs, jogging down the steps to burn off some excitement. A real job being one of the good guys. How about that?

If her parents ever found out, they would flip.

AUDREY drove down Rough Ocean Road away from Olympia. Her blue Honda powered on through the gray drizzle that steadily soaked the west side of Cascades. A thick blanket of dense clouds smothered the sky, turning the early evening gloomy and dark. Trees flanked the road: majestic Douglas firs with long emerald needles; black cottonwoods, tall and lean, catching the rain with large branches; red alders with silver-gray bark that almost glowed in the dusk.

A mile and a half ahead, a lonely subdivision of identical houses waited, cradled in the fold of the hill; meanwhile, the road was empty. Nothing but the trees.

Audrey glanced at the clock. Thirty-two minutes so far, not counting the time it took her to stop at a convenience store to get some teriyaki jerky for Ling and the time she spent driving around to different pharmacies. Getting to work would mean an actual commute.

She loved the job with Milano's investigative agency. She loved every moment of it, from quietly hiding in a car to watch a suspect to running a con on the conmen. They thought they were slick. They didn't know what slick was.

To be fair, most of the suspects she ran across were con-men of opportunity. They got hurt on the job and liked the disability, or they got tangled in an affair and were too afraid or too arrogant to tell their spouses. They didn't see what they were doing as a con. They viewed it as a little white lie, the easiest path out of a tough situation. Most of them went about their deceptions in amateur ways. Audrey had been running cons since she could talk. It wasn't a fair fight, but then, in the world of grifters, "fair" had no meaning.

Ahead, the road forked. The main street rolled right, up the hill, toward the subdivision, while the smaller road branched left, ducking under the canopy of trees. Audrey checked the rearview mirror. The ribbon of pavement behind her stretched into the distance, deserted. The coast was clear.

She smoothly made the turn onto the smaller road and braced herself. Panic punched her in the stomach, right in the solar plexus. Audrey gasped. The world swirled in a diz-zying rush, and she let go of the wheel for a second to keep from wrenching the vehicle off the pavement. Pain followed, sharp, prickling every inch of her skin with red-hot needles, and although Audrey had expected it, the ache still caught her by surprise. Pressure squeezed her, then, just like that, all discomfort vanished. She had passed through the boundary.

A warm feeling spread through Audrey, flowing from her chest all the way to her fingertips. She smiled and snapped her fingers. With a warm tingle, tendrils of green glow swirled around her hand. Magic. Also known as flash. She let it die and kept driving.

Back on the main road, in the city of Olympia, in the State of Washington, magic didn't exist. People who lived there tried to pretend that it did. They flirted with the idea of psychics and street magicians, but they had never encoun-tered the real thing. Most of them wouldn't even see the side road she took. For them it simply wasn't there—the woods continued uninterrupted. Every time Audrey crossed into their world, the boundary stripped her magic from her in a rush of pain. That's why people like her called that place the Broken—when you passed into it, you gave up a part of yourself, and it left you feeling incomplete. Broken like a clock with a missing gear.

Far ahead, past mountains and miles of rough terrain, another world waited, a mirror to the Broken, full of magic but light on technology. Well, not exactly true, Audrey reflected. The Weird had plenty of complex technology, but it had evolved in a different direction. Most of it functioned with the aid of magic. In the Weird, the power of your magic and the color of your flash determined the course of your life. The brighter you flashed, the better. If you flashed white, you could rub elbows with bluebloods, the Weird's aristocratic families.

The Weird, like the Broken, was a place of rules and laws. That's why Audrey preferred to live here, in the no-man's land between the two dimensions. The locals called it the Edge, and they were right. It was on the edge of both worlds, a place without countries or cops, where the castoffs like her washed ashore. Connecting the two dimensions like a secret overpass, the Edge took everyone. Swindlers, thieves, crazed separatists, clannish families, all were welcome, all were dirt-poor, and all kept to themselves. The Edgers gave no quarter and expected no sympathy.

The road turned to dirt. The trees had changed, too. Ancient spruces spread broad branches from massive buttressed trunks, their limbs dripping with long emerald green beards of tangled moss. Towering narrow hemlocks thrust into the sky, their roots cushioned in ferns. Blue haze clung to narrow spaces between the trunks, hiding otherworldly things with glowing eyes who prowled in search of prey.

As Audrey drove through, bright yellow blossoms of Edger primrose sensed the vibration of the car and snapped open with faint puffs of luminescent pollen. By day the flowers stayed closed and harmless. At night, it was a different story. Take a couple of puffs in your face, and pretty soon you'd forget where you were or why you were here. A couple of weeks ago, Rook, one of the local Edger idiots, got drunk and fell asleep near a patch of them. They found him two days later, sitting up on a tree stump butt naked and covered in ants. This was an old forest, nourished by magic. It didn't suffer fools, gladly or otherwise.

She steered her Honda up the narrow road, past her driveway, forcing it to climb higher and higher up the mountain. A shadow loomed ahead, blocking the way. She flicked on her brights. An old pine had fallen across the road. She'd have to hoof it to Gnome's house. The road was muddy with recent rain, and she had new shoes on. Oh well. Shoes could be cleaned.

Audrey parked, pulled the emergency brake as high as it would go, swiped the plastic bags off the seat, and climbed out. Mud squished under the soles of her shoes. She climbed over the tree and trudged up the narrow road, following it all the way up to the top of the mountain. By the time she made it to the clearing, the sky had grown dim. Gnome's house, a large two-story jumble of weird rooms sticking out at random angles, was all but lost in the gloom.

"Gnome!"

No answer.

"Gnooome!"

Nothing.

He was inside. He had to be—his old beat-up Chevy sat on the left side of the house, and Gnome rarely left the top of the mountain anyway. Audrey walked up to the door and tried the handle. Locked. She put her hand to the keyhole and pushed. The magic slid from her fingers in translucent currents of pale green and wove together, sliding into the keyhole. That old ornery knucklehead would probably kill her for this. The lock clicked. Audrey eased the door open smoothly, making sure it didn't creak, more out of habit than real need.

Flash was a pure expression of one's magic. But most people born with it had a talent or two hidden up their sleeve. Some Edgers were cursers; some foretold the future. She opened doors.

Audrey passed through the narrow hallway into the main

room, sectioned off by tall shelves filled with Gnome's knickknacks and merchandise. Being a local fence, he had enough inventory to put Costco to shame. He also functioned as an emergency general store. If Edgers needed deodorant or soap in a hurry and didn't want to drive all the way across the boundary, they stopped at Gnome's. And ended up paying ten bucks for a tube of toothpaste.

A fit of wet, hoarse coughing came from deeper within the house. Audrey slipped between the shelves, like a silent shadow, and finally stepped out into the clear space in the middle of the room.

Gnome, a huge bear of a man, sat slumped over in his stuffed chair, an open book on a desk in front of him and a shotgun by his chair. Flushed skin, tangled hair, feverish eyes, all hunkered down in a blanket. He looked like a mess.

"There you are."

He peered at her with watering, bloodshot eyes. "What the hell are you—" Another fit of coughing shook his large frame.

"That sounds awful."

"What are you—" Gnome sneezed.

"I brought you goodies." She pulled a box of decongestant pills out of the bag and put it on the desk. "Look, I've got canned chicken soup, Theraflu, and here are some cough drops, and here is a box of Puffs tissues with lotion, so you don't scrub all of the skin off that big beak of yours."

He stared at her, speechless. Now that was something. If she'd had a camera, she would've taken a picture.

"And this here, this is good stuff." Audrey tapped the plastic cup of Magic Vaporizer. "I had to hunt it down—they don't make it as much anymore, so I could only get a generic version. Look, you boil some water and put these drops in here and inhale—clears your nose right up. I'll fix you one, then you can yell at me."

Five minutes later, she presented him with a steaming vaporizer and made him breathe it in. One, two, three . . .

Gnome sucked in his first breath. "Christ."

"Told you." Audrey set a hot bowl of chicken soup on his desk. "Works wonders."

"How did you know I was sick?"

"Patricia came down the mountain yesterday, and we ran into each other at the main road. She said you had a cold and mentioned that you undercharged her for the lanterns by twenty bucks."

"What?"

Audrey smiled. "That's how I knew it was bad. Besides, I was tired of hearing you hack and cough all night. The sound rolls down the mountain, you know. You're keeping Ling awake."

"You can't hear me all the way down there."

"That's what you think. Take this generic or Theraflu before bed. Either will knock you out. The red pills are daytime."

Gnome gave her a suspicious look. "How much is all this gonna cost me?"

"Don't worry about it."

Gnome shrugged his heavy shoulders and put a spoonful of soup into his mouth. "This doesn't mean you're getting a discount."

Audrey heaved a mock sigh. "Oh well. I guess I'll have to ply you with sexual favors, then."

Gnome choked on the soup. "I'm old enough to be your grandfather!"

Audrey winked at him, gathering the empty bags. "But you're not."

"Get out of here, you and your craziness."

"Okay, okay, I'm going." He was fun to tease, and she was in such a good mood.

"What is with you anyway?" he asked. "Why are you grinning?"

"I've got a job. With benefits."

"Legit?"

"Yes."

"Well, congratulations," Gnome said. "Now go on. I'm sick of looking at your face."

"I'll see you later."

She left the house and slogged her way through the mud

down to her car. Gnome was a gruff old bear, but he was kind in his own way. Besides, he was the only neighbor she had within two miles. Nobody was around to help them. Either they took care of each other, or they toughed it out on their own.

Backing the Honda down the mountain in the gloom turned out to be harder than Audrey thought. She finally steered the vehicle to the fork where the narrow road leading to her place split off and took the turn. Thick roots burrowed under the road, and her Honda rolled over the bulges, careening and swaying, until it finally popped out into the clearing. On the right, the ground dropped off sharply, plunging down the side of the mountain. On the left, a squat, pale building sat in the shadow of an old spruce. It was a simple structure—a huge stone block of a roof resting on sturdy stone columns that guarded the wooden walls of the house within like the bars of a stone cage. Each three-foot-wide column bore a carving: dragons and men caught in the heat of a battle. A wide bas-relief decorated the roof as well, showing a woman in a chariot pulled by birds with snake heads. The woman gazed down on the slaughter like a goddess from Heaven.

Nobody knew who had built the ruins or why. They dotted that part of the Edge, a tower here, a temple there, gutted by time and the elements, and covered with moss. The Edgers, being poor and thrifty, knew better than to let them go to waste. They built wooden walls inside the stone frameworks, put in indoor plumbing and electricity illegally siphoned from the neighboring city or provided by generators, and moved right in. If any archaic gods took offense, they had yet to do anything about it.

Audrey parked the car under an ancient scarred maple and turned off the engine. Home, sweet home.

A ball of gray fur dropped off the maple branch and landed on her hood.

Audrey jumped in her seat. Jesus.

The raccoon danced up and down on the hood, chittering in outrage, bright eyes glowing with orange like two bloody moons.

"Ling the Merciless! You get off my car this instant!"

The raccoon spun in place, her gray fur standing on end, put her hand-paws on the windshield, and tried to bite the glass.

"What is it with you?" Audrey popped the car door open.

Ling scurried off the car and leaped into her lap, squirming and coughing. Audrey glanced up. The curtains on her kitchen window were parted slightly. A hair-thin line of bright yellow light spilled through the gap.

Somebody was in her house.

Audrey slipped from the seat, dropping Ling gently to the ground, circled the car, and opened the hatchback. A tan tarp waited inside. She jerked it aside and pulled out an Excalibur crossbow. It had set her back nine hundred bucks of hard-earned money, and it was worth every penny. Audrey cocked the crossbow and padded to the house, silent and quick. A couple of seconds, and she pressed against the wall next to the door. She tried the handle. Locked.

Who breaks into a house and locks the door?

She peeled from the wall and circled the building, moving fast on her toes. At the back, she slipped between the stone framework and the wooden wall of the house and felt around for the hidden latch. It sprang open under the pressure of her fingers. She edged the secret door open and padded inside, into the walk-in closet, and out into her bedroom. The house had only three rooms: a long, rectangular bedroom, an equally long bathroom, and the rest of it a wide-open space, most of which served as her living room and kitchen, with the stove, fridge, and counters at the north wall.

Audrey peeked out of the doorway. An older man with curly reddish brown hair stood at the kitchen stove, mixing batter in a glass bowl, his slightly stooped back turned to her.

She would know that posture anywhere.

Audrey raised her crossbow and took a step into the living room.

The man reached for a bag of flour sitting on the counter. Audrey squeezed the trigger. The string snapped with a satisfying twang. The bolt punched through the bag inches from the man's fingers.

The man turned and grinned at her, his blue eyes sparking. She knew the smile, too. It was his con smile.

"Hi, munchkin."

Audrey let her crossbow point to the floor. "Hi, Dad."

"A good shot." Seamus Callahan bent down, looking at the shaft protruding from the bag of flour. "I'd say you killed it. Bull's-eye."

Audrey set the crossbow down and crossed her arms. Inside her, a tiny pissed-off voice barked, *Get out, get out, get out . . .* He was in her house, and she had to clench her fingers on her arms just to keep herself from attacking him and pushing him out.

But she was Seamus's daughter, and twenty-three years of grifting made her voice calm and light. "How did you find me?"

"I have my ways." Seamus opened the bag and poured some flour into the batter. "I'm making my patented silver-dollar pancakes. You remember those, don't you?"

"Sure, Dad. I remember." He was in *her* kitchen, touching *her* things. She would bleach it all after he was gone.

Ling slipped from the back door, scurried around her feet, and showed Seamus her teeth.

"Your little critter doesn't like me much," he said, pouring the batter into a sizzling pan.

"She has good instincts."

Seamus looked up at her, blue eyes like two flax petals under bushy red eyebrows. "There is no need for that."

Screw it. "What do you want?"

Seamus spread his arms, a spatula in his right hand. "My daughter disappears for four years, doesn't tell me where she is going, doesn't call, doesn't write. What, I don't have a right to be concerned? All we had was a little note."

Yeah, right. "The note said, 'Don't look for me.' That was a clue."

"Your mom is worried, kiddo. We were all worried."

Get out, get out, get out. "What do you want?"

Seamus heaved a sigh. "Can we not have a meal like a normal family?"

"What do you want, Dad?"

"I have a job in West Egypt."

In the Weird. The worlds of the Weird and the Broken had similar geography, but their histories had gone entirely different ways. In the world without magic, the huge peninsula protruding from the southeastern end of the continent was known as Florida. In the Weird, it was West Egypt, the Alligator to the Cobra and the Hawk of the triple Egyptian crown.

"It won't take but a week. A good solid payoff."

"Not interested."

He sighed again. "I didn't want to bring this up. It's about your brother."

Of course. Why would it ever be about anybody else?

Seamus leaned forward. "There is a facility in California—"

She raised her hands. "I don't want to hear it."

"It's beautiful. It's like a resort." He reached into his jacket. "Look at the pictures. These doctors, they're the best. All we have to do is pull off this one heist, and we can get him in there. I'd do it myself, but it's a three-person job."

"No."

Seamus turned off the stove and shoved the pan aside onto a cold burner. "He is your brother. He loves you, Audrey. We haven't asked anything of you for three years."

"He is an addict, Dad. An *addict*. How many times has he been through rehab? It was eighteen when I left; what's the number now?"

"Audrey . . ."

It was too late. She'd started, and she couldn't stop. "He's had therapy, he's had interventions, he's had doctors and counselors and rehabs, and it hasn't made a damn bit of difference. Do you know why? Because Alex likes being an addict. He has no interest in getting better. He is a dirty lowlife junkie. And you enable him at every turn."

"Audrey!"

"What was the one rule you taught me, Dad? The one rule that we never, ever break? You don't steal from family. He stole Mom's wedding ring and pawned it. He stole from you, he stole from me, he ruined my childhood. All of it going right up his nose or in his mouth. The man never met a drug he didn't like. He doesn't want to get better, and why should he? Mommy and Daddy will always be there to steal him more pills and pick him up off the street. He gets his drugs and all that attention. Hell, why should he quit?"

"He's my child," Seamus said.

"And what am I, Dad? Chopped liver?"

"Look at you!" Seamus raised his arms. "Look, look— you have a nice house, your fridge is full. You don't need any help."

She stared at him.

"Alex is sick. It's an illness. He can't help himself."

"Bullshit! He doesn't want to help himself."

"He'll die."

"Good."

Seamus slapped the counter. "You take that back, Audrey!"

She took a deep breath. "No."

"Fine." He leaned back. "Fine. You live happily in your nice house. Play with your pet. Buy nice things. You do all that while your brother is dying."

She laughed. "Guilt, Dad? Wait, I'll show you guilt."

She stomped to a bookshelf, pulled out a photo album, and slapped it open on the counter in front of him. In the picture, her sixteen-year-old self stared out from a mangled face. Her left eye had swollen shut into a puffy black sack. Dry tracks of blood stained her cheeks, stretching from half a dozen cuts. Her nose was a misshapen bulge. "What is this? Do you remember this?"

Seamus grimaced.

"What, nothing to say? Let me help: this is when my sweet brother traded me to his dealer for some meth. I had to give him all of the money I had on me and the gold chain grandma gave me, and I had to break into a rival drug dealer's lab and steal his stash so I wouldn't be raped. I had to break into a gang house, Dad. If I got caught, they would've killed me in a blink—if I was lucky. And Cory, the dealer? He used me for a punching bag after. He threw me on the ground, and he kicked me in the face and in my stomach until he got tired. I had to beg—beg!—him to let me go. Look at my face. It was two days before my seventeenth birthday. And what did you do, Dad?"

She let it hang. Seamus looked at the window.

"You did nothing. Because I don't matter."

"Audrey, don't say that. Of course you matter. And I spoke to Alex about it."

She gave him a bitter smile. "Yes. I've heard. You told him that if something happened to me, the whole family would suffer because nobody would be left to steal."

"I said it in a way he would understand: if something happened to you, there would be no more drugs."

"Because it's all he cares about." Audrey sighed. "I left four years ago. I didn't cover my tracks—I just ran clear across the bloody continent to the other side. I would've gone to the moon if I could have, but I would've still left you a nice trail to follow because I kept hoping that one day my parents would wake up and realize they had a daughter. It took you this long to find me because you didn't look until you needed me. I spent years stealing and grifting, so you could put him into one rehab after another. I'm done with you. Don't come here. Don't ask me for any favors. It's over."

"This will be the last time," he said quietly. "If you won't do it for me, do it for your mother. You know that if Alex dies, it will kill her. I swear, this is the very last time. I wouldn't be here if I had any choice, Audrey. Just look at the pictures of the job." He pushed some photographs to her across the table.

She glanced down. The first two shots showed some sort of resort. On the third, a white pyramid rose, its golden top gleaming in the sun. A stylized bull carved from reddish stone polished to a gleam stood before the pyramid. "The

Pyramid of Ptah? Are you out of your mind? You want me to go into the Weird and steal something from a pyramid?"

"It can be done."

"People who rob the pyramids in West Egypt die, Dad."

"Please, Audrey. Don't make me beg. Do you want me to get down on my knees? Fine, I can do that."

He would never leave her alone. If she did this job, he'd be back in six months with another and tell her that it would be "the very last time." She had to find a way to end it now and end it so that he wouldn't return.

Audrey leaned forward. "I'll give you a choice. I'll do the job with you, but from that point on we're strangers. You don't have a daughter anymore, and I don't have a father or a mother. If you show up on my land again, I'll shoot you. I'm dead serious, Dad. I will put a bolt through you. Or you can walk away now and keep me as your daughter. Pick. Him or me."

Seamus looked at the image of her bruised face in the photo album.

She waited. Deep inside her, a little girl listened quietly, hoping for the answer that the adult in her knew wouldn't come.

"I'll see you at the end of the road tomorrow at seven," he said, and walked out the door.

The disappointment gripped her so tightly, it hurt. For a few short, pain-filled breaths she just stood there, then she grabbed the pan, burned pancakes and all, burst out the back door, and hurled it over the cliff.

ONE

KALDAR Mar stepped back and critically surveyed the vast three-dimensional map of the Western Continent. It spread on the wall of the private conference room, a jeweled masterpiece of magic and semiprecious stones. Forests of malachite and jade flowed into plains of aventurine and peridot. The plains gave rise to mountains of brown opals with ridges of banded agates and tiger eye, topped by the snowy peaks of moonstone and jasper.

Beautiful. A completely useless waste of money, but beautiful. If it somehow could be stolen . . . you'd need a handcart to transport it and some tools to carve it to pieces. Hmm, also a noise dampener would work wonders here, and this being the Weird, he could probably find someone willing to risk creating a soundproof sigil for the right price. Steal a custodian's uniform, get in, cut the map, wrap each piece in a tarp, load them on the handcart, and push the whole thing right out the front door, while looking disgruntled. Less than twenty minutes for the whole job if the cutter was powerful enough. The map would feed the entire Mar family for a year or more.

Well, what was left of the family.

Kaldar's memory overlaid the familiar patterns of states over the map, ignoring the borders of the Weird's nations. Adrianglia took up a big chunk of the Eastern seaboard, stretching in a long vertical ribbon. In the Broken, it would have consumed most of the states from New York and southern Quebec to Georgia and a small chunk of Alabama. Below it, West Egypt occupied Florida and spread down into Cuba. To the left of Adrianglia, the vast Dukedom of Louisiana mushroomed upward, containing all of Louisiana and a chunk of Alabama in the south, rising to swallow Mississippi and Texarcana, and ending with the coast of the Great Lakes. Beyond that, smaller nations fought it out: the Republic of Texas, the Northern Vast, the Democracy of California . . .

Kaldar had grown up on the fringes of this world, in the Edge, a narrow strip of land between the complex magic of the Weird and the technological superiority of the Broken. Most of his life was spent in the Mire, an enormous swamp, cut off from the rest of the Edge by impassable terrain. The Dukedom of Louisiana dumped its exiles there and killed them when they tried to reenter the Weird. His only escape had been through the Broken. He traveled back and forth, smuggling goods, lying, cheating, making as much money as was humanly possible and dragging it back to the family.

Kaldar stared at the map. Each country had an enemy. Each was knee deep in conflict. But the only war he cared about was happening right in the middle, between the Dukedom of Louisiana and Adrianglia. It was a very quiet, vicious war, fought in secrecy by spies, with no rules and no mercy. On the Adrianglian side, the espionage and its consequences were handled by the Mirror. He supposed if they were in the Broken, the Mirror would be the equivalent of the CIA or FBI, or perhaps both. On the Dukedom of Louisiana's side, the covert war was the province of the secret service known as the Hand. He had watched from the sidelines for years as the two organizations clashed, but watching wasn't enough anymore.

First, the Mirror woke him up at ten till five, and now he spent fifteen minutes waiting. Puzzling.

The heavy wooden door swung open soundlessly, and a woman entered the room. She was short, with a sparse, compact body, wrapped in an expensive blue gown embroidered with silver thread. Kaldar priced the dress out of habit. About five gold doubloons in the Weird, probably a grand and a half or two in the Broken. Expensive and obviously custom tailored. The blue fabric perfectly complemented her skin, the color of hazelnut shells. The dress was meant to communicate power and authority, but she hardly needed it. She moved as if she owned the air he breathed.

Nancy Virai. The head of the Mirror. They had never met—he had not been given that honor, poor Edge rat that he was—but she hardly needed an introduction.

He'd spent the last two years doing small assignments, challenging but nothing of great importance. Nothing that would warrant the attention of Lady Virai. Anticipation shot through Kaldar. Something big waited at the end of this conversation.

Lady Virai approached and stopped at the desk four feet away. Dark eyes surveyed him from a severe face. Her irises were like black ice. Stare too long, and you'd veer off course and smash into a hard wall at full speed.

"You are Kaldar Mar."

"Yes, my lady."

"How long have you worked for me?"

She knew perfectly well when he had started. "Almost two years, my lady."

"You have open warrants in two provinces, which we quashed when you were hired, and an extensive criminal record in the Dukedom of Louisiana." Nancy's face was merciless. "You are a smuggler, a conman, a gambler, a thief, a liar, and an occasional murderer. With that résumé, I can see why you thought the Mirror would be the proper career choice. Just out of curiosity, is there a law that you haven't broken?"

"Yes. I never raped anyone. Also, I never copulated with animals. I believe Adrianglia has a law against that."

"And you have a smart mouth." Nancy crossed her arms. "As per our agreement with your family and the condition of extracting the lot of you from the Edge, you are now a citizen of Adrianglia. Your debt is being paid in full by the efforts of your cousin Cerise Sandine and her husband, William. You are allowed to pursue any profession you may like. Yet you came to work for me. Tell me, why is that?"

Kaldar smiled. "I'm grateful to the realm for rescuing my family. I possess a unique set of talents that the Mirror finds useful, and I don't want to rely on my lovely cousin and William for the repayment of my debt. William is a nice chap, a bit testy at times and he occasionally sprouts fur, but everyone has issues. I would feel rotten being indebted to him. It would be taking advantage of his good nature."

Nancy's cold eyes stared at him for a long second. "People like you love taking advantage of others' good nature."

He laughed quietly under his breath.

"You lie with no hesitation. The smile was particularly a nice touch. I imagine that face serves you quite well, especially in female company."

"It has its uses."

Lady Virai pondered him for a long moment. "Kaldar, you are a scoundrel."

He bowed with all the elegance of a blueblood prince.

"You were born smart but poor. You view me as a spoiled, rich woman born with a gold coin in my mouth. You feel that I and those of my social standing don't appreciate what we have, and you delight in thumbing your nose at aristocracy."

"My lady, you give me entirely too much credit."

"Spare me your bullshit. You revel in sabotaging the system, you hate orders, and you break the law simply because it's there. You can't help yourself. Yet two years ago you came to me with a bridle and a set of spurs, and said, 'Ride me.' And in two years, your record has been strangely law-abiding. You've been good, Kaldar. Within reason, of course. There was that business with the bank mysteriously catching fire."

"Completely accidental, my lady."

Lady Virai grimaced. "I'm sure. I need to know why you're going through all this trouble, and I don't have time to waste."

The problem with honesty was that it gave your opponent ammunition to use against you. One simply didn't hand a woman like Nancy Virai a loaded gun. Unless, of course, one had no choice. If he played coy now or tried to lie, she would see through him and order him out of the room. He would continue his rotation of small-time assignments. He had waited two years for this chance. He had to be sincere.

"Revenge," Kaldar said.

She didn't say anything.

"The Hand took people from me." He kept his voice casual and light. "My aunts, my uncles, cousins, my younger brother. There were thirty-six adults in the family before the Hand came to our little corner of the Edge. There are fifteen now, and they are raising a crop of orphaned children."

"Do you want the Hand's agents dead?"

"No." Kaldar smiled again. "I want them to fail. I want to see despair in their eyes. I want them to feel helpless."

"What is driving you? It's not all hate. People driven by hate alone are hollow. You have some life left in you. Is it fear?"

He nodded. "Most definitely."

"For yourself?"

In his mind, he was back on that muddy hillside drenched in cold gray rain. Aunt Murid's body lay broken on the ground, her blood spreading across the brown mud in a brilliant scarlet stain. He was sure that's not what he actually saw. Back in that moment, he didn't have time to stand and watch the blood spread. He was too busy cutting into the creature that killed her. This memory was false. It came from his nightmares.

"What are you thinking of?" Lady Virai asked.

"I'm remembering my family dying."

"How did you feel when they were killed?"

"Helpless."

There. She had pulled it out of him. It hurt. He didn't expect it to, but it did.

Lady Virai nodded. "How well can you handle the Broken?"

"I swim through it like a fish through clear water."

She gave him a flat look.

"The Edge is very long but narrow," he told her. "The Mire, where my family lived, is boxed on two sides by impassable terrain. There are only two ways out: to the Weird and the Dukedom of Louisiana, or to the Broken and the State of Louisiana. The Dukedom uses the Mire as a dumping ground for its exiles. They murder any Edger who approaches that boundary. So that border is closed, which leaves only one avenue of escape, to the Broken. Most of my family had too much magic to survive that crossing, so it fell to me to procure supplies and other things we needed. I've traveled through the Broken since I was a child. I have contacts there, and I've taken care to maintain them."

Lady Virai pondered his face.

Here it comes.

"So happens that I can use you."

Aha!

"A few hours ago a group of thieves broke into the Pyramid of Ptah in West Egypt." Lady Virai nodded at the map, where the peninsula that was Florida in the Broken thrust into the ocean. "The thieves stole a device of great military importance to the Egyptians. The Hand likely commissioned this theft. To make matters worse, the thieves were supposed to hand off their merchandise to the Louisianans, and they chose to do it in Adrianglian territory. Their meeting didn't go as planned, and now Adrianglia is involved, and the Egyptians are threatening to send the Claws of Bast into our lands to retrieve the object."

Kaldar frowned. The Hand was bad, the Mirror was dangerous, but the Claws of Bast were in a league of their own. There was a reason why their patron goddess was called the Devouring Lady.

"Can you handle a wyvern?" Lady Virai asked.

"Of course, my lady." Not much difference between an enormous flying reptile and a horse, really.

"Good. You will be issued one, together with funds, equipment, and other things you may require. I want you to use it to fly to the south, find this device, and bring it to me. Find the object, Kaldar. I don't care if you have to chase it to the moon; I want it in my hands, and I want it yesterday. Do I make myself clear?"

"Yes. One question?"

Lady Virai raised her eyebrows a quarter of an inch.

"Why me?"

"Because the West Egyptians tells me the thieves are Edgers," she said.

"How do they know?"

Her eyes flashed with annoyance. "They didn't specify. But it's hardly in their best interests to lie. The Hand hired the Edgers to do their dirty work, and now they have vanished into the Broken. They think they are beyond my reach. Your job is to prove them wrong. You may go now. Erwin will brief you and see to the details."

Kaldar ducked his head and headed for the door. Fate finally smiled at him.

"Kaldar."

He turned and looked at her.

"I'm taking a gamble," she said. "I'm gambling that you are smart as well as pretty, and those smarts will keep you following my orders. Don't disappoint me, Kaldar. If you fail because of lack of ability, I will simply discard you. But if you betray me, I will retire you. Permanently."

He grinned at her. "Understood, my lady."

THE briefing room lay just a short walk from the conference room. Kaldar rapped his knuckles on the door and swung it open. Erwin rose from a chair with a neutral smile.

Lady Virai's pet flash sniper had a pleasant face, neither handsome nor unattractive. His short hair, halfway between dark blond and light brown, didn't attract the eye. Of average height, he was trim but not overly muscular. His manner was unassuming; at the same time, he always appeared as if he belonged wherever he was. Never uncomfortable, never nervous, Erwin also never laughed. During meetings, people tended to forget he was in the room. He would blend right into a crowd of strangers, and once you passed him, his flash would take your head clean off. Erwin could hit a coin thrown in the air with a concentrated blast of magic from fifty paces away.

"Master Mar." Erwin held out his hand.

"Master Erwin." They shook.

Inconspicuous Erwin. When Kaldar had first met him, he'd taken the time to replicate the look and the mannerisms. The results proved shocking. He'd walked right past the security into the ducal palace twice before he decided to stop tempting Fate.

"Would you care for a drink?" the sniper asked.

"No."

"Very well. On with the briefing, then." Erwin turned to the large round table and tapped the console. The surface of the table ignited with pale yellow. The glow surged up and snapped into a three-dimensional image of a large pyramid, with pure white walls topped with a tip of pure gold.

"The Pyramid of Ptah. The Egyptian pyramids started as tombs and slowly progressed into houses of worship and learning. This particular pyramid, the second largest in West Egypt, is devoted to Ptah, God of Architects and Skilled Craftsmen. Of all creation gods of West Egypt, he is particularly venerated because of his intellectual approach. In essence, if Ptah thinks of it, it comes into being."

"A useful power," Kaldar said.

"Very. Ptah's pyramid is the center of research for many magic disciplines. It's the place where discoveries are made and cutting-edge technology is produced. That's why Egyptians guard it like the apple of their eye."

Erwin touched the console, and the walls of the pyramid vanished, revealing its inner structure—a complex maze of passageways.

"This is just what we know about," Erwin said. "The defenses of the pyramid are constantly evolving. It is seeded with traps, puzzles, impossible doors, and other delightful things designed to separate intruders from the burden of their lives. The Egyptians informed us that the thieves entered here, at two in the morning." Erwin picked a narrow metal tube and pointed at the passageway shooting off from the main entrance. The hallway lit up with a bright shade of yellow. "It's a service hallway. It's typically locked at night, and the lock is considered to be tamperproof."

"Until now."

"A fair observation. The Egyptians estimate that a talented picklock could open this lock in ten to fifteen minutes. The entrance is extensively patrolled. The thieves had a window of eight seconds, during which they opened the door, slipped inside the passageway, and closed and locked it behind them."

"They locked it?"

Erwin nodded.

Four seconds to open, four seconds to lock. That was crazy. To break into the Pyramid of Ptah would take incredible talent. Kaldar had looked into it when he was younger and the family was desperate. If someone had asked him this morning if it could be done, he would've said no.

"Then they proceeded down this hallway, leaving three distinct sets of footprints, two large and one small."

"Two for muscle and the cat burglar," Kaldar guessed.

"Probably." Erwin swept the length of the hallway with his pointer, causing sections of the image to light up. "They opened impossible locks in record time. They avoided all of the traps. They escaped detection and ended up here, bypassing both treasury here and armory here." The pointer fixed on a small room, then lit up rooms to the right and left of it. "They took a wooden box containing the device and walked out of the pyramid the way they came. In and out in under twenty minutes.

"That's impossible."

"Our Egyptian colleagues are of the same opinion. Unfortunately, the facts have no regard for their collective sanity."

Kaldar frowned at the pyramid. "Was this the shortest route they could've taken to the room?"

"Yes."

An enterprising thief would've done the research and broken into the treasury. A terrorist would've gone for the armory and the weapons within. But these three went directly to the room, took their prize, and escaped. Someone had hired them to do this job and provided them with the plans of the pyramid. Only a heavy hitter would have access to this sort of intelligence. The Mirror. Or the Hand. That would explain why a thief with a talent of this caliber took a job for hire. The Hand's methods of persuasion rarely involved money. Mostly they showed you your child or your lover strapped to a chair and promised to send you a piece of her every hour until you agreed to do whatever they wanted.

There it was, finally, his chance of a direct confrontation. He would make them pay.

Erwin was watching him.

"What happened after the thieves left the pyramid?" Kaldar asked.

"They disappeared off the face of the world." Erwin fiddled with the console, and the pyramid vanished, replaced by an aerial image of a small town. "This is the town of Adriana, population forty thousand. Two hundred and twenty leagues north, across the border, in our territory. A small, quaint settlement, famous for being the first place Adrian's fleet disembarked after crossing the ocean. It's a popular destination for school tours. Six hours and ten minutes after the thieves left the pyramid, Adriana's prized fountain exploded. The city crew, first on the scene, became violently sick. They reported catching ghost insects on their skin, hot flashes, freezes, temporary blindness, and vomiting."

The reaction to Hand's magic. Kaldar grimaced. The Mirror relied on gadgets to supplement their agents' natural talents, while the Hand employed magic modification. Officially, all countries of the West Continent abided by an agreement that limited how far the human body could be twisted by magic. The Dukedom of Louisiana made all the right noises and quietly manufactured freaks by the dozen. Men with foot-long needles on their backs, women who shot acid from their hands, things that used to be human and now were just a tangled mess of fangs and claws.

Magic augmentation came with a price. Some agents lost

their humanity completely, some held on to it, but all emitted their own particular brand of unnatural magic. If you were sensitive to magic, the first exposure made you violently sick. He'd experienced it firsthand, and he didn't care to repeat it.

Erwin straightened. "The Egyptians believe the Hand hired the thieves to steal the object and scheduled the trade in Adriana, where things went badly for both parties. Your wyvern is on standby. With luck and good wind, you should be in Adriana in an hour. After you review the scene, I'd imagine you will have a better idea of the supplies you'll need. Please stop at the Home Office, and we'll provide you everything you require. This assignment is rated first priority. Should you be captured, Adrianglia will disavow any knowledge of you and your mission."

"But you'll miss me?"

Erwin permitted himself a small smile. "Kaldar, I never miss."

Ha! "What's the nature of the stolen device?" Kaldar asked.

Erwin raised his eyebrows. "That's the best part."

KALDAR surveyed the sea of rubble, enclosed by a line of fluorescent paint and guarded by a dozen undersheriffs. Before him stretched what had once been the Center Plaza: a circle of clear ground, which until this morning had been paved with large square blocks. The blocks had radiated like the spokes of a wheel from the tall round fountain in the shape of a pair of dolphins leaping out from the water basin. He'd picked up a tourist brochure on his way to the scene of the crime. It showed a lovely picture of the fountain.

Now the fountain lay in ruins. It wasn't simply knocked down, it was shattered, as if the dolphins had exploded from the inside out. Not satisfied with destroying the fountain, the perpetrator had wrenched the stone blocks around it out of the ground and hurled them across the plaza. The brochure stated that each block weighed upwards of fifty pounds. Looking at the giant chunks of stone, Kaldar didn't doubt it. A small tea vendor's wagon must've gotten in the way of the barrage, because it lay in shambles, blue-green boards poking out sadly from under the stones.

Blood stained the rubble. Gobs of flesh lay scattered here and there, some looking like they could possibly be human and others sporting weird bunches of fish bladders strung together like grapes. About ten feet to the left, a chunk of an oversized, flesh-colored tentacle curled around a piece of cloth. Long strands of yellowish slime covered the entire scene. And to top it all off, the slime stank like days-old vomit, harsh and sour. The deputies downwind, on the opposite side of the ruined plaza, valiantly tried not to gag.

The tall, broad bruiser, who was the sheriff of Adriana, was giving him an evil eye. His name was Kaminski, and he was clearly having doubts about the wisdom of Kaldar's presence at his crime scene. Kaldar couldn't blame him. His skin was at least two shades darker than most faces in the crowd. He wore brown leather, fitted neither tight nor too loose, and he looked lean, flexible, and fast, like a man who scaled tall fences early in the morning.

The sheriff stared at him. He could just go over and introduce himself, but what fun would that be?

Kaldar grinned. The sheriff's blond sidekick began weaving his way through the crowd toward him.

Strange pair, these two, but probably highly effective. And respected, too. They didn't bother with putting up any barriers, not even a rope. Just a line of paint around the crime scene and a dozen undersheriffs, but the crowd stayed way back.

Cops were the same everywhere, Kaldar reflected. In the Broken, they called you "sir" and Tasered you, while in the Weird, they called you "master" and hit you with low-level flash magic, but the street look—that wary, evaluating, flat look in their eyes—was the same everywhere. Cops noticed everything, and few of them were stupid. He had committed too many crimes in both worlds to underestimate them.

The blond undersheriff stopped before him. "I'm Undersheriff Rodwell. Your name?"

"Kaldar Mar."

"Do you find the destruction of Adrianglian landmarks humorous, Master Mar? Perhaps you would like to visit our jail and spend some time in our jail cell to collect your thoughts and explain to all of us what is so funny?"

"I'd love to," Kaldar said. "But my employer might take an issue with that."

"Who is your employer?"

Kaldar sent a spark of magic through his spine. A faint sheen rolled over the earring in his left ear. It dripped down, forming a dull tear hanging from the hoop. The tear brightened, and Rodwell stared at his own reflection in a mirrored surface.

"Kaldar Mar, agent of the Adrianglian Secret Service." The tear sparked and vanished. "The Mirror is grateful for your assistance, Undersheriff. Thank you for securing the crime scene for me."

"I just want to know one thing." Sheriff Kaminski kept his voice low. "Is the Hand involved in this?"

Kaldar considered before making his answer. He needed their cooperation. It would make things easier, and he needed to build contacts in law enforcement. "Yes."

The sheriff chewed on it for a long breath.

"How do you know?" Rodwell asked.

Kaldar cycled through his options. Neither one of the men struck him as a social climber. They were good at what they did and were happy right where they were. If he came on with an imperious aristocratic air, they'd stonewall him. The buddy-buddy approach wouldn't work, either—their town was on the line, and they were both too grim for jokes. A straight shooter, just-doing-my-job type was his best bet.

Kaldar delayed another half a second, as if weighing the gravity of the information, and pointed at a fragment of a tentacle a few feet away.

The two men looked in the direction of his fingers.

"That's a piece of a Hand operative, *pieuvre* class. Six to ten tentacles, amphibious, weighs in close to five hundred pounds. A nasty breed." He clipped his words a bit, adding a touch of a military tone to his voice.

"You've seen one before?" Rodwell asked. The hint of challenge in his voice was a shade lighter.

Kaldar pretended to think for a moment and grasped the sleeve of his leather jacket. The clasps on his wrist snapped open, and he pulled the sleeve down, revealing his forearm. Four quarter-sized round scars dotted his forearm in a ragged bracelet, the reminder of a tentacle wrapping around his wrist. The suckers had burned into his skin, and not even the best magic the Mirror had at its disposal had been able to remove the scars. He let them see it and pulled the sleeve closed. "Yes. I've seen one."

"Did it hurt?" Rodwell asked.

"I don't remember," Kaldar answered honestly. "I was busy at the time." He heard people say that you couldn't kill a *pieuvre* operative with a knife. You could. You just had to have the proper motivation.

The sheriff stared at the wreckage. "What do they want here?"

Kaldar gave him a flat look and clamped his mouth shut. Giving up the information too easily wouldn't do. Kaminski didn't like him and didn't trust him. However, if Kaldar risked his neck and broke the rules to put his fears to rest, well, it would be a different story. But no straight shooter would break the rules without serious doubts.

A wise man far away in a different world once said, "Give me a lever long enough and a fulcrum on which to place it, and I shall move the world." Kaminski was worried about his town. It was written all over his face. That worry was the lever. Apply the proper amount of force, and Kaldar could shift the sheriff to his side.

The silence won.

"Look, Master Mar, I know you're breaking regulations," Kaminski said. "I just need to know if my people are safe."

Kaldar rocked back on his heels, looked at the sky, and sighed. "I don't normally do this."

Kaminski and Rodwell took a step closer, almost in unison. "It won't go anywhere," the sheriff promised. "You have my word."

Kaldar took another breath. "Eight hours ago, the West Egyptian authorities discovered that a group of thieves broke into the Pyramid of Ptah. The perpetrators stole a magic device of great strategic value. It was a theft for hire, and the Dukedom of Louisiana's Hand was the intended recipient of the device. In the early-morning hours, the thieves crossed the border and arrived here, to meet the Hand's operatives. The Hand is infamous for double-crossing the hired help, so the thieves picked a public, well-known location for their own safety. As you can see, their fears were justified."

"So Adriana was never the intended target?" Kaminski asked.

"No, Sheriff. It was simply the closest public place. Your people are safe."

"Thank you," Kaminski said simply.

"If the city was never the target, why is the Mirror involved?" Rodwell frowned.

"Because the attempted exchange took place on our soil, West Egypt requires our assistance in recovering the device. It's a diplomatic nightmare already. We must resolve this and quickly, or they may take matters into their own hands. Nobody wants to have half a dozen of the Claws of Bast running around in the realm."

The undersheriff winced. Even Kaminski looked taken aback for a moment. The Claws of Bast had a certain reputation.

Kaminski surveyed the rubble. "All those pieces look like they belong to the same body, and according to you, they're pieces of a Hand operative. No other body parts. The thieves got away."

Kaldar nodded. "Indeed. Somewhere out there, in that mess, is a clue that will tell me where they went."

"I can have my men pull the rubble apart," Kaminski said. "I can put sixteen undersheriffs on this. We'll throw up a grid, work in shifts through the night, and have every crumb and rock cataloged for you by morning."

Kaldar grinned. "I appreciate the offer, but time is short."

The two men stared at him. Showtime.

"Do you have any coins on you, Undersheriff?" Kaldar asked.

Rodwell dug into his pocket and came up with a handful of change. Kaldar plucked the small silver disk of a half crown from the man's palm and held it up with his thumb and index finger. The rays of the morning sun shone, reflecting from the small disk of silver. "I bet you a half crown that I'll walk out there and find this vital clue in the next three minutes."

Rodwell glanced at the half crown and back at the sea of debris. A small smile bent his lips. "I'll take that bet."

A spark of magic pulsed from the coin in Kaldar's fingers. It shot through him like lightning, awakening something lying hidden deep in the recesses of his being, just on the edge of consciousness. The strange reserves of magic sparked to life and solidified into a tense, shivering current that burst through the coin, through his spine, up through his skull, and down through his legs and the soles of his feet. The current speared him, claiming him, and he shuddered, caught like a fish on the line. This was his own special talent. If he got someone to accept a bet, his magic skewed the odds in his favor.

The current pulled on him, and Kaldar let it steer him. The magic led him, guiding each step, maneuvering him around the pitted pavement, over the heap of shattered marble, to a cluster of splintered wood. The coin tugged him forward. Kaldar bent. Something shiny caught the sun in the crevice underneath a twisted wreck of metal that used to be a tea-making machine. He reached for it. His fingertips touched glass, and the current vanished.

Kaldar pulled a handkerchief from his pocket, wrapped it over his fingers, and gently pried the glass object free. A six inch long tube with a wide bulb on the end. Dark soot stained the inside of the bulb. How about that?

He turned and brought his find back to the two men. "What is that?"

"That's an 'I Love You Rose.' These tubes are sold in certain shops." Namely, the gas stations near ghettos in the Broken. "There is usually a cheap fake flower inside. They're bought by addicts who drop cheap narcotics into the bulb and smoke the tube like a pipe."

Kaminski raised his head. "Bring the *goleeyo!*"

A young woman, whose blond hair was carefully braided away from her face, hurried over, carrying a contraption of light bronze resembling a long flashlight. She glanced at the pipe, snagged a small leather book chained to her belt, tore a piece of thin paper, and looked at Kaldar. "Hold it up, please!"

He raised the meth pipe. Most of the Weird's gadgetry was still new to him. He hadn't seen this one before.

The blonde clicked the flashlight. A bright beam of pale green light stabbed the pipe, highlighting dirty smudges, specks of dirt, and, on the bulb, one large, beautiful finger-print. The woman placed the paper between the light and the fingerprint, holding it an inch away from the glass, and clicked the flashlight again. The flashlight whirred. Its back end split, the metal plates lifting up, revealing the interior: a series of small gears speckled with tiny gems. The gears spun. The flashlight clicked loudly in a measured rhythm. With each click, the light turned darker and bluer. Thin lines appeared on the paper, growing darker and darker. The beam of the flashlight turned indigo and winked out. The blond woman handed Kaldar the piece of paper with the fin-gerprint squarely in the center.

He hit her with a dazzling smile. "Thank you, m'lady."

She smiled back. "You're welcome, m'lord."

If he didn't have to leave, he could've asked her to share a meal with him, and she would say yes. Kaldar checked the hint of a smile hiding in her eyes. She would definitely say yes, then he would get her to say yes to a night together, and it would be a lot of fun for them both. Unfortunately, he wasn't his own man at the moment.

"So what's next?" Kaminski asked.

"Next, I'll go hunting," Kaldar said.

Fifteen minutes later, Kaldar finished with the pleasantries, shook the hands, thanked and was thanked, and finally headed to his wyvern, waiting for him on the edge of town. Addicts in the Weird didn't use meth pipes, which meant the West Egyptians were right. The thieves must have come from the Edge or the Broken. Almost four months had passed since he had visited either place. The hop back across the boundary was long overdue.

Of the three people involved, the picklock had to be his best bet. A man with a gift like that wouldn't stay idle for long. Somewhere, somehow, that man had left a trail. All Kaldar had to do was find it.

He couldn't wait to meet the talented bastard.

THE fallen tree still blocked the road. Audrey sighed, put her parking brake on, and started up the mountain. The evening sky sifted gray drizzle onto the forest. Soon June would come and with it heat and crystalline blue skies, but for now the world was still damp, its colors, except for the brilliant green, muted. A far cry from Florida. Traveling through the Weird meant crossing four countries, impossible without a wyvern. She had flown from Seattle into Orlando instead. The plane had landed late, and they pulled the job off that night, but when they had driven to Jacksonville, she got to see the sunrise through the windshield of a stolen car. It started as a pale glow of purple and red near the horizon, just over the smooth expanse of silvery ocean, then, suddenly, it bloomed across the sky, pink and orange and yellow, a riot of color, huge and shocking. If it had a sound, it would've deafened everyone on the road.

Audrey sighed. She wished she could've stayed longer, but common sense had won. Every moment in Florida put her in danger. Besides, seeing Alex again was like ripping off a scab. He hadn't changed, not even a little. Same sneer, same hollow eyes, same junkie-contempt for everyone and everything. She abandoned Dad—no, *Seamus*, since he hardly was her father anymore—and Alex to their scheme and took the first available plane from Jacksonville. Ended up with a six-hour layover in Atlanta, just like everyone else. She was pretty sure that if you died in the South, you'd have a layover in Atlanta before you reached the afterlife. But now, almost fifteen hours later, she was finally home.

The pyramid had been a hell of a challenge. Complex locks weren't a problem, but three doors had heavy bars. Lifting a bar by magic felt harder than lifting her own weight. The three reinforced doors had nearly drained her dry, but she had done it. It was over now, and she was living the first day of the rest of her life. Free life.

Audrey conquered the fallen tree, crossed the clearing, and knocked on the door of Gnome's house. A rough growl answered. "Come in!"

Audrey tried the door handle. Locked again. A little test, huh. She put her palm against the keyhole, and the door clicked. Audrey opened the door, wiped her feet on the little rug, and went inside. Gnome sat in his chair. His thick eyebrows furrowed as she approached. Audrey took a seat across from him, reached into her bag, and pulled out a bottle of AleSmith Speedway Stout. She set the bottle on the table.

"Thank you for feeding Ling for me while I was gone."

"No trouble. All she needed was a cup of cat food." Gnome shrugged his huge shoulders. "The little beast hates me, you know."

"No, she's just weary. She's been beat up by life," Audrey said.

"Haven't we all?" Gnome took the bottle by the top and turned it, this way and that. "That's some talent you've got there."

"It comes in handy." What was he getting at? If there was a job offer on the end of this conversation, she'd turn it down flat.

"Did your talent have something to do with this urgent business you left on?"

Audrey nodded.

"I thought you got a legal job in the Broken."

"I did. It was a special one-time thing. For the family."

"Family, huh." Gnome gave out a gruff snort. "I knew your father."

"He mentioned you."

Gnome studied the beer bottle. "What did he say?"

"It was some years back. He said you knew just about everything there was to know about the Edge business on this coast. He didn't like you much. He thinks you're a tough fence to con."

"Well, I don't like him much, either." Gnome grimaced. "You see all this around you?" He indicated the shelves with a sweep of his hand. "That's over a hundred years of the right decisions."

It didn't surprise her. Gnome looked sixty, maybe, but a lot of Edgers were long-lived. A couple of centuries wasn't out of the question, and Gnome knew the Pacific Edge too well to have gotten into this business only a few years ago.

"I bargained for every item here, and I know I can sell it for a profit. Those batteries over there cost me nine dollars and ninety-eight cents. I sell them for three bucks apiece. Make fifty dollars and two cents in profit. I don't force foolish people to pay three dollars for a double-A battery. I just provide the opportunity, and they buy it because either they're too lazy to drive five miles down to the store or they don't have the gas, or they don't have the money, but they've got something to trade. Why should I charge less because they can't make enough to feed their kids and buy gas at the same time? This is *business*. You build it little by little, and you hold on to what you've got. Your father can't get it through his thick skull. He wants big money now, and when he gets it, he blows it all because he is too damn stupid to pace himself. He had you with your gift, and he's still penniless."

"I won't argue with you there." Childhood in the Callahan family had been feast or famine. One day steak, the next mac with imaginary cheese.

Gnome leaned forward, poking the table with his finger. "I'm not in the business of giving advice. I'm in the business of making money. So you listen to me good because this is the only time I'll say this. You're a nice girl. Not many of you are left out there. You're an endangered species. Your father's trouble. He's a selfish asshole, and his turkey is cooked—he ain't gonna change for nobody." Gnome made a cutting motion with his hand. "He'll drag you into a mess and run the other way. You've got a good thing going here: you've got a house, you've got a good job, and you're your own person. Don't let him screw it all up for you."

Audrey rose. "I won't. This was the last time."

"That's what they all say."

She smiled at him. "Yes, but I mean it. I will never do a job again for Seamus Callahan."

"You see to that."

Oh, she would. She most definitely would. If any of the Callahans ever showed themselves on her lawn again, she would meet them with a rifle in her hands. If she was feeling charitable, they'd get a warning shot, but chances of that were slim.

TWO

JACK sheathed his knife, tied the dressed hare to a stick, and slung it over his shoulder. It wouldn't do for the meat to touch his school uniform. Might make the kill dirty.

He headed down the forest path. It was a nice rabbit. No bugs. No sickness—all the innards smelled right. He'd killed it quick, by breaking its neck with his fangs. Best that way because the hare didn't suffer, and the meat wasn't contaminated. Jack had changed back into a human, washed the hare in a stream, and taken care to field-dress it properly.

He always brought a gift when he came to see William. He was going into his den, and William didn't have to let him in. It was polite to bring a present.

Jack grimaced. He wasn't very good at polite, according to his sister, Rose. But William and he never had an issue. They were both changelings, and some things were unspoken but understood: bring a gift, don't show your teeth, don't stare at Cerise for too long. Not that he liked Cerise like that. It was just that she was William's wife, and when Jack tried to explain things, it made sense to her. When he tried to explain things to his own sister, he got chewed out.

And that was precisely the problem.

Around him, the late-summer forest teemed with life. Tiny squirrels chased each other through the branches, chittering in outrage at some perceived slight. Forest mice scurried between the roots of huge Weird oaks. Butterflies floated on the breeze like bright petals. Although Jack had been born in the Edge, he liked the Weird's forests. They were old and powerful and held magic secrets. Still, he missed hunting in the Edge woods, creeping up on soft paws along the branches of a huge tree, smelling the moss, and hunting Edge critters in the dusk. It was the last time he remembered being really free.

A small yellow butterfly glided closer, bouncing up and down on air currents above his head. He paused, frozen.

Up and down, bright yellow wings. Bounce, bounce, bounce . . .

Jack jumped a couple of feet into the air and swatted at the butterfly with his hand. Ha! Got it.

He opened his fingers carefully. The butterfly crawled up his palm, fluttering the lemony yellow wings. It climbed the heel of his hand, onto his thumb, spread its wings, and glided off, leaving a faint yellow dust on his skin. He watched it fly away with an odd longing. It was not that he wanted to be one. Butterflies couldn't hunt, couldn't speak, and their lives were short. But butterflies could fly about carefree. They didn't have to worry about being sent off to military prison schools.

Jack sighed, sniffed the traces of powder on his palm—they smelled dry and flowery—and went on his way.

Four years ago, he, George, and Rose had lived together in the Edge, a narrow strip between the Broken of no magic and the Weird of too much magic. They lived in an old house. They were poor. Really, really poor. He didn't understand how poor they were until they came to the Weird. Their mother had died. Jack didn't remember her that well, except for a faint scent. He had smelled something similar once, in the perfume of a girl at a ball, and that scent had opened a big gaping hole inside him. He'd had to leave right then, so he'd gone over the top-floor balcony into the trees, and when he'd returned in the morning, he had to go into Declan's office and explain himself.

With their mom dead, their dad had run off. Jack recalled him but only vaguely, just a blurry, man-shaped thing. He remembered the voice, though, a rough, funny voice. Their dad went to look for some treasure and never came back. It was just him, Rose, George, and Grandma. Rose worked all the time. George and he had to go to school in the Broken. George had been slowly dying because he couldn't let things go. Every time George had found something that had died, a bird, a kitten, Grandpa, he'd bring it back to life—but it took his own life force to keep it going. Right before they moved to the Weird, George had brought back so many things, he was sick all the time.

Jack sighed. People had picked on George, but he'd always fight for him. That was his job, Jack reflected. He protected George and Rose. He was a changeling, a predator. Stronger and faster than other people even in the Broken, without magic.

And then Declan came from the Weird. Big, strong, wearing armor and carrying swords, and blowing houses up with a flash so powerful it was like white lightning. Declan wanted Rose. He fixed George's problem, defeated the monsters, protected everyone, then Rose fell in love with him, and off they went into the Weird.

Grandma didn't want to go. She came to visit every summer, so it wasn't all bad.

In the Weird, changelings didn't live with normal people. Most of the time, their parents gave them up for adoption by the government, and they were sent off to Hawk's Military Academy. William had gone through Hawk's. He said it was like a prison: no toys, no books; nothing except seven changes of clothes, towel, toothbrush, and hairbrush. Changelings at Hawk's lived in small, sterile rooms. It was a life of studies and constant drills, designed to turn them into perfect soldiers. Jack read an article about it once—it said that changeling children couldn't understand how regular people interacted. "A controlled low-stimulus environment" was better for them.

There was nothing worse than Hawk's. Jack felt an odd tightness in his back and shrugged to get rid of it. Rose and Declan had both told him that he would never be sent there. But the older he got, the more he screwed up.

Last night, Declan sat him down and told him that they couldn't keep going on like this. Changes had to be made. He didn't say anything about Hawk's, but Jack could read between the lines. He wasn't a baby.

William was his only hope. William was Declan's best friend. If anyone could come to Jack's defense, it would be him.

He had to make William understand how things were before it was too late.

WILLIAM'S house sat in the middle of a vast grassy lawn, bordered by ancient ashes and oaks. It was a big place, three stories with an attic on top, all brown stone under a roof of green clay shingles. Four round towers, two stories high, sat at the corners of the house. Each tower had a round balcony with a stone rail on the second floor. Their other place was even bigger, a mansion the size of Declan and Rose's house, but William and Cerise both hated it. They still went there once in a while because it had a bigger pool.

Jack left the tree line, crossed the lawn, and stood in front of the arched entrance, letting William catch his scent. One minute, two . . . Long enough.

He went to the arched front door. It swung open under his fingertips, admitting him into the dark stone entrance-way. The door shut behind him, and darkness took him into her black mouth and gulped him down. Jack crouched on instinct, letting his eyes adjust.

William could kill any intruder while he stood there, blinking like an owl. When Jack got his own house, he'd have an entrance just like this one.

Jack's pupils caught the weak light and the glint of a trip wire strung across the way just at the right height to trip an unsuspecting attacker's ankle. Jack stepped over it, went through to the next door, and out into the courtyard. The bright light of the day shocked his eyes again. He blinked until he saw a blue pool on the left, surrounded by a stone pathway. Around the path, flowers bloomed in curvy flower beds, yellow and blue blossoms catching the sun with delicate petals. His nostrils caught wood smoke. Cerise was cooking.

Jack headed down the path to the back of the house,

through a side door, and into the large kitchen. The huge solid table took up most of the room. William lounged at the other side of it in a big chair, close enough to touch Cerise, who stood at a stone counter. Like Declan, William was tall, but where Rose's husband was blond and buff, William was black-haired, lean, and hard. Their stares met. William's eyes shone with yellow once. Just a friendly warning. Jack looked to the floor for a second to let him know he didn't have a problem with his authority.

When he looked up, Cerise was grinning at him from the counter. She was short and tan, with long dark hair, and she wore a blue apron. "A hare! Is that for us?"

Jack nodded and offered her the hare. Cerise took it. "That's perfect, Jack. Just in time. And so nicely cleaned, too."

Jack grinned. She liked it.

"Come, sit." William pushed a glass of Adrianglian tea in his direction. Jack swiped the cup and landed in the nearest chair. Cerise set a pan on the fire, threw some chopped bacon into it, and started peeling an onion.

"How's it going?" William asked.

"Fine." Jack kept his voice flat. He'd have to go about this conversation very carefully.

"How's school?" Cerise asked, chopping the onion to pieces.

"Fine."

William and Cerise looked at each other.

"How's the school really?" William asked.

Jack looked at the table. He was one week into his first year of the Royal College. The College was a big deal. It cost a lot of money and had the best teachers, and he had to pass a load of exams to be admitted. George was two years ahead of him, and he loved it. If someone else had asked him, Jack would've said the school was fine because Rose and Declan were paying for it, and he didn't want to be ungrateful. But this was William's house, which meant he didn't have to lie.

"It's strange."

"Strange good or strange bad?" Cerise added onion and garlic to the pan. The aroma tugged on Jack. He licked his lips. Cerise cut the rabbit into bite-sized chunks and swept the meat into the pan, too. *Mmmm, smells good.*

"Strange strange," he said. "People don't talk to me, that's fine. I don't need to talk to them, either. But they talk behind my back all the time. The girls are the worst. They huddle and whisper things, and when I try to be nice and talk to them, they get all weird. They're calling me Brother of the Cursed Prince."

William sat up straight. "What?"

"They call George the Cursed Prince because he does necromancy. And I'm his brother."

Cerise sighed and stirred the meat. "Girls at your age are odd. I know, I was one. Adults expect them to have little romances, and they kind of think they ought to have them because that's what grown-up women do, but really they're little girls, and they have no idea how to go about it. Boys are a mystery. Ask Lark. She will tell you."

Lark was Cerise's younger sister. Jack looked down at the table again. "Lark and I aren't friends anymore."

Cerise stopped stirring the rabbit in the pan. "Since when?"

"Since two weeks ago."

"What happened?" William asked. "Did you do something?"

Jack shook his head. "She said that she and I were too much of the same. She said I was wild and she was wild, and when we got together, we were crazy. She says she isn't mad at me, but she won't go to the woods to hunt with me anymore. She spends time with George now. She says he's civilized."

He wasn't even sure what the hell that meant. One day, Lark was there; the next, she wasn't. It pissed him off and made him sad, until he was too confused to do anything about it.

William fixed him with his wolf eyes. "Lark is broken in the head."

"Damaged," Cerise said with steel in her voice.

"Damaged," William repeated. "Sorry. You know about the slavers?"

Jack nodded. Years ago, slavers had come to their house in the Edge and tried to kidnap Rose. His sister had the strongest magic in the Edge. Her flash was pure white, and she still practiced with it at least an hour every day. The magic made her valuable.

"Slavers stole Lark," William told him. "They put her in a hole in a ground and didn't feed her. One of them got into the hole with her to molest her."

Jack bared his teeth. "What?"

"She killed him with her magic," Cerise said. Her face looked strained, as if she was trying to keep herself calm. "They stopped feeding her. It was just her and his body for over a week. She didn't know how long she would stay in the hole or when we'd find her."

They both looked at him. This was an adult thing or a human thing, and he wasn't getting it, so he just waited.

"She might have eaten the slaver," William said.

Jack nodded. It was a fair kill. It was gross, but if he were stuck in a hole in the ground for a week, surrounded by enemies, he might have eaten human flesh, too.

"It's different for not-changeling people," William said. "It damages them."

"Why? Is there poison in the meat?"

"It's not that kind of damage," Cerise said. "Lark thinks that she is a horrible monster because of what she did. She hates herself a little, and she is trying to forget about it. Have you noticed how she is always wearing pretty dresses now, and her hair is always brushed really well?"

He'd noticed. He also noticed that she wouldn't go to the woods with him anymore. They used to have fun. They'd hunt and hang out. Now she wanted to sit on the chair on the balcony and have tea with Rose.

"She wants to be normal right now," Cerise told him. "She wants to forget the ugliness, so she is making every-thing around her pretty."

"And I am ugly," Jack said.

Cerise put her hand over her face. "Oy."

"You're not ugly," William said. "You're violent. You like to hunt and kill, and she can't handle the blood right now. Let her work it out on her own. When she's ready, she'll find you."

"Girls just don't like me," Jack said. "They prefer George."

"The girls at school like George because he is safe," Cerise said. "George has perfect manners, he is calm, and they know that if they are alone with him, nothing will happen. Don't try to be George. The kind of girls that like him are the wrong girls for you. You're looking for the girls that are attracted to a boy with a dark, dangerous side."

"I don't have a dark side," Jack said.

"Of course you do. At this age, it's all about the roles you play. When William and I do work for the Mirror, we often have to be somebody else. We have to put on different costumes and look the part."

"But I don't want to be somebody else."

"That's not what I am saying." Cerise sighed. "Let's take George. He puts on his costume, goes to school, and plays the role of the Tragic Prince."

"Cursed," Jack corrected.

"Cursed. But at home he's normal, right?"

Jack considered it. True, George was a bit weird at school. He rarely laughed, and sometimes he would stand by the windows and stare into the distance, looking sad, while a gaggle of girls whispered about him nearby.

"Yes," Jack said. "I get it."

"You just need to find your role. George is a Cursed Prince, and you might do better as the Mysterious Dark Loner."

William stared at his wife. "You thought way too much about this."

Cerise waved her hand at him. "You hush. Jack, look, it's very simple. You just have to keep to yourself and look nonchalant."

Jack blinked. "What?"

"William does a really good nonchalant look." Cerise turned to William. "Do the nonchalant for him."

William sighed and looked at Jack. It wasn't any sort of special look. It was just flat.

"So I have to look bored?"

"You have to look like you don't care. Like you would rather be somewhere else."

"I would! I would rather be anywhere else."

"Then it shouldn't be too hard. Don't tell people about yourself. Try not to get excited about anything where people can see you. If someone challenges you to a fight, shrug and keep going. If they persist, kick their ass. And once in a while, be yourself and do something randomly kind, the way you usually do, like help a smaller kid. If someone asks you why you do something, look nonchalant and tell them they just wouldn't understand and that there are things about you they're better off not knowing. Girls will eat it up."

Jack glanced at William for confirmation. William shrugged and looked nonchalant.

"Give it a shot," Cerise said. "Jack, you have to go to school. Trust me, you can't do anything in the Weird without at least a third-degree graduation scroll in your hand."

Jack inspected the table for a bit. "Nonchalant won't work on Rose and Declan," he said.

"What happened?" William leaned toward him and fixed Jack with his wolf stare. It was a hard, merciless stare that pinned Jack in place like a knife. If he met a wolf who looked at him like that in the forest, Jack would've puffed his fur out and snarled. And if that didn't work, he'd take off as fast as he could.

"There was a ball," Jack said, trying to keep his voice monotone. "Or a banquet. One of those things Declan does because of his job as Marshal. A lot of people came. I walked around. They never notice me because I am quiet. Some people were standing there eating shrimp and those crab things on toast. I walked up behind them. They were talking about Rose. An older man said that Declan had all those women he could've picked and he had to go to the

Edge to get himself a whore, and why do they suppose he had to do that?"

His voice was building. Jack knew he should keep calm, but the fury he'd felt last night woke up again inside him, like an animal that rose to find himself caged. He remembered every word and every sound of that conversation. William had told him before that it was a changeling thing, and his perfect memory was spurring him on now.

"And then the woman in blue on his left said that maybe there was something wrong with Declan, physically. He had to get the kind of woman who was dependent on him completely, so she wouldn't say anything."

The anger was scratching at him now, trying to rip him up from the inside out and escape. The skin between his knuckles itched, eager to let his claws out.

"And the other woman, in yellow, she said, 'Like mother like son. His mother was an Edge woman of ill repute.' And the man said that he questioned the wisdom of associating with a woman who brought two mongrel children with her and that there must be something really valuable in the services she performs in the bedroom for Declan to keep her around. And then I said . . ."

His voice snapped into a deep, ragged growl. The fury broke and took him off his chair. He knew his eyes were glowing, and he didn't care. "And I said that the Edgers take care of themselves and don't come to other people's houses looking for handouts and insulting people who're feeding them, like fat ticks leeching off their hosts and complaining that the blood they're stealing doesn't taste right. I said, you think my sister is an Edge whore? Then don't come here to eat her food."

"Oh, Jack," Cerise whispered.

"And then everyone was shocked." Jack paced up and down, snarling. The hair on his arms was standing on end. He remembered the man's scent, vivid and sharp, his face, his voice. "I wanted to kill him. They should've let me kill him! I would snap his neck with my teeth!"

"What happened next?" Cerise asked.

"Declan got this crazy look, and he said, 'Either the boy is lying, which he never does, or you've insulted my wife.' The man said, 'At our house, we chain our animals before the arrival of guests. Perhaps you should do the same.' Then Declan said, 'Leave or I will throw you out.' The man said, 'Is that a threat?' And Declan said, 'Would you like it to be?' The man said, 'If you insist,' and put his hand on his sword. And then Rose did her flash. It was shooting around her in spirals like white lightning, and her eyes were glowing with white, and she said, 'This is over! Leave before I slice you and your family into ribbons.'"

Jack kept pacing. "And then the banquet was over, and I had to go to Declan's office. He was really mad. I said, 'I was defending my family! He was a bad guy.' Declan said that he knew the guy was bad. I asked him why he invited him, and Declan said that he wanted to see who was friendly with this guy, so Declan could learn who his enemies are, and that I pretty much stabbed that plan through the heart. He said that he didn't expect me to be perfect, but we can't keep having these catastrophes every time I show my face in public. He said it's causing problems between him and Rose, and he doesn't want those kinds of problems, so we couldn't keep going on like this, and something had to change. He also said that I needed more supervision and that I left him no choice. And then he told me I could go."

Jack took a deep breath. "I know what this means. He doesn't have to spell it out. He's sending me to Hawk's! For supervision!"

"Sit down!" William barked, his eyes glowing with green.

Jack landed on the floor and shut up.

"The animal thing inside you, the Wild. Has it ever taken over?"

Jack shook his head.

"You ever see red?"

Jack nodded.

William glanced at Cerise. "He needs to rend and soon, and we don't have time. The first time is always the hardest." He turned back to Jack. "Listen to me. We have a thing inside us, the Wild. The Wild sleeps in a den deep in you. When you get angry, or worried, or excited, the Wild wakes up, and if you let it, it will break out. When the Wild takes over, you forget that there are rules. If it ever happens, you will kill in a frenzy, and you won't stop until you're dead or exhausted. It will take you to a place without gods. This is called rending. We all do this from time to time. There is the right way to rend and the wrong way. Rending in the middle of dinner filled with civilians is the wrong way. Do you understand?"

Jack nodded. "Yes."

"You must keep the Wild in check until you and I can find a way to release it safely."

"How?" Jack asked.

"I told you, the Wild sleeps in its den. When you see red, it's about to escape. That's when you push it back into its den and make it stay there. If the red ever goes black, you're gone. Don't let it drag you under, Jack. You get me?"

Jack nodded again.

"Next, Declan won't send you to Hawk's. That's not the kind of man he is. Even if he did, they probably wouldn't take you. You're too old. You wouldn't survive—they would have to crush your spirit completely, which would make you a lousy soldier and useless to them."

Yeah, yeah. They would take him if Declan asked, but now didn't seem like the best time to mention that.

"But the Camarine Castle might not be the best place for you for the next few years, no matter how much Declan and Rose love you. Their house is the house of the Marshal. Cerise and I are leaving tomorrow morning. We have a mission for the Mirror. When we come back, I'll speak to Declan about it."

The full enormity of the statement crashed on Jack. William was leaving. There would be no help. "Where are you going?" Jack asked in a small voice.

"You know I can't tell you where or how long we'll be gone." William leaned forward.

A weak hope flared in Jack's mind. "Can you talk to Declan tonight?"

"No. It's a long and complicated conversation."

The hope died. A mission for the Mirror could take a week or a month or half a year. He needed help *now*.

"So what am I supposed to do?" Jack asked. His voice sounded defeated even to him.

"Keep your head down, and don't do anything stupid," William said. "Stay out of trouble until I come back."

"Not going to happen," Jack said. He couldn't stay out of trouble because he had no idea where normal ended and trouble began. "I can't do that. I don't know how."

"Yes, you can," Cerise told him.

A faint noise tugged on Jack, the dull hum coming from above. William rose and walked out of the kitchen. Jack followed. Outside, the hum grew louder. Jack squinted at the sky. A small dot darkened the clear blue, growing in size.

Cerise stepped out behind them. "A wyvern."

"Mhhhm. Air Force." William growled under his breath, and he and Cerise strode across the inner yard to the gate. Jack trailed after them. They passed through the dark gateway and out into the light again.

The wyvern dropped lower, a huge, scaled creature with massive leathery wings that spread so wide, their shadow covered the entire clearing. Its two muscled legs were bent close to its scaled belly, pale purple, like the sky at dusk. The beast circled the house, tilting as it turned, and Jack caught a glimpse of green scales on its back and the tightly woven wicker shelter of the cabin. The air had a dry, bitter wyvern scent. It made Jack's nostrils itch, and he sneezed.

The wyvern banked, flew over their heads, and landed in the wide field in front of the house, its wings spread, its two legs digging into the soft soil. It shifted in place, settling down, spread its wings, dipping them down to rest on the grass, and lowered its head to the ground. The door of the cabin swung open. A dark-haired man emerged and slid down the wyvern's side to the ground, like it was a play-ground slide. The wyvern stirred, sending a gust of air their way, and Jack caught a familiar scent. "Kaldar."

William growled under his breath, looking as if he had bitten something sour.

"Cousin!" Cerise waved. "Long time no see!"

Lean and light on his feet, Kaldar landed in the grass and strode to them with a big smile on his face. He wore jeans and a blue T-shirt that said WORLD'S BEST UNCLE on it in black letters written in the Broken's English.

Kaldar was Cerise's cousin. The last time they had met, Jack and Lark were still friends, and she told him to watch Kaldar at dinner. While people ate and mingled, Kaldar stole things from their pockets, then put them back.

"Hello, hello!" Kaldar grinned wider, showing white teeth. Cerise hugged him; he laughed and held his hand out to William. William unclenched his teeth and clapped Kaldar's hand and made some sort of quiet snarl that could've been *hello* or could've been *I'll kill you*, Jack wasn't sure.

Kaldar pumped William's hand and turned to him, palm out. "Jack!"

Jack took his hand and gave it a squeeze.

Kaldar's eyebrows crept up. "Easy now. Don't break my fingers."

Jack hid a smile. Heh-heh.

"I've come to beg for help," Kaldar said. "Professional, not personal."

"What is it?" Cerise asked.

"I'm tracking the theft of an item for the Mirror. The trail led into the Edge, so I ran some evidence I had by a buddy of mine in Baton Rouge PD."

"Did sirens and blue lights go off when you walked into the police station?" Cerise asked.

"Very funny." Kaldar grimaced. "I had a fingerprint I lifted from a crime scene in Adrianglia. He ran it through the database. One of the thieves popped up. He is in California in a drug rehab facility." Kaldar grimaced again. "To get to him, I have to fly to the Democracy of California on the Weird's side. You know what it's like. I need backup."

William showed Kaldar his teeth. "Not happening. We're leaving tomorrow."

"Business?" Kaldar asked.

William nodded.

Kaldar sighed.

"You could request assistance from the field office," Cerise said.

"And work with a stranger? Please." Kaldar frowned. His eyes lit up. "Wait. Give me the boy."

"He's twelve!" Cerise reached over and gently popped Kaldar on the back of the head.

"Not Jack. Gaston."

Jack bared his teeth. He liked Gaston about as well as William liked Kaldar. Gaston was William's ward and Cerise's nephew or cousin or something. He was bigger, stronger, older, and he wasn't all human, either.

William shrugged. "He isn't a full agent."

"He's been trained by the Mirror for three years, he's nineteen, and he can lift a cow. I am not exaggerating. I've seen him do it. Let me take him."

"I'll think about it," William said.

"Why is everything so difficult with you?" Kaldar raised his left eyebrow.

"I'm responsible for him," William growled.

Kaldar's face turned serious. It was like someone had jerked the funny mask off his face. "William, I was there when he was born. I changed his diapers. Do you honestly think I'd let any harm come to him?"

"Let me think . . ." William leaned forward. "Yes!"

"That's ridiculous. I just need an extra pair of eyes and ears. Consider it his final exam, Professor. I can look after him much better than you."

William took a step toward Kaldar. His eyes got a predatory glint.

"All right!" Cerise declared. "Why don't we go to the

house and have some delicious rabbit before I pull out my sword and have to separate you two."

She put her hands on the arms of both men and pushed them toward the house. "Come on, Jack."

There was nothing to do but follow.

JACK trotted down the path toward the woods, away from William's house. His belly was full of hare. It should've made him happy, but it didn't.

The wind brought a familiar scent of lemon. Jack stopped at a large oak and leaned against it, his back to the bark. Above him, branches rustled. A moment later, George climbed down, holding a small spyglass in his hand. He wore a white shirt, a pale brown vest, brown pants, and dark brown boots. A short rapier hung from his waist. His hair was pale blond and cut longish. His eyes were big and blue, and he looked like a girl.

"How did you know where I was?" George asked.

"You put lemon juice in your hair again."

"The juice makes it lighter." George leaned against the maple to Jack's left. "How did it go?"

"William and Cerise are leaving tomorrow," Jack said. "Mirror mission, and he doesn't know when he's coming back. William said he'll talk to Declan when he comes back. He says to stay out of trouble until he comes back."

"Not going to happen," George said.

"Yeah."

"So what are we going to do?" George asked.

"I can't stay at the house. I'll do something or say something, and they'll ship me off. With William away, nobody will tell them no."

"Rose wouldn't do that," George said.

Jack glanced at him. "She's mad, George. Really mad. I'm going to get my bag tonight and go into the woods. I'll wait it out until William comes back."

"Jack, you have to think ahead." George shook his head. "What happens if you disappear?"

Jack shrugged. He would be in the woods, that's what would happen.

"Declan and Rose will think that you ran away. They'll search for you. They won't find you, because you're good at hiding, so more people will get involved. Rumors will spread: Lord Camarine, the Marshal of the Southern Provinces, has lost his changeling brother-in-law. Obviously, he can't control him, because the beast took off into the wild. Lock your children, or he'll break into your house and devour them at night. Maybe we should hunt him down with torches." George shook his head again. "They will send you to Hawk's after that for sure. No, we need an actual plan."

"Well, I don't have one," Jack growled.

George peered through the trees. "You said William and Cerise are leaving tomorrow. Who does the wyvern belong to? I got stuck at fencing, and when I made it here, the wyvern had landed already."

"Kaldar. He has a mission in the Democracy of California. He came to ask them for help, but they're leaving on their own thing tomorrow, so he's taking Gaston with him instead."

George thought about it. "When?"

"Tomorrow evening. He has to give the wyvern time to rest before the long trip." What did that have anything to do with it?

"That's a large cabin," George said.

"So?"

"If they're flying to California, they'll pack it full of supplies, right?"

Jack looked at the wyvern. It was a large cabin. Large enough to hide in, especially if it was packed with crates and bags.

"Let me talk to Gaston. We can't pull it off without him. If it goes well, we pack tonight," George said. "We'll tell Declan and Rose we have an overnight camp for school. By the time they realize we're gone, we'll be in California."

"Gaston won't help," Jack said.

"Let me worry about that."

Jack stared at his brother. "If we go, it will be the same thing as if I ran away. The search and the torches."

"We'll tell Lark where we're going, and she will tell Declan and Rose when the time comes. They won't be happy, but Kaldar is on a Mirror mission, and Declan and Rose won't jeopardize it. Besides, it's clear across the continent. Did you see the pile of stuff on Declan's desk? It's not like he can just take off and leave the Southern Provinces to be overrun by criminals. Lark will tell them that Kaldar will take care of us." George smiled. "There will be hell to pay when we get home, but they can't send you off while you are in California. This will work."

"And if it doesn't?"

"We'll think of something else. Now we have to go home and quietly pack. Tomorrow, we have to go to school, like normal, and be very well behaved."

They started down the forest path.

George's leather boots creaked as he walked. He needed to oil them or something, Jack reflected.

If George came with him, they would both be in trouble.

"You don't have to do this," Jack said. "I can do this by myself."

"You remember when you beat up Thad Mosser?"

Thad was a mean Edger kid. He had it in for George, but it was years ago, back when they lived in the Edge. Besides, it only took one fight and some stitches to get it settled. "Yeah."

"We leave tomorrow evening," George said.

They didn't talk any more until they got home.

THE cabin was cramped. Jack stirred in his small space, squished between the wall of the cabin and the wall of wicker trunks Gaston had stuffed into the cabin. Across from him, George leaned against the cabin wall. His eyes were closed.

They had been flying for most of the night. At first, Kaldar and Gaston talked. Something about some thieves from the Edge stealing a magic thing from West Egypt and trying to sell it to the Hand. Things didn't go well because they broke a fountain, and one of the Hand's people had been blown to bits. Kaldar had found something called a crack pipe, whatever the hell that might be, and taken it to the cops in the Broken. They found a fingerprint on the pipe, and it belonged to someone named Alex Callahan, who was checked into a "rehab" in the Broken's California.

"How much did that nugget of information cost you?" Gaston had asked.

"A few trinkets from the Weird," Kaldar had told him. "Turns out our boy has a rap sheet a mile long. The State of Louisiana got him for possession and burglary. He also earned a couple of warrants in Florida: theft and possession with intent to distribute. And his rickety 1990 Nissan Sentra was involved in a high-speed chase and somehow gave the cop cars the slip."

"That tells me nothing," Gaston had said.

"He outran a racehorse on a donkey."

"You think he went into the Edge?"

"He had to," Kaldar had said. "The high-speed chase netted him another heap of charges. Then he popped up in Alabama and Tennessee, theft and possession again, and right now his fingerprints show him checked into the Rose Cliff in northern California. The Rose Cliff is where you put your addict relatives when you have money."

"This guy seems mostly small-time," Gaston said.

"'Seems' is the key word here. We only know about the things he got caught on, and on each one, he was so addled, it's a wonder he could find the ground with both feet. You and I were both Edgers once. You know how they operate."

"Family," Gaston agreed. "Somewhere in the Edge, someone knows him."

"Exactly. And that someone suddenly got a lot of money and checked Alex into rehab. Most Edgers don't have forty grand lying on the shelf somewhere."

Gaston whistled. "That's serious money."

"One has to wonder how Alex's family came by it. If I

had time, I would knock on some doors in the Edge around Macon where he first blazed a trail, but we don't have that luxury. We know where he is, so we go to him and we ask him how his crack pipe ended up in the town square in the Weird next to the bits and pieces of the Hand's agent."

None of it made a lot of sense, and now everyone was quiet.

Jack fidgeted. It would've been much cooler to sit up front, where he could see the sky and the clouds and the ground far below. The heat rising from the wyvern's back and the blankets Gaston had given them kept the cabin warm, but it wasn't exactly toasty. He fidgeted again. Bored. Bored, bored, bored. He'd slept, he'd read through the book he'd packed in his bag—it was all about the Weird's nobles on the Old Continent fighting against the ancient raiders. The book was okay, and the hero got to cut the bad guy's head off at the end, which was fine.

They had stopped a few times, and Gaston snuck them out to relieve themselves, but that was hours ago.

Jack stretched his legs, bumping his brother. George opened his eyes, and mouthed, *"Stop it."*

"You stop it," Jack mouthed back.

George raised his arm and pretended to scratch his armpit. *"Ape."*

Jack kicked him. George kicked back, and his heel landed on Jack's thigh. So that's how it is? Fine. Jack lunged across the space and grabbed George by his arm. George elbowed him in the gut. Jack rammed his fist into his brother's side.

"Did you hear that?" Kaldar asked.

"I'll check on it."

George sank a fist into Jack's ear. Pain exploded in his head. Ow. Jack punched him in the ribs.

A huge fist landed on his head. The world got fuzzy for a second, and Jack went down. Half a second later, George sprawled next to him, clutching the back of his head. "Nothing, just some crates shifting," Gaston called out.

Jack pointed to the front of the cabin and put his fist into his palm. George nodded. When they got out of here, Gaston would be in for a treat.

"How long till we land?" Gaston asked up front.

"A couple of hours. Almost there," Kaldar said.

"So what's the plan?"

"The plan is for me to visit Mr. Alex Callahan and ask him some questions."

"Do you think he'll answer?"

"Not without some persuasion," Kaldar said. "As it happens, persuasion is my specialty."

"I take it I'll be staying with the wyvern?"

Kaldar laughed. "Unless you want to panic the entire city of Red Grove with your serrated teeth."

"Are you sure? One look at me, and Alex will spill his life story. If that fails, I could always be convincing."

"By breaking one of his limbs?"

"If necessary."

"It may come to that."

"Is something bothering you, Uncle?" Gaston asked.

"This guy. Alex Callahan. He's a junkie. A rap sheet a mile long, all of it with drug charges over the last six years."

"Aha."

"The Pyramid of Ptah is a tough nut to crack even for the best picklock. These guys walked in and out. Popped fourteen locks in record time. It would take me days."

"You're thinking magic?" Gaston asked.

"Probably. That means if Alex is the picker, he would've never done the job."

"How do you figure?"

"Anytime he wants a hit, he can break into anything in the Edge or in the Weird, sell it, and get high. If this lockpicking talent is magic, then it only works in the Edge and the Weird. So why does Alex Callahan have a trophy wall of theft charges in the Broken? Why steal where you're at a disadvantage?"

"Maybe he's stupid."

"Junkies are clever; they have to be to keep the addiction going, and long-term junkies are too far gone to plan ahead.

They're only thinking of the next high. An addict will steal anything, and he will sell it to you for twenty bucks. That's the going price of a meth hit. No matter what the item is, the fence will offer the addict twenty bucks for it, and the addict will take it. To them a five-hundred-dollar DVD player for one hit is a fair trade because they have no use for the player. The Pyramid of Ptah is a risky and compli- cated job. The chances of getting caught are high, and to top it all off, whoever took the item sold it to the Hand. Cal- lahan wouldn't have done the job by himself, and even if he had, he would've unloaded the item at the first fence along the way. No, Alex might have been there, but he wasn't the picklock. Someone else set this job up."

"Well, we'll find out in a couple of hours, right?"

"Right. Whoever this picklock is, I can't wait to meet him."

Gaston laughed. "Remember, you work for the Mirror, Uncle."

"I remember. Still, the possibilities are intriguing. I'm sure this guy and I could come to an understanding."

The voices fell silent.

Jack stirred in his small space, sighed, and curled up. Two hours. He could sleep for two hours.

IT was more like three hours before the wyvern dipped down and another fifteen minutes or so before they landed. Jack sat quietly while Kaldar got out, changed clothes, and gave some final instructions to Gaston. Finally, a thump resonated through the cabin as Gaston's fist pounded on the wood and wicker. "Up, ladies. He's gone. I'm going to get some water and mix catalyst feed for the wyvern. Piss, stretch your legs, do whatever you need to do. And stay the hell away from the boundary. We're really close."

Jack looked at George. They were close to the boundary. They hadn't been in the Broken for almost three years, not since the last time they went to visit Grandma, and they hadn't been in California ever.

The light of the early morning glowed ahead, sifting through the front windshield of the cabin. Jack leaped over the crate, pushed the wicker door open, and stopped. A few steps ahead, the ground plunged down in a sheer cliff, and beyond it, a vast ocean spread to the horizon, blue and pale silver. A wind gust shot from under the cliff and hit him in the face. A thousand scents exploded all around Jack: the smell of pine resin and eucalyptus; the fragrance of small blue flowers, hiding between the crags; the distant stench of seagulls screaming overhead; salt; wet sand; ocean water, clean and slightly bitter; seaweed; and, as an afterthought, a faint aroma of smoked fish flavoring the breeze.

For a second, Jack couldn't process it all, then he jumped, arms open wide like wings, and dashed down the near-vertical slope to the waves below.

THREE

THE Rose Cliff Rehabilitation Center could only be described as posh, Kaldar reflected, walking through the glass door into a foyer. Huge windows painted the cream and pale peach walls with rectangles of golden sunlight. The floor was brown marble tile, polished to a mirror sheen, and as he walked across it to a marble counter, his steps sent tiny echoes through the vestibule. Normally, he preferred shoes that made no sound, but the set of Broken clothes had to be obtained quickly, and he didn't have a lot of choices. Now he felt like a shod horse: *clack, clack, clack*.

The mirrored wall behind the receptionist presented him with his reflection: he wore a dark gray suit, a white shirt so crisp he was half-afraid the folded collar might nick his neck and draw blood, and the cursed black shoes. His dark hair was slicked back from his face. He'd shaved, trimmed his eyebrows, and dabbed cologne on his skin. He smelled expensive, he made noise as he walked, and he projected enough confidence to win a dozen sieges.

The blond receptionist behind the counter smiled at him. "May I help you, sir?"

"My name is Jonathan Berman." He held out his business card. She took it and studied it for a second. Silver foil cursive crossed the dark blue card printed on the best stock money could buy. It read: SHIFTING THE PARADIGM. Below it his name was printed, followed by a phony Los Angeles address.

"Good morning, Mr. Berman."

Kaldar nodded. Amazing how the Broken worked: all

those forms of identification, but hand someone a business card, and they forget to ask you for your driver's license. He'd had business cards in twenty different names, one for each region of the country. Each communicated something different. This one said money, confidence, and success, and, judging by her even wider smile, this fact wasn't lost on the receptionist.

"How may I help you, Mr. Berman?"

"I'm here to see Alex Callahan."

The receptionist glanced at her computer screen. Her fingers with very long nails colored canary yellow flew over the keyboard. "Mr. Callahan was admitted three days ago. Normally, we recommend that our guests refrain from distractions during the first two weeks of treatment."

Kaldar leaned on the counter and gave her a knowing smile. "What's your name?"

"Bethany."

"Well, Bethany, Alex is my cousin. I understand he came in with his parents."

That was a wild stab in the dark, but who else would make a deal with the Hand, then blow all of that hard-earned cash on a rehab for an addict? That kind of love came only from parents. If Alex had a woman, she was either an addict like him or penniless like him.

"His father, actually," Bethany said.

Kaldar felt the first hint of excitement. He was right; there was a family, and they were in this theft up to their eyeballs. Alex was probably too far gone to care, but they cared. They had something to lose. That meant he could lean on them.

Everyone had a lever . . .

While his mind processed and calculated, his lips were moving. "Just between you and me, did Alex's father strike you as a man who can simply drop forty thousand dollars on this marble counter and walk away?"

"I can't say." The receptionist leaned back, but he read the answer in her eyes. "It's not proper."

"Who will know?" Kaldar leaned closer and made a show of glancing around. "I don't see anyone, do you?" His voice dropped into a conspiratorial, intimate half whisper. "So just between you and me, he looked like a man who hunts for spare change in his couch."

Bethany blinked, big eyes opened wide.

"You have to ask yourself, Bethany, where does a man like that get this kind of money. He borrows it, of course. No bank would give him a loan, so he has to turn to family." Kaldar smiled magnanimously.

Understanding crept into Bethany's eyes. "Oh."

"All I want is to make sure that I've made a correct investment in Alex's future. I'd like to speak to him and let him tell me if he is treated well and that his needs are being seen to. I promise I carry no contraband." He raised his hands palms out. "You may search me if you'd like."

He slipped just enough suggestion into that last phrase to make Bethany blush a little. "That won't be necessary." She pointed to the right, where a group of blocky leather chairs and couches surrounded a glass cube of a table. "Please wait here."

Kaldar turned on his heel and clacked his way across the floor to the leather chairs. A hollowed-out wooden dish, shaped almost precisely like a canoe, sat on the table. The canoe held three spheres about the size of a large grapefruit made of smoky glass shot through with veins of gold. Odd decoration. He pictured himself swiping a sphere, its comforting weight heavy in his hand. In a pinch, he could use it to shatter the windowpane and give himself a head start if he had to leave in a hurry.

Two men emerged from the side hallway. One was middle-aged and blond, going gray, with the slick, clean look of someone accustomed to dealing with people of money and making a good living from it. The other was Alex Callahan. Tall, lanky, with longish hair on the crossroads of dishwater blond and faded red, Callahan walked oddly, as if he didn't fully trust the ground to support his weight. His cheekbones looked sharp enough to cut, his cheeks caved into his face, and his neck, left bare by the collar of a too-big T-shirt, stuck out, thin, long, and bony.

A mean, arrogant sneer bent his lips. His eyes radiated a manic energy and contempt. It was the look that said, "You think I'm shit because I'm a junkie, but guess what? I am better than you."

Kaldar had seen that same look on the faces of spoiled addicts before. This wasn't a desperate soul in need of help debasing himself for a fix. This was a man surfing the edge of violence, who saw himself as a victim and the rest of the world as owing him.

Callahan was too far gone. Threats wouldn't work. He simply didn't care about himself or his family.

"Cousin!" Kaldar grinned at Alex.

Callahan didn't miss a beat. "Didn't expect to see you here, cousin."

The older handler held out his hand. "I'm Dr. Leem. I want to assure you that Alex is being well looked after. Isn't that right, Alex?"

"Sure," Callahan said.

"Let's sit down?" Leem suggested.

They took their places on the leather furniture, and Leem launched into a long overview of the facilities. Kaldar pretended to listen, watching Callahan. Callahan watched him back. The file back in Louisiana said he was twenty-eight; he looked forty-eight. His foot tapped the floor; he picked on the skin around his nails; he rolled his mouth into different variations of his sneer, which was probably semipermanent. He'd been in the facility for over forty-eight hours. They had detoxed him. Alex Callahan was sober, and he hated it.

Finally, Kaldar raised his hand.

"I'm sorry to interrupt, Doctor, but my time is limited. I'm due in LA for a meeting. Would you mind giving Alex and me some privacy? This won't take long."

"Of course." Leem rose and moved to the counter, keeping them in plain view.

Callahan leaned back, bony knees straining the loose fabric of his jeans. "What do you want, dear cousin?"

Kaldar flicked his fingers. A small clear packet appeared

between his index and middle finger as if by magic. Inside the packet, a small purple flower spread three petals. Bromedia. The most potent herbal hallucinogenic the Weird had to offer. The purest of highs. He'd procured it during one of the jobs he'd done for the Mirror. It involved a caravan of illegal contraband trading between the Edge and the Weird, and in the chaos of the arrest, nobody ever realized that some of the illegal goods had gone missing.

Callahan's eyes fixed on the packet, on fire with greed. Kaldar closed his fingers for a moment and opened them, showing Callahan an empty hand. The packet with the flower had vanished.

"How did you get out of Adriana?" Kaldar asked.

"I ported us. That's my thing," Callahan said. "Can only do it once in a while and about twenty feet tops. It went sour, the Hand's freaks were closing in, so I got me and my old man out of the square, then we ran."

A teleporter. Kaldar had run across them before—it was a rare talent and very useful, but teleporters could only move a few feet at a time, and most of them couldn't do any magic for a day or two after.

"What happened to your third partner?"

"Audrey had left before we got to Adriana."

A woman? Of course. Fate had decided to have a little fun with him. Very well, he could take a joke.

"She said she was done." Callahan shrugged. "My dear sister doesn't care for me very much."

I wonder why. "Where is the box?"

"Don't know, don't care. Old man found a buyer somewhere. All I know, he dropped me off here to 'get clean.'" Callahan's voice dripped with derision. "That's the last I've seen him."

"Where would your father go to hide?"

Callahan rocked back and laughed, a dry humorless chuckle. "You won't find him. Old man's a legend. They call him Slippery Callahan. He's got a hideout in every settlement in the Edge. Anyway, he isn't who you want. You need Audrey."

"I'm listening," Kaldar said.

Callahan leaned forward. "The old man is good at planning. That's his shtick. But to pull off the heist, you go to Audrey. She's the picker. Any lock, any door, she can open it like that." He snapped his fingers. "She doesn't like me because of some business back, but the old man, him she hates. Daddy issues, blah-blah-blah. My sister is anal. She'd know who he sold it to, and she would be the one to get it back for you."

Whenever a woman got involved, things instantly became more complicated. Kaldar flipped the packet of Bromedia back into view. "Where can I find Audrey?"

"That's the funny part. She's up in Washington, near some town called Olympia. The old man said she'd gone law and order on us. Works for some PI firm under her real name. Can you believe that shit?" Callahan laughed again.

Kaldar rose and held out his hand. Callahan got up, shook it, and Kaldar slipped the packet into his fingers. Callahan palmed it with practiced ease and let go. The whole thing took a second at most.

"Half a petal in hot water," Kaldar murmured. "Any more, and you'll regret it."

"Don't school an expert," Callahan told him.

Kaldar headed for the door, nodding at Bethany and Leem in passing. There was no need to exchange threats and promise to return in case he was lied to. Callahan had been around long enough to know the score.

"THIS wasn't one of my better ideas," George murmured.

"Yes, but it's fun." Jack strode down the street. The sun shone bright, and he squinted at it. Kaldar's scent floated on the breeze, spiced with the deep, resin-saturated aroma of eucalyptus. "When was the last time you've had fun, George?" He stretched "George" out the way Adrianglian blueblood girls did.

George looked sour. "I'm too busy making sure that you don't kill anybody or get killed to have fun."

"Blah-blah-blah."

Around them, tan, white, and pale brown stucco buildings lined the street. They passed a gas station, followed by a furniture store, and some sort of restaurant emanating a smoky, charred-meat smell that made him drool, and now they marched along a low stone wall, behind which houses rose, each with a small square of a yard.

Jack stopped. Kaldar's scent lingered at the curb and vanished, replaced by the bitter stink of gasoline, rubber, and a foul burned smell. He shook his head, trying to clear his nose.

"What's the matter with you?" George asked.

"The fumes. All that time in the Weird with no cars made my nose extrasensitive. He got into a car here."

"Which way did it go?"

Jack puzzled over the faint marks of rubber on the pavement. "Right."

George surveyed the intersection up ahead. "That would've put him into the right-turn lane. Come on."

"Why are we following him?" Jack trotted down the street. When he first mentioned that he wanted to go to the Broken, he'd expected George to shoot him down, but his brother jumped on the chance. At first they had to follow Kaldar to get to the boundary, which made sense. The crossing had been harder than he remembered. The magic squeezed him and ground, not wanting to let go, but, finally, he won and made it through into the Broken. Then they followed Kaldar's scent so they wouldn't get lost, which made sense, too. But the trail led them deeper and deeper into the city, and now Kaldar had gotten into a car. They were still wearing the Weird's clothes: he wore a dark brown shirt, George wore a white shirt with loose wide sleeves, and they both sported brown practice leggings that passed for sweatpants in the Weird.

"I'm fourteen," George said. "You're twelve. Gaston is only five years older than me."

"Yeah?"

"Gaston gets to run around with William and do cool shit."

Jack gave him a sideways glance. "Do cool what?"

"Do cool shit."

Jack peered at George.

"What?"

"Waiting to see if your face will crack after saying 'shit,' Cursed Prince."

"Whatever." George waved his hand.

Jack turned the corner. Ahead, a long street rolled into the distance, bordered on the right by a tall, dense hedge. The scent of the car continued up the street. Jack followed it.

"The point is, Gaston fights the Hand, he gets weapons, and he hasn't spent a day stuffed into a boarding school," George said.

"You like school."

George stopped and gave him an icy look. "I don't."

Jack turned on the ball of his foot to face George. "You rule that damn school." While he could do no right.

"I know the rules, and I follow them. It doesn't mean I like it. I can't just punch everyone who calls me Edge Trash, because both of us can't screw up all the time. The more you throw your fists around, the less freedom I have to make mistakes."

Oh, really? "Exactly how is it my fault?"

"We're the two brothers from the Edge. When the blue-bloods look at us, they lump us together. If we both screw up, then they'll completely despise us."

"And this way they just despise me." Jack stopped. A short side street sliced through the hedge. Through the break, he could see a parking lot. Whatever Kaldar drove, he had taken it in there. Why steal a car to drive it only a mile?

Jack turned into the parking lot. George followed. Rows of cars greeted them. To the left, five older boys loitered on the edge of the lot.

"Yes, please, do feel sorry for yourself." George rolled his eyes. "Oh, poor Jack. Oh, he just doesn't understand."

Jack growled.

"When he grabs a guy by his hair and smashes his face

into the wall, he is just reacting to being bullied. He is sensitive."

Jack spun and launched a quick jab, aiming for George's stomach. George blocked and danced aside.

"And then he runs and hides in his room, and his poor sister has to go and take his plate to him because he is brooding there . . ."

Jack snapped a quick hook. George dodged, and the blow whistled past his chin.

". . . Crying into his pillow . . ."

Jack veered left, right, rocking on the balls of his feet, and sank a quick powerful punch. George saw it, but too late. All he could do was turn in to it, and Jack connected with his brother's shoulder. *Ha! Landed one.* And then the heel of George's left hand slammed into his nose. Jack staggered back. Ow.

"That's right, solve all your problems with violence."

"Don't worry, I won't hit your pretty face." Jack stood on his toes and bowed, twisting his hands as expected before you asked a girl to dance. "We wouldn't want to mar that delicate beau—"

George's fist slammed into his face. Pain exploded in his jaw. The world blinked. He locked his fingers on George's wrist, jerked his foot up into his brother's stomach, and rolled back, heaving George over him. George slapped the asphalt with his back. The air burst out of him in a loud gasp. Jack rolled up, clamped George's right arm between his legs, scissoring it, and leaned over George's torso with his back, pinning him down, right forearm across the windpipe.

George squeezed out some hoarse noises.

Jack leaned closer and grinned. "Hi. How are you doing?"

George tried to jab the fingers of his free left hand into Jack's neck. Jack ducked out of the way. He could still remember, five years ago, when George was dying, and he fought all of his fights for him. Jack had the upper hand now, but there was a second or two back there when, if they had been playing for real, George could've won. He had been practicing, and not just with the rapier. Jack had to figure out what George was doing and do that, or he'd be left behind.

Jack leaned a little harder.

George growled.

"You know I can lie here all day. It's not hurting me at all. How long do you practice every day? Two hours? You should practice more. Don't struggle now. You might get your hair dirty."

"Hrgff."

"What's that?" Jack eased the pressure.

"In the Edge, I would've killed you by now."

"With your flash, yes. Don't kid yourself. If this was for real, you would've broken your neck in the fall."

A desperate high-pitched squeak jerked Jack's attention to the end of the parking lot. Straight ahead, the five guys crowded around a tree growing from a square flower bed. The thicker kid with brown hair held a rope. Another squeak. Jack focused on the end of the rope coming from beneath the hedge on the other side. The kid on the left looked back at him and George, said something, and laughed.

A fist landed on his ear. Jack ignored it and sat up. George sat up next to him.

The thicker kid jerked the rope and pulled, dragging a small gray shape into the light. It was bedraggled and filthy, its fur smeared with some sort of mud or paint.

Jack forgot where he was.

The little cat shook and hugged the ground, trying to break free of the rope. The asshole on the other end kept pulling, dragging the limp body across the asphalt.

Red flooded the world. Jack exhaled rage through his nose. Suddenly, he was on his feet and walking, and he didn't remember how he got there.

Next to him, George caught up with him, reached out, and snapped an antenna off the nearest car.

The world snapped into crystal clarity, the smells too sharp, the sounds too loud. Jack floated through it, light as a feather.

"Don't kill anyone," George said.

The bastards noticed them and turned toward them.

"You two done making out?" a tall blond kid asked.

The little cat lay on its side. He wasn't moving. A long stripe of bright green paint ran along his back, gluing his fur into small, sharp spikes. They had painted the cat. Those fucking bastards had painted the cat and then tortured it.

The Wild snarled inside him. He strained, pushing it back into its den.

"I'll make it simple," George's voice rang out next to him with icy precision. "Give us the cat, and you can go."

"Man. What a fucking dumb-ass." The blond kid snorted. "Get the hell out of here, fags."

"What's with the clothes? Are you from some sort of fag cult?" the asshole with the rope asked.

"No, man, they're from a Renaissance fair."

"Maybe they need the cat for their fag sacrifice!"

The Wild retreated into its lair and stared at him with glowing eyes.

"Yeah, be careful, they might pull some crazy satan shit on you, man." The bigger dark-haired kid laughed.

The smaller kid on the right raised his hands and crossed his index fingers. "Stay back, the power of Christ compels you!"

Jack looked at George. "Now?"

"Ooh, I am so scared." The blond kid raised his hands. "So scared . . ."

"Now," George said.

Jack charged.

OUTSIDE, the California sun hit Kaldar. He kept walking, down the path and out into the street, through the open iron gates, past the cream-colored wall bordering the rehab facility. He turned left, heading for the parking lot. He'd left his stolen vehicle there. Men in pristine black shoes did not walk; they drove expensive cars, and so he'd procured one on an off chance someone might see him arrive. And now he needed one to depart quickly because a man in his outfit would draw attention jogging down the street.

He had to find Audrey Callahan. Kaldar imagined a female version of Alex Callahan. Ugh. Likely an addict as well. If Callahan was to be believed, she hated him, so she wouldn't have helped them with the heist out of love or from a sense of obligation. No, their father must've dangled money or drugs before her, and she took it.

Family was the last line of defense. No matter what Kaldar had done or would do, he could walk through the gates of the New Mar house and be welcomed with open arms, food, and friendly proposals to rearrange his face. They would lament and bellyache and whine, but in the end, crossbows and rifles would come off the walls, and the Mars would ride out to fix whatever he'd wrought.

The Callahans couldn't stand each other. Alex despised his sister and thought his father was a sucker. Since Audrey returned the hate, using her brother's safety as leverage was out of the question.

Audrey wasn't an obnoxiously common name, and the list of PI firms in Olympia had to be somewhat limited. It shouldn't take him too long to find her . . .

Ahead, a vicious snarl ripped through the afternoon. It sounded inhuman, but he'd heard it before. That's how William sounded when he cut through people like they were butter. Kaldar sped up.

A scream of pure terror followed. A changeling here in the Broken? William could cross back and forth, so it was plausible . . . Was someone else from the Weird or the Edge here for Callahan?

Ahead, an adolescent boy, around fifteen or sixteen, stumbled out from between the hedges bordering the entrance to the parking lot. His nose was bloody, and both of his eyes sported red puffy bags that promised to develop into spectacular shiners. Red whip marks crossed his forearms and neck.

The boy stared at Kaldar, looking but not seeing, his eyes two pools of fear, and took off down the street, limping. Kaldar broke into a run.

A moment, and he turned the corner into the parking lot.

Four adolescent kids rolled on the ground, clutching various limbs as a result of a savage beating. In the center of the carnage Jack stood, his arms raised in a trademark South Adrianglian style. Next to him, George brandished a car antenna.

Damn it all to hell.

The bigger of the boys moved. George let him rise halfway and whipped the car antenna. Right, left, right. The kid tumbled down.

George glanced up, saw Kaldar, and grabbed Jack's shoulder. The two kids froze.

He had to get them away from the damn parking lot before someone called the cops. Escape first, explanations later. Kaldar moved past the prone bodies to the first decent older vehicle he saw and slid the long narrow strip of metal from his sleeve. The boys followed. A second to pop the door open, another three seconds to hot-wire the car, while Jack slid into the back, clutching a small cat that looked dead, and George hopped into the shotgun seat.

Another second, and they pulled out of the parking lot and merged into the current of cars, heading out of the city toward the boundary and the safety of the Edge.

Fuck. Fuck, fuck, fuck. He had the two wards of the fucking Marshal of the fucking Southern Provinces in a stolen car. An entire continent away from where the two of them were supposed to be. In the Broken. Where they had beat up some Broken children. Well, if those children weren't broken before, they were surely broken now.

Fate, that bloody, vicious, fickle bitch. Sometimes she loved him, and he could do nothing wrong. And sometimes she stuck a knife in his back.

Kaldar adjusted the rearview mirror until Jack's face swung into view. "What the hell are you doing here?"

"They were torturing the cat," Jack said.

That explained volumes and nothing at all. "Who else knows you're here?"

"Why are you asking?" George asked.

"So I would know if I could kill you and dispose of the bodies." That ought to shake them up. For all he knew,

Declan was scouring the countryside looking for these precious darlings and breathing fire. How the hell was he going to get out of this?

In the rearview mirror, Jack gathered himself. Kaldar was suddenly aware that sitting with his back to the boy left his neck vulnerable.

"You won't kill us," George said from the front seat. His voice trembled slightly.

"Why not? Cerise is mildly fond of you, but I have no emotional attachment to either of you. I could slit your throats and toss you into a ravine. Nobody would know. You can be sure I would be sad and express my condolences to your sister at the first opportunity."

George paled and stared straight ahead. No tears, no hysterics. Some sort of calculation was taking place behind those blue eyes. At least the boy was thinking. That was usually a positive sign.

"We told Lark that we had stowed away on your wyvern. She will wait until Declan and Rose panic, then tell them where we are."

It wasn't enough that Fate had stabbed him with a knife. No, the blade had to be poisoned. Kaldar feverishly sorted through the possible outcomes. How in the world would he explain this? And it would have to be explained and justified. Instead of wondering where his brothers-in-law had disappeared to, Declan would know that some distant, no-good cousin of his best friend's wife had taken them to the Democracy of California, the place that made Convict Island seem like a walk in the park.

He would need Richard, Kaldar decided. His older brother and Declan were cut from the same cloth. The two of them would sit down, sip some wine, share stories of their siblings' regrettable behavior, commiserate with each other's family issues, and in the end the Marshal of the Southern Provinces would see the light and perhaps condescend not to murder him.

The two boys sat completely quiet. Idiots. "I'm waiting for an explanation," Kaldar ground out.

"Jack might be sent to Hawk's," George said. "William promised to intervene on his behalf."

The light dawned. "But he's gone on a mission, and the two of you are trying to buy some time at my expense."

"Yes." George nodded.

Perfect. Just perfect. "I understand why Jack would run away. Why are you here?"

The kid looked at him as if he were stupid. "I'm his brother."

Of course. Why did I even ask? "How much time do we have before your brother-in-law loses his grip on his temper?"

"At least a week," George said. "I informed them that we had a weeklong camp at College. It's an annual tradition, and since I told them about it, they won't have any reason to doubt it."

"And why would that be?" Kaldar made a left turn off the highway onto a country road. Two more miles, and they were in the clear. "Is it because you never lie?"

"No, it's because I only lie when I know I won't get caught."

Good answer. Kaldar considered his options. He could load them on the wyvern and take them back, which would take two days there and two days back. Too long. He had no reason to trust Alex Callahan. For all he knew, the junkie was calling his supposedly hateful sister right now with a warning. If he delayed, he risked losing Audrey. Not to mention that Lady Virai would be less than pleased. In fact, after she was done with him, they wouldn't even be able to harvest his organs.

He could load the kids on the wyvern and send them off with Gaston while he made his own way up the coast to Washington State. Going through the Edge on his own was out of the question—it was a wilderness. Going through the Weird was too dangerous—the Democracy of California consisted of a collection of baronies only loosely organized into a country. Each baron had his own private army at his disposal. They disliked their neighbors, but they hated outsiders. That left him with traveling through the Broken in a stolen car, ready to be pulled over by every highway patrolman with half a brain.

He could also just take the kids with him. It was the only solution that still permitted him to do his job. There would be hell to pay, but he would worry about it when the time came.

Kaldar leveled a heavy stare at George. "Tell me why I shouldn't load you on the wyvern and send you back to the loving arms of your sister?"

"We can be useful," George said.

"How? You think that you're smarter than everyone around you, and he"—Kaldar pointed at the backseat—"he can't control himself and starts breaking legs if someone looks at him for half a second too long. What I do requires perfect timing, resolve, and cold temper, none of which you've demonstrated so far."

George blushed.

"The fact that you're turning pink, like a happy bride, tells me you aren't well suited for my line of work."

The blush died. "We can be useful."

"Nobody pays attention to us because we're kids," Jack said from the backseat. "I can go anywhere. I can climb a wall, listen to the conversation, and tell it back to you word for word. George can animate a mouse, send it to a locked room, and tell you what's inside."

"We can speak three languages fluently," George said. "We're trained in self-defense, we know the protocol, and we're motivated."

"By what, exactly?" Kaldar asked.

"We're Edge Trash," George said. "No matter how perfect we are, we'll never be accepted completely. I can never hold a political post like Declan, and if I could attain it, I wouldn't have the kind of influence he does."

Kaldar glanced at him. Now that was interesting. "What makes you think that?"

George looked back and held his gaze. "Declan's uncle tried to enroll me into Selena University. It's the best school in Adrianglia. I scored in the top one percent of nine hundred applicants. I was denied admission. They know that Declan can pay for my school. They just don't want the likes of me on their admission scrolls."

Welcome to the real world, kid. The Weird ain't all it's cracked up to be. For all of their reforms and talk of equality, pedigree still mattered in the Weird.

"Jack can at least do the military, but he has to get his temper under control. I can't," George said. "I'm fast and strong, and I can fight well; but I don't have the endurance. I've worked on it for two years, and a ten-mile run leaves me nearly dead. I can't put on a fifty-pound backpack and march thirty miles in one day. I will never be good at it. But I could be good at this."

"The Mirror doesn't care if we're Edge Trash," Jack said. "It doesn't care that I'm a changeling, either."

This was ridiculous. These two kids thought they were good enough to go up against ruthless killers, augmented with magic and trained to murder. Two fools, full of innocent arrogance. Was he ever that young? No. No, he wasn't.

"This isn't an exercise or a drill. Nobody will blow the whistle and make the other side stop shooting while we huddle up and review what we did wrong. This is the real shit. People I go up against kill children. They won't hesitate. They will slit your throats and never think about it again. Your lives mean less to them than the life of a mosquito."

"We're not children," George said. "You killed your first man when you were fourteen."

He would have to wire Gaston's mouth shut.

"I was fighting in a family feud. It was about pride and hate and survival. And I had my family around me. It's different when you're in a group. Crowd mentality kicks in."

Kaldar made a right turn and slowed. The boundary bit down on them with its blunt teeth. The kids gasped. The car kept rolling, the pressure grinding him, compressing his bones, then, suddenly, they were through. George coughed.

"We're a crowd," Jack said.

Kaldar sighed. "More like a gang of idiots, and I am the biggest moron in it."

George coughed carefully. "Would that make you the Chief Moron then?"

Kaldar parked the car under a tree and rapped his knuckles against George's head. The boy grimaced.

"Gaston does that, too," Jack reflected.

"Family punishment." Kaldar got out of the car. "You will come with me to Washington. I need to find a woman there. You will not get in my way. No more unsupervised outings, no more field trips, and no more fights. You do as you are told, when you are told, or I will hog-tie you, load your scrawny behinds onto that wyvern, and have Gaston hand-deliver you home to your sister with a pretty little ribbon tied over your mouths. Understood?"

"Understood," the two voices chorused.

As they headed up the path, he checked the gray shape in Jack's arms. "How's the cat?"

"He'll be okay," Jack said. "He just needs someone to take care of him for a while."

Don't we all, Kaldar reflected. *Don't we all.*

FOUR

HELENA d'Amry inhaled the evening air. It smelled of the woods and dampness. She leaned against a large cypress, her cloak mimicking the color of the cypress bark so precisely she was practically invisible. In front of her, the road stretched into the distance, sectioned off by a weak shimmer. The boundary.

Helena closed her eyes and felt the reassuring current of magic. It was weak here, in the Edge, much weaker than in the Dukedom of Louisiana, but beyond the boundary, it didn't exist at all. Beyond the boundary, she would be dead. She could see the different dimension, but she could never enter it. The Edge was her limit. Very few of the Hand's agents could cross into the Broken. The Hounds were differently augmented, and yet barely a third of her crew had been able to cross the boundary.

This place, it was too damp, too rainy, too . . . verdant. Her Louisiana estate was verdant as well, but there the nature served her will, shaped by the tools of her gardener. Here it ran wild, like a bull out of control.

Still, it was good to be back. She had grown up in the Dukedom of Louisiana, on the family estate, and although her duty took her from the colony all the way to the capital of the Empire of Gaul, she had missed it. The air here smelled different from the atmosphere of the sprawling monster cities in the Old Continent. She hadn't planned to return, but her uncle needed looking after. To uphold the family name, she had stepped in to fill his shoes. They were rather large shoes to fill.

A faint noise made her turn. Three men approached from the Broken, running at an easy jog and carrying a bundle. Helena watched them enter the boundary. They slowed. One by one, they stepped through it, inching forward, their faces contorted, their legs bowing under the pressure. A long, torturous minute passed. Finally, the first man was through.

Helena peeled from the cypress trunk and stepped out into the road. Her cloak reacted, the long feathery strands contracting. Without an environment to mimic, they turned pale brown, each strand darkening toward the end. The strands fluttered weakly in the wind, as if she wore a mantle of owl feathers.

The men dumped the bundle on the ground.

To the left, Sebastian dropped thirty feet off a pine, landing in a half crouch. Jasmine stepped from behind the trunk, her bow aimed at the bundle. All around Helena, her unit, twelve of the Hound's finest, congealed as if by magic from the forest.

The largest of the three men who'd arrived from the Broken, an enormous giant with hair the color of eggshell, dropped onto one knee. Sebastian, her second-in-command, moved to stand by her side, hovering over her and emitting menace. The two men couldn't have been more different. Karmash, seven and a half feet tall, pale, with long hair so light it was nearly colorless, perfectly manicured nails and a penchant for finer things in life. Sebastian, barely five-ten but weighing nearly the same, darker-skinned, his dark hair cropped short. The ribbon of tattooed words around his neck spelled out FIERCE TO THE END. Monstrously strong and layered with hard, bulging muscle, Sebastian gave the words a new meaning. He was devoted to her the way a dog raised from a puppy is devoted to a kind but firm master. He didn't trust Karmash, and the albino giant couldn't stand him. It would be an excellent fight, Helena reflected.

Karmash was a loan, just like Mura, her new slayer shadow, but while the woman fit neatly into the chain of command, Karmash didn't. He was too used to running the show, and Sebastian hated him with silent, violent fury. That was fine. Sebastian was becoming too secure in his position. He needed some unfriendly competition. Besides, Karmash could enter the Broken, and apparently he got the job done. She had expected nothing less from one of Spider's operatives.

"My lady." Karmash's head was bowed, but his eyes watched her and Sebastian to her left.

"Rise."

He got up, towering a foot and a half over her. She walked over to the bundle and pulled down her hood. Her hair fell down over her shoulder in a long blond ponytail. "Open it."

The other operative crouched and sliced through the canvas, dumping a man out in the road. The man rolled up and sat in the dirt. "Hello."

Helena paced before him, tilting her head to get a better view. Thin. Almost emaciated. Bloodshot eyes. Feverish tint to the skin. Twitching hands. An addict.

"I can't say I appreciate the treatment." The man spat in the dirt.

What a sad, ugly wreck of a human being.

She crouched by him and stared into his eyes. He returned her gaze. Most people couldn't hold it: her pale green eyes with a cat pupil made them uncomfortable. Spider once told her it was like looking into the eyes of a demon and knowing you were about to be devoured. Her uncle always had a flair for the poetic. Sadly, this man was either too addled, too stupid, or too arrogant to cringe.

"Were you bruised?" Helena asked.

"I'm tender in places." The man sucked mucus back into his nose. "But I could see a way to forgiving this sort of thing, provided you make it worth my while. You did get me out of rehab, after all."

"Mmm, I see. Do you know who we are?"

"The Hand. The Mirror. Honestly, I don't give a shit."

Profanity in the presence of others. Expected of a low-born mongrel but rude all the same. "Where is the box?"

He raised his chin a bit. "What have you got for me?"

Helena almost laughed. He sat surrounded by the Hounds,

and he expected them to bribe him. She leaned closer, her voice quiet. "Are you for sale?"

"Sweetheart, everyone is for sale." The man shrugged. "You're new at this? Let me explain to you how things work. I'm not expensive. I know what you're looking for. You want my sister. Give me what I want, and I'll tell you all about her."

"Is that so?" *What a worm. No honor. No dignity. No loyalty. Pathetic.*

"Like I said, if the price is right, I'm your man. I'll tell you everything. I'll even let you in on another guy who beat you to me."

Helena straightened and glanced at Karmash. The big man yanked the captive to his feet, slid his arms under the man's stick arms, and locked his hands on the back of the man's head, jerking him up, off the ground.

"Hey, hey, hey!" The man squirmed in Karmash's grip. "Come on."

Helena pulled off her glove, unfastened her cloak, and let it fall. Behind her, Mura, dark-haired, sharp and narrow, like the blade of a dagger, took a step and caught the living fabric before it hit the ground. The cloak shimmered, turning an unhealthy shade of orange, straining to duplicate Mura's magic-altered skin.

Helena stood before the man. She wore supple leather and dark cloth. A leather belt clasped her tunic to her waist, together with custom-made sheaths which held her two curved swords. She pulled a black knife from her waist and took a step toward the addict.

The captive stared down at her. "What, you're going to work me over now? What for? I'm trying to make a deal here."

She arched her narrow eyebrows. "I don't do deals." She pinched the thin fabric of his shirt and sliced it open, baring his bony chest.

"Listen, you're making a mistake here. You'll waste all your time and energy with me, and for what? Just give me my little piece of the pie, and I'll tell you everything.

Helena pulled back her sleeve and showed him the blue

fang etched into her muscular forearm. "I'm a Hound of the Golden Throne. Do you know what that is?"

She could tell by his face that he had no idea. "Do you know that the Dukedom of Louisiana is a colony of the Greater Empire of Gaul?"

He nodded. "Sure."

"When the throne of Gaul wishes to slice open a boil, it calls upon me. I don't make deals. I don't bargain. I don't spare. I destroy for the glory of my country. Look into my eyes, sirrah."

He stared into her blue-green irises. She looked at him the way a tiger looks at her prey until she saw the first shiver of fear in his face.

"Tell me if you see any mercy." Her magic rose around her, like a smoky cloak of darkness.

The addict froze like a frightened bird. Finally, she had his attention.

Helena bowed her head for a brief second, her eyes closed. "I'm a Hound of the Golden Throne. I have the right of judgment within the Empire of Gaul and all of its colonies, and I find you, Alex Callahan, guilty. You are an enemy of Gaul."

Magic sparked. Karmash dropped Callahan, and the man blinked out of existence and reappeared twenty feet away. He hit the ground running and dashed down the path, squeezing every last drop of speed out of his worn-out body. Interesting power. More interesting was the fact that Karmash had sensed something amiss and acted to save himself rather than hold on to the prisoner.

Helena waved her fingers. Soma and Killian sprinted down the road after Callahan. In two breaths, the hunters overtook the running man. Killian crashed into the addict, pinning Callahan to the ground. The Edger's nails clawed Killian's arms and slid off harmlessly. Killian was one of her more enhanced hunters: his skin was thick like leather. Together, he and Soma jerked Callahan off the ground and carried him back.

"Nail him to the tree," Helena said.

The two hunters yanked the Edger upright. Sebastian pulled two daggers from the sheath on his waist and stabbed both through the man's shoulders, just under the collarbone. Callahan screamed, pinned to the oak like an insect.

Helena approached him, holding her knife. It was an excellent blade, razor-sharp and strong, like all of her tools, human or otherwise. She flicked it across the Edger's torso. The blade barely touched the pallid flesh, but its razor-sharp point painted a vivid line of red across the man's skin.

"Help!" Alex screamed. "Help me! Help me!"

The knife flashed once, twice. She used to paint like this in her study: fast strokes of brilliant red paint across the pale canvas.

Alex screamed and buckled, but the knives held him tight.

"Betrayal is bought with agony. When you betray your partners, especially if these partners are family, you should do it only after much suffering. Flesh is weak. When the pain is too much, most people do break. The greater the betrayal, the more terrible the pain the captive will endure."

Helena slid the point of her knife into the first cut she'd made, hooked the skin, and jerked it down in a sharp move. Alex shrieked a desperate, pain-filled howl. Red muscle glistened bare on his chest. She was always an excellent skinner.

"Don't worry. I will make sure that the pain you experience is equivalent to your betrayal." Helena raised her left hand, still in the soft brown glove. "Salt."

The vial of salt was deposited into her fingers.

"Now then. Let's talk about your sister."

JACK looked out the window. Outside, gray rain sifted onto a Broken town called Olympia. It was in the State of Washington, which was like a province but larger. Kaldar had stolen another car—this one was blue and smelled of some bitter fake-pine scent—and Jack got the front seat this time. The view from the window was wet and dreary.

"Does the sun ever shine here?"

"Sometimes," Kaldar said. "If you wait for a few hours and squint just right."

In the backseat, George shifted around. They both wore plain brown shirts and loose pants. They still didn't look like they belonged in the Broken, but at least it was an improvement over George's poofy shirts, Jack decided.

His side ached. He discreetly rubbed his bruised ribs. Gaston had been less than happy to find out that the two of them had taken off into the Broken and gotten themselves caught by Kaldar. Words like "morons," "spoiled babies," and "made me look like a total imbecile" had been said. And then words turned into punches. To be fair, he did throw the first one, Jack reflected. But there was only so much baby name-calling one could take. He and George had double-teamed Gaston, but Gaston was strong like a bull. Still, he hadn't won by much. It was fine now. They had made peace. He'd just have to be careful with the ribs for a couple of days.

Jack had left the little cat with Gaston. It had taken them a few hours to fly to Washington, and they spent the night in the Edge. Until they'd crossed back over to the Broken, Jack had carried the little cat around in a basket he'd found in the wyvern's cabin. The cat drank but didn't eat. That was usually a bad sign.

Gaston would take good care of it. He'd stayed behind to watch over the wyvern, and he promised he would check on the little cat. Of course he would.

"Where are we going?" George asked.

"We're looking for a thrift store. Anything would do. Goodwill, Salvation Army . . ."

"Salvation Army?" Jack perked up. "Crusaders?"

"No, not that Salvation Army," Kaldar said. "A second-hand clothing store."

"What's that?"

"You've been rich for too long." The thief sighed. "Does Rose do any charity work?"

"She gives alms to the poor," George said.

"How does that work?"

"We ride up to the Helping Hand building," Jack said. "We get out and carry the food crates inside. Rose talks to the people in there. They look at accounts for a while. She gives them money. We go home."

"Okay." Kaldar nodded. "A secondhand store is like Helping Hand: it's a store that raises money for the poor. In the Broken, they are usually attached to houses of religion."

"Churches," George said.

"Among others. People bring in clothes and furniture they no longer need and donate them. The stores sell them and use the money to feed the poor."

Jack frowned. "Why would you want to wear clothes somebody else had worn?" The scent alone would drive him mad.

"Because you can't afford anything else," George said quietly. "Rose used to shop at the secondhand store."

"I never got clothes that somebody else wore," Jack said. "I would've known."

"Not for us, you dolt. She shopped for herself. You don't remember because you were seven."

Jack bared his teeth. "I remember just fine."

"Another word, and it's back to Adrianglia for both of you," Kaldar said. His mouth smiled, but his eyes were dead serious.

Jack turned around and shut up.

"A thrift shop is the place where people shop when they don't have money or when they're looking for a bargain. Men of doubtful legality, such as ourselves, shop there for three reasons. First, the clothes will be clean, but they'll look worn, which is what we need. Fresh-off-the-rack stuff draws attention, and that must be avoided at all costs. The idea is to blend in. Be one of the guys. Second, the regular stores have surveillance cameras. They record your image, which means someone can track you down. For the same reason, we will stay away from any shop that has a camera in the window, TV screens, electronics, convenience stores, ATMs . . ."

"What are those?" Jack asked.

"Small automated banks that give out money."

"Why doesn't anyone steal the banks?" Jack asked.

"They are very, very heavy."

Jack grinned. "You tried?"

"Yes, and I don't recommend it. You need a sturdy truck with a wheelchair lift and a dolly. A rental truck with a ramp is good, too. And that's if said ATM isn't bolted to the ground. Anyway, we want to find a thrift shop like that one, for instance." Kaldar made a left and parked in front of a plain concrete building. The sign above the door said MISSION STORE.

"When we go in, keep your heads down. Don't stare at anyone, don't make eye contact, and shuffle a little. This is the third reason to shop here: people who work in these stores are either kindhearted or recovering from their former life: ex-addicts, ex-drunks, ex-homeless. They know what it's like to be on the wrong side of the poverty line. All they will see is a man down on his luck trying to find his sons some clothes. They take cash and don't look too closely at the faces. If cops come asking, they won't remember seeing you. Remember: heads down, think humble, and don't draw attention. Jack, no getting excited and running down the aisle like a damn idiot because you saw a cat or a mouse or some such. George, try to remember what it's like to be poor. One sneer, and I'll tan both of your hides. This is your test, boys."

Kaldar got out of the car. Jack followed. Humble, right. He could do that.

Thirty minutes later, they were on the road again. Jack sniffed at his new clothes. His faded black hoodie smelled of one brand of soap, his jeans of another. At least Kaldar let him keep his own boots. In the backseat, George wore a gray hoodie with a pocket in front and ripped jeans that needed to be thrown away. Kaldar had also bought him a used skateboard, a plank of wood on four wheels.

George caught him looking. "What?"

"You look ridiculous," Jack told him.

"This from a guy who strips naked and runs around in the woods."

"I'm not ashamed of my human or my lynx form. I wear clothes because people force me to. I don't need to put on a costume every morning to feel better about myself."

"That's right. You're a simple creature, aren't you?"

"Simple" in the human world usually meant "stupid." Jack grinned. "Why don't you lean closer, so I can explain to you exactly how simple I am."

"So help me Gods, I will turn this car around," Kaldar said. His face was relaxed, but his stare had gained a sharp, dangerous edge. Not good.

"You're different," Jack told him.

"Different how?"

"You're a lot more easygoing when you come to visit Cerise."

"That's because when I visit Cerise, I'm her funny, charming, favorite cousin. The hardest challenge I face there is how much I can annoy my dear cousin-in-law before he turns into a wolf and tries to rip my throat out. Right now, I'm an agent of the Mirror, saddled with two children, which means if someone jumps out in front of this car and tries to kill you, I will shoot him through the heart before he has a chance to blink."

Jack clicked his mouth shut and sat straighter.

"I understand, believe me," Kaldar said. "I have an older brother, and I make it a point to disappoint him at least once every month. But you are on my time now. You need to get out of this childish mind-set, because it will get you killed. You can do this stupid sibling-rivalry bullshit on your own time."

It seemed like a really good time to be quiet, so Jack did just that. The city rolled by his window. On the way from the boundary, they had passed through some woods. Old, scarred trees that looked like they belonged in the Weird rather than the Broken. The woods had encroached on the city—he could see places where they had snuck in—patches never cleared between the groups of houses, a huge tree somebody forgot to cut down growing from a small patch of dirt left bare by the pavement, parks . . . It seemed strange that people would want to live here, in a place where it always rained, fighting free of the woods.

Kaldar kept driving: right, left, turning down the gradually widening streets until he finally pulled the car into a large parking lot in front of a tall tower of glass and stone.

"Audrey Callahan works in that building."

"How do you know?" George asked.

"While you were getting pretty and picking out clothes, I made some calls to local PI firms listed in the phone book. I asked for Audrey. This firm transferred me to her office answering machine." Kaldar looked pleased with himself, like a cat who'd gotten into some sweet cream. "Here's the plan: I go in. The two of you wait here. Look like you're loitering but watch the doors. I doubt Audrey will be happy to see me."

"Are you going to torture her?" Jack asked.

Kaldar stopped and gave him an odd look. "No. If you see us come out together, you wait until we get to the car. If you see a young woman with red hair come out alone, like she is in a hurry, that means things didn't go smoothly."

Kaldar reached into his bag and pulled out a small metal box with a flower engraved in its top. He pushed the center of the flower. The metal petals sprang up with a click. Jack inspected the edges. Razor-sharp and serrated at the bottom.

"This is a magic tracker. It works only in the Weird or in the Edge. It's designed to attach to carriages, but it's magnetic and should stick to a car as well. George, take this tracker. If Audrey comes out alone, follow her and stick the tracker to the back or bottom of her vehicle. Use the skateboard as a diversion." Kaldar looked at Jack. "While he is doing that, you will follow my scent into the building, find me, and . . ."

"Save you?" Jack asked.

"*Assist* me. Don't get ahead of yourself, there."

"Assist." That was a nice way to put it.

"Are we clear?" Kaldar asked.

Jack nodded.

"Off we go, then."

* * *

ANY day that started with a check was a good day. Audrey grinned and checked the folder in her hands as she walked through the long, carpeted hallway of Milano Investigations. She wore a beige pantsuit that did lovely things for her skin tone, her hair was braided away from her face, and inside her folder a blue pay stub showed $822 deposited into her account. Honest money, honestly earned. She didn't even begrudge the government biting a chunk off in taxes.

In eighty-two days she would be eligible to apply for benefits. And today promised to be good. She would play second fiddle to Johanna Parker on an attorney case. She'd met Johanna yesterday—she was forty-five, dark-eyed, gray-haired and proud of it, and retired from the Seattle PD. Apparently when a defendant retained a private attorney in a criminal case, that attorney in turn often retained a PI, especially if that PI was a retired cop. The PI would do the legwork, talk to cops, talk to witnesses, review police reports, and so on. And Audrey would get to sit in on all of it and see how the other side worked.

Oh yes. Today would be good. If she wasn't trying to be professional, she'd run down the hallway squealing, "Wheeeee!" like a four-year-old who had just been told she would get to go to the water park. She reached for her office door.

"Audrey!" Johanna's voice called behind her.

Audrey turned on her heel. "Yes, ma'am?"

Johanna was leaning out of her office two doors down the hallway, half-in, half-out. "You have a client. Serena put him in your office because George has the conference room."

A client? Already? "Thank you!" Audrey took the door handle.

"He said he's a friend of your brother."

A little ball of ice burst inside Audrey and petrified her in place. Nothing connected with Alex could be good. It wasn't her father—Seamus was too vain. He would've said he was her father. No, this was either some drug dealer or someone who had gotten wind of the heist and wanted his money.

She stared at the door. Her instincts said, "Walk away." Let go of the door handle, turn around, walk away, and keep walking.

"Anyway, I need you at ten, so you have about an hour," Johanna said. "Do you think you can wrap it up by then?"

Audrey heard her own voice. "Yes, ma'am." *Go into your office so I can escape. Go into your office.*

Johanna laughed. "You can stop calling me 'ma'am.' We're less formal here on the West Coast. Just 'Johanna' will do."

"Okay, Johanna." Audrey forced a smile. *Go away.*

Johanna turned to stop into her office and paused.

Now what?

Serena was walking down the hallway with a pack of folders. Oh no. *Keep walking. Keeeep walking.*

Serena stopped by Johanna's doorway and held out a file. She would have to go by them to get outside. Her escape route was gone.

Why now? Why when everything is going so well? Am I cursed or something?

Audrey swallowed. That was fine. She was a Callahan. She would handle it.

Audrey opened the door. A man stood by the window, looking out. He wore faded jeans, tan leather work boots, and a charcoal hoodie. She could walk outside and find ten men wearing a variation of the same thing. People on the West Coast took it easy and didn't bother with too much formality. Out here, he could be anyone: an older college student, a college professor, or the CEO of a multimillion-dollar company.

His hair was neither too long nor too short, tousled, and very dark, almost black. His shoulders were wide, his waist mostly hidden by the sweatshirt, but his butt looked like he'd spent a fair amount of time running. Hair and butt said younger than forty, shoulders said older than teens. Probably late twenties. Her entire assessment took about a second.

Audrey beamed a bright, pretty-girl smile, and said, "Hi!"

The man turned.

Oh sweet Jesus.

He had a narrow, strong face, good cheekbones, and a full mouth. If she covered the top half of his face, she'd say he was a very handsome man. But his eyes, they were devil eyes. Light brown like clover honey, smart, and framed in long eyelashes, the man's eyes brimmed with wicked humor. They lit his whole face, changing him from a handsome man to the kind of man any woman with a drop of sense would stay away from. He toned it down almost right away. The only reason she saw it at all was because she had caught him off guard, but it was too late. *Nice try.* She'd spent her life in the Edge, among con artists, thieves, and swindlers. *Don't you worry. I've got your number.*

This man was a rogue, not because circumstances forced him to be a criminal but because he was born that way. He was probably conning his mother out of her milk the moment he could grin. He'd charm the clothes off a virgin in twenty minutes. And if the poor fool took him home, he'd drink her dad under the table, beguile her mother, charm her grandparents, and treat the girl to a night she'd never forget. In the morning, her dad would be sick with alcohol poisoning, the good silver would be missing together with the family car, and in a month, both the former virgin and her mother would be expecting.

Whatever he wanted, it was bad. She had to get the hell away from him. He wasn't one of Alex's junkie buddies, and he wasn't one of her father's "friends." Seamus Callahan knew his limits. This man would run circles around him, and Seamus never partnered with anyone smarter than himself. Well, except for the family.

No, this man was too dangerous to be a common Edge rat. He was working for someone in the Edge or, more likely, in the Weird, and he probably wanted the box she had stolen from West Egypt. If he had found her, others would follow. They would never leave her alone, and they wouldn't think twice about killing her.

She was finished. Her job, her life, it was all over.

* * *

THE girl was beautiful.

Kaldar had expected a junkie or a long-suffering victim, a woman with a haggard face, toughened by life, and bitter. He'd seen some pretty girls in his time, a lot of them in their entirety, but Audrey was in a class by herself. She was golden. Her tan skin almost glowed. Her dark eyes sparked under narrow eyebrows. Her hair, pulled away from her face, was that particular shade of dark red, more brown touched with gold rather than orange. And when she smiled at him, showing white teeth, it was infectious. He wanted to smile back and do something amusing so she would smile at him again.

She walked up to him. Big smile, wide eyes, no hesitation. Nice outfit too; professional, true, but tight enough to show off her long legs and hug her butt, and her red shirt under the jacket was cut just low enough to pull the gaze to her breasts, which were very nice to look at. He'd bet there were men in this building who spent too much time picturing themselves peeling off her clothes and pondering the color of her panties. The question was, did she know it, and if she did, how did she use it?

"Hi!" she repeated, all sunshine and roses. "My name is Audrey. How can I help you?"

Her voice was golden too—smooth with a light touch of the South. He should've gone for a different type of disguise, something warmer and more folksy, instead of Seattle grunge. But too late now. Either she was really good, and he was in trouble, or she was an airhead, and he was unbelievably lucky.

"Hi, Audrey." Kaldar smiled back, dropping a hint of his own South into his voice as well. "My name's Denis Morrow."

"So nice to meet you, Denis."

"The pleasure's all mine."

Audrey shook his hand, and he caught a whiff of her perfume: citrus, peaches, and sandalwood, fresh, sensual, but not overpowering.

Her fingers squeezed his for a second and slipped out of his hand. He'd expected it, but his pulse sped up all the same. She was good.

"Please sit down."

"Don't mind if I do."

Kaldar sat in the wooden chair in front of her desk. She went to her desk, sashaying a little, sat, and smiled at him. It was a sweet and completely innocent smile. He half expected flowers to sprout from the carpet and small birds to spring into song.

Audrey slid the top drawer of her desk out. Kaldar tensed. She took a small box of Altoids out and set it on the desk. "Mints?"

Probably poisoned. "No, thank you."

Audrey pried the box open with her slender fingers. "Sorry, I just had coffee. My breath is . . . phew!" She waved her hand in front of her face.

"I don't mind. Go right ahead."

She plucked a mint out, put it on her pink tongue, and closed her mouth. "Mmm. I love Altoids."

Aaand his thoughts went off the map. Nicely done again. He wondered how often she'd used that little trick. He could picture a conference room full of men simultaneously shutting up to watch her eat Altoids. No sister of Alex Callahan could be a complete innocent, but he didn't expect this.

She leaned forward, her face earnest. "So, how can I help you, Denis?"

"I've visited your brother," he said, testing the waters. "Alex."

"Alex?" Her eyes went wide. "How is he? Is he okay? Did something happen?"

Her face showed genuine concern, even.

"Did he OD?"

And that was genuine fear. If he were a little less jaded, he would've bought it. Callahan wouldn't be the first addict to have a persecution complex. Maybe Audrey was Daddy's little girl, and Alex was the family's bitter black sheep, who was lying through his teeth.

And maybe pigs would fly and rich men would grow a conscience.

"Papa said he was in a nice place. The doctors were supposed to take care of him!"

Moisture wet her eyelashes. Crying on cue. Adorable. Kaldar had to say something before she teared up, or things would get messy. He held out his hand and put on a guilty smile. "Audrey, please, you misunderstood. It would break my heart to see such a lovely woman upset. Your brother's fine."

Audrey drew back. "That wasn't nice. You scared me."

Now he was a mean, rotten man, yes he was. He almost clapped.

She drew herself upright. "What is it that you would like from me, Mr. Morrow?"

Well, it was a great performance, but all good things had to come to an end. Kaldar leaned forward, and said in an intimate, quiet voice, "I want you to cut the bullshit and tell me what your daddy has done with the device you stole from West Egypt."

She jerked her hand toward him, blindingly fast. A sharp jolt exploded in his chest, as if he had hit his funny bone, and the shock overwhelmed his whole body. Kaldar's muscles locked. He willed himself to move, but he remained trapped in the chair, rigid like a board. The words gurgled in his mouth.

A Taser! She had Tasered him! *Damn it all to hell.*

Audrey slipped from behind her desk. He felt his arms yanked, then the pain was over. His body snapped back to normal, all functions restored, and he spat the first word that popped into his mouth. "Fuck."

Audrey slapped a piece of duct tape over his lips. He growled and lunged at her, but his arms didn't move.

She'd zip-tied him to his chair.

He'd been had. She'd tricked him like he was a sucker. Like he was a child. The moment he got free, she would regret it. He would make her deeply regret it.

Audrey bent over him, running her fingers through his clothes with practiced quickness, and pulled his knife from the inner pocket of his hoodie. The slightly curved black blade was almost six inches long and razor-sharp, but thick enough to parry one or two sword strokes.

"Nice knife."

The point of the black blade pricked the skin just below his eye. She bent over him, her voice shaking with quiet rage.

"You have no idea what you've cost me. I worked for months to get this job, and you ruined everything. Do you know what it's like to have to start over? Do you know how hard it is to get legal in the Broken?"

The knife cut his skin. He felt a drop of blood slide onto his cheek. Kaldar held very still. No need to agitate her.

"I've worked so hard. I've been so good. I like this job. I was supposed to get benefits in three months. And you and that pathetic excuse for a human being crushed it all. What did you give Alex to get to me, huh? Couldn't have been money. He doesn't care about money. No, it had to be drugs, didn't it? That bloody moron would sell me out for a dime bag of pot. If he told you, he'd tell anyone. The Hand, the Claws, anyone!"

Audrey raised his knife. If she stabbed him, he'd lunge right and hope she missed the heart. For a moment, she looked like she would plunge the knife into his chest, then she leaned over him, her face an inch from his and spoke, each word a furious promise.

"Don't follow me. If I ever see you again, I'll cut out your eyeballs and make you swallow them."

Audrey turned and marched out of the office, carefully closing the door behind her. The door clicked. She'd locked him in.

Kaldar surged to his feet, spun his back and the chair toward the heavy desk, and braced the chair's legs against it. If his luck held, the chair was as old as it looked. He strained. The wood groaned. He'd done this a couple of times before. The trick was enough pressure at the right angle.

The last thing he wanted was for Jack to find him tied up. He would never hear the end of it.

* * *

JACK crouched on the curb and surveyed the parking lot.
The tall glass-and-concrete building rose in front of them.
From his vantage point, the front door was clearly visible. Next to him, George kept messing with the skateboard.
He had good balance from fencing, and if he pushed with
one foot, he could stand on it while it rolled; but Kaldar had
said there was a way to make it roll faster by rocking side
to side. So far nothing George had tried worked, but he was
entertaining to watch.

Jack inhaled the scents. The parking lot smelled of many
things, but through it all he sensed the vivid trail of Kaldar's
track. This was fun, Jack reflected. Even waiting was a lot
more fun than school.

"Door," George murmured.

Across the parking lot the glass door of the building
swung open. A pretty woman with copper-colored hair
stepped out and started out down the sidewalk. She walked
another ten feet, out of view of the door, and broke into a jog.

"Go!" George said. Jack shot across the parking lot at a
dead run. He burst through the doors, following Kaldar's
scent. An older man behind the counter yelled, "Where are
you going?" Jack ignored him and turned right. The scent
trail led him past the elevator to the stairs. Jack bounded up,
taking the stairway two steps at a time. Smart of Kaldar to
take the stairs. Can't track scent through the elevator.

Seven floors, eight, nine, ten. There! Jack slapped the
door open and jumped out into the hallway. The scent said,
"Left!" He turned left and dashed down the hallway. Doors
punctured the walls. Not this one, not that one, no, no, no.
This one. He gripped the door handle. Locked.

Jack took a step back and hammered the heel of his foot
into the door. It popped open. Jack ducked inside and almost
ran into Kaldar, who for some reason had pieces of wood
dangling from his wrists. They looked like chair pieces.
Kaldar jerked his arms up, exposing pale plastic things

wrapped around his wrists. Jack pulled his knife out and slashed at the ties. Chunks of chair crashed onto the floor.

"Where is your knife?" Jack asked.

Kaldar's face was frightening. He grabbed a small sliver of wood and headed out of the office, "She took it."

"What do you mean, she took it?"

Outside in the hallway a woman with gray hair blocked their way. "What are you doing? Where is Audrey?"

Kaldar spun away from her and marched to the stairway. The woman chased them.

"She took it after she Tasered me and tied me to the chair."

They went through the doorway, and Kaldar slammed the door shut and shoved the piece of wood he was carrying under the door.

"Oh, so you gave her your knife so she wouldn't kill you."

Kaldar stopped and stared at him. The woman shoved the door from the other side and cursed.

"Too bad," Jack said. "It was a nice knife. I really liked it. But it was a good trade."

"You have an odd mind."

"Is that bad?" Jack asked.

"Not at all. It makes you unpredictable. That's an excellent quality." Kaldar shook his head and kept walking.

"So what now?"

"Now I get my knife back."

FIVE

IT was ruined. Audrey clenched her teeth. Everything she had worked for, everything she had tried to accomplish. All of it was ruined.

She took the turn too fast. The Honda careened, threatening to veer off the road. She gripped the wheel and steered it back into the lane. Why was it that every time things went well, someone showed up to shatter it all to pieces? Her father, her brother, this idiot. She was so mad, she had almost run over some blond child in the parking lot. He actually fell off his skateboard in his rush to avoid her. She'd stomped on the brakes so hard, she'd hurt herself. The boy had scrambled off before she had a chance to ask him if he was okay.

It was good that she had no superpowers because she would have burst into flames and left a trail of charred trees in her wake.

She didn't even ask "Denis" who he worked for. It wasn't the Hand—all of Louisiana's spies were so twisted by magic, none of them would make it through the boundary into the Broken. The more magic you had, the harder it was to travel into that world, and he seemed damned comfortable in it. Wasn't a Claw, either. He didn't look Egyptian.

She wasn't sure what nationality he did look like. Dark hair, honey-colored eyes—those she remembered very well—Caucasian features, but there was something else in there. Some Native blood, maybe? Whatever it was, he had an interesting face. Handsome. Really handsome. He used it well, too. He probably thought his smile was dashing.

Moron.

For a moment, when he sat there and listened to her with that smile on his face, she almost thought he bought her naive Georgia peach act. She even pulled out her best "sweet tea" Southern for the occasion. But no. God alone knew what Alex had told him.

"That sonovabitch." She slapped the wheel with the heel of her hand. "That damn bastard." It wasn't enough he had screwed up her childhood. He kept screwing up her adult life, too. She'd moved across the bloody continent to escape her family. Wasn't far enough.

The Honda jumped over the roots and popped out into the driveway of her house. Audrey shut off the engine and jumped out. Her getaway bag waited in the closet, already packed. It was always packed. She ran across the lawn to the front door, unlocked it, and ducked inside.

"Ling!"

She hoped Denis would buy her cold killer act. Either way, her life here was over, but extra time would be a great thing right about now. Even if he didn't, it would take him at least a few minutes to break free. He didn't seem the type to call for help. He'd want to get out all by himself, except that she made sure the zip ties on his hands were nice and snug. Eventually, he'd call for help, then there would be explanations, delays, and so on. By the time he was on her trail again, she would be long gone.

Audrey yanked the getaway bag out of the closet and pulled the zipper. "Ling!"

Money in a Ziploc bag, clothes, camping kit in another Ziploc bag: matches, Band-Aids, painkillers, wound disinfectant, antibiotic ointment.

"Ling the Merciless! Where are you?"

No answer. Where had that raccoon gotten off to? They didn't have time to waste.

Audrey threw the bag out onto the porch, grabbed Ling's carrier out of the bedroom, set it on the porch, added two full five gallon gas cans—the less she stopped in places with people and cameras, the better—and went to grab the bow from the bedroom. The crossbow was already in the car, securely hidden under the tarp. She had briefly considered taking it out that morning, not sure if she would be expected to chauffeur Johanna around. She didn't want to answer awkward questions if the older woman had glanced into the backseat, but her paranoia had won, and she'd kept the crossbow where it always was.

Awkward questions. Ha!

Audrey swiped the bow and quiver from the shelf and marched onto the porch.

"Ling, I swear, if you don't appear this instant—"

A familiar figure stood by the car. Denis.

Audrey planted the arm of the bow into the porch boards and strung it in one swift movement. How the hell . . .

"Leave, or I will kill you."

He gave her a bright predatory grin. "Now, you know, I can't do that."

She notched the arrow and let it loose. The arrow sliced through the air with a long whine and buried itself at the man's feet.

"A warning shot. Just one. That's all you get."

He spread his arms. "Audrey, let's talk."

"Let's not."

She notched the arrow, took aim, and shot. He spun out of the way. The arrow glanced off the door with a screech. *Damn it, now I've dented the Honda's door.*

"I'm beginning to suspect you don't like me."

"Really? What gave you that idea, I wonder?"

"You don't want to kill me. I'm your ticket out of this—"

She fired again.

"—mess. Could you stop shooting at me for a moment?"

"No." That last one had to have nicked his thigh. She plucked another arrow from the quiver.

He swiped the first arrow off the ground. "I bet you this arrow against the knife you took from me that I will make it onto your porch unharmed."

There were sixty feet between him and the porch, and she had a full quiver. "I'll take that bet."

He grinned. Clearly the man was some sort of deranged lunatic with a death wish. Audrey shot again. The arrow pierced the air, heading straight for the man's chest. At the last moment he jerked out of the missile's path with unnatural quickness, almost as if he had a rope attached to his waist and something had yanked him out of the way.

He took two steps forward.

"Oh no, you don't."

Fire. Miss.

Missed.

Missed.

Missed, God damn it.

Missed again.

He put his left foot onto the first porch step. Panic swelled inside her, a feverish stupefying jitter that threatened to turn off her brain. Audrey stared past him at the line of arrows neatly puncturing his trail.

"My knife," he said.

"You cheated." It had to be magic.

"I did no such thing."

She pointed at the trail with the arrow in her hand. It shook in her hand. "Yes, you did."

"You are a lousy shot."

Audrey jerked the bow and fired an arrow point-blank into his chest. The string snapped in her fingers. The arrow went sideways. It was magic.

She pointed the bow at him. "Cheated."

In her head a tiny voice cried, *Run, run away! He could be anyone. He could be the Hand, he could be a California robber baron. He could be a slaver. Run!*

For all she knew, Alex had told him that she still had the West Egyptian box. Or worse, her brother had sold her to him, just like he had before. Audrey felt a phantom hand squeeze her throat. She would not be anyone's punching bag again. Never again.

He stepped onto the porch. "I'm still waiting for my knife."

She pulled the knife out. The beautiful black blade curved from her hand. "Come and take it if you can."

"If I can, huh." The man rolled his eyes and lunged for her.

She sliced across his arm, cutting the heavy fabric of the sweatshirt rolled up at his sleeves. Red stained his sleeve. Audrey reversed, sliced again, quick. Somehow she missed. His fingers clamped her wrist. She rammed her knuckles into his throat. He stumbled back and turned sideways, falling into some sort of fighting stance.

His left hand snaked out, too fast. A punch rocked her shoulder. He punched again, quick combination, left, right, left. She lunged into it, aiming to cut his forearm. If she bled him enough . . .

His fingers clamped her wrist like a steel vise. Audrey swung to punch, but he caught her other arm, stepped forward, and drove her back, tripping her. She knew exactly what he was doing; she just couldn't stop it. A moment, and he was on top of her, pinning her to the boards.

"Let's review," he said. "So far, you Tasered me, tied me to a chair, shot me, cut me, and punched me. Did I miss anything?"

She pushed against him, trying to throw him off, but he outweighed her by at least sixty pounds, and those pounds seemed to be made of steel because he wasn't budging.

"Have I hurt you in any way? Did I threaten you?"

She tried to kick him, but he clamped her leg with his thigh.

"Audrey, I just want to talk like two civilized people. If I let go, will you gouge my eyes out?"

"Probably."

His face was too close, and his eyes looked straight into hers. She searched his face for cruelty, anticipating a punch in the gut or a jab in the face, but found none. He was pissed off, but he didn't have that icy reptilian coldness she'd seen in Alex's drug dealer.

She was breathing hard, and he was, too. Time to end it before he got any ideas. Audrey jerked her head up and rammed her forehead into his nose.

"Damn it, woman, I said I just wanted to talk."

The accent broke through his words, and she caught it. "Louisiana." Oh crap.

"What?"

"You're from Louisiana. You're the Hand."

"I'm from the Mire, in the Edge." The silver earring in his ear flowed into a single mirror drop. "And I work for the other side."

She strained, trying to jerk her arms free. "You're all the same."

The sound of someone clearing his throat made them both turn. A boy stepped out from behind the tree across the lawn. The stray ray of sun breaking through the cloud cover played on his blond hair. The skateboard punk from the parking lot.

What in the world . . .

The blond boy called out. "I'm terribly sorry, but is there any way we could grab that cage off the porch? We won't disturb your dalliance."

Dalliance?

Another boy emerged carrying a fuzzy gray creature by the scruff of its neck. "You can keep making out," he called out. "We just want the cage. This raccoon is really hard to hold, and she doesn't like me."

They had Ling, and they thought that she and this idiot were getting hot and heavy on the porch. "Get off of me, you fool!" Audrey squirmed. "Get off, get off, get off!"

The man let go, and she rolled to her feet. "Let my raccoon go!"

The second boy looked at the man next to her. Audrey glanced at him, too. He was holding his knife. She hadn't seen him pick it up. The "dashing" smile was back, too.

"Tell him to release my raccoon."

An evil spark flared in his eyes. "Trade: raccoon for some answers."

"Fine," she ground out.

"Let the little beast go," he called. The boy dropped Ling, and she streaked across the lawn and hid behind Audrey's legs, hissing and spitting.

"My name is Kaldar, by the way," the man said.

"Not interested," Audrey told him. "This is strictly a business conversation. You step a hair out of line, and I will hurt you."

He tossed the bow to the ground. "With what? I took my knife back, and your bow is gone. You're out of weapons."

She headed for her door. "Oh, I have more inside. Don't you worry. I always have more."

AUDREY leaned against her kitchen counter, arms crossed. Kaldar sat on her love seat, as relaxed as he could get. Mr. Smooth Operator. The man was handsome, he knew it, but if he was waiting for an acknowledgment from her, he would be old and gray before he got it.

The boys had taken the chairs. The blond sat with an inborn elegance, back straight, one leg over another. A shockingly pretty kid. A few years, and he would be crushing hearts left and right. Of course, if he kept hanging out with that fool, he might not survive that long.

The brown-haired boy sat in the chair like it was a rock in the middle of a raging river, and he had to defend it from gators. As she watched, Ling snuck closer to him and showed him her teeth. The boy's eyes flashed amber. He hissed, and Ling beat a strategic retreat. A changeling. Well, at least Kaldar was telling the truth. The Louisianans murdered changelings on sight. Kaldar probably was Mirror, which didn't explain anything. The Mirror had no reason to get involved.

The four of them looked at one another. Inside Audrey, irritation fought with her sense of hospitality, but the South was too deeply ingrained into the core of her being, and it won.

"Would you like some iced tea?"

"Sweet?" Kaldar asked.

"Well, of course it's sweet. Who do you take me for?"

Kaldar arranged his face into an angelic expression. "I'd love a glass."

Wicked. That was the right way to describe him. Wicked to the core and full of himself. She had to get him out of her house. Audrey took out four glasses. The blond boy rose. "Please let me help."

"Sure. What's your name?"

"George."

"Nice to meet you, George." She distributed the ice into the four glasses and poured tea into each one. "Did I hurt you in the parking lot?"

"No, m'lady. I fell, so I could put a tracker on your car."

Great. At least that explained how they had found her. She took two glasses, George took the other two, and they brought them to the table.

"Should I check it for poison?" Kaldar asked.

"I would," she told him. *Waste your time, go ahead.*

The blond boy passed a glass to the dark-haired boy. The changeling sniffed, took a sip, held it in his mouth, and swallowed. "It's clean."

"First you let one child get hit by my car, now you make the other one act as your human poison detector. You really have no conscience, do you?"

Kaldar leaned back. "*I* didn't ask him to check for poison. His *brother* asked him."

Audrey shook her head and turned to the changeling boy. "What's your name?"

"Jack."

"Jack, there are poisons that are tasteless and odorless, the kind that even a changeling can't detect. Next time, let Kaldar drink first. If he dies, no big loss."

Jack snickered.

Kaldar sighed. "Tell me about the heist."

Audrey shrugged. "My father needed money to put my asshole brother into rehab. Yet again. I agreed to help them for the last time. My father and I took a plane to Orlando and met Alex there. We crossed into the Weird through the Edge in Florida, broke into the pyramid, and nabbed the box. It was a plain wooden box, about a foot and a half long, a foot wide, eight inches tall. We took it, popped back into the Broken, and drove up I-95. When we reached Jacksonville, I left them and flew back to Seattle."

"Did you know who commissioned the heist?" Kaldar asked.

"No. I suspect it was the Hand. Am I right?"

"Yes."

Oh, Seamus. You moron. "I told my dad it was a bad idea. But no, he had stars in his eyes. They'd promised him a small mountain of gold, and he figured if he flipped it into US currency, he'd get a little over fifty grand. I take it his buyer double-crossed him?"

Kaldar reached into his bag and pulled out a small contraption of pale bronze-colored metal. A bowl, formed by several circular bands sat on a narrow stem, which widened into a base resembling tree roots. She'd seen high-end gadgets from the Weird before, and it had that polished look: beautiful, with an attention to detail that was usually paid only to fine jewelry. You could sell it to some art gallery in the Broken. They'd auction it off and never know what it was.

Kaldar squeezed the stem. A whisper of magic shivered through the air. The metal panels of the stem rose, revealing the insides of tiny, fine gears in a dozen of shades. The circular bands rose, turning slowly. A faint glow coalesced above them. Kaldar leaned closer and said, pronouncing the words with crisp exactness, "Adriana. Fountain."

The glow snapped into a ghostly three-dimensional image of a cobbled square with some sort of ruin in the center that might have been a fountain at some point but now was mostly a heap of broken marble. Flesh-colored remains dotted the scene. Alex's handiwork. He must've teleported out, and someone held on to him half a second too long.

The Hand didn't get their goods, which meant they would be hunting both her father and Alex. And her. Her heart skipped a beat.

"Is my father dead?" Audrey asked. Her voice came out flat. She wished she would've felt worry or fear. Something. But she felt nothing at all. A better daughter should've wondered if she shouldn't have left them alone, but she wasn't that daughter. *You reap what you sow, Dad.*

"I don't know," Kaldar said. "If he is, he lived long enough to deliver your brother to the rehab center and pay for it, which means he found another buyer."

"I have no idea who that would be." Audrey shrugged. "My involvement ended in Jacksonville."

"He didn't contact you?" Kaldar peered at her face. "Shouldn't you get some reward for this venture?"

"Ha! My reward was that I would be left alone to live my nice life, which you've ruined."

"Oh no, darling," Kaldar shook his head. "You ruined your own life when you took that job. Every Edger knows to keep the hell away from the Hand. This was a high-risk/low-reward heist. There are much easier ways of getting money. Were you born yesterday?"

Just who does he think he is? "I'm not your darling. It was a family matter."

"When family insists on being stupid, you steer them away from it. It's not that difficult."

"You don't know me." Audrey crossed her arms. "You don't know my father. Don't come here and tell me how to live my life. You can't steer Seamus Callahan. You can only bargain with him."

He leaned back. "So the two of you did strike a bargain. He got forty thousand dollars. What did you get?"

"I got to never see my family again."

Kaldar frowned. "Come again?"

"I got to be cut off. Left in peace. I want nothing to do with them or with their stupid schemes. I don't have parents, and they don't have a daughter. That was my condition."

Kaldar reeled back a little. She could almost feel gears turning behind that pretty face.

"I've met your brother. If anyone should be cast off, it should be him."

"That's not how it works in our family. He is the heir, the pride and joy, who carries on the family name. I'm his younger sister." And she wasn't bitter about it. Not at all.

"Anyway, my life is none of your business. Did you have any more questions about the heist? If not, you should go now. My patience is all worn down."

The moment he was out the door, she'd grab Ling and bail.

"I need to find out who bought the box."

"No clue."

"Where can I find your father?"

"No clue, either."

"Audrey, I really need your help." Kaldar smiled at her. Now there was a work of art. If she were just a girl and he were just a man, and they met at a party, that smile would've guaranteed him a date. The man was hot. There was no doubt. But right now, all it would get him was a solid punch in those even teeth.

Audrey laughed. "Aren't you sweet? Tell me, do girls usually throw their panties at you when you do that?"

He grinned wider, and she glimpsed the funny evil spark in his eyes. "Do men throw money when you do your little Southern belle?"

Pot calling the kettle black. "Men enjoy my 'sweet tea' Southern. Nobody here is enjoying that stupid grin on your ugly mug."

"Ugly."

"Hideous."

The kids snickered.

"You have no idea what you've gotten yourself into." The Mirror agent sat straighter. "Do you know what you've stolen?"

"It wasn't my job, and I wasn't paid to know." She waited for a jab. No good thief ever did a heist without knowing every detail, especially what and why. "We were paid to obtain the box and deliver it to the buyer."

He didn't say anything.

"The box had four seals on it, anyway," she said.

"Did you look in the box, Audrey?"

"I said it had four seals on it."

He just waited. *Oh, for Christ's sake.* "Of course I looked in the box."

He leaned to his gadget, whispered something, and nodded. "Did it look something like this?"

A pair of ghostly metal bracelets appeared above the table. At first glance they looked silver, but where silver leaned toward a gray shade, this metal blushed with warm tones of peach and pale pink. The wider part of each bracelet bent and flowed, thin and wide, like a ribbon. A smooth border tipped the edges, which otherwise would've been too sharp. At the other end, tiny pebbles of metal encrusted the narrow edge of each bracelet, seeded so close together, sometimes on top of each other, almost like barnacles on the bottom of the ship. The two bracelets together were an elegant piece of jewelry, unique and beautiful. She would wear them in an instant, with a flowing gown of pure white. But it was just jewelry. A hunk of metal, yet the Hand, the Mirror, and the Claws were after it, and now, curiosity was killing her. She had to know why.

"Yes, that's what we stole," Audrey said. "I don't see what all the fuss is about."

"It's a portable Gorleanean diffuser," Kaldar said.

"What is that?"

The blond boy, George, stirred. The kids had been so quiet, she had almost forgotten he and his brother were there at all. "A Gorleanean diffuser functions like a magic battery," the boy said. "You can charge it with a blast of magic, like flash, for example. It holds the magic for a while, but it starts leaking the charge into the environment right away. Also, they're huge. The size of a house."

"Not anymore." Kaldar nodded at the bracelets. "These hold only a very small amount of magic."

"What's the purpose of having one?" George leaned closer and peered at the bracelets. "Some sort of last resort in battle, when you overflash? To keep from dying?"

Kaldar drew his hand over his face. "You are too bright for your own good. That was the original plan, yes."

Audrey stared at the bracelets. She'd heard about flashing so much magic that your body gave out. But she had always thought that you simply passed out. "I never heard of people dying from flashing out."

"Our sister almost did," Jack said.

"You said it was the original plan?" George asked. "What is it used for now?"

"It holds just enough magic to help an augmented being cross through the boundary," Kaldar said.

The room was suddenly quiet. Audrey caught her breath. The Edge had two boundaries: the first with the Weird and the second with the Broken. The boundaries barred the passage between the worlds. If you didn't have enough magic, you couldn't cross from the Broken into the Edge without help. If you had too much magic, the crossing from the Weird into the Edge would leave you convulsing in pain. The threshold to leave the Edge and enter an opposing world was even higher. Most magic heavyweights couldn't make it into the Broken. The crossing killed them. And if people stayed too long out of their own world, the way back disappeared forever. The Edgers who moved to the Broken permanently lost their magic after a while. Some of them couldn't even see the Edge anymore.

George cleared his throat. "So does this mean that someone with strong magic, like a Hand agent, can cross into the Broken with these?"

"That's exactly what it means," Kaldar said.

Audrey put her fist against her mouth, thinking. No wonder the Hand wanted them. If they manufactured enough of these, they could send their goons into the Edge and into the Broken. The boundary had always shielded the Edgers from harm. Their magic was weaker than that of people in the Weird. If any magic-wielding creature could just pop back and forth, it was all over. Her imagination served up the Hand's agents trotting across the boundary, all spikes and tentacles and poisoned needles on twisted human bodies . . . *Jesus Christ.*

She sat down. She didn't know too much about the Hand or the Mirror and their politics, but she knew that both the

Dukedom of Louisiana and Adrianglia were large and strong, while the Edge was tiny and defenseless.

"If the Hand obtains this . . ." Kaldar started.

She held up her hand. "Now you listen to me. This isn't my problem. I didn't make the thing, I didn't know what it was when I stole it, and I don't give a damn what the hell it does now. If you think I'll fall over myself in a rush to fight the Hand for it, you're crazy. Do you know what they're capable of?"

All mirth had vanished from Kaldar's face. Only grim determination remained. "The Hand took two-thirds of my family from me. I watched people I loved being slaughtered. I will do everything in my power to make the Hand pay. And if it means I have to knock you down and walk over you to get to them, I will."

He wasn't kidding. A slight touch of insanity flared in his eyes. Audrey felt a pang of the familiar fear.

"Don't sugarcoat it," she told him.

"I won't. The Hand will keep looking for the diffusers until they find them. I will find them first, and I need you to help me. If you do it willingly, the terms will be better for everyone."

"And if not, what? You will make me?"

"If I have to."

Fear squirmed through her. She clamped it down. "So there is no real difference between the Mirror and the Hand, is there?"

Kaldar held her gaze. "There is a woman in Adrianglia. Her name is Lady Nancy Virai. She isn't the most patient woman in the world, and some find her methods frightening. If I were to drag your ass over to her, she would extract the information from you. But if you told her everything you knew, you would likely walk away on your own two legs. If I delivered you to the Hand, they would get the same information out of you as well. Then they would rape you and torture you for the fun of it. If you were lucky, they would kill you afterward. But most likely they would wring every drop of pain from you and simply wait for you to die. Most of them aren't human anymore. They drink agony like fine wine. Run if you want—the Hand will find you. Sooner or later, your brother or your father will sell you out again, they will catch your scent, and you'll wake up with monsters standing over you. You have contacts in the Edge. Ask any of them if I'm lying."

Run if you want . . . Yeah, right. His eyes told her that she wouldn't get very far. He had no intention of letting her go. Just like before, when she was a child, technically she was given a choice, but practically things had been decided without her.

"It's not my mess," she told him.

"You stole the stupid things. You made this mess; you're in it up to your eyeballs."

"No."

"Audrey, weigh the odds."

She had. Audrey looked away. Her gaze snagged on the book of Greek myths she had been reading yesterday. Like Odysseus, she was stuck between Scylla and Charybdis: the Hand on one side and the Mirror on the other. Each would swallow her without a moment's hesitation.

She liked her place. It wasn't much, but it was so cozy and comfortable. She liked her old couch and reading her books with Ling curled by her feet. She just wanted to be left alone. That was all.

"You may not like my ugly mug," Kaldar said, "but as corny as it sounds, I am your best hope for survival. I've fought them, I've killed them, and I will do it again."

This had gone from bad to the end of the world in a hurry. "And if I help you?" Audrey asked.

"I can't promise that you will survive. But I promise that I will do everything I can to protect you, and if we succeed, the Mirror will see to it that you won't have to fear the Hand again."

"Is that code for 'the Mirror will kill me'?"

"No. It's code for they will do for you what they've done

for my family. They will give you enough funds and space anywhere within Adrianglia to make a brand-new start in comfort."

He really did think she was born yesterday.

Her family finally screwed up so badly, they put the whole Edge at risk, and she was the one who had made it happen. She could deal with it, or she could walk away and be known as the girl who destroyed the Edge. It stretched like a ribbon from ocean to ocean, all across the continent. How many people lived in the Edge? It had to be thousands. Thieves and swindlers and conmen. Her people and their children. All at risk because of Seamus Callahan's greed and her daddy issues.

Audrey raised her head. "I will help you find where Seamus unloaded the diffusers. That's all. The moment you know your next target, I am out. Do we understand each other?"

Kaldar smiled, and this time his smile was savage. "Perfectly."

SIX

AUDREY had a conscience. She was good at hiding her motivation, but Kaldar had practiced reading people for way too long to miss the subtle tightness in the corners of her mouth, the eyebrows creeping together, and the glimpse of sadness in her eyes. She felt guilty. Probably even ashamed, although of her own involvement or of her family's stupidity, he couldn't tell.

Kaldar pondered it, turning it over in his mind. Conscience was a virtue he tried very hard to avoid. True, there were things that were just not done: injuring a child, forcing a woman, torturing a dog. But beyond those basic rules, everything else was just a cumbersome guideline he strived to ignore. He supposed it made him amoral, and he was fine with that.

His world was clearly divided: on one side was the family. Family was everything. It was a shelter in the storm. A place where he would be welcome no matter what he'd done or would do. On the other side lay the rest of the world, like a ripe plum, ready for plucking. Between them ran the line of demarcation. When he crossed it to the family's side, he was a devoted brother, cousin, and uncle. When he crossed it to the other side, he became a villain.

The heist was the Callahan family's responsibility. Audrey was a Callahan, and she had stepped up to take it— that he understood. He would've done the same. But considering how much she loathed her family, he would've thought self-preservation would be a much stronger motivation for her. He'd misread her, and now it bugged him.

Audrey was a puzzle. He quietly examined the place, cataloging her possessions. A solid fridge, dented but clean. Same with the stove. Worn but plush furniture. The chair under Jack sported a very neatly sewn seam where something had torn the upholstery. He bet on the raccoon.

The three windows he could see were narrow, and each one had a heavy-duty shutter, lockable from the inside. A functional dagger hung on the wall between the kitchen cabinets. A small bow waited unstrung on the shelf above the plates, and below it a pair of yellow work boots, streaked with mud, sat on the floor.

Her three bookcases held an assortment of books, all well handled and shopworn. A dozen plastic horses each about six inches long sat on one of the shelves. A few had wings, and at least one sported a horn. On the top shelves, tucked away from raccoon paws, lived a collection of stuffed animals: a pink kitten, a panda, a frog with a yellow helmet marked with a star, a wolf. Daggers and stuffed frogs.

Her decorations made no sense: a blanket in a bright Southwestern style that clashed with everything, a *Star Wars* movie poster, some sort of potted flower, a scented candle, and a tomahawk. She was like a little magpie: if it struck her fancy, she brought it home.

He'd seen this before, in Cerise's husband, William. Kaldar's cousin Cerise was practically his sister, which made the changeling wolf his brother-in-law. The man was a trained, savage killer. He killed with no doubt or remorse and suffered no pangs of conscience after the deed was done. And then he went home and played with toys. His childhood had been pure shit. William had essentially grown up in a prison, barely disguised as a school. It was the fear of that same prison that had driven Jack to stow away on Kaldar's wyvern.

This house, with its sturdy walls, weapons, and fluffy pink kittens, didn't belong to an infantile, child-like woman. It belonged to an adult battered by life. She had survived it all, and now she was trying to recapture the childhood she'd never had.

Someone had hurt Audrey, and it had left lasting scars. Kaldar looked at her again. She was golden, not just pretty, but funny and vivid, like a ray of sunshine in the room. There was something good about Audrey, and at least some of it was real. Most women he'd come across in the Edge families that were down on their luck were like haggard dogs: bitter, vicious, devoid of any joy. But she was like a summer day.

What sort of twisted bastard would hurt her so much that she decided to live alone in the woods, in a house with foot-thick stone walls? This was her haven and her shelter. Pulling her out of this place would be next to impossible. Why, in fact it would be a challenge. And Kaldar loved challenges. They kept his life from being boring.

The way she sat now, leaning forward frowning, biting her pink bottom lip, her shirt dipping to reveal a hint of her cleavage . . . He wondered idly if he could get her to bend over a little farther . . .

"Just what are you staring at, exactly?"

Kaldar snapped back to reality. "You. You've been thinking hard for the last five minutes. It's not good for you to strain your pretty little head like that. I'm waiting for the steam to shoot out of your ears to relieve the pressure on your brain."

"Aha." Audrey glanced at Jack and George. "What you have here is a man who was caught gaping at my breasts, and now he's trying to cover it up with rudeness."

Kaldar lost it and laughed.

"Don't get any ideas," Audrey told him. "I'm helping you to get your bracelets back, and that's it. Most of Seamus's contacts are back East. He did unload some hot merchandise in the West before, but I have no idea where. He's a creature of habit. If a deal went well, he'd stick to that buyer like glue."

"He wouldn't have gone back East," Kaldar said. "Too hot with the Mirror and the Hand both hunting him down, looking for the diffusers." Judging by his actions so far, Seamus Callahan was a man with some talent but many flaws. He planned too much, he hustled too much, he lost both of his children and had chosen to save the wrong one. But even Seamus would know better than to run headfirst into a lion's maw.

Audrey tapped her nails on her glass. "So the question is, who around here would buy such a thing? It must have been somebody who understood the diffusers' true worth, because they paid over forty grand in Broken money for it." Audrey frowned. "How long ago did Alex go into rehab?"

"Three days," Kaldar said.

"So Seamus and Alex barely had time to make it to the rehab facility after that craziness with the Hand. Seamus would've gone through the Broken for sure, probably by plane. I doubt he could've flown in with a caseful of money. Too risky." Audrey rose.

"He would've had to fence the merchandise here," Kaldar said.

Audrey rose and headed to the fridge. "I need to see Gnome. He's the local fence, and he'll be our best bet."

"Does he live in the fridge?" Jack asked.

Heh. Of course, with Jack there was no way to tell if he was joking or being literal

"No." Audrey pulled out a large brown bottle. "But he loves beer. Especially AleSmith Speedway Stout. I keep a bottle for him. Just in case."

Kaldar squinted at the dark champagne-sized bottle filled with jet-black liquid. "Why is it black?"

"I don't know. Maybe because they put coffee in it." Audrey went to the door. "I won't be long."

"Nice try." Kaldar rose. "I'm coming with you."

"Gnome doesn't trust outsiders."

"What do you want to bet that I'll get him to talk?"

She narrowed her eyes. "You like betting a lot, don't you?"

Careful. "Even a perfect angel like me has to have some vices."

"Angel? Please." Audrey looked at George. "George, could you get a can of Pepsi out of the fridge for me?"

George extracted a can.

"Throw it."

The boy tossed it at her. Audrey caught it and shook it up. The can landed in front of Kaldar on the table. Audrey waved her beer bottle. "I bet you this stout you can't open it without foam spilling all over."

"I don't have to bet." Kaldar tapped the can and opened it. Foam rose and fell back down. "See?"

She gave him a suspicious look. "Mhhm."

Kaldar crossed the room and held the door open. "I can take that bottle."

She thrust the stout at him. "Why thank you, sir." Boom, a thousand-watt smile. She couldn't possibly be trying to con him—all the cards were already on the table. It must've been force of habit.

He raised his hand, shielding his eyes. "Smile . . . too . . . bright . . ."

"You're going to be a pain to work with, aren't you?"

"Oh, I don't know. I might grow on you."

She furrowed her pretty eyebrows. "Like a cancer?"

"Like a favorite vice."

"Don't count on it."

Audrey swept outside, and he nodded at the two boys. "On the double."

The two boys exited. A moment later, Ling the raccoon darted out and shot across the porch to Audrey's feet. Kaldar pulled the door shut, and they were off.

KALDAR climbed up a steep forest trail. Around him, the ancient forest shimmered with vibrant green. Giant spruces spread their branches. Emerald moss, sparkling with a dusting of tiny brilliant red flowers, sheathed gray boulders. Strange flowers, yellow, large, and shaped like three bells growing one within another, bordered the path. A weak haze hung above the forest floor, present even in the middle of the day. The whole place seemed ethereal, otherworldy, like a glimpse of some fairy kingdom in the fog.

Kaldar hid a grimace. He knew the Mire. He understood

it—the ever-changing labyrinth of mud and water, the herbs, the flowers, the animals. This forest was different, sprawling atop rugged mountains that cut through the soil like the planet's bare bones.

Audrey kept moving with practiced quickness, stepping over roots protruding over the trail and pushing ferns and branches out of her way. She kept a brisk pace, but Kaldar didn't mind. From his vantage point, he had an excellent view of her shapely butt. It was a butt that deserved some scrutiny.

"If you're waiting for my behind to do a trick, you're out of luck," Audrey called over her shoulder.

"How the hell did you even know?" Did she have eyes on the back of her head?

"Woman's intuition," she told him.

"Aha, so it wouldn't be the fact that I stumbled twice in the last minute?"

"Not at all."

George cracked a smile. To the left, Jack laughed. The boy moved through the woods like a fish through water, climbing over boulders and fallen tree trunks with unnatural ease. The raccoon raced after him, sometimes ahead, sometimes behind.

"Does she always follow you around?"

"Ling the Merciless? Yes. I found her bleeding by my porch. She was so tiny then, she fit into a tissue box." Audrey glanced at the raccoon. "She follows me around now, and sometimes she brings me dead bugs because I'm a bad hunter, and she tries to feed me. If I hide, she'll find me."

"Always?"

"Always."

As the path turned, the trees parted, revealing a long, wooded slope dropping far down. They were on the side of the mountain.

"They're prone to rabies, you know," Kaldar said. "And this one is out in the daylight all the time, too. That's not typical. Are you sure she isn't rabid?"

"This one has been taken to the vet to get shots."

"They can carry rabies for months before it ever manifests."

"Kaldar, leave my raccoon alone, or I will push you off this mountain and laugh while you try to grow wings." Audrey turned away and kept walking.

"How much farther?" Kaldar asked.

"Are you tuckered out already?"

"I bet I could beat you there."

"No."

"You're sure?" Kaldar grinned.

"No more bets."

"As you wish."

Audrey pointed up and left, where a cliff thrust out, bristling with ancient trees. "He lives around there. Another fifteen minutes, and you can rest your delicate footsies."

He let the footsies comment pass. "Why do they call him Gnome, anyway?"

"Because of his size, of course," Audrey said.

Fifteen minutes later, they emerged into a narrow clearing. A huge structure stood at the far end: a two-story ruin built of the same gray stone as the framework of Audrey's house. A collection of columns stretched out to the sky, each carved with some sort of battle scene, forming a precise rectangle, with two smaller squares at each end. A wooden house had been built within the stone skeleton, in some places inside it, in some places hanging over it, its walls and rooms protruding under odd angles. Windows of all shapes and sizes punctuated the wooden walls at random, as if some toddler had mixed several construction sets and thrown together a structure with his eyes closed. Moss and flowering vines climbed over the timbers, and some sort of small furry beast, with charcoal fur and a long tail with a puff on the end, scurried up the vines to the roof.

"Come on." Audrey headed toward the house.

"Anything I need to know about this Gnome?" Kaldar asked.

"He doesn't like outsiders much. Let me do the talking, and we'll be fine."

They approached the building. "Hey, Gnome! Gnooome!" Audrey turned to the boys. "Okay, kids, make some noise. He's hard of hearing sometimes. Gnoome!"

"Hello!" George yelled. "Hi!"

"Open the door!" Jack roared.

Kaldar put two fingers into his mouth. A piercing whistle rang through the forest. Jack stuck his finger into his ear and shook a bit.

A misshapen window swung open on the top floor. Someone moved in the gloom.

"Hey, Gnome!" Audrey waved.

"What do you want?" A male voice called out.

"I have a question I need to ask you!" Audrey called.

"I'm busy now."

"I brought payment." Audrey turned to Kaldar. "Show him the beer."

He raised the bottle.

"Is that Speedway Stout?"

"Yes, it is," Audrey confirmed.

The shadowy figure heaved a sigh. "All right. I'll be right down."

A cascade of thuds and banging echoed inside the house.

Kaldar leaned to Audrey. "Is he falling down the stairs?"

Audrey grimaced. "No, he just has . . . things. Many, many things."

Kaldar's imagination served up a hunchback gnome struggling to climb down the stairs among stacks of dirty pots. Why he'd imagined pots, he had no idea. Hopefully, they wouldn't have to climb in there to rescue the man.

A section of the wall slid aside. A huge man emerged into the sunlight. His oversized jean overalls barely enclosed his enormous frame. Thick defined muscle strained the sleeves of his white T-shirt. His hair was a reddish curly mess, and his face, with sunken eyes and a massive jaw, looked menacing enough to frighten away rabid wolves. He could've been sixty or eighty; with the Edgers, it was hard to tell. Some of them lived to a couple of hundred.

The giant ambled over to Audrey, towering a foot over

her, and held out his shovel-sized hand. Beer. Right. Kaldar thrust the bottle into Gnome's hand. The giant bit the cork with his teeth, twisted the bottle, spat out the cork, and took a deep gulp.

"Good." Gnome peered at him. "I know her. I don't know you."

Kaldar opened his mouth.

"He's my fiancé," Audrey said.

What?

Gnome blinked. "Fiancé?"

"Yep," Audrey confirmed.

"When's the wedding?" Gnome asked.

Kaldar stepped closer to Audrey and put his arm around her. She didn't stiffen; she even leaned into him a little. He caught a hint of her perfume again and grinned, squeezing her closer, as his hand slipped into her pocket. His fingers caught something metal and Kaldar pinned the object between his index and middle fingers and withdrew his hand. "Not for a while. We've been living in sin and enjoying every bit of it."

"And they are?" Gnome jerked his chin at the boys.

"My cousins," Kaldar said.

Gnome pondered the four of them for a long moment. "Okay, come."

Kaldar took a step forward, his arm around Audrey. Gnome held up his hand. "The changeling stays outside. I've got a lot of glass in there, and I don't want it broken."

Jack was a child, not a wild dog. Kaldar hid a growl. "Fine."

Gnome turned and went back into the house.

Audrey sank her elbow into his side.

"Ow," Kaldar winced.

"Keep your paws to yourself," she murmured, and followed Gnome.

"It was worth it," he called after her.

She turned around, her eyes indignant, punched her left palm with her right fist, and kept walking.

"I don't think she likes you," Jack said.

Kaldar ruffled his hair. "You have a lot to learn about women. Jack, Gnome doesn't want you inside."

Jack wrinkled his nose. "That's fine. He doesn't smell right anyway."

Ling tried to dart past them, following Audrey. Kaldar scooped the beast off the ground by the scruff of her neck. The raccoon snarled and raked the air with her claws. "Hold her." He held out Ling, and George stepped up to grab her. Kaldar hesitated. He'd expected Jack to take Ling. The little beast would scratch George bloody.

George's hands closed about the raccoon. Ling snorted and sat on his arm, perfectly calm.

They had to be the strangest children he'd ever come across. "Can either of you sense magic?"

"Yes," George nodded. "I feel it, and Jack smells it."

"If you sense a lot of magic coming, let Ling go and run to get Gaston. No waiting, no hesitation." His luck had held out—without realizing it, they'd landed the wyvern only half a mile from Audrey's house. He'd left Gaston there with instructions to be ready for takeoff at a moment's notice. It would take the kids less than fifteen minutes to get there. "Just run to Gaston as fast as you can."

"What, I don't get to fight?" Jack asked.

Kaldar appraised the indignant note in his voice. Now was the time for finesse. "We have Audrey with us. If people are coming to kill us, we may have to get out of here in a hurry, and the best way to keep Audrey safe is to load her onto the wyvern. Make sense?"

Jack thought about it. "Yes."

At the door, Audrey called, "Are you coming?"

"No, just breathing hard, love." He glanced at her and was rewarded by an outraged glare, followed by, "Oh, my God!"

Kaldar took a moment to look at both boys. "No heroics. Do exactly as you are told. The mission is our first priority."

"We understand," George said.

"Good."

They took off for the trees. Kaldar glanced at the object he'd taken from Audrey's pocket. It was a simple gold cross on a chain. In the middle of the cross a tiny black stone winked at him. He wondered why she didn't wear it. Pretty Audrey, full of secrets like a puzzle box. Now he'd have to find an excuse to touch her again to put the cross back.

The boys reached the trees and melted into the brush. Kaldar slipped the cross and the chain between his fingers, turned, and caught up with Audrey. "You could've warned me he was a giant."

"And spoil the fun? Please."

Kaldar swiped a chunk of rock and wedged it between the door and the frame.

Audrey raised her eyebrows.

"For your raccoon," he told her. "In case of emergency, the kids will let her go. You said she always finds you, so she'll run right back here."

She gave him a long, suspicious stare that said plainly that she trusted him about as far as she could throw him. "I bet you scheme even when you sleep."

"That depends on who I'm sleeping with."

Audrey laughed and went inside. Somehow, it didn't seem like a "with him" kind of laugh. More like "at him." *That's all right, love. You'll come to see my point of view.*

Kaldar followed and found himself in a large room. Shelves occupied every available inch of wall space and cleaved the room in long rows, their content protected by glass. Some were filled with books; others held vials in a dozen shapes and sizes. Colored bottles, green, brown, and red, stood next to Weird gadgets and gears. To the right, two shelves contained teapots. Under them rested an army of aromatic candles, then a dozen sticks of deodorant, twenty bottles of assorted shampoo, kerosene lamps, Nintendo game systems, a Sony PlayStation, two or three hundred game cartridges and CDs, sun catchers, laptops, old toys, animal skulls, cowbells, Blu-ray movies, assorted metal parts from engines, and above it all a dried-up baby wyvern, mummified into a skeletal monstrosity, spread its dead wings, suspended from a ceiling by a cord. Each item had a tiny price tag. Not a speck of dust marred the place.

Charming. A pawnbroker's paradise.

Gnome took another long swallow from the bottle and strode between the shelves to a beautiful antique coffee table, surrounded by plush red chairs. He settled into one and indicated the other two with a sweep of his hand.

Audrey perched in a chair. Kaldar sat next to her.

"So what can I do you for?"

Audrey leaned forward with a charming smile. "You've done business with Seamus."

"Yeah." Gnome shrugged. "What of it?"

"If he had to unload a hot item on the West Coast, where would he go?"

"How hot?"

"The Hand wants it," Kaldar said.

Gnome grunted. "What the hell . . . Okay, what sort of item?"

"It's a gadget," Audrey said. "With military applications. He got at least forty grand for it."

"US currency?"

"Mhm."

"Well, he didn't sell it to me, I can tell you that much. I won't touch anything the Hand wants. Isn't worth the risk. And if you and your fiancé have any sense, you will leave this thing alone." Gnome rose and disappeared between the shelves.

"Fiancé," Kaldar mouthed at Audrey and wagged his eyebrows.

She shrugged. *"Don't get any ideas."*

"Too late."

Oh, he had ideas, and if the circumstances were different, he would explain them to her. In a lot of detail. With practical demonstrations.

Gnome returned, carrying an enormous book, four feet tall and at least six inches thick. He pulled a book pedestal from behind the shelf and lowered the book onto it. "There are about ten people on the West Coast who would buy Hand-hot merchandise." He opened the book and flipped through the pages. "Of those, six could come up with forty grand on short notice. We can rule out Vadim Urkovski."

"Why?" Audrey asked.

"He got himself jailed in Sacramento for running a stop-light while roaring drunk, then punching a cop." Gnome grinned. "His wife refused to post bail. Apparently, he wasn't alone in the car. He'll get out of it, but it will take time."

"That leaves us with five," Kaldar said.

"That it does." Gnome flipped the old page. On it a large photograph showed a woman with flowing brown hair. "We can rule out Vicki as well. Seamus is superstitious. He once did a deal with her and got pinched right after. Wouldn't work with her since. So we're down to four." Gnome flipped another page. On it, a tall blond man in a pale fisherman sweater and jeans leaned against a Mercedes. "Kaleb Green. Operates near Seattle. Will buy anything for the right price."

"Too far," Audrey said. "Alex is in rehab in northern California, and Seamus wouldn't travel over a long distance with a lot of money."

Gnome turned the page. A woman in a bright skirt and a pale beige vest over a white blouse smiled into the camera. A pair of rose-tinted glasses perched on her nose. A layered necklace with large wooden and turquoise beads hung from her neck. There was something deeply predatory in her eyes. The outfit said hippy. The eyes said deepwater shark.

"Magdalene. She's near San Diego."

Audrey frowned. "She is a possibility. I never heard him mention her, but that's neither here nor there."

Gnome flipped a couple more pages. "Morell de Braose. He probably isn't your guy. He deals mainly in jewelry and art."

Jewelry. Like bracelets, for example. Kaldar leaned forward, focusing on the photo. The man on the page wore a pricey suit, that dark, expensive shade of gray that worked equally well for luxury suits or red-carpet gowns. He appeared to be in his early forties, blond, with a carefully trimmed beard on a youthful, tan face. He had the athletic build of a man who either belonged to or owned a gym and had copious leisure to attend it. Behind him, a luxurious office spread, all dark, polished furniture, decorated with antique statuettes and daggers with gilded hilts on the walls.

Audrey frowned.

"This is the man," Kaldar said.

"How do you know?" Gnome raised his furry eyebrows.

"A feeling I get."

Gnome rolled his eyes and lifted the page.

"Hold on." Audrey got up off her seat and leaned over the page. "He's right."

"Why?"

Audrey pointed to the picture. "See that marble statue of a half-naked woman? The one on the gold pedestal?"

"Yeah." Gnome squinted.

"That's *Aurora* by Ciniselli."

"And?" Kaldar asked.

Audrey turned to them with a look of triumph on her face. "I stole her. Eight years ago. Seamus sold her for ten grand. We needed money in a hurry, and I remember him saying the man he sold it to was good for quick cash in a pinch. It was a pain-in-the-ass heist, too. Took two weeks, and I got hit by a car at the end of it."

Now there was a story. Kaldar made a mental note to ask her about it later.

Gnome shrugged. "Hate to tell you, but he got ripped off. The statue *Aurora* has been appraised between thirty-five and fifty."

Audrey stared at the picture and swore.

KALDAR leaned back in his seat and hung one leg over the other. Audrey watched him out of the corner of her eye. The man was a chameleon, who changed personalities the way a teenage girl changed outfits, trying to find the right one before a big party.

Why was she still here? He had gotten what he wanted—they figured out where Seamus must have unloaded his merchandise. She should go, grab Ling, and disappear.

Audrey eyed Kaldar. Back at the house, when he spoke

about his family, his eyes had turned merciless. A little of his true self had showed—that was the real man, ruthless and resolute. All the rest were just disguises.

Kaldar caught her glance and smiled. Yes, yes, you are a handsome devil. Emphasis on devil. He was flirting with her, either because he liked what he saw or, more likely, because he had decided it would be an easy way to keep her agreeable. He went from *I'll walk over you* to *I can't take my eyes off your butt* kind of quick.

A small annoying thought nagged at her. If she hadn't taken the job, none of this would've happened, and the Edge wouldn't be at risk. Which was stupid because had she not taken the job, her dad would've just found somebody else. She wasn't the only picklock in the Edge. Well, she was probably the best, but not the only one.

What was she thinking? Seamus wouldn't have had a prayer of breaking into that pyramid without her. The lock on the first door, which led to the passage, was easy enough, but some of the inner locks had taken her a full ten minutes each. Complicated locks weren't a problem, but if the tumblers were heavy, opening them took a lot of effort. The bolts and bars were the worst. Sliding an inch-wide bar by magic felt like trying to lift a truck. When she finally swung open the final door, her nose was bleeding and she had to lie down. She had made this whole burglary possible.

Okay, fine. Fine, but it didn't mean she had to run head-first into the Hand's jaws to fix it. She might have pulled off the heist, but Seamus had put it together. It was Seamus's mess. He had dragged her into this predicament. Kaldar should've found him, not her.

In all of her twenty-three years, Audrey had never seen anyone die. Sure, there had been an occasional punch or a slap, but violence was never a part of her childhood. Well, not until Alex had sold her for some coke. That was not how her family had operated. They were thieves, yes, swindlers, yes, con artists, but they had always stayed away from murder. No matter what Kaldar said, she knew both the Hand and the Mirror had no compunction about killing left and right, cutting people down like weeds. The danger the Edge was in wasn't her problem unless she made it her problem. And Audrey didn't want to be a hero.

"So what do you know about this Morell de Braose?" Kaldar asked.

"That information would be extra." Gnome shook his bottle. "I'm out of stout, so I'll take cash."

Kaldar reached inside his hoodie and pulled out a gold coin. An Adrianglian doubloon. Five hundred dollars. Gnome's gaze fixed on the coin. Kaldar set the coin on its edge and spun it with a quick flick of his fingers. It whirled in place.

"I know de Braose owns a castle," Gnome said. "And six thousand acres of the Democracy of California to go with it. He came on the scene about twelve years go. Nobody knows where de Braose is from for sure, but he did away with the baron who owned the estate before him, killed off a few of his neighbors, and remodeled the castle. About a third of his land is in the Edge, and he pops back and forth across the Broken and the Weird at will. He likes the Broken's antiques, and he hobnobs with the bluebloods from the Weird."

Well, that was neither here nor there. How was Morell de Braose funded? Where was his castle? How many people did he employ? How did he make his money? Those would be the questions a competent thief would ask. She settled back to watch Kaldar. *Here's your test. Let's see how good you are.*

Kaldar appeared to be in no hurry. "How did he get his money?"

"There are rumors." Gnome shrugged. "People say he traffics in weapons, art, and other merchandise."

"Human merchandise?" Kaldar asked.

"Like I said, there are rumors, but every robber baron in California comes with those kinds of rumors. They're a lawless crowd. Anything goes. De Braose was never caught in the act, so I don't got anything concrete."

A slaver. Audrey fought a shudder. There was no worse

scum in either world. They already had the Hand and the Mirror—apparently this mess wouldn't be complete without a robber baron/slaver in the mix.

"How big's his army?" Kaldar asked.

"Garrison's forty men, give or take. Plus a special guard. How many he can raise in a pinch is anybody's guess."

Too many. Way too many.

"Why such a large force? Is he ambitious?" Kaldar asked.

"He isn't land-greedy, if that's what you mean. De Braose holds art auctions once every few months," Gnome said. "He sells everything, outlawed automatics from the Weird, stolen art, weapons and medicine contraband from the Broken. These are invitation only; if you don't have an invitation and a million or two in liquid cash, you shouldn't bother even showing up. The army's there to make sure the guests arrive safely and depart safely. It's a big deal: the whole thing takes three or four days, and he throws banquets and balls as part of it."

"When is the next one?"

"In eight days. Trust me, you ain't getting in."

If Morell de Braose had bought those stupid amplifiers from her father, he'd sell them at the auction. They were too hot an item to hold on to indefinitely. Kaldar had to get into that auction, which sounded pretty much impossible. Well, good luck. It would be his problem and not hers.

"What about this special guard?"

Gnome grinned. "He's got himself twelve of the Republic of Texas's finest sharpshooters. A mercenary outfit called Eagle Eye. They don't miss. And if the guns don't get you, he also imported himself sixteen of Vinland's veekings. I've seen a picture once. They're all seven feet tall and carrying axes that would cut a tall tree down in one blow."

Kaldar kept playing with the coin. "Does he have any enemies?"

Gnome flipped the page, and the hippy woman looked back at them. That was some stare. It would give a seasoned murderer the creeps.

"Magdalene Moonflower."

Magdalene Moonflower, right. And that wasn't a fake name, not at all.

"She hates him. She'd be your best bet."

Kaldar rolled the coin across the table. Gnome swiped the little gold disk and grinned. "Pleasure doing business with you."

Ling shot between the shelves and leaped onto her lap.

Someone was coming. Audrey tensed. Kaldar rose to his feet. Gnome reached to the top of the nearest shelf and retrieved a shotgun.

Audrey got up and ran through the house to the window overlooking the forest. A moment and Kaldar joined her, standing too close. They scanned the woods.

Nothing. No movement troubled the Edge wilderness.

Behind them, the shotgun clanged as Gnome chambered a round.

A green human-shaped shadow detached from the gloom between the cypress branches, about twenty feet above ground.

Audrey caught her breath.

The shadow leaped. It flew thirty feet, its wide, tattered cloak flaring behind it, and landed at the top of a pine.

What the hell was that? "Why jump around in a cloak?" Audrey whispered.

"That's not a cloak," Kaldar said next to her, gently nudging her aside. "That's his wings. The Hand is here. We have to go. Now."

Another person appeared between the trees. He was unnaturally lean and painted in swirls of green and brown. The man looked at a cedar trunk and scrambled up the bark like he had suckers on his hands.

Gnome pulled a box of ammo off the shelf. "You go ahead. There's a door out back. I'm not going anywhere."

"Don't be a fool," Kaldar snapped. "You see that man in the cedar? That's a *lesarde*-class operative right there, and that over there is a *boddus*. Those two are never let off the chain because they're both so twisted by magic they're unstable. That means there is a Hand officer out there, pulling the strings, and they come with a commando unit, twelve operatives, maybe more. You stay here, you die."

"They aren't getting into my house." Gnome locked his teeth.

Idiot. Audrey thrust herself in front of him. "Gnome! Are you crazy? Come with us! All this stuff isn't worth your life."

He bared his teeth at her. "This stuff *is* my life. You two get the hell out of my house."

Something thumped on the roof and scrambled across it, fast, scratching the shingles. *Oh God.*

"Go!" Gnome growled. "Out the back door."

Kaldar's hand clamped around her wrist. "Come, Audrey."

She shook him off. "So you're just going to die here? Why?"

"Because I spent my life working my hide off for this house and everything with it," Gnome said. "That's fifty years of trading and bargaining right here. I know every single thing on these shelves, and the Hand ain't getting it. None of you are getting my shit, not you, not them."

"You stupid old fool!"

Gnome waved her off with an angry jerk of his hand.

Kaldar grabbed Audrey's hand and yanked her, pulling her with him through the house.

"Let go of me."

"He made his choice. You stay, you die with him."

"I said let go. You don't know where you're going."

He released her hand and she ran, zigzagging between the shelves, Kaldar a step behind. They passed the pedestal with the book still on it. It was still open to Magdalene Moonflower's portrait. If they survived this, she would be their next stop, and the Hand didn't need to know that. Audrey lunged for the book, nearly colliding with Kaldar.

"The page," he barked, bumping into her.

"I know!"

Audrey grabbed the book and ripped a handful of pages free. Kaldar ran his fingers along the seam, pulling little clumps of paper out, until no evidence of the pages remained, and shoved the pedestal. The giant volume crashed to the floor, closing. Audrey dashed to the back of the house, through a side room, and to the small door. Kaldar grabbed the handle and strained.

"Locked."

No dead bolt, only a keyhole. "Let me." Audrey pressed her palm against the keyhole and let her magic seep into the lock. Three, two . . .

The lock clicked. She pushed the handle and ran out into the open air. Ling sprinted into the forest, passing her.

Kaldar drew even. "Keep moving," the agent murmured. "Keep moving."

They scurried into the trees.

"Which way is the cliff?" he whispered.

What? Had he lost his mind? "Straight on."

"Lead the way."

She broke into a run.

Behind them, something clanged with a heavy metal thud. Audrey glanced over her shoulder. The metal shutters on the house were snapping closed one by one, locking it down. Anxiety squeezed her chest. She remembered when Gnome first showed her his "defense system." He was trapped within the house, like a sardine in a can.

She looked back again. People in green and brown converged from the grass and trees, climbing onto the house, one from the left, the other two from the right. A man crawled over the roof, moving on all fours. He raised his head. His eyes bored straight into her.

For a second she stopped in her tracks, frozen by the sudden fear. A strange, revolting feeling flooded Audrey, grasping her stomach and throat and crushing both. Nausea writhed through her. The tiny hairs on the backs of her arms rose.

The man opened his mouth. A long black tongue flailed among a forest of long, needle-thin fangs.

Magic washed over Audrey in a sickening miasma, clinging to her skin. Tiny jaws nibbled on her flesh, trying to worm their way inside. Audrey spun and dashed through the woods. Tree trunks flashed by. She ran like she had never run before in her life, all but flying over the forest floor, trying to get away from the awful magic. Her feet crushed undergrowth. The magic chased her. She could feel it flooding the woods behind her.

A shotgun barked, its fire like thunder: *Boom! Boom!*

A high-pitched shriek tore through the forest, spurring her on. Something had caught the full blast of Gnome's fire.

Boom!

Glass shattered. Something thumped.

Boom!

A hoarse howl lashed her ears, and she knew it was Gnome screaming his life out.

The trees ended, and she skidded to a stop on a carpet of brown pine needles. Ahead, the ground stopped, as if cut by a giant's knife. A vast blue-green valley stretched far below.

Kaldar shot out of the woods, and she caught him and spun him around.

"What now? They're coming."

Kaldar pulled his bag open and took out a small bronze sphere the size of a tennis ball. He squeezed its sides, lifted it to his mouth, and exhaled. The sphere buzzed like an angry beehive and unrolled into a metal wasp.

"Gaston," Kaldar said.

The wasp shivered. Thin golden membranes of twin wings rose from its back. With a faint whir, the insect took to the air and streaked away, behind the mountain.

Kaldar pulled a coin from his pocket. "Do you trust me?"

"No!"

"Well, you're going to have to." He gripped her hand. "Whatever you see, hold still. If you move, it's over. Not a sound."

The coin in his hand turned white. A transparent shiver spread from the coin, sliding over his hand, his elbow, his shoulder, and rolling over her. She thrust her left hand into her pocket. The reassuring cold of Grandma's cross slid against her fingers.

The coin's magic swallowed them. Colors slid over the outer surface of the spell bubble and snapped together, mimicking the fallen log and the trees around them. They blended into the forest, invisible.

She'd heard about this. The mirror spell, the one that gave the Mirror its name. So Kaldar hadn't lied after all.

Tiny needles pricked her skin. Fear slid down her back like an ice cube melting along her spine. Audrey froze.

The foul magic caught up with them. It seeped through the mirror barrier and dug at her skin, trying to pry her open.

Kaldar squeezed her hand.

The bushes rustled.

A man stepped out into the clearing. He moved hunched forward, neck stretched out, as if he were a hunting dog who had somehow learned to walk upright and was tracking its prey. Green-and-gray camo paint swirled on his face. His long brown hair fell on his back in dozens of tiny braids. He was so close that if she took three steps, she could have touched him.

Heat streaked along her skin, and Audrey had the absurd feeling that she was about to burn alive. She could almost feel the tiny hairs on the backs of her arms curl from the heat. Kaldar's fingers pressed into her hand gently.

It's just like a regular job. You're just standing there, waiting for the security guard to pass before you open the door.

Breathe easy. Breathe easy. You don't want to get busted, do you?

The man pulled back his cloak, letting it slip off his shoulders. Muscle corded his nude upper body. His frame had no fat at all, and his tan skin hugged his bones, too tight, like a latex glove.

Audrey exhaled slowly through her nose. A familiar calm settled over her. She forced herself to relax muscle by muscle until she simply stood next to Kaldar, as if the two of them were on a date, watching the beautiful mountain view.

The Hand's agent turned, raising his arms, holding curved narrow knives in each fist. The flesh along his sides, right over his ribs, split.

The disgusting magic smoldered around her, threatening to burn her.

The skin over the man's ribs rose in two flaps, like fins on a fish. Spongy red tissue lay underneath, moist and veined with blood vessels.

Jesus Christ.

The magic slammed into her like an avalanche, overwhelming her senses. It slid against her skin, scraping it like the edge of a sharp blade, burning, hotter and hotter. Nausea came. Her stomach twisted. Acid washed her throat.

Breathe easy. Audrey held completely still, concentrating on inhaling and exhaling. Her heart slowed down.

The man turned left, then right, slowly. The red flesh on the man's sides fluttered like a fish's gills. He was smelling the air, Audrey realized. She glanced at Kaldar. The bastard was smiling, watching the Hand's monster like he was the biggest lollypop in a candy store.

All these people were crazy. The Hand, the Mirror, all of them.

The man took a step closer. Another.

Another.

They were face-to-face now, less than two feet from each other. She saw every detail of his face: wide overdeveloped jaw, large nose, and eyes so dark they were nearly black. Like staring into the beady button eyes of a shark: nothing but cold, merciless hunger.

The agent sucked the air into his lungs, his nostrils fluttering. He raised his foot. If he took another step, he would run right into them.

A pissed-off growl almost made her jerk. Audrey turned her head a fraction of an inch. To the right, two feet above them, Ling bared her small fangs on a tree branch.

The Hand's freak stared at the raccoon with his dead eyes.

Ling coughed and snarled, biting off sharp chitters. Stupid, stupid raccoon.

The man turned and took a step toward Ling. If he touched her raccoon, she would charge right into him.

Kaldar gripped her hand tighter.

She couldn't let him get Ling.

A long, piercing cry came from the right, behind the mountain.

The Hand's agent spun toward it, the raccoon forgotten.

Kaldar jerked a black gun from inside his sweatshirt. The spell around them tore like wrapping paper. Kaldar stepped behind the freak and squeezed the trigger. The gun spat thunder. Blood and chunks of bone sprayed, splattering her with tiny drops of human gore.

Her brain refused to process it, as if it were happening to someone else.

The agent spun around, his eyes wide, somehow still alive. Kaldar fired again, straight into his face. The freak stumbled, veering toward her, a gaping red hole where his forehead used to be. As if on autopilot, Audrey leaned back and kicked him in the chest. The Hand's agent tumbled over the edge and fell to the valley below. Her stomach lurched, and Audrey vomited into the grass and forced herself back upright. No time to waste.

The revolting magic still burned her. The Hand's agent was dead, but his magic ate at her, fracturing into a thousand tiny jaws that gnawed on her skin, trying to chew their way inside. She rubbed her arms, trying to wipe them off, and failed.

Wild ululating howls rocked the forest. The Hand was coming.

The gunshot had been too loud. "They know where we are."

Kaldar shook his head and glanced over the edge of the cliff. "It doesn't matter."

Audrey looked down, following his gaze, and every hair on the back of her neck stood on end. An enormous blue dragon circled the mountain, coming toward them, its massive wings held rigid as it glided. Huge, larger than a semi, it surfed the aerial current, majestic and unreal. A wicker cabin rested on its back. As she watched, its roof split in half. The two sides rose and opened, like the petals of an unfolding flower.

It was a wyvern, she realized. She'd only seen them twice, soaring high above in the clouds, on the rare excursions she'd made into the Weird.

There was no way it could land. There was no space . . . *Oh no.* Kaldar expected them to jump.

The Hand's magic had gotten inside her somehow and begun mincing her insides into mush. She could actually see it in her head, her heart and lungs turning to wet clumps of red sludge. *I must be going insane . . .*

The wyvern was coming in too low. They would have a drop of at least twenty feet. Audrey glanced down. The tree-tops below were so far, the haze that clung to them looked blue from here. If they missed, they would fall for several seconds. She would know she was about to die.

Kaldar gripped her shoulders. "Audrey! Look at me. We can make it!"

The howls sounded closer. Another moment, and the dragon would be right under them. They had mere seconds.

"Ling!" she yelled.

The raccoon launched herself into the air. Audrey caught her and hugged Ling to her chest. She yanked a hair band out of her hair. "I bet you this hair band we can't land safely on the wyvern. Bet me."

Kaldar grinned an insane grin.

The first of the Hand's people broke into the open. She was tall with a long ponytail of blond hair and piercing light eyes that seemed to glow. Behind her, a dark-haired man charged out, broad, powerful, muscled like a bull. Black tattoos twisted around his throat.

Kaldar swiped the hair band from her fingers and gripped her hand. "It's a bet!"

Dear God, please don't let us die.

"Jump!" Kaldar barked.

Audrey sailed off the cliff, gripping his hand as tightly as she could. They plummeted through the air, weightless, then, suddenly, the cabin was there, and Audrey crashed down onto a pile of wicker boxes, Ling still clutched to her chest with her other arm. Kaldar fell next to her and rolled to his feet.

Up above, the blond woman thrust her hands out. A phantom wind stirred her hair, lifting her ponytail.

"Dive!" Kaldar screamed. "Dive now!"

The wyvern dropped, and Audrey's stomach dropped with it.

Magic shot from the woman in a whip of a blinding white lightning. It snaked toward them. Audrey hunched, shielding Ling with her arms.

The magic singed the air mere feet away and melted harmlessly into nothing.

Audrey exhaled.

The wyvern beat its wings, rising. Audrey let go of the raccoon. They were in the clear.

"The guy with white hair! I know him!" a voice said in a guttural snarl from the front cabin.

Audrey turned and saw a giant man next to the blond blueblood woman up on the cliff. He towered over her, his mane of white hair shifting in the wind.

"I see him," Kaldar said. "Karmash, Spider's lieutenant. I thought we killed the sonovabitch the last time."

"I'll fix that," the guttural voice barked.

"Not now, you won't. Steer, Gaston."

The dark-haired tattooed man next to the blueblood woman heaved something with his right arm. Huge muscles flexed as he hurled it at them. The dark object flew through the air, right at Audrey. She caught it by pure reflex and fell to her knees.

Bloodstained and slick with gore, Gnome's decapitated head stared at her with dead eyes.

HELENA watched the wyvern soar into the endless sky. They truly were beautiful creatures. If the sky could dream, it would dream of dragons.

A shot popped, like a firecracker. Magic whipped from her, her flash snapping into a glowing white barrier, shielding her and her team. A spark flared to the left—the bullet disintegrating, bitten in half by the flash shield. If not for her magic, it would've hit Sebastian in the face.

Helena held the barrier for a few seconds, but no more shots came. She let the magic die. She could resurrect the shield at any moment without pausing for conscious effort. Her bloodline stretched back over a thousand years. Magic was so deeply ingrained in her, its use was as instinctive as breathing.

"They are gone," Sebastian said next to her, his voice a deep, guttural growl.

And they had murdered her tracker, too. It would be a loss keenly felt. Sobat could find a drop of blood in a gallon of water. Taken down by surprise by a gun. How appallingly stupid. Sobat was more than capable of a low-grade flash shield, which would disrupt the flight of a bullet. Now they had to rely on Emily, and her talents were, while not bad per se, not on par with Sobat's. Inside, Helena grimaced. She hated to rely on second-best.

"No matter." Helena shrugged. "The book?"

Sebastian waved a clawed finger. Suzanne appeared, carrying the dead man's book.

"Emily."

The thin, petite tracker stepped forward. Wiry and always nervous, with reddish hair that looked odd with her bronze skin and hazel eyes, Emily reminded Helena of a skittish ermine. It had to be the combination of large wide eyes, always looking surprised, and round ears slightly protruding from her head.

"M'lady?"

"Find the page with the most recent scent signature on it."

Emily motioned downward at Suzanne. The two women knelt. Emily opened the book and leaned close, inhaling. She turned the page, sniffed it, turned the next one.

This would take a while. Helena looked away, into the distance. The wyvern all but melted into the blue.

Karmash cleared his throat. "M'lady?"

Sebastian bared his teeth.

"Yes?" Helena said.

"I recognized the man, m'lady. He is a mud rat from the Mire."

The Mire. The memory of Spider sitting in his wheelchair on the balcony flashed before her. That godforsaken clump of muddy water where mongrels dared to oppose the peers of the realm. They had cost the best agent the Hand ever had the use of his legs. Her emotions must've reflected on her face, because Karmash took a step back.

"Is he a Mar?" The name of the family left a foul taste on her tongue.

"He is. He killed the head of the second unit your uncle took to the swamp. His name is Kaldar."

The name blazed in her head.

Helena dropped by Emily. The agent shrank back.

"I know that you are trying to hurry because you think that they are escaping and time is short," Helena said. "I need you to slow down. Don't rush. Take all the time you need."

Emily blinked at her.

"Make sure there are no mistakes, even if it takes hours. Accuracy is more important. Do you understand?"

"Yes, m'lady."

Helena rose and fixed Karmash with her demon stare. The giant swallowed.

"Tell me more," Helena ordered. "Tell me everything."

SEVEN

GNOME'S head lay in her hands. Audrey stared at it for one painful, horrified moment and dropped it on the floor of the cabin. Gnome's head rolled and came to rest against a trunk.

They threw his head at me. Gnome is dead, and it's my fault.

"Stubborn, greedy fool." Kaldar picked up the head and deposited it in a wicker box.

A weapon. She needed a weapon. A crossbow hung on the wall of the cabin. Audrey lunged for it and saw a rifle. Even better.

"Audrey," Kaldar said.

She ripped the rifle off the wall, flipped the safety off, chambered a round, took aim at the tattooed asshole standing on the cliff, and fired, all in the space of two breaths. The recoil punched her shoulder.

A screen of white lightning burst from the blond woman. The bullet exploded against it. The tattooed man grinned at her, muscles bulging on his frame like body armor.

"Damn it."

Audrey chambered another round. If only the repulsive magic would leave her alone for one second, she would make this one count.

Kaldar's hand clamped on the rifle. "You're wasting your bullets. That's a blueblood. She can stop a shell from a bazooka with her flash shield."

Audrey let go of the rifle. Anger filled her so hot and intense, she had to scream, or she would've exploded. The

Hand's magic, still burrowing into her flesh, only made her fury hotter. "What kind of a sick fuck throws a severed head? What the hell are those people?"

"That's what the Hand does." Kaldar shrugged.

"And you! You don't seem surprised by any of this!"

A man shouldered his way into the cabin, his hair a glossy black curtain. The man sat next to Jack and George in the corner, and she saw his face: powerful jaw, strong line, slightly slanted eyes of pale silvery gray. Slabbed with thick muscle, he looked strong enough to wrestle a bear, but the eyes were young. He couldn't have been more than twenty. The man smiled, displaying serrated teeth. "This ought to be good."

A small separate part of Audrey realized she ought to be shocked, but right now Kaldar was more important.

"I've told you, I've dealt with the Hand before," Kaldar said.

"No, there is more to it than that. It's like you knew that they would be coming. You even sent the kids to keep watch." She pointed to where George and Jack sat. A new thought occurred to her. "You sent the kids to keep watch!"

"I think we've established that," Kaldar said.

"You knew that the Hand was coming, the Hand who murders people, then throws their heads at their friends, and you sent *children* as lookouts right into their jaws?"

"Um." Kaldar took a small step back.

"Are you insane? Did your mother drop you on your head when you were a baby? What were you thinking?"

"I think it's a very reasonable question," the black-haired man said. "What were you thinking, Uncle?"

Kaldar pointed at him. "You stay out of this."

"And what if the kids didn't get a chance to escape? That blond bitch would've cut them into tiny bite-sized pieces, and we would be picking up their heads now instead of Gnome's." Audrey shuddered. "I can still feel their magic. It's crawling all over me. It feels like someone doused me in lighter fluid and set me on fire."

Kaldar stepped toward her. "The Hand's magic causes an allergic reaction. If you hold still—"

"I don't want to hold still!" she barked. "Don't touch me!"

Kaldar stepped back with his hands raised. "It will go away, Audrey. Everybody gets it the first time. You have to wait it out."

"How did you know the Hand would be coming?"

"I didn't know," Kaldar said. "I suspected."

Oh, please. "I don't believe you. You lie all the time."

"No, I don't."

"You kind of do," George murmured.

She pointed at the boy. "See!"

Kaldar growled under his breath. "Now you listen to me. The Hand is following the same trail of crumbs I did. We can't find your father, which leaves you or your brother as a target. The only way to make sure that the Hand didn't get to you would have been to kill your brother. I could've done it, but I didn't. I just gave him some drugs."

"You gave an addict in rehab drugs, and you want credit for it?"

"Of course it sounds bad when you put it that way."

"It sounds bad whichever way you put it. I know Alex. Drugs fried his brain, and he thinks the whole world owes him. He would've tried to bargain with the Hand." She stopped. "My brother is dead, isn't he?"

"Yes," Kaldar said.

Two people had been murdered because she had been too weak to say no to her dad. Alex had it coming. But Gnome was just a neighbor. He could be mean sometimes, and he was an ornery old bastard, but he had always helped her. Now his head, with glazed-over eyes, was sitting in a wicker trunk in the corner of the cabin. She shouldn't have taken that job. She should've convinced Gnome to run with them when the Hand showed up. Should've, could've, would've . . .

The kids were looking at her, as quiet as two birds.

"Audrey?" Kaldar asked.

Alex was dead. She had prepared herself for that possibility years ago, but now it finally hit home. She would never see him again. Deep down in the hidden recesses of her being lived a tiny hope that Alex would get better, that one day he would walk across her threshold, clean and sober, grin that handsome grin, and say, "I'm sorry, sis. I was an ass. Let me make it up to you."

The Hand's magic had burrowed so deep into her, it finally reached that hope, and Audrey felt it die. Something vital shattered at her very core. Her own magic, so familiar and easy, rebelled and bucked inside her like a runaway horse, fighting back in self-defense. The pain almost took her off her feet.

Audrey cried out. Her magic burst out of her body in a sweeping wave. Every bag and box in the cabin flew open. Jack jumped a foot in the air. George gasped.

"Leave!" Kaldar barked, and the three boys scurried out to the front.

"I killed Gnome, and I killed Alex." Her voice came out dull and creaky. "And more people will die because I was selfish, hurt, and stupid. I was always so smart. How the hell could I be so stupid?"

"Happens to the best of us," Kaldar said. "How the hell did I get stuck with the Marshal of the Southern Provinces' teenage brothers-in-law and a woman who thinks I'm ugly?"

"You have to send them back," she said. "They will be killed, Kaldar."

"It's too late now," he said. "It was already too late by the time I found them because the Hand has their scent. To go home, they'd have had to fly over Louisiana territory, and Gaston doesn't have a lot of experience with piloting wyverns and doesn't know how to avoid detection. The Louisianans would track them down at the border, and without me, they would kill them or worse."

"What could be worse?"

A grimace twisted his lips. "Like I said, their brother-in-law has unprecedented access to matters of Adrianglian security. The Hand would torture the boys to gain influence over him."

This was just getting better and better. "Then put them on a plane in the Broken and have them cross into Adrianglia through the Edge at the eastern coast."

Kaldar sighed. "Being in the Broken didn't protect your brother. Besides, even if I bought tickets and made them go through security, they'd escape the moment our backs were turned. They're here because they want to be here, and they are clever enough and well trained enough to be trouble. Trust me, I've spent two days thinking it over, trying to find some way to get out of this blasted screwup. The kids have to remain with me. That's the safest option."

Audrey couldn't handle being responsible for the deaths of two kids. In her head, it wasn't even George and Jack specifically; it was all the Jacks and all the Georges who lived in the Edge. All the lives her stupid caper had put at risk.

Some things even a Callahan couldn't live with. "Then there is only one solution."

Kaldar crossed his muscular arms. "Please. I'm all ears."

"I have to get the diffuser bracelets back."

She had to set it right. She would fix this, whatever it took.

"Why the sudden change of heart?"

Audrey shrugged. "Who else is going to do it?"

"Me."

She gave him a *drop-dead* stare. "Please. You got yourself Tasered and tied to a chair because you were too busy watching me eat little mints."

Kaldar grabbed her. One moment he was there, and the next he clamped her to him in a firm grip. Suddenly, his face was too close. His eyes were pale brown, like old whiskey, and he looked at her the way a man looked at a woman when wanting her had pushed every other thought out of his brain. A little electric thrill danced through her. She was pretty sure that if a volcano suddenly erupted in the cabin, neither of them would've paid it any mind.

"Mmm, Audrey," he said, his voice low and intimate. The sound of her name caressed her like velvet against her skin. Tiny hairs rose on the back of her neck.

"You should let go of me now."

"You know what the difference between you and me is?"

"I can think of several." Oh yes, yes she could, and what fun differences they were. And at a different time and in a different place, she might even consider exploring them, but not now.

Kaldar leaned over her. His whisper touched her ear. "The difference is, I don't need a Taser."

He turned, his mouth so close to hers, the distance between them suffused with heat. He looked at her, drinking her in, his gaze sliding over her eyes, her cheek, her mouth . . .

She felt his breath on her mouth, the first light, teasing touch of his lips on hers, then the stronger, insistent pressure of his mouth, and, finally, the heated touch of his tongue. She let her lips part, and he slipped his tongue into her mouth. They met, and his taste washed over her—he tasted of toothpaste and apricot and some sort of crazy spice, and he was delicious. He chased her, teasing, seducing, and she pretended not to like it, then teased him back again and again, enticing, promising things she didn't intend to deliver.

They broke apart slowly. Her whole body was taut as a string stretched to its limit, and just before she took a step back, one of those differences he mentioned earlier pressed hard against her stomach.

Audrey looked straight into his smug eyes and slapped him. It was a good slap, too, loud and quick. Her palm stung.

Kaldar let her go and rubbed his face. "Really?"

"I told you no, and you still did it." And it had been glorious. When she was old and gray, she'd remember that kiss.

Kaldar looked at her, amused and slightly predatory. All of his smooth polish had vanished, and the part that was left was dangerous, reckless, and very much up to no good. Audrey had heard about the Mire before. It was a savage place, and Kaldar had grown up there, which made him both savage and crazy. Now all his sleek manners had sloughed off, and the real man emerged. And he was hot.

He must've been a feral terror at eighteen, especially with that face. Now he was older and wiser, and he hid his crazy better, but it was still there, buried deep under the surface, and he had let it out for her benefit. Well, wasn't she privileged.

Kaldar winked at her. "You enjoyed it. It made you feel alive. You were looking kind of green."

You bastard. "Oh, so it was a lifesaving kiss."

"Well, if you want to put it that way . . ."

Arrogant jackass. "Do me a favor: next time you think my life needs saving, just let me die. I'd really prefer it."

He laughed.

She shook her head. "I'm going to the front with the boys. Don't follow me. You and your paramedic kisses need time to cool off."

Audrey swiped Ling off the floor and marched to the front of the cabin.

THE wyvern dipped down, banking above the clearing, which felt only slightly less thrilling than plunging down a drop in a roller coaster. Audrey clutched on to her seat. The front of the cabin offered only two seats, and the boys had graciously let her sit next to Gaston and the enormous windshield, which she now sorely regretted.

"It will be fine," Gaston told her. "The wyverns are difficult to stop, so we're just going to spiral down for a minute. Landing is actually kind of fun."

Jack bared his teeth at her from his perch on top of a trunk. "He just says that because he isn't human."

Gaston laughed.

Audrey tried to look anywhere but at the rapidly approaching trees. "Not human?"

"His grandmother had sex with a thoas," Jack told her.

"Why thank you, Jack." Gaston showed him his fist. "You're so helpful."

"I like to be helpful," Jack told him.

"I have strange teeth, and my eyes glow, while you turn into a lynx and run around spraying your spunk on bushes. And you're calling me not human? That's rich."

George cleared his throat.

Gaston looked at him. "What?"

George nodded at Audrey.

"What is it?"

George heaved a sigh. "We have a lady in our company."

"I'm aware of that. I am not blind."

"He's telling you to watch the crude language," Kaldar said, emerging from the cabin. He stopped between their two chairs, leaning on the backs with his arms. "How does it look?"

"Looks good," Gaston said. "We're in the clear."

"Take him down."

Gaston leaned forward to a complex, polished set of levers and knobs and pushed several switches.

"So how does the wyvern know what you would like him to do?" Audrey asked.

"He's wearing a receiver device over his spark glands, just under his chin," Kaldar told her. "When Gaston adjusts the magic frequency of the console, the receiver sends the new signal through the glands. The wyvern is trained to recognize the specific commands."

"Just like a dog," Gaston told her. "He knows 'sit' and 'stay.' Except in his case, 'sit' takes about five minutes."

"Why?" Audrey asked.

"He's very large," Kaldar said. "So for him to land, everything has to align just right: approach, speed, wind, and so on."

"What if he decides that 'sit' means turn upside down in the air?" she asked.

Kaldar leaned closer to her. "Then we all die a horrible death."

Great. Audrey squeezed the chair's seat, willing the wyvern not to fall out of the sky.

"Afraid of flying?" Kaldar asked.

"No, I'm afraid of falling to my death."

"If it will make you feel better, I could hold you."

"In your dreams . . ."

The wyvern plunged down. Audrey gasped. The ground

rushed at her as if she were in the cabin of a train hurtling at full speed.

Audrey dug her nails into the seat cushion.

The trees jumped up. The cabin jerked, and the wyvern's feet smashed into the ground, skidding. The huge reptile careened and stopped.

Kaldar leaned toward her ear. "You can breathe now, magpie."

Magpie? "I don't need your permission, thank you very much."

"You're welcome."

Argh.

"Beautiful landing," Kaldar told Gaston. "Your best thus far."

Gaston grinned.

If that was the best, what in the world did the worst feel like?

"Let's go," Kaldar called. "We need to make camp. The sky is clear, so we'll be sleeping outside today. Audrey can have the cabin."

"That's all right," she told him. "I can manage. I can sleep outside just fine."

Four pairs of eyes looked at her with a distinctly male skepticism.

"It's only proper that you have the cabin," George said.

"You're the only lady," Jack added.

"What they said," Gaston said.

"Then it's settled." Kaldar pointed at the cabin. "Quilts, pillows, sleeping bags. Once we're done, Jack, you find us something to eat, and George, you set up some sentries. Let's go."

Fifteen minutes later, their sleeping bags were on the ground by the wyvern. Audrey had always pictured dragons as fast and agile. But lying in the grass, the wyvern appeared barely alive, like some monolith carved from blue stone, with a blanket of green moss on his back.

Kaldar extracted a foot-long bronze box from one of the

trunks and opened it. Inside, on a bed of green velvet, rested a large mechanical insect. Another gadget. The people from the Weird called them automatics.

Kaldar opened another box, pulled out a small printer with a cord sticking out of it, and plugged a camera into it. The printer whirred and spat out a picture. Audrey peered over Kaldar's shoulder. The blond blueblood woman stared at her from the cliff. Her haughty face radiated scorn.

"You took a photo? When?"

"When we landed in the cabin. I don't know her, and she isn't in any of the Hand's roster available to me. I would've recalled that face, but I need to identify her, and I can't simply patch myself through the Mirror's network." Kaldar waved the photograph around to dry the ink. "Any magic contact will be intercepted, and given that we're in the field, we're under strict orders to limit our communications."

He took the insect out of the box, flipped it on its back, and gently pressed the thorax. A bronze panel slid down, revealing a small, clear crystal. Kaldar held the photograph to it, rattled off a string of numbers, and said, "Activate."

Tiny gears turned within the insect with a faint whir.

"Scan."

A ray of light stabbed through the crystal from the inside. The light slid over the photograph, and the crystal went dull.

"Encode," Kaldar ordered.

The insect's long legs moved and trembled. The panel over its thorax slid closed, hiding the crystal. Kaldar flipped it back on its feet.

"Home base."

The insect's back split. Gossamer wings emerged, shook once, and blurred into movement. The insect rose from the box, hovered above the grass, and streaked into the sky.

"We'll get an answer in a few days." Kaldar stood up. "Gaston, you and I have to see to the wyvern."

A moment later, Kaldar and Gaston went to get some water to mix some sort of special food for the wyvern.

Jack walked up to Audrey, holding Ling. "Could you please put her in the cabin for the next hour?"

"Of course." She took Ling from him. "Why?"

"Because I need to change, so I can hunt, and I don't want her to freak out." Jack went behind the cabin. Audrey took Ling inside and deposited her into a large wicker trunk where the quilts had been stored.

"Now stay here."

She shut the lid. Thin tendrils of magic extended from her hand, and she clicked the lock shut and went back outside.

A lynx trotted out from behind the wyvern on massive paws. As big as a large dog, his fur thick and luxurious, the big cat glanced at her with green eyes.

Audrey held very still.

The lynx's large ears with black tufts on the ends twitched. The lynx opened his mouth, showing her his pink tongue, winked, and took off for the trees.

Wow.

She turned to George, who was unrolling the sleeping bags. "Was that Jack?"

"Yes, my lady."

This was getting weirder and weirder and not in a good way.

Audrey perched on top of a heap of blankets. "You know, you really don't have to call me 'my lady.' I'm just an Edger."

George gave her a small smile that lit his angelic face. "I'm just an Edger, too."

"But I thought Kaldar said you were a blueblood?" That wasn't exactly what Kaldar had said, but fishing for more information never hurt.

"Our sister married a blueblood. We're just Edgers. People in the Weird remind us of where we come from quite often. In case we forget."

Ouch. They must've had a bad time of it. "I'm sorry."

"It's fine," George told her. "We're well taken care of. We go to a very good school, we have a large allowance, and Rose, our sister, and her husband love us very much. Someone would dislike us because of all that one way or another. The Edge is a convenient excuse."

Audrey sat next to him on a quilt. "If you're so well taken care of, why did the two of you stow away in Kaldar's cabin?"

"Because of Jack. The Weird has problems with changelings." George smoothed the sleeping bag in place. "Jack is difficult. He cares about other people, and he's kind, but he doesn't always get how people think. And he's very violent, which scares people. In Adrianglia, changelings like him are sent off to a military school. It's a very bad place. Jack is in a lot of trouble right now since he almost killed someone, and he thinks that Rose and Declan—that's her husband—are getting ready to ship him off. He thinks that Declan's best friend, who is a changeling, can convince them otherwise, but he's gone on a trip. We're buying time until he returns."

She caught the faint hint of disapproval in his tone. "So that's what Jack thinks. What do you think?"

George grimaced. "Jack is spoiled. Things are hard for him, but he isn't the only one who doesn't have it easy. He gets away with crazy things because he's a changeling and he's different. Jack could behave better, but he stopped trying. He decided that he's worthless and that nothing he could do would make any difference."

George rose and reached for a large cooler sitting by the wyvern. The muscles on his arms bulged. He strained. Audrey got up and took the other handle of the cooler, looking straight ahead without meeting his eyes. No need to make the boy self-conscious.

The weight of the cooler nearly toppled her over. The stupid thing was huge and likely full of ice. Eighty pounds at least. They dragged it over to the patch of clear grass.

George knelt by the cooler, and she sat in the grass across from him. Neither of them mentioned dragging the cooler, as if it hadn't happened.

"When we were little, Rose worked a really crappy job," George said. "It made her bone-tired, but she did it because she wanted us to have a better life. You asked me what I thought. I think Rose would work herself into the ground just so she wouldn't fail me and Jack. My brother misinterprets things. I don't know what he heard, but I doubt he's getting sent off. My sister loves him too much, and Declan never came across a problem he didn't attack straight on. He wouldn't palm Jack off on someone else. It would mean giving up."

Talking to George was almost like talking to an older wise adult. At fourteen, she supposed he was almost an adult by some standards, but still, his maturity was startling. Was there a fourteen-year-old boy somewhere in there, hiding behind all of that logic?

"I get why Jack ran away, but why did you?"

George popped the cooler open. "Because he needs someone to look after him. We barely know Kaldar, and Gaston and Jack don't care for each other."

She grinned. "You don't say."

"Jack baits him all the time until Gaston loses his patience and hits him, and then it's on." George rubbed the back of his head. "Gaston hits very hard."

"Speaking from experience?"

"Yes. I don't take it personally. We are a pain in his . . . head. I came because without me, my brother would do something rash and stupid. Wouldn't you do the same for your brother?"

Audrey shook her head. "No."

"Why?" George reached into the cooler and pulled out a big bird. It was black and very dead.

Audrey stared at it. Another bird joined the first one on the grass, then another. What in the world? "It's a long story, and you probably don't want to hear it. What are these?"

"The sentries," George explained. He picked up the first bird and closed his eyes for a moment.

The bird shivered.

Oh, my God.

The bird rolled on its feet. It spread its large wings.

"Go on," George murmured.

The bird flapped its wings and flew into the woods. George watched it go. "I'm a necromancer. The birds will keep watch, and I'll know if anyone comes close."

Wow. They were some pair. One was a lynx, and the other one brought corpses to life.

"I would like to hear your story." George picked up the second bird.

"My childhood wasn't nearly as bad as yours, so this will sound like I'm throwing myself a pity party, and I am. To you, my problems might be small, but to me, they're huge. Funny how it always works that way. Ask a man how much a dollar is worth, and he'll tell you, 'Almost nothing.' Try to take a dollar away from him, and you'll get yourself a fight." She smiled.

"You're right, my problems are the biggest problems ever," George said. "No, honestly, it's horrible to be me. I'm rich, talented, and I make girls cry."

"How do you make girls cry, exactly?"

George turned to her. His blue eyes widened. His lovely face took on a forlorn, deeply troubled expression. He leaned forward, and, in a theatrical whisper, said, "My past is tragic. I wouldn't want to burden you with it. It's a pain I must suffer alone. In the rain. In silence."

She laughed. "That was pretty good, actually."

George shrugged, back to his normal self. "It works sometimes. Still, I'd like to hear about your parents. Please?"

Oh well. Why not. "My parents were grifters. I don't think either one of them earned an honest dollar in their entire lives. Every day there was a new con or a new heist. Sometimes we'd have a ton of money. Dad would check us into a great hotel, we'd have steak and lobster, and he'd buy Mother jewelry. And the next week we'd be sleeping in some abandoned car. It was chaotic, but it was fun.

"My brother was eight years older than me. He was handsome and so funny, and I thought he could do anything. All the girls fought over him." Tears heated her eyes, and she blinked them away. "Alex could teleport short distances. That was his special talent. He was a really good thief, too. He would steal ice-cream bars for me from gas stations. I thought he was so cool.

"We worked a lot, my brother and I. We'd steal things,

and our parents would sell them. And then, when Alex was twenty, it all went to hell. He became a drug addict. And it was our own father who got him addicted. Dad was always looking for that big score. Every con was supposed to make us rich for life, just like the one before it." Audrey paused, then asked, "Do you know what the Internet is?"

George nodded.

"People in the Broken sometimes use debit cards instead of money. They're small plastic cards with a magnetic strip. When you swipe one through a card reader, it subtracts the price of whatever you bought from your bank account. Criminals steal the debit-card numbers and the little code you have to use to authorize the money. It takes some technical skill to do it. Then they sell the card numbers on secret forums on the Internet. You can buy the numbers, sometimes for ten or twenty bucks each, and you can make your own cards. You can take these cards to ATMs—do you know what those are?"

George nodded again. "Automated banks that give out money. They're very heavy."

"That's right." Audrey nodded. "I once tried to steal one, and they have to be made of lead, because we tried to winch it onto our truck and the winch broke. But anyway, if you have fake cards loaded with debit-card numbers, you can go to ATMs and withdraw money straight from the people's accounts. You could clean out one ATM, then go to the next, for several days even, until the banks caught on. You could make thousands. My dad loved this idea. In his head, it was ridiculously easy free money. You see, the bank insures people's accounts, so if the money is stolen, the insurance company replaces it. My dad thought it was a victimless crime. Oh, if only we'd get in on this scam, we would all be rich and happy forever."

KALDAR paused behind the wyvern. Audrey's voice carried over. She was talking about her parents. She kept it light, but he heard the underlying tension in her tone.

Kaldar put down the two buckets of water he'd carried from the stream and held up his hand. Behind him, Gaston stopped, and murmured, "What?"

"Shhh. I want to hear this."

Gaston shrugged, set his buckets on the grass, and sat near the wyvern, his long, dark hair spilling down his back.

Kaldar leaned against the wyvern's scaled side. The boy had talent. Getting Audrey to talk must've been difficult. She was smart, and she guarded herself carefully.

Her reaction to the Hand's magic might have played a part. The Hand's agents were so twisted by the magic, they emanated it. Magically, they stank like roadkill left to bake in the sun for a few days, and most people "gagged" when they came into close contact with them for the first time. The reaction lasted a few hours, depending on the intensity and brand of magic and how sensitive the victim was to it. Some exposed felt invisible bugs on their skin; some panicked; some went into convulsions. Audrey was the burn type: they reported the feeling of being set on fire and the sensation of being skewered or chewed on. That reaction came coupled with lowered inhibitions. Whatever brakes Audrey had were malfunctioning. She was hurtling out of control down an emotional highway, and Kaldar wanted to be there for that ride. Curiosity was killing him. He wanted to know what she liked, what she didn't like, what made her happy. He wanted to know why she lived in the Edge by herself.

The more he knew about her, the easier it would be to impress her. The more impressed she became, the more she'd like him. And he wanted Audrey to like him. Standing next to her was like standing in the sunlight.

AUDREY'S voice caught a little, and she cleared her throat.

"My parents never understood the Internet. They didn't realize you couldn't just go on to the debit-card forums to buy the numbers. You had to be introduced or get a password from someone.

"Dad found this guy—Colin—a real scumbag. Colin was a big shot on one of the forums, so Dad told Alex to make friends with him and get the password. He told him to do whatever it took. 'Get the password, Alex. Just get that password.'"

She sounded so bitter. Audrey felt bitter too, bitter and angry "Colin was a cokehead, and the only way to get to him was to supply him with drugs. So Alex would sell him coke, and Colin wanted him to sit there and do it with him, so that's what Alex did for two months. Finally, Colin ODed. He took too many drugs, and they killed him. We did get the password to the forum, and Dad bought a bunch of numbers. Drained our reserves completely. And then on the fifth ATM he hit, an off-duty cop noticed him feeding a bunch of cards into the machine, and Dad got arrested. It was a huge mess. When Dad got out three months later on some technicality, he and Mom put Alex into rehab, but it was too late. He likes . . . liked being an addict. It was an easier life than being Dad's errand boy all the time, and he would guilt-trip Dad into buying him drugs. He never stopped after that. All we did from that point on was work to get enough money to put Alex into a new rehab."

Audrey paused. She didn't want it to sound all "oh-poor-me," but there was no help for it. "Sometimes I went to school, but mostly I didn't. I didn't have friends, I didn't get to do any of the normal things twelve-year-old girls do. I guess I still had hope that my brother would come back to us. Then, when I was almost seventeen, Alex sold me to a drug dealer. He wanted some prescriptions, and he didn't have the money, so he told the guy that he could do anything he wanted with me. The guy cornered me as I was coming back to the Edge. I've never been so scared in my whole life."

SO that was it. Kaldar clenched his teeth. How could you trade your own sister? How could you trade Audrey? Beautiful, sunshine Audrey. His mind understood, but the part of him that was a brother and an uncle seethed at the thought. That was not done.

In the Mire, he would've put Alex Callahan down like a rabid dog.

"The drug dealer took everything I had on me," she said. "And then he told me that I could either steal more drugs for him, or he would rape me and kill me. So I did it. He took me to a bad neighborhood to a drug house owned by a gang. I snuck inside, stole the drugs, and gave them to him. Then he beat me. The first punch knocked me to the ground, and he kicked me for a while. Broke two ribs. My face was messed up for months. Still, I got off easy."

"That's fucked up," George said.

The profanity startled her, coming from him. Audrey cleared her throat. "I came home and told my parents about it. My face was all black-and-blue. I couldn't have hid it if I'd wanted to, and I didn't want to. They did nothing. That night I decided I had to leave. From that point on, I saved up my money. I had to hide it very carefully because Alex was very good at finding whatever money we had. I actually left a few bucks hidden somewhere obvious so he'd find it and not look for my stash. Here." She reached into her pocket and pulled out the cross. "This was my grandmother's. She gave it to me when I was little. I stole it back from the drug dealer when I made up my mind to leave. It took me almost two years, but I finally escaped."

"What about your mother?" George asked.

Kaldar shook his head. George needed more experience. With a conversation like this, you didn't push. Audrey might catch herself and stop talking all together.

"My mother liked pretty things," Audrey said. "We moved a lot, and in every new place, she'd plant flowers and hang pretty curtains. She liked jewelry, makeup, and nice clothes. She'd make herself up just as pretty as she could be every morning: hair brushed, war paint on. We'd be stuck in some hovel, but she'd make it all spotless, plant flowers, and send us out to steal pictures to put over the holes in the walls. She would always make sure that my clothes were clean, and I had my hair just right, and my makeup was perfect. But she couldn't really deal with any kind of crisis and ugliness. She just pretended it didn't exist. When Alex hit rock bottom, it got really ugly. She'd let him have one room, and the rest of the house would still be perfect."

"She wasn't much help," George said.

"No. She ignored me until my face healed. When I finally gathered enough money and escaped, I went as far as I could and started to build my own life. It took me three months to get the house up, and when I did, for half a year I didn't do anything. I was just happy. By myself in my little house. Then I worked and got enough money to apply for a driver's license, and eventually I bought a car, and then I got a better job. I kept making improvements to the house. I was perfectly happy for years, then my father showed up. For the first few moments, I thought maybe he had come to tell me he was sorry, but no, he just wanted me to do a job for Alex. So I told him that either he could have me do the job for the very last time, or he could have a daughter. Well, we all know what he picked."

"I'm sorry," George said.

"Thank you," Audrey told him. "I didn't tell you all this as a play for sympathy. My life wasn't that bad. Many people have it way worse. My parents never beat me or abused me. I never had to sell myself on the street. No matter how low we fell, we always had food. I just . . ." She hesitated. "Gnome was my neighbor, and now he's dead because of me. That's a terrible thing, and I'll have to live with it. It's tearing me up inside. I just wanted someone to understand why."

"I understand," George said. "You didn't steal the diffusers because you were greedy."

"Right. I stole them because my father made me so mad, I couldn't think straight. I was selfish and stupid. I had daddy issues and a chip on my shoulder, and I wore all of it like a badge. It seems very small now, compared to Gnome's life."

Kaldar picked up the buckets and retreated a few steps. Gaston watched him with an amused grin on his face.

Pretty Audrey. Honed into a tool. Used like one, then shoved into a drawer and forgotten until she was needed again. He had the strong urge to punch the entire Callahan clan in the face one by one.

Snap out of it, you fool. A pretty face and a sweet smile, and you've lost all common sense.

Kaldar kicked some bushes, forcing them to rustle.

"Hurry up, Gaston!"

His nephew pushed to his feet, swiped the buckets off the ground, and croaked in a choked-up voice. "Yes, master."

Kaldar rolled his eyes and carried the buckets to the wyvern's mouth to feed him.

EIGHT

KALDAR squinted at Magdalene Moonflower's lair. The Center for Cognitive Enhancement and Well-being occupied a large three-story building in northern San Diego. The white stucco walls rose, interrupted by huge windows. The whole structure nearly floated off the pavement, sleek, modern, and somehow light, almost delicate. The salt-spiced wind blowing from the coast less than a mile away only strengthened the illusion.

He'd given Gaston a pocketful of money and sent him out on a fishing expedition with the locals. If Magdalene had dealings in the Edge, he would soon know all about it. But in the meantime, they had to approach her directly. The wheels of time never stopped turning; sooner or later, they would bring the Hand and the blond blueblood closer to them. The blonde troubled Kaldar. She wasn't on any of the Hand's rosters he had in his possession.

"Magdalene's building looks like an ivory tower," Audrey said next to him.

"Pretty much. You see it?"

She nodded. "Yeah."

Just beyond the tower, the boundary shimmered, cutting off a section of the building. A person with no magic would see only the tower. Kaldar and Audrey saw the tower and the long two-story-high rectangle of the rest of the building behind it. Magdalene operated halfway in the Edge.

"Clever," Audrey murmured.

"It is. The Edge Gobble."

"Yep." Audrey nodded.

The Edge wasn't a stable place. It shrank and expanded, sometimes forming bubbles in the Broken—holes in reality, invisible to those without magic. The Edgers called the bubbles the Edge Gobble. San Diego had more holes than a block of Swiss cheese, and this one was of a good size, at least as large as a football field. Normal passersby would just walk by it, completely unaware it existed.

"You think if you crashed a car into that hole, chunks of the building would fly out into the Broken?" Audrey asked.

"I don't know. They might bounce off the boundary back into the Edge."

"We should test that theory sometime."

Kaldar snuck a glance at her. Her clothes from yesterday had been too bloodstained to salvage, so after they had stolen a car, they drove to an outlet mall. He wore black jeans, a black T-shirt, and a leather jacket. He'd thought she would choose something similar, but no. She came out in pale capris that molded to her behind in a very interesting way and a light, blue-green, teardrop blouse. The blouse tied at the clavicle with two cords, and the teardrop cutout fit perfectly between Audrey's breasts, promising a glimpse but never giving one. He was focusing way too hard on that teardrop, and it was screwing up his concentration.

Audrey's red hair gleamed in the sunlight. Her makeup was barely noticeable, except for her lipstick, which was a shade lighter than raspberry and gave him an absurd impression that her lips would taste sweet. Her face wore an easy, carefree expression, as if she skated through life completely unscathed and untouched by any tragedy. Considering that they had just buried Gnome—well, what was left of him—and she had cried her eyes out, her control was impressive.

"Admiring my blouse?" Audrey asked.

"It's a nice shade of sea foam. Goes well with your hair." A potato sack. He needed to put a potato sack over her, then it would be fine.

"Most men wouldn't know that sea foam is a color, let alone what it looks like."

Kaldar shrugged. "For one of my assignments, I had to

be a butler to a blueblood noble. The Mirror put me through two months of intensive preparation. If you show me a gown made in the Weird in the past five years, I'll tell you in what year and what season it was made."

Audrey laughed. "Were you very proper as a butler?"

All the tears, all of the hurt, where did it all go? He had to give it to her: she hid it well. She had a lifetime to learn how to do it. He just had to pray it didn't boil out of her again under the pressure.

He slipped into a clipped, upper-class version of Adrianglian English. "I was simply a very competent butler. It was, after all, what my employer deserved. Would my lady care to cross the street?"

"She would."

They crossed to the other side. "How shall we play this?" she asked.

"Straight." He held the glass door open for her.

She grimaced.

"You disagree?"

"It's your show."

He fired a test shot. "Oh, come on, Audrey. You know I need you to pull this off."

She glanced at him. "Kaldar, I told you I'd help you. I still think it's a stupid plan."

"Trust me."

"Ha! I'd rather give all my money to a snake-oil salesman."

They walked through the long lobby to the counter. Kaldar took a mental inventory of the place. Let's see, floor of gray tile streaked with softer brown, calming white walls, large, enhanced photographs in gallery frames: vast Arizona vistas, serene mountain lakes, tangled green forests. At the counter, a deathly pale young man looked up at them. His hair was long, brushed to the side in a ragged cut that probably cost an arm and a leg, and his clothes, designer khaki pants and a high-end olive shirt, would've set him back two weeks of a normal receptionist's pay.

The man smiled. "Hello. My name is Adam. How may I help you today?"

"Hello, Adam."

Audrey gave a tiny wave and smiled. "Hi!"

Adam's gaze snagged on her blouse. Kaldar hid a grin. At least he wasn't the only sucker out there. He brushed against Audrey, slipping the cross from her pocket, palmed it, and pulled a blank business card from his pocket, black on one side, white on the other. "Say, friend, do you have a pen?"

Adam produced a pen. Kaldar took it and wrote "Morell de Braose" on the card. "Do me a big favor and deliver this to Magdalene. We'll wait."

Adam retreated behind the door for a moment, then resumed his post behind the counter. Kaldar held the cross in his hand for luck. Just in case. Not that he doubted himself.

Two minutes later, the door opened, and another man stepped out, this one older, with a careful gaze of an Edger. He didn't just expect trouble; he knew with absolute certainty it was coming. "Come."

They followed him through the first door and out the other. A long hallway stretched between them, severed by the shimmer of the boundary. Kaldar stepped into it. Pressure clasped him, and, a moment later, magic bloomed inside him, surging through his veins in a welcome flood. Kaldar smiled. Audrey kept her pace. A few more steps and they were through, neither of them breathing hard.

The man kept walking. They followed him up the stairs and into a large rectangular room. Tall walls, white and pristine, rose sixteen feet high, adorned at the top with an elaborate white lattice that cascaded down, like rows of falling snowflakes. The tiled floor swirled with a dozen shades of beige and brown, supporting a long white rug shot through with streaks of gold. Clusters of white furniture sat here and there, chairs, small sofas, all overstuffed and soft. Eggshell and white planters hung from the lattice, containing emerald green plants, mimosa, and Edge vines dripping down to meet palms, carefully trimmed shrubs, and flowers growing in large planters on the floor. Finally, the ceiling of translucent glass sifted sunshine onto the entire scene, setting the lattice and walls aglow.

A woman rose from one of the chairs at their approach, closing her laptop as she got up, her long white skirt swirling around her legs. She wore a beige blouse and looked pretty much like her picture: about forty, narrow face framed by short brown hair, tan skin, rose-tinted glasses. Kaldar checked the eyes behind the rose-tinted glasses. Cold and hard. Predatory. Yep, Magdalene Moonflower in the flesh.

Magdalene held up his card. A small explosion of magic burst from her fingertips, sending a silver spark across the black surface, turning it into a silvery mirror. A moment, and the mirror faded back to black.

"An agent of the Mirror in my humble abode. Imagine that."

Kaldar executed a small bow.

"Cute. What is it you want, blueblood? And make it quick. I have an appointment later this evening, so if I have to kill you, I'll need to do it fast."

KILL you fast, blah-blah-blah. Audrey pretended to be preoccupied with a plant. Someone had a rather high opinion of herself. Magdalene called Kaldar a blueblood, and he didn't correct her, either. What was he playing at?

"The Mirror is interested in Morell de Braose," Kaldar said.

"Mhm." Magdalene flipped the card between her fingers, pretending to watch the light play on it. She was assessing Kaldar out of the corner of her eye, and the way she adjusted her pose, one hip out, shoulders back to put her breasts on display, meant she liked what she saw.

Not that anyone would blame her. Kaldar wore black Levi's and a black T-shirt that showed off his carved arms. His hair was doing this wild unkempt thing that made Audrey picture him just rolling out of bed. He'd grown a day's worth of stubble, which just made him look hotter. Magdalene was definitely pondering if she should take him for a test drive.

You're barking up the wrong tree, woman. Then again, if Magdalene promised to deliver what Kaldar wanted, he would sleep with her in a blink. He was a man, after all, and he'd do anything to get what he wanted. And that thought shouldn't have bothered her. Not at all.

"And what did Morell do to warrant the Mirror's attention?" Magdalene asked.

"Rumor has it, he bought the wrong item."

"Are there other interested parties?"

"The Hand, the Claws, the usual." Kaldar smiled, a quick, sly curving of lips. He was keeping eye contact, his shoulders squared, his body facing Magdalene. He was working her hard. Magdalene probably knew it, but she still enjoyed the attention.

The two of them might as well have forgotten that Audrey was even there. She felt a tiny pinch of jealousy. It shouldn't have mattered. She and Kaldar had nothing, would have nothing, even if he'd promised her the moon and delivered it on a silver platter. Men like Kaldar were fun to kiss but impossible to keep. Why in the world Audrey was annoyed because he was paying attention to this cobra in a white skirt she had no idea.

Magdalene smiled. "So Morell finally stumbled. Good to know. What do you want from me?"

Kaldar slipped a hint of confidentiality into his voice. "People say that Morell isn't universally loved."

"People say a lot of things."

"If someone who disliked Morell, a direct competitor of his, let's say, were to help us with information or assist us in gaining access to his person, well, such a person would benefit when Morell was brought down."

"Heh." Magdalene leaned forward. "Suppose I help you do this. Then what if you're captured and you give up my name? That might put me in an awkward position." She gave Kaldar another once-over. "As much as I might enjoy that under different circumstances . . ."

Audrey almost slapped her. *For Heaven's sake, woman, have some dignity.*

". . . I don't cherish having Morell's goons showing up at my doorstep."

"Is that a no?" Kaldar tilted his head. The light sparked off the silver earring in his ear. Mmm, that was exactly what he would look like after a wild night, raising his head from the sheets.

And now both of them were staring at him googly-eyed. Audrey returned her gaze to the plant. She'd have picked at it to keep herself occupied, except it was an Edge Mercy flower, and it would peel the skin off her fingertips.

"That's a maybe." Magdalene snapped out of her Kaldar-stupor and looked at the card again. "I'd like you to do a job for me. In return, I will give you an invitation to his auction. It's a foolproof way to get into Morell's castle. In fact, his guards will let you in through the front gate."

"I'm listening," Kaldar said.

"I have particular talents," Magdalene said. "In the Edge, they call people like me soothsayers."

Figured. Now the snake stare made sense.

"Everyone has problems," Magdalene said, her voice light. "Your boss is driving you mad, your job puts you under pressure, your hair is falling out, you're carrying an extra fifty pounds, and you suspect your wife is banging a used-car salesman. You're worn-out, so you come to me. Two nice employees walk you through that hallway, and you find yourself here."

Well, of course. A couple of Edgers could get almost anybody into the Edge through the boundary. They'd just feed their own magic into the person to get them through.

"You tell me about your problems, and after we chat for twenty minutes, you start feeling better. The longer we talk, the easier your life becomes. People think happiness is about money. It's not. It's all about perception. A doughnut-shop clerk who makes twenty grand a year is often more content than a boardroom desk jockey making two hundred thousand because the clerk appreciates every break he gets. Those who come to me focus only on the negatives, so I simply realign them to see their lives through rose-colored glasses."

"And they tell you all of their secrets in return." Audrey clamped her mouth shut. *Oops.*

Magdalene spared her a single look, as if seeing her for the first time. "Yes, they do."

You went to soothsayers at your own peril. They made you feel so good. But the next thing you knew, you had told them all about your affair with Bob down the street, and that time you lost your temper with your kids, and the twenty thousand dollars Aunt Hilda left you. Soothsayers traded in information. Most Edgers knew this.

"I've done well for myself over the years. But now I have a problem."

Magdalene took a remote off the nearest table and clicked it. A section of the wall slid aside, revealing a flat screen. Magdalene opened her laptop, typed something in a quick staccato, and the flat screen ignited, showing a smiling man in a suit. Early thirties, healthy tan, bright white teeth, salon-bleached hair. Handsome, but not overly. He had the kind of face that would make him a good vacuum salesman or a successful serial killer: open, honest, confident, and pleasant. Old ladies would judge him to be a "nice boy" and open their doors to him, no problem.

"Edward Yonker." Magdalene crossed her arms on her chest. "Also known as Ed Junior. He runs the Church of the Blessed. He's a prosperity preacher."

Kaldar nodded. "I see."

"Ed's like me, except his specialty is crowds. If he were a carnie, he'd be a sky grifter."

Audrey looked at the plant some more. She'd met a few tent-revival preachers, and none of them were any good. They'd preach hell, whip up the crowd into hysteria, pull off a couple of cheap tricks, then pass the collection plate around. Sky grifters—nothing but show.

"Ed's power isn't that impressive, so I didn't pay him much attention. Two years ago, he got himself a gadget from the Weird, and suddenly his church started growing. He's moved twice, and now he's got himself a nice new building. Ed's aiming for megachurch status, and he's moving in on my clients."

"Does he lift their burden as well?" Kaldar asked.

Magdalene grimaced. "Happiness is infectious. I teach

them to be kinder and more compassionate, because that in turn makes people around them happier."

Audrey almost snorted. Magdalene Moonflower, the new Mother Teresa. *Be kind to your fellow man and tell me about that impending business acquisition so I can call my stockbroker . . .*

"Ed tells them it's okay to be a rich bastard. He tells them Jesus wants them to be happy." The soothsayer stared at the screen. "I've warned him before to stay away from my people and my client list. I had a girl working for me. A nice sweet girl, not too bright but very diligent. Very earnest. She had some trouble in her life, and, for whatever reason, she didn't come to me; she turned to his church instead."

No surprise, Audrey reflected. She had barely spent half an hour with the woman, and she'd rather have her teeth pulled than let Magdalene rummage in her head.

"Ed got his hooks into her. She stopped coming to work. The next time one of my people saw her, she was singing in Ed's choir. She's one of his Blessed Maidens now. He has these *retreats*." Magdalene spat the word like it was poison. "For his special contributors."

"So what is it that you want?" Kaldar asked.

"I want his gadget. Bring it to me, and I'll get you into Morell's castle."

Kaldar bowed. Magdalene held out her hand, and his lips brushed it lightly.

Ew.

"We have a deal," Kaldar said.

THE moment she stepped outside Magdalene's lair, Audrey gulped the fresh air. Kaldar put a light hand on her back, trying to steer her across the street.

She stepped aside. "Kaldar, don't touch me with that hand."

"Why?"

Audrey crossed the street. "You touched Magdalene with it."

Kaldar chuckled. "It's not contagious."

"You have no guarantee of that."

They reached the Ford they had "borrowed" that morning from a used-car lot. "She really rubbed you the wrong way, huh?" Kaldar popped the locks open and held the door out for her. She went to sit down, and his hand brushed against her hip.

"I steal things. It makes people sad, but in the end they're just things. They are replaceable. She steals memories and secrets, and she ruins people who take her into their confidence. She's a snake."

"I thought a shark myself."

They got into the vehicle, and Kaldar started the engine.

"You're not serious about this?" she asked.

"I'm very serious."

"Kaldar, jobs like this take time. Did you forget that we have a homicidal blueblood on our trail?"

"She doesn't know where we went. We have a couple of days." He pulled out into the street.

"We need two weeks minimum to pull this off, and you know it."

"Well, we'll just have to do it fast."

She stared at him.

"I have a feeling Fate will be with me on this one," he told her.

"Fate?"

"Mhm. She's sucker punched me twice since this job started. I'm due for a kiss. Why don't we go spy on Yonker? You might change your mind."

"What about the kids?"

"They are safe with the wyvern. Besides, Gaston should be back from talking to the locals by now. He'll keep them from doing anything stupid. They will be fine."

She shook her head. "That's your general approach to life, isn't it? Wing it, and it will be fine."

"Hey, it's worked so far."

"You are impossible," she told him.

Kaldar laughed.

NINE

KALDAR passed the binoculars to Audrey. They were parked out of the way, in the back lot of Vans, a large grocery store, their stolen car just an anonymous vehicle among all the others. A few hundred yards down, a large brown-and-beige building sat in the back of a parking lot, couched in large California sycamores and flame trees, blazing with bright red flowers. The Church of the Blessed. Sturdy, solid, brand-new, with large, spotless windows and a large portico before the double-doors entrance. The building had no steeple, no bell tower, nothing to mark it as a church. If anything, it resembled a small convention center.

Audrey took the binoculars. Her fingertips brushed his hand. In his head, he was kissing her, tasting those raspberry lips. Of course, in his little fantasy she loved it. Idly, he wondered if she wanted him to kiss her. Would she pull back, would she melt into the kiss, would she . . .

"Children," she said, passing the binoculars back to him.

He looked. A throng of adolescent boys made their way to the doors, each carrying something pale . . . Kaldar zoomed in. "Flyers. They're carrying flyers."

Audrey reached for the binoculars, and he let her have them. "They're a skinny lot," she murmured. "Probably runaways. It's warm here. The city is full of them. He's using them as walking advertisements."

A man in his early thirties, carrying a placard, followed the kids. The doors opened, and two women brought out a cart filled with sandwiches. The children lined up. The man thrust his placard into the lawn and joined the end of the line.

"Come to Jesus and live an abundant life," Audrey read. "He's a prosperity preacher, all right. Ugh."

"I meant to ask you about that," Kaldar said. "What is a prosperity preacher?"

Audrey took the binoculars from her face. Her eyes were huge with surprise and outrage. She looked hilarious.

"You don't know what a prosperity preacher is, but you took the job anyway?"

"I have you to explain it."

"Kaldar!"

He leaned closer. "I like the way you say my name, love. Say it again."

She plucked a paper map off the dashboard. "No."

"Auudreey?" He toyed with a lock of her hair. His voice dropped into the quiet intimate murmur that usually got him laid. "Say my name."

She leaned toward him, her eyelids half-lowered, her long eyelashes fanning her cheeks. She tilted her face to his, close, closer. Her lips parted.

Here it comes.

"Dumb-ass."

Ouch.

She tapped his forehead with the map. "Focus on the job."

The woman drove him crazy. "I would focus, but I've been rejected and must now wallow in self-pity. So prosperity preachers. What are they?"

Audrey sighed. "How much do you know about Christianity?"

"I've read the Bible," he told her. "The good parts."

"Let me guess, the ones with wars and rich kings and women?"

He gave her an innocent look. "We've barely met, and yet you know me so well."

"The New Testament, that's the one with Jesus, in case you didn't know, doesn't care for rich people. There is a story in the Gospel of Matthew, where a rich prince visits Jesus and asks him how he could get into Heaven. And Jesus tells him to keep the Commandments, and if he really wants to ensure his place in Heaven, to give away all his possessions to the poor. That's where that famous verse comes from, 'It is easier for a camel to go through the eye of a needle than for a rich man to enter into the kingdom of God.' There are more things in the same vein. Mark and Luke and James, all of them basically said that the richer you are, the harder it is to go to Heaven because rich people fall into temptation and surrender to their greed."

" 'The love of money is the root of all evil.'" He had read the Bible, and the quote had stuck with him. He took it as a warning.

"Timothy 6:10." Audrey shrugged.

"From the way I'm looking at it, poverty doesn't lead to love and happiness, either."

She waved her hand at him. "Bottom line is, Christians are supposed to be rich in spirit, not in money. Well, if you're doing well for yourself and you're a Christian, that kind of leaves you with two choices: either you can keep giving away your money to get into Heaven, or you can pretend that everything will be okay anyway and hope you won't go to Hell. Prosperity preachers prey on that fear: they preach that God wants us all to be rich and happy, and it's okay to have extra money and live a good life full of luxuries."

"It's a good gig," Kaldar reflected. "Nobody wants to go to church and be condemned every Sunday, and the congregation is either rich already or—"

"Hoping to get rich," Audrey finished.

"Good works aren't necessary—besides giving generously to the church, of course."

"Of course." Audrey wrinkled her nose. "The church needs money."

Indeed. "All that guilt and all those assets, wrapped in a lovely package."

"Delicious, like a chocolate truffle." Audrey licked her lips, and he had to yank his thoughts out of the gutter and back on target. "Outside a hard shell of moral decency, inside creamy, decadent bank accounts."

Kaldar tapped the wheel. "Sign the check, send it to the business office."

"Better yet, give us your account number, we'll do the heavy lifting of withdrawing funds for you."

"Easy money."

"Yep. The whole church full of suckers."

They looked at each other and grinned.

"If we joined forces, how quick do you think we could clean out this town?" Audrey asked.

Kaldar calculated in his head. "We'd be millionaires in six months. Faster if you did your Southern bit."

They both looked at the church and the children in front of it. "So does the Mirror pay you well?" Audrey asked.

"Not enough to buy any mansions," he said.

They looked at the church some more. "Being good guys sucks sometimes," Audrey said.

"Would you really go through with it?" he asked.

She shook her head. "No. A church should be a place of solace. For some people, that's all they have to lean on when tragedy happens. You'd have to be a special kind of scumbag to prey on that."

There was an echo of something personal there; but he knew if he probed, she'd slam all her doors shut.

"Plenty of scumbags out there." Kaldar started the car. A plan had formed in his head.

"Yes, we never seem to have a shortage of those."

"We need someone on the inside to figure out how this whole Yonker dog and pony show works."

"You want to pull off a Night and Day scam and use the boys for the Night team, don't you?"

The way she picked up his train of thought was uncanny. The two kids were the perfect age to blend in with the runaways.

"They can handle it."

"And if they can't?"

"Those kids have been through more than most adults. I ran cons at their age. Don't tell me you didn't."

"You and I had no choice," she told him.

"I will ask them. I won't order."

"Right, what fourteen-year-old would turn that adventure down?"

He understood exactly where that worry was coming from. Audrey felt used by her family. It had left scars, and she was trying to make sure the boys weren't exploited. She didn't realize both kids had been in combat training for the past four or five years. She didn't know that Jack killed game on a regular basis, and George could sever a body in half with a burst of his flash. To her, they were children, and she looked at them through the prism of her own experience.

"Don't underestimate them," Kaldar said. "George looks fragile, but he is well trained. Gaston put them through their paces, and George can hold his own. The kid is brilliant. He is truly, all jokes aside, brilliant. He's an Edger, and the bluebloods never let him forget it. Things other children of his social status take for granted are out of his reach."

"It's not enough to be good," Audrey said. "He has to be the best. But George doesn't worry me. Jack does."

Kaldar shrugged. "Jack is a teenager with a chip on his shoulder. I was one, you were one, I'm sure everyone has been there at one time or another. Once he snaps out of his 'the world is against me' rut, he's a resourceful, smart kid. And unlike most changelings, he's pretty sharp when it comes to figuring out what drives other people. He likes to pretend he understands less than he does."

"Why?"

"He's a cat," Kaldar said. "It's in his nature, I suppose. Don't worry. He will hold his own."

"You seem awfully sure of that. George said you barely know the two of them."

"I know William," Kaldar said. "He's married to my cousin, Cerise, who is more like my baby sister. If her life and happiness were at stake, William would burn the world just to see her smile. Jack is a changeling like William. He would move the earth and the moon to protect his brother.

"So you're using one child to manipulate another." Audrey shook her head. "Do you have any conscience at all?"

"No. I didn't ask them to come with me. They want this, and they're old enough to understand the risks."

Audrey looked away from him and through the window. He studied her profile out of the corner of his eye. *Pouting? No, calculating.*

"If you and I are the day, I'll need to go shopping," she said. "It won't be cheap. Do we have to grift for the money?"

Their minds ran like two trains on parallel tracks. Kaldar had never come across anyone like her. He didn't have to explain himself, or justify anything, or convince her that his scheme would work. She just snapped his ideas out of thin air and ran with them. Even when he worked a con with his family, he still had to sell them on it, taking them through the plan bit by bit, but then most of his family excelled at killing or magic, often both. He excelled at burglary, grift, and making money by any means necessary. It wasn't that they didn't love him or trust him, but none of them understood him. Audrey did. He wanted to sit her down and ask questions until he knew everything there was to know about her, down to the most minute detail. But the moment he did that, she would run like a deer. That was what he would do in her place.

And she was so damn pretty. He rifled through adjectives: "sexy," "hot," "desirable," none of them was right enough. Delectable. Delicious. No, she was a woman, not a pastry. He ran out of words and gave up. He wanted her. He needed her like a man in a room full of smoke needed a breath of fresh air. He wanted to peel off her clothes and kiss those lovely breasts and . . .

"Earth to Kaldar?"

"Yes, love?"

"Do we have to grift for the money? And don't call me 'love.'"

"Why spend our own if we don't have to?" He was dying to see her work. This was his chance. He looked at her and tested the waters. "Is that a problem, *love*?"

Audrey turned to him, a sly little spark hiding in her eyes. "The only man who gets to call me 'love' would be waking up next to me after a very, very fun night."

Fun night. Oh yes.

"Guess what?" She leaned closer. "You will never be that man."

Kaldar laughed. "If I wanted to, you would be waking up next to me, lying with my arm around you every morning. You would wiggle closer to me in bed just so I could pet your butt."

"My goodness, you think you're God's gift to women, don't you? You poor, deluded man."

He hit her with his best smile. Her eyes widened. She took a deep breath. "Oh no, not that seductive face. I'm overcome with the need to take off these awful clothes. What is happening? I do not understand. Oooh. Ahhh." She touched her wrist to her forehead. "Somebody help me. I'm being drenched with my own fluids."

Evil woman.

"See now, you shouldn't have done that," Kaldar said.

She gave him an innocent look.

"You've made yourself into a challenge. Now I'll have to seduce you out of principle."

"You can try. Not that you'll get anywhere. If you were in love, that would be one thing, but we both know this is pride talking." Audrey patted his forearm. "It's all right. I won't tell anybody about your shameful failure. I'll keep it completely confidential." She pretended to lock her lips and throw away the key.

"I'll remind you of this when you're collapsing on my sheets, all happy and out of breath." He leaned closer. "I'm picturing it in my head. Mmm, you look lovely."

"Whatever fantasies help you get through the day," Audrey said.

"So kind of you."

"I'm all about being charitable when it doesn't cost me anything."

Charity? For me?

Before this was all over, either they would be lovers or they'd kill each other. Right now, he had no idea which it would be.

* * *

AUDREY stared out the window. The car suffered from a
desperate lack of space, especially when it came to the front.
Specifically, the front seats. Specifically, Kaldar in the front
seat, who was sitting entirely too close.

And Kaldar was getting hotter by the minute. When
they'd first met, he was handsome, then hot, and now he had
moved into the irresistible category. When he'd leaned
toward her and said her name in that bedroom voice, every
nerve in her body came to attention. She actually got the
shivers. If he'd leaned in and kissed her, she would've kissed
him right back, then she would've slapped him again, just
so he wouldn't get any ideas. She liked looking at him. She
liked the sound of his voice. She liked when he paid attention to her. They were in the Broken, which meant that Kaldar's increasing hotness couldn't be magic, and that left only
one explanation: she was falling for him.

Audrey glanced at him. He turned to her right when she
looked and gave her his evil grin. *Wow.* She was in so much
trouble. Audrey rolled her eyes and looked back through her
window.

If they were strapped for cash, they could just sit Kaldar
on a street corner with an empty coffee can and a phone
book to read. They'd make decent money until the cops
chased them off because crowds of women were obstructing
traffic. It wasn't just his looks. Looks alone she could resist.
It was the wicked glint in his eyes. He was a smart, sly bastard, quick on his feet and equipped with a silver tongue.
He could run circles around the best professionals she knew.

Audrey hid a sigh. Before her grandmother died, she
had given Audrey only one piece of advice: never fall in
love with a conman. Conmen couldn't stop grifting. It was
like a drug, an addiction, like her lock picking. And born
con artists like Kaldar grifted for the hell of it. Everything
was a game to them, and pretty soon the game became not
just "can I take this poor sucker's money" but "can I fool
my wife into thinking I'm where I'm supposed to be." Even-

tually the game would turn into "can I keep my ball and chain from knowing about all of my women on the side," and you would end up with your heart crushed into dust. She'd seen her father do it, she'd seen Alex do it when he was still sober, and she'd seen other conmen do it. They lied, oh how they lied.

Kaldar was too talented, too clever, and too full of pride not to play the game. She didn't even know the real him. He showed her what he thought she wanted to see. And he would expect her to be okay with all of it because she knew the score from the start. All the girls in the business knew it. Marry a mobster, take collect calls from prison. Marry a gambler, hide your paycheck. Marry a conman, nurse a broken heart. You made your bed, and you had to lie in it.

No, thank you. No matter how fast her pulse sped up when he played with her hair, she didn't want that kind of heartache. Nor did she want to be somebody's "ball and chain" or "old lady." If a man thought she cramped his style that much, he could go and find himself someone else. She needed someone straightforward and dependable—but then those guys were boring. Audrey smiled to herself. There was always time to settle down to boring and dependable. Flirting with Kaldar was fun. She might even dip her toes into those waters, but she wouldn't be taking a swim anytime soon. Unless, of course, she wrapped him around her finger first.

Now that would be a challenge.

JACK perched on the wyvern's back and watched the scrubby forest around them. The little cat he'd rescued in the Broken lay next to him, curled into a tight, furry ball. He wasn't as skinny now, and Jack had cut and washed most of the green paint off his fur. The little cat still didn't meow or purr, but he followed Jack around the camp like a baby duck after his mother. Not that Jack minded.

A little farther off, closer to the wyvern's hips, Ling the Merciless watched them with alert, suspicious eyes. Kaldar and Audrey were gone, and without Audrey, the raccoon turned into a nervous, listless ninny. Usually if a raccoon was out in daylight, it was sick, desperate, or rabid. This one sat out right under the sunshine and didn't care. Weirdo.

Below, George was going through his fencing routine. Lunge, scoot back, lunge, scoot back. Gaston had been gone for most of the day, too. He said he was going to gather information from the locals, but now he was back, writing something down in a notebook.

The sun baked the wyvern's back. Jack stretched. Mmmm, warm. Strange creatures, wyverns. The schoolbooks said that they were extremely smart, smarter than dogs, smarter than foxes, but Jack couldn't see how one would find out how smart a wyvern was. When he wasn't flying, the wyvern lay still, like a rock. The only time he came to life was when Gaston dumped buckets of food paste into his mouth in the morning.

Jack stirred. The little cat twitched an ear, opened one yellow eye, and looked at him. Jack raised his finger to his lips, and told him, "Shhh. Stay." The little cat closed his eyes.

Jack slid off and padded to the wyvern's head, silent like a shadow. Smart, right. Let's just see. He passed the blue shoulder, the long neck, as thick as a century-old tree, the brilliant blue fringe that protruded from the corner of the wyvern's jaw.

The heavy eyelids snapped open. Jack froze.

A huge gold-and-amber eye, as big as a dinner platter, stared at him. The dark pupil shrank, focusing.

Jack stood very still.

The colossal head turned, the scaled lip only three feet from Jack. The golden eyes gazed at him, swirling with fiery color.

Jack breathed in tiny, shallow breaths.

Don't blink. *Don't blink* . . .

Two gusts of wind erupted from the wyvern's nostrils. Jack jumped straight up, bounced off the ground into another jump, and scrambled up the nearest tree.

In the clearing, Gaston bent over, guffawing like an idiot. "It's not funny!"

"He knows you're there, you dimwit. He just chooses not to care."

The wyvern lowered his head.

George straightened and sheathed his rapier. "Kaldar and Audrey are back."

Jack climbed down from the tree before anyone asked him any uncomfortable questions. That's all he needed. Especially since Audrey would be there. Audrey was . . . pretty. Really, really pretty.

Ten minutes later, when Kaldar and Audrey came up the path, he was sitting on the wyvern again. That way, nobody would think that he was scared. Not that he was. He was just cautious.

"We have a job," Kaldar called out. "Come here."

Jack slid down the wing and came over to sit by George. It took Kaldar about fifteen minutes to explain about Magdalene and Ed Yonker.

"I may be overstepping myself," George said, "but why don't we just steal the invitation?"

"It won't work," Audrey told him. "First, we don't know where it is."

"Second," Kaldar continued, "if we steal it, she would let Morell know we have it. We'd walk straight into a trap."

"I thought she hated him," George said.

"Hate doesn't mean 'doesn't do business,'" Kaldar told him.

"He's right. It's a very costly mistake to make," Audrey said.

Kaldar turned to his nephew. "Gaston, did you get anything on Yonker?"

Gaston flipped open his notebook. "Ed's a local. Born and bred in the Edge. His parents still live about six miles east of here. The Edge here looks like Swiss cheese—you know, the one with holes. Bubbles of the Edge pop up all over in the Weird and in the Broken. The boundary is very thin, and the Edge itself isn't that wide, but there are a lot of people living here, and there are several powerful merchant families. The families keep the peace."

"Makes sense," Kaldar said. "Conflict is bad for business."

"Ed's not too well liked. The expectation was that when he made it big, he'd hire his buddies, but he brought in outside talent instead. The locals aren't getting any crumbs of his pie. Magdalene isn't that well liked, either. She isn't exactly trustworthy. Here's an interesting tidbit: Magdalene and Yonker almost had themselves a feud a couple of times, and they were seriously warned that if they started any sort of fighting, the families would squash them. All their fun and games would be over."

"So they have to play nice," Audrey said. "And Magdalene is using us to walk around the rules."

"Pretty much. Yonker's got a compound in the Edge, about twenty acres, fenced in, and guarded like there are state secrets inside. There are a lot of guards, and they're well trained. That's where his Wooden Cathedral is."

Audrey rolled her eyes.

"The scam works like this." Gaston checked his notes again. "He invites wealthy people into his church, flirts with them for a while, and if they've got the dough, he invites them to his private retreat, to the Wooden Cathedral. They go in normal, and they come out thinking he's a prophet. Whatever gadget he's got in there, it works."

Kaldar looked at George.

George frowned. "Crowd-control devices are illegal except in Gardens of Bliss, and there you have to sign a liability form."

"Is a Garden of Bliss as bad as it sounds?" Audrey asked.

"No, but when I first heard the name, I thought it was a brothel," Kaldar said. "It's a last resort for people who are depressed and suicidal. You sign a consent form and splash around in a garden with pretty flowers and ponds of warm water while good feelings are being pumped into you by magic."

Audrey blinked. "Oh."

"It could be a Vilad Lantern," George said. "Or some sort of emotional emitter. I'd have to see it to say for sure."

"Anything more about Ed?" Kaldar glanced at Gaston.

"Not much. Ed's greedy, and he likes nice things: expensive cars, good clothes, bling—that's apparently something to do with flashy jewelry. He likes women too, but all those are collateral vices. Ed ultimately gets off on crowds worshipping his every footstep. He wants to be a big shot. He actually gives money to the San Diego Children's Center, and he attends the charity dinners and all that."

Kaldar and Audrey glanced at each other.

"Explains the kids," Audrey said.

"The Blessed Youth Witness," Gaston said. "He gets street kids to work for him. They give out flyers, and he gives them a place to stay in his Witness Camp during the summer at his compound. Middle-aged women with money love it."

"Do we know where the camp is?" Kaldar asked.

Gaston shook his head. "No. But we do know he's got people with rifles and live ammo guarding it. Also, it's protected by enough defensive spells to hold off an army. It used to be his old family place. The Yonkers were a really strong Edge family a few years back, but now only Ed and his parents are left. The wards on that puppy are a century old."

"Nice." Audrey sighed. "So breaking in and stealing the magical brain-cooking device is out of the question."

Kaldar glanced at George. "How complicated are these devices usually?"

George shrugged. "Well, the inside is complicated, but most of the time they're designed to look like normal objects. When you want to manipulate someone's emotions, it's better that people don't know they're being manipulated. They tend to take that sort of thing badly."

"So what are we talking about?" Gaston asked. "Like a vase or something?"

"Not exactly." George got up. "Usually it's jewelry. For the emitter to work, I'd need to position it between me and the person I wanted to influence. So let's say I want to manipulate Kaldar." He turned to Kaldar. "I could probably have a bracelet emitter and lean on my fist or something, so the bracelet faces him." George bent his arm so his wrist faced Kaldar.

"You look stupid," Jack told him.

"Exactly," George agreed. "The object has to be something inconspicuous. And usually the object will be inert until the user focuses their magic into it."

"So wait," Gaston said. "It won't work for just anyone?"

"No," George said. "You have to have some magic talent in emotional manipulation already. These devices just make that kind of magic stronger. Since Yonker manipulates a crowd, you're looking for something with range, so the magic goes out at a wide angle. Like a crown or some sort of device he holds between himself and them."

"He wouldn't wear a crown," Audrey said. "This is an American congregation we're talking about. They wouldn't stand for that.

"So first we have to find out what the device looks like," Kaldar said. "Then we make a copy."

"Out of what?" Audrey stared at him.

"Memory plaster," Kaldar said. "The Mirror gave me a tub of it. If you expose it to the right magic, it will mimic glass, metal, or wood. Gaston is very good with it."

Audrey frowned. "And again, to get that close to Yonker very fast, we'll need money. Lots and lots of money."

"I am confused," Jack said.

"So am I," George said.

"Yeah, can we be in on the plan?" Gaston asked.

"Let me explain," Kaldar said. "Yonker has a magic gadget that manipulates people's emotions. He is probably keeping it in the camp in the woods. We need to steal that gadget."

"I got that part," Jack said. "But how do we steal it?"

"There are two ways," Kaldar continued. "First, we must find out where and how the gadget is guarded. To find that out, we'll need to infiltrate Yonker's camp, which is why we're going with this plan."

"You're getting them more confused," Audrey said. "Can I step in here for a second?"

"Sure." Kaldar invited her with a sweep of his hand.

"This heist is called Night and Day," Audrey said. "There are two teams: Day team and Night team. The two teams pretend not to know each other. Jack and George will be the Night team.

Jack exhaled. *Finally. Something to do besides sitting on the wyvern. Yes!*

Audrey continued. "Yonker's church takes in runaway children. You boys will pretend to be runaways, get Yonker church people to let you work for the church, and try to get into the camp. Once in the camp, George, you can use your necromancy to find the gadget and figure out how heavily it's protected. You have to be sneaky and avoid attracting attention."

"Meanwhile," Kaldar added, "Audrey and I will be the Day team. We will approach Yonker out in the open and draw a lot of attention to ourselves. Yonker will concentrate on us."

"Here comes the fun part." Audrey smiled. "If the gadget isn't well protected, then the Night team will either steal it or tell us, and we'll sneak in and steal it together."

Kaldar nodded. "If the gadget is too well protected, then the Day team will swap the real gadget for the fake one in broad daylight, pocket the real item, and walk right out of there."

Gaston raised his hand. "Question: what happens when Yonker figures out that the gadget is a fake?"

"All hell will break loose," Kaldar said. "But the gadget switch should buy us enough time to get out."

"And if it doesn't?" Gaston asked.

"Then we go to Plan C and cut our way out," Kaldar said.

"I like that plan," Gaston said.

"Let's hope it won't come to that." Audrey looked at George, then at Jack. "This heist usually takes a lot of time. We don't have time because that blond bitch is on our trail.

We'll be very rushed. There can be no mistakes, guys. No room for error. Do you understand?"

Jack nodded. *No mistakes, got it.*

"And if we tell you to get out, you run," Audrey said. "You run, and you don't look back."

"Listen to her," Kaldar said. "If we pull the plug in the middle of the heist, you two walk away. Clear?"

Jack nodded again.

"Can the two of you handle pretending to be runaways for a couple of days?" Kaldar asked.

George nodded. "We can do it."

"You don't have to if you don't want to," Audrey said. "These are unscrupulous people. We don't know what they will do, but we may not be there to help you. It's real, and it's dangerous."

And they were not babies. "We'll be fine," Jack said. "I'll take care of George."

"I'm not worried about George." Kaldar stared at him. It was a dominant, hard stare. Jack felt invisible hackles rise on his back. To the right, Gaston rose, his jaw set, and moved to stand by Kaldar's side. Gaston's silvery eyes glared at Jack. Ready to fight.

"Why would you worry about me?"

"You're a whiny baby," Gaston said.

What?

"You like to feel sorry for yourself, Jack," Kaldar said. "It's all about Jack, all the time."

Inside him, the Wild gathered itself into a tight ball, all fur and teeth.

"Poor, poor Jack," Audrey said. Her voice was sweet, but her eyes mocked him. "Everyone's mean to you. What will you do? There is no room to run away to this time, and Rose won't help you."

How does she know about my sister?

The Wild snarled. They had all ganged up on him. Jack's heart hammered in his chest. His claws prickled the inside of his hands. He glanced at George. His brother stood there, his face calm, like he was a complete stranger.

"Selfish and stupid," Kaldar said. "That's you."

"Good for nothing," Gaston added.

The Wild screamed and scratched inside Jack, straining to break free. He wanted to grow teeth and claws and dash into the forest. No, he had to stand his ground. Changing in the Edge wasn't like changing in the Weird. It hurt, and it lasted half a minute. They would kill him before he was done.

The world distilled itself to painful clarity. He had to defend himself. He couldn't let them take him.

Why? They were friends—why would they do this? Why didn't George do anything?

"You're on your own," George said. "Don't ask me for help, crybaby."

Traitor. Jack looked into his brother's eyes. They were blue and calm, almost peaceful. George always helped him. Always. Even when everyone else turned away.

This was wrong. George would never turn on him.

It's a test, he suddenly realized. They were testing him to see if he would snap and give himself away. They were watching him carefully, trying to gauge what he would do.

Jack's instincts told him to bite back as hard as he could. But that was what they expected of him, then he'd be stuck in that clearing by himself, while George went out to spy and probably fight. George was good with his rapier but not that good.

Jack pushed the Wild back into its hole. It clawed him, refusing to go, and he had to force it, step by step. It hurt. His mouth tasted bitter. Finally, he shoved it deep inside, into its usual place. It must've taken only a couple of moments, but to him it felt like forever.

The colors lost some of their sharpness, the scents faded just a fraction. He stepped away from the edge of the cliff.

Jack took a deep breath and forced himself to smile. "That's okay. If I get in trouble, I'll just mop up my tears with George's hair."

It was a lame joke, but that was all he could manage.

Audrey was looking at him, and her eyes were kind again.

"Good man," Kaldar said. "There is hope for you yet."

Gaston walked over and punched his shoulder.

Jack breathed. He was terribly tired all of a sudden.

"Okay, now we'll need money," Audrey said. "And a lot of it. Preferably owned by some ass, so I won't feel bad stealing from him. Gaston, any candidates?"

Gaston raised his black eyebrows. "How do you feel about a slaver? Rumor says he doesn't believe in banks. He keeps all his money in his mansion in the Edge."

Kaldar raised his hand. "Sold!"

"Oh, really?" Audrey crossed her arms. "So I guess you'll be breaking into this mansion all on your own without my help."

"I could," Kaldar said. "But I would get caught."

"In that case, how about I decide if we're sold or not?"

Gaston waved his notebook. "Maybe the two of you should let me tell you about the guy first."

Jack heard them bicker, but the words barely sank in. His legs grew weak, as if all his muscles had turned to mush. He took a couple of steps back and half sat, half fell, on the grass. Exhaustion claimed him. He took rapid, shallow breaths.

George came over and sat next to him. "The Wild?"

Jack nodded. He had beat it back that time. But it was so hard, much harder than it had been before in the parking lot. He had won this time. There would be a next time, and he wasn't sure who would win then.

TEN

KALDAR lay on a low ridge, wearing one of the Mirror's night suits. The fabric, painted with swirls in a dozen shades of gray, hugged his body, formfitting but too elastic to hinder his movements. With the hood hiding his hair and his face painted gray and black, he supposed he resembled a ninja.

It was good that nobody could see him because he looked completely ridiculous.

Although, come to think of it, the suits did have their advantages. For example, if one had decent night vision, he could admire the way the stretchy fabric clung to Audrey's incredibly shapely ass . . .

"Kaldar," Audrey hissed. "Stop looking at my butt."

Behind them, Gaston made some choked-up noises that might have been coughing but really resembled chortling.

She had a sixth sense. That had to be it. He would never again take woman's intuition lightly.

She leaned closer, her whisper so quiet he had to strain to hear it. "Do you ever take anything seriously?"

"No."

Audrey shook her head and raised her binoculars to her eyes, looking down on the house three miles below. Kaldar picked up his binoculars and looked, too. The full moon ducked in and out of torn clouds, dappling the building with patches of silvery light and deep shadow. The house sat in the middle of the shallow valley, surrounded by palms and greenery. The building rose two stories high, with white arches sheltering a long front porch under a bright orange roof. Five thousand square feet, at least. A tennis court stretched in front of the house. To the left, a fenced-in field contained a horse course with white gates. Farther back, a barn loomed, and next to it a caretaker's house. To the right, a picturesque pool gleamed in the weak moonlight. Except for a gun tower behind the house and the ring of metal spikes circling the house, which served as anchors for the defensive spells, the place looked like a tropical resort built by a Spanish family with unlimited funds.

The humble abode of Arturo Pena. Kaldar gritted his teeth. If houses could tell stories, this one would bleed.

According to Gaston, Arturo Pena prayed on coyotes, the human traffickers who ferried illegals from Mexico into the embrace of the State of California. Arturo and his band of hired lowlifes ambushed the coyote vehicles, extracted the cargo, and sold the people in the Democracy of California's slave markets. Half of the people died making the crossing into the Weird. The other half followed shortly thereafter. There was a reason why the robber barons always needed fresh bodies to till the fields, build their castles, and fight in their armies.

Nobody ever missed Pena's victims. The Broken's California didn't know they existed; the Broken's Mexico lost jurisdiction once they left its borders, and the victims themselves had no idea where they were taken. Those who ran away never found their way back across the boundary.

Pena was a sonovabitch of the first order. His name was spoken in whispers. The local Edgers feared him, but for the most part, he left them alone, and they did the same—which said something considering that Arturo Pena didn't believe in banks and was rumored to keep large sums of cash in his house. It made sense, Kaldar decided. Putting money in the bank resulted in questions. Money earned interest, which was reported. Arturo Pena avoided all that transparency by hiding all of his blood money in his house, in a supposedly unbreakable safe. A tempting ripe plum for any Edger.

Kaldar focused the binoculars at the circle of iron spikes. The ward extended in a rough oval shape around the house, not including the barn or the caretaker's dwelling. The ward couldn't be very old—the house looked too new. Still, the defensive spell presented a problem. It kept out anything magical, including people with magic and sometimes even those without. Screwing with it would be like ringing a warning bell because anyone with any magic sensitivity would come running.

This was impossible. They should've gone with his plan: stroll up to the front door and con their way in. He had tried suggesting that, but both Audrey and Gaston refused. It seemed that Arturo Pena had a habit of shooting visitors in the face first and checking identification second.

Next to Audrey, Ling crouched on the slope.

Kaldar leaned to Audrey, and whispered, "I still don't understand why we had to bring that creature."

"Because she helps," Audrey told him "You really should use her given name. You might hurt her feelings."

And she nagged him about not taking things seriously. "How exactly is she going to help?"

Audrey nodded at Ling. "See how she's quiet? This means Pena has no dogs. Don't move. I'll be back in a minute."

She slithered backward and, bending low, ran to the right along the ridge. Ling followed her. He watched them go, then Gaston landed in her place, his dark hair obscuring his field of vision.

"If you keep taking her side instead of mine, I'll have to disown you," Kaldar murmured.

"I'm crushed." Gaston pantomimed being struck in the heart.

"That's right. Don't forget whose rolpies are pulling your boat." Walking up to the front door was still a better way to go. Getting through the wards without noise would be impossible. Suppose something went wrong with Audrey's brilliant plan. How many guards would they have to deal with?

"Uncle?"

"Mmm?"

"Arturo Pena. He's a slaver. A scumbag."

"Yes?"

"Why don't we just kill him?"

Kaldar paused.

Gaston shrugged. "With the equipment we have, we could slice through that ward. Walk in, kill him, and once his guys realized that their paycheck was dead, they would scatter."

"You've spent too much time with the wolf," Kaldar said.

"William is efficient."

"He is that." This would have to be said just right. "What's the difference between you and me and a murderer?"

"A murderer kills out of passion or for money. We kill for our country."

Kaldar shook his head. "We kill to keep our people safe. 'Country' has a nice ring to it, but it doesn't really get to the heart of the matter. Families, Gaston. Our family. Your brothers, your cousins, uncles, aunts, grandmother. We do this so they can sleep in their beds at night, worry about their daily problems, and have delicious berry wine on their porch while their kids play in the grass."

Gaston smirked. "I never knew you were all about noble purpose and grandeur."

"I'm not. Tell me, what do you want out of this life?"

"Vengeance for our family."

"And then?"

The boy shrugged again. "I don't know."

"You think, eventually you might want to be like those people we're protecting and start a family?"

"Sure."

"You might find some funny girl to be your wife, have some kids, someone to come home to?"

"Yeah, I guess it would be nice."

"This job, if you let it, will burn every shred of humanity out of your soul. It will chew you up and spit out an empty husk. If you don't take care, you'll be hollow like an empty casket. No pretty, funny girl for your wife, no home, no love, no laughter, nothing." Kaldar paused to make sure it sank in. "You've seen the old Mirror agents. They walk jingling enough medals on their chests to be their own marching bands, but their eyes are dead. That isn't what you want."

"At the end of the day, they know they've done their job."

"That satisfaction doesn't keep them warm at night. It's no substitute for a life or a clear conscience." Kaldar pointed at the house. "Every time you get into a situation like this, I want you to think of our family. If one of us asks you why you killed or maimed or tortured, you need to be able with a clear conscience to say, 'There was no other way.'"

"William . . ."

"William has Cerise," Kaldar said. "And she has a temper, and she kills, but she is also kind and compassionate. Cerise seeks balance in all things. William listens to her because he knows she has something he lacks. It's not his fault; the Adrianglians did their best to murder any humanity he had in him when he was a child. And even he has some lines he won't cross. I once saw him run into an open field, in plain view of the enemy's guns and bows, to save Lark, with no regard for his own life."

"That was different! Lark is a kid."

"Can you tell me for sure that there are no children in that house? Can you tell me that one won't run out and be caught in the cross fire? Are you prepared to murder Pena while his family watches?"

Gaston opened his mouth and closed it.

"You must hold on to your humanity, nephew, so when it's time to return to your house for a family dinner, you can do so as a happy man. At some point, you will have a son or a daughter. When you come home, you need to be able to look your wife and children in the eye."

Gaston looked at the house.

"We kill only when we have no other choice. Is Pena a scumbag? Sure he is. But he's outside of the scope of our job. We are not judges. Remember, we do only what is necessary. We need his money, and we'll take it—because it's dirty and we can. But until he levels a gun on another human being, we will not take his life. Am I clear?"

"Yes, Uncle."

"Good."

They fell silent.

Gaston stirred. "If it helps, Audrey checked your ass out before she took off."

"She did?"

Audrey slipped next to Gaston. "I did what?"

"Nothing!" Kaldar and Gaston chorused.

"Shh." Audrey glared at them. "Will you two nincompoops stop screwing around?"

"Yes, m'lady." Kaldar ducked his head in a half bow.

Audrey tapped Gaston's shoulder with her finger. "Think you can get into that barn?"

Gaston shrugged his muscular shoulders. "Sure."

"I need you to get down there, open the stalls inside, and panic the horses."

" 'Panic'?" Gaston asked.

"Smile at them or something."

He gave her an insane grin. "I can do that."

"What about me?" Kaldar whispered.

"You lie here and look pretty. I'll be back."

Look pretty, huh. She'll pay for that.

Gaston and Audrey melted into the darkness. Audrey and his nephew seemed to be made of the same stuff: she flittered over the ground, completely silent, almost weightless, and Gaston snuck around like a big cat, noiseless despite his bulk. Kaldar turned to the house. Well, he did want to see her work. All he could do was hope that she didn't get the lot of them murdered.

Breaking into the house in the middle of the night just wasn't his style. He did his best work in plain view, and, usually, his tongue was doing most of it.

Now that was an interesting thought. *Heh.*

He made a mental note to drop that one on Audrey. Maybe he'd get another "Oh, my God!" out of her.

She hugged the ground next to him.

"Where is my nephew?"

"Watch," she told him, and pulled her mask on.

A long minute passed, then another. They lay in silence atop the hill. Kaldar leaned closer to her until their faces almost touched. "Take your mask off."

"Why?" she whispered.

"I miss your face."

Her eyes widened. *Aha!* He had finally scored one.

"We've got a few minutes," she whispered. "Do you want to make out?"

It was a trap. A one hundred percent, genuine Audrey trap. If he fell for it, he'd be sorry. But then there was that slight, one in a thousand chance that she was serious. He'd be an idiot not to take it.

Kaldar reached over and gently tugged her mask from the lower half of her face.

She flicked her fingers, hitting him lightly on the nose. "You're so easy."

"No, just smitten." He leaned closer. His lips almost brushed hers.

Audrey didn't pull away. "Now, remember what happened the last time you tried that?"

"Worth it," he whispered.

The door of the barn below flew open with a thud. Horses burst into the night. Audrey turned toward the herd, and he grabbed her and kissed her. She tasted just like Kaldar remembered, like a sunny day in the middle of a dark night. For a moment, Audrey didn't respond, as if they had both paused on the edge of a skyscraper with the ground far below, and she was too scared to move. He pulled her closer, kissing her, reassuring, loving. Suddenly, Audrey melted into his kiss, so hot, so welcoming, and they fell off the edge into the empty air; but instead of plummeting down, they floated, wrapped up in each other. Kaldar lost all sense of time and place. He just wanted more of her.

She hit his shoulder with a closed fist. Pain shot through his biceps. Kaldar let go. "Ow."

Audrey glared at him with sincere outrage. He might have overstepped just a smidgen.

"What the hell? We're working!"

She took everything so seriously. "For luck," he told her.

Audrey yanked her mask over her face. "Follow me and try to be quiet."

They descended the slope, the raccoon sneaking through the night a few steps ahead of them. At the house, horses dashed to and fro, galloping along the driveway and jumping fences. The ward meant nothing to them, and they dashed back and forth, trampling the flower beds in their frenzy.

A long, ululating call of a pissed coyote rolled through the night. Gaston was always good at imitating animal calls.

Floodlights snapped on, bathing the scene in harsh white light. Men spilled from the caretaker's house, yelling. At the guard tower, a sentry dressed in black yanked a rope. A siren wailed. The horses lost what little calm they had left. The scene turned into complete pandemonium. It was glorious.

Kaldar laughed soundlessly and padded through the brush, making less noise than a fox. The Mire didn't suffer loud guests.

Audrey dropped behind a dense clump of brush. He landed next to her.

"Can you strut louder?" she whispered. "I think there might be one or two guards who haven't heard you yet."

"Lies," he told her. "Nobody heard me. Not even you."

A huge, pale horse charged out of the barn, scattering the guards like a pike scattered a school of fish. The horse veered left, galloping toward them, its mane like white silk. A stallion. Kaldar wasn't a horseman, but even he had to admit: the stallion was one hell of an animal.

A door opened, and a half-naked man marched out from between the porch arches into the open, three guards following at his heels. The man waved his arm, pointing a gun at the guards outside the ward. The wind brought tatters of his voice from the distance. "What do I pay you for . . . get the fucking horses . . ."

Hello, Arturo Pena.

The guards set down their rifles. Pena bent down, grasped an iron spike, and pulled it out of the ground. The flow of magic around the spikes vanished. Pena pointed at the guards next to him. Two men chased after the herd while the third went back inside. A moment later, the guard from the tower slid down and joined the pursuit. Pena surveyed the scene, spat, and went back into the house.

Audrey moved, slinking through the darkness with Ling as her silent shadow. He followed. Together, they ran toward the house, angling to the right, away from the horses and guards toward the darkness of the pool. A few moments, and they sank into the deep shadows by the glass patio door.

AUDREY touched the lock on the glass door. Locked. Her face burned under the mask. She wished she could take it off, but that would've been foolish. The Mirror's suits were beyond cool. They made her practically invisible. Kaldar wouldn't be getting this one back. Not in a million years.

When Kaldar kissed her, she hadn't reacted quickly enough. She'd been focused on the horses, and the bastard ambushed her. All her nerves had been keyed up, and the kiss had sung through her, hot and sudden. Kaldar kissed like the world was ending. And after she came to her senses, his face was so full of self-satisfaction that she knew she'd stumbled. It had been a crucial blunder, and now he'd be insufferable.

Her magic slid off her fingers in translucent tendrils of deep, beautiful green. The tendrils tasted the lock, seeped into the tiny space between the door and the frame. She pushed. The lock clicked, and she gently swung the door open and slipped inside. Kaldar followed and shut the door behind them. She had to give it to him: when the man closed his mouth, he could actually move quietly.

The living room lay shrouded in inky night shadows. Across the room, a wet bar of mahogany spanned the wall. Between the bar and her, a set of plush couches circled a coffee table, facing a colossal flat screen on the wall. A handful of pinpoint lights in every color of the rainbow glowed under the TV, where assorted electronic equipment sat on glass shelves. For an Edger, this was unimaginable luxury. Amazing what selling other people into slavery could buy you.

Ling trotted along the wall, sniffing at the air. Audrey kept still, listening.

Hello, house.

The house answered: the tiny buzzing of electronic gadgets, the whisper of the air-conditioning, the murmur of the generator filtering from the outside, the faint creaking of the walls . . . The sounds enveloped her, blending into a calm white hum, and she committed their pattern to memory. Any stray noise, no matter how tiny, would sound the alarm in her head.

Audrey padded through the room, toward the right-hand end of the bar, where the hallway led deeper into the house, diving under a wide staircase. The safe would be on the first floor. Gaston's intelligence claimed the safe was large enough for a man to fit inside. Most of the larger varieties weighed thousands of pounds and required reinforced flooring, which wasn't likely judging by the first floor's ceiling. Besides, the logistics of dragging a safe of that size and weight up the stairs would drive anyone mad. You needed a forklift to move it.

A quiet creak announced a door swinging open above. Her mind snapped into overdrive, thoughts firing off in rapid succession. Heavy footsteps—male. Coming down to the first floor, fast, but not running or sneaking—not alarmed. Stomping—irate. Her gaze snagged on the bar. Arturo Pena wanted a nightcap. That had to be it.

Audrey crouched, pressing against the outer edge of the bar, and put her hand on the floor. *Hide.* Ling darted under the couch and lay down. Kaldar dropped down next to Audrey.

Arturo Pena jogged down the stairs. She caught a flash of hairy tan legs under a short white robe and a black muzzle of a handgun in his left hand, pointing down. The lights came on with a click.

Breathe in and breathe out. Nice and calm.

The cabinet door creaked, opening. A heavy glass clinked as it was set on the marble bar.

Breathe in.

A heavier clang—probably a crystal decanter. Swiveling top sliding out with a barely audible sound as it was being spun. The scent of scotch spread through the air, alcohol fumes mixed with a distinct aroma of burned honey.

Breathe out.

Glass clinked against glass, Arturo swallowed in a long gulp, exhaled, and headed back upstairs, hitting the light switch with a casual swipe of his hand. Arturo climbed the stairs. A moment, and he was out of their view.

The door thudded shut.

He had never let go of the gun. Talk about paranoia. She waited another moment and waved her hand at Ling. The raccoon emerged from under the couch and slunk into the hallway. Audrey paused, but the raccoon didn't return. The way was clear. She rose and moved into the hallway, Kaldar a ghost behind her.

The safe sat in the back of a small room, on the right side of the hallway, a solid black tower. She crouched by it. Hello, old friend. TURTLE60XX, Super Vault, 76.25 tall, 39.25 inches wide, 29.0 inches deep. Capacity of 20.4 cubic feet. Weighing in empty at fifty-nine hundred pounds. The multi-layered door was eight and a quarter inches thick. It would take hours to break through it with a drill, and if you did, at the end you'd hit a plate of tempered glass, which shielded the locking mechanism. Any attempt to access the locking mechanism by a tool would shatter the glass and activate the relocking mechanism. It was a monster of a safe, the kind diamond dealers used.

Audrey touched the door. Three locks secured the safe. A combination lock, standard antitheft precautions, but nothing major. An auxiliary key lock and a huge one, too. She'd seen one before: the locking mechanism connected to four steel rods, each as thick as her wrist. It would take a lot of pressure to open it. Finally, a digital lock, an optional feature. Not that it did anything superfancy, but the digital display looked awesome enough to impress Pena, because he'd paid an extra chunk of cash to have it installed.

Magic slipped from her fingers. The green numbers on the digital panel blinked and vanished. Bye-bye computer defenses. One down, two to go. Unfortunately, the other two locks would be harder. Audrey motioned Ling to the hallway. The raccoon padded out. Audrey pulled a stethoscope out of her suit and slipped it on, pressing the sensor to the door.

Kaldar bent over her, his lips barely moving. "Magic?"

"The key lock's too heavy," she breathed. "The heavier the lock, the more magic it takes. A quarter of a pound feels like five hundred. Need to save the juice."

"A problem?"

"No problem. I'm not a one-trick pony."

She touched the wheel gently. One, two, three, four, five . . . turn, turn, turn . . . with a faint click the false tumbler fell into place. It was a dry sound, clear and distinct, designed to fool an average picklock. Audrey touched the dial again. Turn. Turn. A tiny muffled sound traveled to her ears through the stethoscope. There it was, the real tumbler. It was an almost imperceptible sound, but she'd practiced on these combination locks as long as she could remember.

Ling dashed into the room and crouched in the corner.

"Someone's coming," Audrey whispered.

Kaldar nodded and took a step back, moving into position by the door.

Audrey turned the wheel in another direction.

Footsteps came down the hall. She willed herself to ignore the approaching person.

Turn, turn, click. Turn, turn. Tumbler. Reverse.

A tall, large man walked into the room, dressed in dark clothes and carrying a rifle, pale blue disposable booties on his shoes. Her stethoscope was still pressed against the door of the safe.

They stared at each other. The guard jerked his rifle up. Before the barrel moved an inch, Kaldar snapped a lightning-fast punch to the guard's throat. The man had no time to react. The second punch caught the guard in his solar plexus. Kaldar grabbed the man, pulled him forward, bent him, guiding him into position with fluid grace, almost as if the guard were made of Play-Doh, until somehow Kaldar was behind him, with his arm barring the guard's throat, cutting off the blood flow to the brain. The guard jerked, flailing. Kaldar held him, almost carefully. The man went limp.

Wow. That was kind of beautiful.

Kaldar lowered him to the floor and pulled tape and plastic ties from his pocket.

The last tumbler clicked. Audrey rose, pulled the stethoscope off, and spread her arms, bent at the elbow, palms up. The magic bubbled from inside her and out, sliding down her shoulders in a weightless wave of crystalline green. The translucent color encased her palms. Audrey pushed. The magic shot from her to the lock, flowing through the keyhole. The safe trembled but stayed locked.

She braced against the pain and pushed harder.

The lock resisted.

Harder.

Pain began deep inside her, growing hotter and hotter, the price of too much magic expended too quickly. The weight of the lock ground on her, like someone had piled a ton of rocks on her shoulders. *Come on . . . Come on . . .*

Metal slid against metal. The door swung open on well-oiled hinges, revealing four shelves filled with cash.

The pain ebbed. Audrey exhaled. Kaldar grinned like an idiot. The way he looked at her almost made her blush, and for a Callahan, that was saying something.

He leaned over to her, and whispered, a little too loud, "Audrey, you are magic."

She had no way of knowing if he was being sincere. But she really, really wanted to believe that he was.

JACK sauntered down the street next to George, squinting at the early-morning sunshine. They were gloriously filthy.

They'd both rolled down the hill twice, and now George's hair looked like a dirty mop. Swirls of dust stained their arms and faces. The memory of Kaldar's voice resonated through his head. *Less happy, more hungry.* Hungry. Right.

"Doode," George said.

He'd practiced all morning but still didn't get it quite right. "Nope, more *u*, less *oo*. Duuude."

"Dude."

"Dude."

"Okay, dude." George nodded.

"How's it hanging?" Jack asked.

"How am I supposed to answer that?" George looked at him.

"I don't think Kaldar said anything about that. I guess 'good'? I don't get it. What's hanging anyway?"

George shook his head. "Your stuff, you nimwit."

His stuff . . . *Oh. Ha!* "In that case, it's hanging long!" Jack dissolved into giggles. "Long, get it?"

"My brother, everyone." George bowed to an invisible crowd with a martyred expression. "A refined and sensitive creature."

A beat-up red car turned the corner and swung into a parking lot ahead. Audrey was driving, with Kaldar in the passenger seat and Gaston in the back. He barely recognized any of them. Audrey wore a baseball cap that covered her hair. Kaldar and Gaston looked like two beggars in ripped-up clothing. Jack forced himself to ignore the car. They were the backup. If anything went wrong, the adults would run to rescue them. When he told them that if something went wrong, they would have to rescue the other guys instead, nobody seemed amused.

Jack hid a sigh. He was under strict orders to do nothing violent unless it was absolutely necessary.

They strolled up the street. Out on the sidewalk, kids traveled in pairs, handing out little pieces of paper. George and Jack stopped, leaning on the building, and watched them for a while. The kids worked the street up and down, targeting women mostly. They had it down pat: a suck-up smile, a few quick words, hold out the paper, a sad dog face if they didn't take it, a giant smile if they did, and on to the next victim. A tall, lean man watched the whole thing from the side. He held a placard that said, COME TO JESUS! LIVE AN ABUNDANT LIFE.

Jack didn't fully get Jesus. Audrey tried to explain it, and he could repeat it back to her, word for word, but he still didn't comprehend most of it. The best he could gather was that Jesus lived long ago, told people to be nice, and they killed him for it. At the end, he asked who was Jesus' necromancer and if he was in the Bible, then Kaldar couldn't stop laughing and had to sit down.

The man with the placard noticed them. The next time a pair of kids passed him, he handed the placard to them and started across the street toward the two of them in an unhurried fashion. George tensed next to him. A nervous burst of alarm dashed through him, and Jack squared his shoulders. Kaldar and Audrey had made them practice the conversation for the last three hours. This was the real thing, and he was so excited, he had to fight to keep himself from jumping and yelling something stupid.

A faint scent of cinnamon fluttered on the wind. Placard Man. Declan smelled like a pie, but this man's scent was slightly bitter, spiced with cloves. It wasn't that Placard Man was that powerful or had that much magic, but he'd definitely been around it.

The man stopped a few feet away, hands in plain view. "Hey there."

Showtime. Jack gave him the kind of look bluebloods unleashed when they first found out he was a changeling: half suspicion, half derision.

George just stared at the man, his face flat and unfriendly, tense as if ready to bolt any second. Kaldar had explained the street-prostitute thing to them. He said it was the easiest way to go, and they both agreed they could do that.

"I saw you standing here," Placard Man said.

Jack bared his teeth at him. "We can stand here."

"It's a public street," George said.

"That's an interesting accent," the man said. "You boys are English?"

Aha, they had practiced that one. "Canadian," Jack said, while George said, "None of your business" at the same time.

"Canadian." The man nodded in appreciation. "You're a long way from home. Does your family know where you are?"

"What do you want, dude?" George asked.

"I want to help," the man said.

"Right." George laughed, cold and bitter.

"We don't need any," Jack told him.

"From what I'm looking at, you do. Do you boys know about Jesus Christ, our Savior?"

"I don't know, does Jesus have food?" Jack smirked.

"Yes," the man said. "Yes, he does. When's the last time you two ate?"

"Look, why don't you bugger off," George told him. "We aren't bothering you."

Placard Man smiled. "I tell you what, I'm shorthanded today. If the two of you give out flyers for me for the next two hours, there will be a sandwich and a bottle of water in it for each of you. And a cookie."

"What kind of cookie?" Jack asked.

George put a restraining hand over him. They didn't practice that, but Jack went along with it. "What else do we have to do for the food?" A warning note crept into his voice. Heh. George was kicking ass and taking names.

Placard Man sighed. "Nothing else. Definitely nothing like what you're thinking of. Nobody will touch you or force you to do something you don't want to do. Just simple payment for two hours of honest work. And the cookie is chocolate chip, by the way."

George pretended to think it over.

"I'm starving," Jack said.

"We just hand out flyers," George said. "Nothing else."

"Nothing else."

"We're not going into any buildings with you, dude."

"That's fine," Placard Man said. "No buildings."

George hesitated for another moment. "What sort of sandwich?"

"Ham or turkey. You get your pick."

"Come on." Jack let a little whine into his voice.

"Okay," George said.

"THEY'RE in," Audrey murmured. On the street, the two boys accepted a stack of flyers each. Look at George go. The kid did everything right: the weary, suspicious look, the distrust, the jumpiness. George was a born actor, and Jack wasn't bad himself.

"Go," Kaldar said.

Gaston slipped out of the car. He wore a tattered trench coat and a filthy panama hat that hid his face and most of his hair, which Kaldar had sprinkled with white powder. His face and hands, what little could be seen of them, had been dyed brown with one of the plant dyes from Kaldar's collection. As she watched, Gaston slipped a small glass vial from his sleeve and splashed some liquid on his coat.

She glanced at Kaldar.

"Cat urine."

Ugh. Cat urine stank to high heaven. Nobody would come within six feet of Gaston.

All this trouble so they could get an invitation to the auction of the man who had bought the bracelets. And to think Audrey had the stupid things in her hands a week ago. She should've never taken that job. But whatever regrets she had, she would have to live with them. Regrets never did anyone any good. She would fix this mess. She was smart, good at what she did, and she had Kaldar, who was possibly the best conman she had ever met.

The glass vial vanished into Kaldar's nephew's sleeve. Gaston slumped against the wall in the corner of the parking lot and slid down to the ground. He looked like an old Hispanic homeless man.

"Nice job," she approved.

"One of the first things the Mirror teaches field agents," Kaldar said. "The best way to hide is to do it in plain view."

If anything happened to the kids, Gaston would get them out. It didn't make her feel any better. The whole plan was made of bubble gum and lint and hinged on luck. When she told Kaldar that, he grinned, and said, "Trust me," as if that was supposed to make everything okay. She argued against it until Kaldar suggested a vote. All male members of the party voted against her, which meant everyone. She had a feeling that if the wyvern and the cat could've understood what was going on, they would've voted against her, too. She was surrounded by fools with too much testosterone, and there wasn't a thing she could do about it.

"Why the sour face?" he asked. "Still worried about the kids?"

"You know they need to simmer for at least a week." She merged into traffic, heading toward the nearest mall. "We're rushing this."

"We have no choice. The Hand won't keep spinning its wheels forever."

Audrey shook her head. They were moving too fast. They had cash, that was true, but some things couldn't be fixed with money alone.

They'd taken $187,000 from Arturo Pena's safe. They had also taken the stack of maps that showed his slave routes, which maps Kaldar had delivered in a neat bundle to the doorstep of a friend of a friend, whose business car seemed to have government plates. Even if Arturo Pena managed to pull himself back together, he would never regain the respect of his crew. They had effectively put him out of business. It was the least he deserved. And now they would spend his blood-soaked bill.

"How long will you need at the mall?" Kaldar asked.

"At least four hours."

He blinked.

"Manicure, pedicure, wax, hair, makeup, clothes, jewelry. You'll be lucky if I'm out of there by three in the afternoon."

"I'll count my blessings," he said. "Don't buy anything tasteful."

"Shut up. Do you think this is my first time?"

THE buzzer on the intercom sitting on Kaleb Green's desk chimed with a silvery note. Kaleb Green opened his eyes. His head throbbed with the beginnings of a spectacular migraine. He could take the pills, which would turn him into a zombie for the rest of the day. Unfortunately, he had to stay lucid and upright.

The Bosley deal was going down today, which, if the die fell right, would net him a quarter of a million dollars in the Weird's gold. Personally, he could see no point in arming anyone in the Weird with AK-47s. Any blueblood with a decent flash would simply deflect the bullets and mince the troops into sushi. But the robber baron wanted the guns, and Kaleb would deliver and endure. He'd taken three Excedrins and four Advils, but the migraine persisted, so he had retreated into his private office and told his secretary he wasn't to be disturbed.

The intercom chimed again. For a moment, he considered throwing it against the wall. But then, his curiosity won. Perhaps there was a deal of the century waiting on the other line. Kaleb reached over and pressed the button. Tamica's voice came through. "Mr. Green?"

Kaleb sat up. His secretary had worked for him for six years. They were on a first-name basis. "Mr. Green" meant a client or trouble. Considering that they were currently in the Edge part of the building, the latter was more likely.

"Yes?"

Tamica's voice shook slightly. "You have visitors."

He pulled a Colt .45 from the desk drawer and let his magic cloak him in a pale sheen of green. His wasn't the strongest of flashes, but it would shield him from a hail of bullets.

"Can they wait?"

"No, sir. They would like to see you now."

She hadn't used the code word, or he would be already gone, out through the back.

"Very well. I'll see them."

The door swung open, and a blueblood woman entered, her cloak flaring behind her. Tall, gorgeous, lithe like a cat, with hair the color of golden silk and radiant eyes of such pure intense green he forgot to breathe. A short, muscled man who looked like he could bench-press a car moved to her left. His dark hair had been cropped short, and a long line of tattooed symbols wound about his neck, like a snake, looping over his bare arms only to disappear under his clothes. Long, black claws protruded from his fingers.

To the right, a giant of a man, pale like an albino, loomed over the blueblood's head. A woman came to stand next to him, slender, dark-haired, with pale gray eyes and skin the color of orange peel. A bald man stepped forward, carrying Tamica, one hand around her waist, the other on her throat, carrying her horizontally, like she weighed nothing. Tamica's hazel eyes stared at Kaleb in silent panic.

For the first time in his life, Kaleb seriously considered prayer.

The blueblood woman looked at him. He saw the slit pupils contract in her emerald irises. An enhanced blueblood. This was bad. This was extremely bad.

"Are you Kaleb Green, the fence?"

His throat had gone dry like a shriveled-up leaf. Somehow, he made the words come out. "I am much more than a simple fence."

The blueblood arched her perfect eyebrows. "Are you familiar with your competitors?"

"Of course."

She reached into her cloak and pulled out a purse. For a moment, she let it dangle from her long fingers, sheathed in leather gloves, and Kaleb wondered what her hands looked like. Then the purse landed on his desk with a telltale metallic clink, and he focused on it.

The woman raised her hand. "Killian."

The bald man jerked Tamica up. His mouth gaped open, the lower jaw unhinging like the gaping maw of a snake. His lips circled back, baring huge triangular teeth.

"No!" Kaleb gasped.

Tamica screamed.

The man bit Tamica's throat, ripping out half of her neck with his teeth. Blood drenched the floor. Her scream died in mid-note. The man bit again, tearing out red flesh and shreds of muscle, and dropped Tamica's body on the floor. It dropped with a soft thud onto his prized carpet.

"I require your services," the blueblood woman said. "If you agree, the money is yours. If you refuse, I'll skin you alive."

He was still frozen. *Move, you moron. Do something, or you'll be next.*

The blueblood woman watched him, waiting.

Kaleb licked his lips. His voice came out hoarse. "What can I do for you, my lady?"

The albino giant stepped aside. A woman with pale skin tinted with a sickly shade of green approached his desk, carrying an enormous book. She flipped the pages, and he stared at the photograph of himself, complete with his name, contact information, and a short list of his accomplishments. Kaleb's heart hammered faster. He'd never seen it, but he'd heard of it. This was Gnome's book. If the Hand had it, that meant the old bastard was dead, and if Kaleb wasn't careful, he would be joining him. Just like Tamica.

"This book contains profiles of your major competitors," the blueblood woman said. "A page has been torn from it. I need you to tell me who is missing."

OUTSIDE, the night air felt cool against Helena's skin. The Mar had torn out more than one page. The book was missing Magdalene Moonflower from the south and Clive Keener from the north. The two Edgers lived a thousand miles apart. Clever, Helena reflected. *It won't save you, swamp rat. The Hound of the Golden Throne is coming for you.* Dogs killed rats, and she would crush this one and take his head to Spider. It would make a fitting tribute.

Karmash and Sebastian waited for her. The situation mandated only one possible solution. She had to split her team. They both knew it, and each waited to see who would be chosen.

Clive Keener operated only a few hundred miles from their last encounter, while Magdalene Moonflower made her den all the way in the south of the continent. Of the two, Clive was a better bet.

"Karmash."

The large man stepped forward and dropped to one knee, his head bowed, his white hair dripping down. Sebastian's face was carefully impassive.

"Take Soma, Mura, and Cotier and pay a visit to Magdalene Moonflower. You may have the smaller wyvern. If you find this Mar, inform me immediately and do not engage. Observe only and do not let him know he's been found. Am I clear?"

"Yes, my lady."

"You may go."

Karmash rose, spun, and walked away, barking orders. The three agents she had named followed him into the night.

Sebastian said nothing.

"You are more capable," she said quietly.

"Thank you, my lady." Sebastian's voice was a deeper snarl than usual.

She didn't often condescend to explain her reasoning, but fostering resentment in her second-in-command would lead to a disaster. "It doesn't matter who scouts an enemy. It only matters who apprehends him. Kaldar Mar is a snake, and like a snake, he's smart and calculating. If Karmash manages to find him and stay undetected, he will wait until we arrive to capture. If the Edger outsmarts Karmash, your reputation with our people will remain untarnished by failure."

Sebastian stared at Karmash disappearing into the Edge. A low, half-suppressed growl reverberated in his throat.

"I don't trust him. He doesn't care about the security of the country or the mission. He thinks only of himself."

Helena glanced at him. "He's one of my uncle's lieutenants. Do you question Spider's judgment?"

"No, my lady." Sebastian bowed his head.

She smiled at him. "You should. I question everyone's judgment, including my own. You must remember, Sebastian, Karmash is part of the Hand, which protects the colony. We're the Hounds, who defend the throne. We have a more refined sense of purpose and duty. That's why I am here, stepping into my uncle's place until he can return to active service. I must uphold the honor of our family name and do my duty to the Empire. I count on you to fight by my side."

Sebastian bowed his head. "Always, my lady."

She had expected nothing less. "Come. We travel north."

ELEVEN

KALDAR sat in a Starbucks across from the mall's Sears entrance, sipped coffee—it was slightly burned and bitter—and contemplated his sanity. Or rather, the lack thereof.

Audrey was right. They were rushing the scheme. They needed ten days. Two weeks would have been better. But the Hand wouldn't be delayed for long. In every con, there came a time when the plan fell apart, and one had to improvise. This was no different. He was used to flying by the seat of his pants; he welcomed it most of the time. Often, when he was under pressure, things miraculously snapped into place. But he wasn't flying solo.

First, there were the kids. As much as he reassured Audrey, there was a small chance one of them would stumble. True, both of them could defend themselves, but having the potential didn't always mean guaranteed results.

Then there was Audrey herself. Beautiful, sweet Audrey. Distracting Audrey. Audrey who monopolized his brain when it should be concerned with other things, like planning and calculating. Leaving her father and brother he understood, but walking away from a talent of that caliber to chase cheating husbands and insurance frauds in the Broken? She loved what she did; back in Pena's house, she had enjoyed every moment of it. The memory of her, cool, collected, and smooth as silk, popped into his head. *Mmmm. Audrey, Audrey, Audrey . . .*

Why had she stopped stealing? If there was ever a woman born to be a cat burglar, she was one. She could live like a queen in the Broken or in the Weird. But something had made her stop cold. The violent episode with the drug dealer damaged her, but it didn't break her. She'd made a conscious choice to walk away from her talent. Curiosity was once again killing him.

He'd tried to steal a kiss again before dropping her off, and she gave him a flat stare that slammed the door in his face.

In his experience, women fell into two categories: those who were too old or taken, and those who were up for some fun. With the right approach, most available women could be seduced. It had nothing to do with their character or their gender and everything to do with the basic human need for recognition and attention. He was a grifter. Seducing, whether it was to separate people from their money or to entice them into friendship or an affair, was his art. He was expert in it.

He wanted Audrey. He'd used the correct combination of flattery and playfulness. He complimented her. He said all the right things and employed all the right touches, and yet here they were in the exact same place they had been the moment they'd met. She still wouldn't give him the time of day. He won a battle here and there, but mostly he lost. He was tired of losing. He was tired of obsessing about her. It left him irritable and off-balance. And worst of all, Kaldar knew that the moment she reappeared on his horizon, his irritation would evaporate, and he'd be all wrapped up in trying to earn a smile. Like some puppy.

He was thirty-two years old. Way too old to be thinking in circles about some redhead with a plump cleavage.

His mug was empty. Kaldar looked up, considering if he should get another coffee. A brunette in oversized shades smiled at him from two tables away. *Hmm.* Denim shirt, baring toned arms; low-cut white pants, secured on her narrow hips by an expensive belt; Ariadna Alto shoes with a sky-high heel—he'd seen them on the cover of a tabloid when he went to a store to pick up a few things to complete his own transformation. A chunky necklace of caramel glass beads completed the look. She had money, and she was unsuccessfully trying to pretend to be carefree and casual.

He was wearing his businessman persona, the same one he wore when he'd come to trade for information with Alex Callahan. Most likely, she was just reacting to the right combination of signals his hair and clothes were sending. He smiled back at her, pleasant but not beguiling enough for an invitation.

"I leave you alone for a few hours, and you're off flirting."

Kaldar turned. His mouth fell open. A pale pink suit bordered with black embraced Audrey's perfect figure. Her hair was brushed and sprayed until it looked glossy and slightly stiff. A wide hat perched on her hair at an angle. Her makeup was heavy and flawless. Her jewelry would've made any self-respecting conman come to attention: bloated gold rings encrusted with diamonds; a tennis bracelet so iced, it was bordering on vulgar; diamond earrings; and, to top it all off, a heavy chain of gold beads studded with tiny diamond dots. She looked like a politician's trophy wife, full of money and ready to take "shop until you drop" to the next level. She was absolutely perfect, from the hat to the pointed toes of her thousand-dollar spiked heels.

Audrey cleared her throat and raised her eyebrows, pointedly looking at the chair in front of her. Kaldar got off his ass and held it out for her. She landed, one leg over the other, her French tip manicured fingers holding a tiny pink purse. He sat next to her, and the heavy scent of roses emanating from her almost made him sneeze.

"Jonathan Berman," he said, inclining his head.

"Olivia Berman." She held her hand out, and he kissed her fingers.

"Charmed."

"So do I look like I'm ready to spend some money I didn't earn?"

"You look divine," he told her, and meant every word. "Former beauty queen marries a wealthy asshole; all the means, none of the taste. Yonker will eat it up."

Audrey examined him, leaned over, and adjusted the knot on his tie. "You look pretty good yourself. The slicked-back hair is a nice touch."

"I was going for rich sleazeball."

"You got it."

They looked at each other for a long moment. She smiled, and he grinned back, unable to help himself.

"Why did you walk away from stealing?" Kaldar asked. And he just blurted it out. Brilliant move. Simply brilliant. Such finesse, such perfect timing.

"A lady never reveals all of her secrets," Audrey told him with a smug wink.

He probably could've come up with some clever retort if his mind had stopped imagining peeling off her clothes.

"Any word from the boys?" she asked.

"Nothing." Nothing was good; it meant the plan was proceeding as scheduled.

"What happens if Ed Yonker tries to check us out?"

Kaldar shrugged. "While you were getting the war paint on, I checked on a few things. Ed Yonker just put in a bid on the Graham Building. It's an old theater and a perfect location for him: its back faces an Edge bubble. I imagine he now ferries people into the Edge. If he obtains Graham's, he'll be set up just like Magdalene. He put in the highest bid—eleven million."

"And?"

"I put in one, too."

She stared at him.

"It's Friday afternoon. It will take them at least a business day to run credit checks and other things. I've spent a long time building up this identity. Jonathan Berman has rock-solid credit and owns enough fictitious real estate to buy Donald Trump. If they dig deeper, we're in trouble, but they won't until Monday, and by Monday, we need to be gone. Shall we?"

"We shall."

He tossed some bills on the table, rose, and held out his hand to help her from her chair. She put her hand in his, and he gently led her down to the parking lot.

"It must hurt to burn an identity like that," Audrey said.

"Small price to pay."

"How do you do it? How do you keep up with things in the Weird and in the Broken?"

"A gentleman never reveals all of his secrets."

She laughed, leaning her head to the side, and Kaldar wanted to kiss her neck. "Please. You're dying to boast."

"All right." He shrugged. "I've spent most of my life trading with the Broken. I know many useful people, and I make it a point to remember their names and the names of their wives or husbands. I'm pleasant and charming, and I always come bearing gifts, so they don't mind doing me small favors."

"Why do you do this, Kaldar? Is it for the thrill?"

"That's part of it."

"And the rest?"

"I want the Hand to suffer," he said. "I'd burn all my identities and start clean if I had to."

"To kill one of them?"

He knew his face had gone predatory, but he didn't bother to hide it. "Oh no. I want the whole thing."

"The entire Hand?"

"Yes. I want to end the entire organization as we know it."

Audrey blinked. "You're aiming high."

"The last feud my family endured lasted for over a century." He allowed himself a small smirk. "Mars hold grudges."

"I'll have to take care never to feud with you," she said.

"I wish you would feud with me. Then, when I won, I'd reap sweet rewards."

"Picturing me as your love slave?" Audrey laughed.

Kaldar nodded. "And you are divine."

"And what if I won?"

"Then I would be your love slave, of course."

"So you'd win in either case."

"Precisely."

Audrey searched his face for something, then bit her lip. "Did you get us new wheels?" she asked.

Kaldar gave her a flat look. "Please." He dipped his hand into his pocket, pulled out the remote, and pressed the button. A black Hummer answered with a short beep.

"A Hummer?" Her Southern accent was getting thicker by the second. "Shooog, you shouldn't have."

"Only the best for my doll."

She reached over and patted his cheek. "It's too bad this partnership will be over soon. We'd own this town."

Huh. "It doesn't have to be over soon."

"Oh no, it does. It definitely does."

JACK watched the huge, shiny car swing into the street. They had been giving out flyers for most of the day. The two of them kept to themselves, and they had gotten most of their flyers handed out and had had to go back to get a second stack. Paul, the guy with the placard, even complimented them. At lunch, George and he got a sandwich each and some bottled water. The sandwich was okay, but nothing like Rose's cooking.

He missed Rose. It stabbed at him suddenly. He missed his sister, her voice, her scent, his room, his stuff. He missed the smell of the house. He even missed Declan. It all seemed so far away somehow. Jack shook his head, trying to clear the memories. Now wasn't the time to get all sad and whiny. George had let Paul talk them into a few more hours of work with the promise of a hot dinner. Jack had made all the right "I want more food" noises, and George finally reluctantly agreed.

The large black car slowed down a few feet away in front of two kids. The window rolled down, and Audrey's voice rang through the street. "Oh my goodness! Shoog, look at the children. You boys are adorable. What are you doing?"

"We're giving out flyers," the smaller kid said.

"Is this for a school project?"

"We don't go to school," the bigger kid said.

"That's silly. How can you not go to school? What do your parents think about this?"

The bigger kid shrugged. "We don't have parents."

"You're orphans? Oh, my God! Honey, give the children some money."

Kaldar's voice said something gruff. Audrey reached through the window and handed two twenty-dollar bills to each of the boys.

The other children abandoned their customers and made a beeline for the car. George grabbed Jack by the shoulder, still acting. "She's giving out money, come on!" They ran to the vehicle.

"We have no parents." The smaller kid at the window was sniffing for emphasis. "The church makes us hand these out to earn our lunch."

"What? Who makes you do this?"

Several hands pointed at Paul, who stared at the whole scene with owl eyes. "He does!"

"Is that nasty man forcing you to *work for your food*?"

Heads nodded.

The car door swung open, and Audrey stepped out onto the pavement. She was wearing a ridiculous pink outfit, and her hair was shiny and hard like a helmet. She tucked her purse under her arm. "We will just see about that. Hey, you!" She pointed at Paul. "Yes, you over there! How dare you exploit these children?"

Paul raised his arms. "No, ma'am, look, that isn't what this is."

The other door opened, and Kaldar stepped out. He looked the way he looked when he'd gone to Rose Cliff, dressed in a suit, with his hair slicked back.

Audrey put her hands on her hips. "Well, is it or isn't it?"

"Is it what?"

"What this is?"

Kaldar walked over to them, looking exactly the way Rose looked when Jack forgot to wipe his feet and tracked bloody mud all over the carpets.

Paul blinked again. "Look, you got it wrong. We're trying to help the kids."

"By making them work for their food? I have news for you, Mister, slavery has been abolished in this country in eighteen ninety with the Immunization Proclamation," Audrey said.

"You mean Emancipation and 1863 . . ." Paul murmured weakly.

Behind Audrey, Kaldar shook his head at him.

"Don't try to confuse me! You're using these boys as slave labor. Maybe they should go and pick cotton for you next."

"Umm . . ."

"Well, I am telling you, these kids won't have to work tonight." Audrey looked over the kids. "Who wants McDonald's?"

Jack stuck his arm out with everyone else, and yelled, "Me, me, me!"

Audrey swung to Kaldar. "Honey?"

Kaldar sighed, opened his wallet, took out a thick wad of cash, and deposited it into Audrey's hand. Audrey waved it around. "Let's go, children! I saw a Mickey D's around the corner."

She marched down the street, everyone following her.

"Wait . . ." Paul called out. "You can't do this."

"Trust me," Kaldar told him. "It's best to just go with the flow when she's like this. Come on, I'll buy you a cup of coffee."

KALDAR walked next to Paul through the shiny, polished hallway of the Church of the Blessed and pretended to listen to the man droning on about the camp and the runaways, while keeping an eye on Audrey and the gaggle of children ahead. They had gone to McDonald's, and, afterward, Audrey insisted on seeing where the "poor boys" were sleeping. She made it sound like she expected them to be chained to the walls in some cell somewhere, which caused their handler no end of distress. Paul was a true believer. He was honest and hardworking, and he genuinely wanted to help the children.

"You see, most of them really have no place to go. It's horrible what they're reduced to on the streets. Drugs, violence. Some of them even prostitute themselves. I had two boys just today standing there, looking as hungry as could be, and I had to promise that nobody would touch them, or they wouldn't come near me. What is the world coming to, I ask you? These children, they're suspicious of charity. I mean, wrap your mind about that one, will you? Childhood should be a happy thing. At least this way they get two decent meals a day."

Ahead, the double doors opened, and Ed Yonker entered the hallway. He looked exactly like his photograph: well-groomed, tall, with clear blue eyes and a well-oiled smile. Kaldar disliked him instantly.

"Paul, what's going on here?"

"Immunization," Audrey proudly told him, and kept walking.

"What?"

Kaldar sighed.

"She means emancipation," Paul said helpfully.

"I see. Who is being emancipated?"

Paul launched into a long explanation, complete with arm waving. Kaldar studied Ed Yonker, and Ed was clearly doing his best to study him. His gaze slid from Kaldar's shoes, to the expensive suit, to the Rolex on his wrist, to the three-hundred-dollar tie, then, finally, to his eyes.

Paul was winding down.

"You must excuse my wife," Kaldar said. "She has a soft spot for underprivileged children, and she gets carried away. We'll be on our way shortly."

"It's no trouble. No trouble at all." Ed Yonker stuck out his hand. "Edward Yonker. Everyone here just calls me Ed Junior. We're not very formal here."

Kaldar took the hand and shook it. "Jonathan Berman. As I said, Mr. Yonker, we'll be on our way soon."

"Please, just Ed will do." All three of them looked after Audrey's retreating behind, clasped in a skintight skirt. Yonker raised his eyebrows a bit, appraising Audrey like a piece of meat in the market, and Kaldar felt a powerful urge to hit him in the mouth.

"If your wife wants to make sure the boys aren't mistreated, then I say more power to her. In our day and age, it's so rare to find people who take interest in God's less-fortunate children."

"Thank you for understanding," Kaldar said.

"Come, I'll show you around." Ed strode next to him, shoulders back, firm gait. No trying to dominate, but secure in his authority all the same. They went through another set of double doors, down the hallway, and entered a small dormitory.

Ahead, Audrey called, "Y'all don't rush now, I don't want any of you falling."

"Is that a Southern accent, if you don't mind my asking?" Ed asked. "Georgia perhaps?"

"Florida," Kaldar said, just out of spite.

"Oh. What brings you to sunny San Diego?"

"Business. Real estate."

"There is plenty of that around here." Ed gave a hearty laugh.

"Indeed."

Audrey inspected the dormitory, letting the boys lead her.

"Your wife is very passionate about doing good works, I see."

"She is very generous," Kaldar nodded. "Luckily, I'm in no danger of bankruptcy."

Ed chuckled. If he had been a cartoon, his eyes would've ignited with dollar signs.

Audrey came full circle and headed back toward them. Her eyes shone, and her face was slightly flushed, just enough to put all sorts of interesting thoughts into a man's head. She held on to Jack and ruffled his hair. "Isn't he just the most adorable thing you've ever seen? I want to take him home."

"Feel better, doll?" Kaldar asked her.

Audrey let go of Jack, leaned forward, and Kaldar kissed her, carefully so as not to smudge her lipstick. Their lips barely touched, but for once he was grateful for the tailored trousers of his suit. Most men didn't go erect from a casual kiss from their wives.

"Yes, I do. Thank you, darling."

"Livie, this is Ed Yonker. He's in charge here."

"Nice to meet you, preacher."

Audrey beamed. Kaldar was prepared for the smile, but it took even him off guard. Ed Yonker blinked. Paul had to have a private moment studying the floor. Kaldar slid his arm around Audrey and cupped her butt possessively, a fact Ed Yonker noticed and obviously filed for further reference. Dear Gods, Audrey had a nice ass.

"I do miss going to church," Audrey prattled on. "Jonny has been so busy lately. One day we're in Seattle, then in Nevada, now here. We never get to worship anymore. Especially in such a lovely church. Y'all seem like such nice people, and your kids are darling."

Ed finally collected his wits. "As you can see, only a small group of our younguns stay here. Most of them stay with us at the camp."

Audrey opened her eyes wider. "What kind of camp?"

"That's where most of our services take place. The Blessed Youth Witness Camp and the Wooden Cathedral."

Audrey turned to Kaldar. "Can we see the camp, darling?"

"Not today, doll," he told her. "I have a business meeting."

"I don't mean to be rude or to upset you," Ed said. "But the Wooden Cathedral is a special place for our congregation. That's where we worship and meet in fellowship. One must aspire to be a member of our church to visit there."

They were losing Ed's attention.

Audrey pretended to pout and made a small dog noise. Nicely done, but Ed still didn't seem involved.

"No, Livie," Kaldar shook his head. "As I said, I have an auction to attend today. Ed has his congregation to look after. He can't exactly give us a grand tour. I do apologize again for the interruption."

"No problem at all." Ed nodded, amicable. The hint had flown clear over his head. Ed was swimming away and fast. "What is it you said you did?"

"Real estate," Kaldar said.

"My husband provides housing for poor people," Audrey said proudly, petting his shoulder. "He owns apartments, and when people can't pay their rent, he buys them back and turns them into stores."

Kaldar grimaced. "Livie . . ."

"It's something to be proud of," she said.

Slum lord, tons of money, beautiful wife without a brain, and loads of guilt. Come on, Ed. Come on. Take the bait.

Ed considered it. The thought flashed in his eyes for a moment and dulled. "Well, it's a pleasure to meet you folks. Paul here will show you out."

Damn it.

"Later!" Kaldar raised his hand and steered Audrey to the exit.

"I really wanted to see the camp," Audrey pouted.

"Sorry, doll. Besides, tonight we have to go visit Magdalene, remember? Your brother recommended her?"

Behind them, Ed Yonker came to life like a shark sensing a drop of blood in the water.

Three.

Kaldar put a little pressure on the small of Audrey's back. *And we're walking away. Walking away . . .*

Audrey let out a cute sigh. "I suppose. It will be boring. Those people are always boring."

"It's supposed to be inspiring," Kaldar said. "I'm sure you'll like it. Supposedly, she gets great results. One session, and your mind is sharper. Your brother swears by her."

Two.

"You're already the sharpest man I know." Audrey leaned into him, slipping her arm around his waist. It felt like heaven.

"Thank you, doll."

One.

"Mr. Berman!" Yonker called.

Audrey squeezed his side a little. Kaldar turned. "Yes?"

Yonker came toward them. "If you folks attend tonight's service, I can see to it that you can come and worship with us tomorrow at the Wooden Cathedral."

Got you, you greedy sonovabitch.

"We don't want to be a bother," Kaldar said.

"Please!" Ed raised his hand, as if blessing them. "As a fellow Christian, I'd hate for you to miss out on the opportunity to witness God's glory. I won't take no for an answer. Tonight at seven. I'll be looking for you."

Fifteen minutes later they were out in fresh air. They stayed in part, strolling leisurely to their Hummer. Kaldar opened the door and helped Audrey into her seat, then unhurriedly got in, started the engine, and pulled away from the curb.

The church disappeared behind the buildings.

"The kids did great," Audrey said.

"The kids did fantastic," he agreed.

"Risky mentioning Magdalene," Audrey said.

"We were losing him."

"Still risky. You take chances, Kaldar."

"Fortune favors the brave."

"Or the prepared." Audrey pulled a prepaid cell from her purse and punched in a number.

"What are you doing?" he asked.

"Calling Magdalene to let her know we're canceling our evening appointment. Who knows how long Ed's reach is? He might have someone in her office."

JACK watched Kaldar and Audrey exit the building.

"The Witness work is over for the day," Paul called out. "Go on."

The kids around them scattered. Some went back to the dormitory, others headed for the exit. In a moment, only Jack and George were left standing. Farther down the hall, Ed Yonker stuck one finger into his ear and raised his cell phone to the other.

"No dinner today. Sorry, boys." Paul spread his arms. "That rich woman messed up all of our plans. But you had McDonald's anyway."

"It's fine," George said.

Jack grimaced. "Thanks for nothing. We'll be going now."

Paul reached into his pocket and peeled off a small rectangle of paper. "This is the address of the Children Services Center. If you go there and register, you can come here and hand out more flyers. If you do really well, you can sleep in the dormitory here, too."

"Dude!" George leveled a look of pure scorn at him. "We'll find our own place to sleep."

Ed Yonker snapped the cell phone closed and stomped down the hall toward them. A heavy stink of cloves clung to his clothes and hair. Jack moved out of Yonker's way. George occasionally smelled like that after a session in the estate laboratory. Ed was playing with heavy-duty magic.

Ed's gaze snagged on Jack. "You!"

Jack cringed. "I didn't do nothing."

"Leave my brother alone!" George moved forward.

Ed pointed at Jack. "The Berman woman likes you." He turned to Paul. "Clean them up. I need them on their best behavior tonight and tomorrow."

"What? But they aren't registered with the Center . . ."

"I don't give a goddamn if they're registered or not. That bastard Berman is trying to buy the Graham Building from under me. No wonder that slick sonovabitch was trying so hard to slip away. That's fine. He might have fifteen million, but I've got my hooks into his wife. Before long, he'll be signing Graham over to me. Mark my words." Ed stabbed his finger in Jack's direction. "Get them cleaned up, Paul. I want them at tonight's service and tomorrow at the camp front and center." He turned and stomped down the hall.

Paul stared at them helplessly.

"A hundred bucks," George said. "Fifty for my brother, fifty for me."

Haeh-heh. "For fifty bucks we'll be nice to the rich lady." Jack nodded. "She likes my hair."

"And if we stay overnight, we get our own room. With a lock," George said. "And we sleep light."

Paul shook his head. "Fine. A hundred bucks and a separate room it is."

"Deal!" George stuck his hand out, and Paul shook it.

* * *

THE church service was boring and tedious, Jack decided. George had once dragged him to a lecture Declan's grand-uncle Tserebus was giving on the practical applications of flash. This was only slightly less dull.

It started exciting enough. Paul herded them into a huge room and made them sit next to Audrey and Kaldar. Jack sat on Audrey's side and George on Kaldar's side. Then a big choir came out and sang "hallelujah," at first quiet, then louder and louder, until Ed Yonker appeared from the back and walked through the aisle, shaking hands and hugging people.

"He thinks he's a rock star," Audrey murmured under her breath. Her mouth was still smiling. Jack couldn't figure out how she could talk like that, with her mouth stretched out.

Yonker kept hugging people until he got all the way to the stage. Then he picked up a microphone and started talking. And talking. And talking . . .

". . . God wants us to live a full life. Let's think about it for a moment. What does living a full life really mean? It means being healthy, in spirit, in body, and in your work. God loves us. And that love, oh that love is all-encompassing. We are His special children. We are the chosen ones." Yonker waved his arm. "God has chosen us above aaaall of his creations. Above the beasts of the forest, above the fish of the sea, above the birds in the air, above the angels in Heaven! God wants us to succeed! Are we a success if we're not healthy?"

Yonker held the microphone out to the audience.

The crowd answered, "NO."

"No." Yonker got terribly serious. "Are we a success if we're not happy?"

"NO."

"If we are God's chosen, than how can we glorify His Name if we're sad and wretched? How can we be a witness to His Power if we are weak and lacking? We can't. We must stand strong. We must stand united. We are the Blessed. We must provide an example of His Love for us, for we are His Will upon this Earth. We must spread His Glory to the farthest corners, so those who don't know Him look at us and seek Him out."

Jack pondered if he could get away with sneaking out to "use the washroom" and decided he couldn't.

"People come to me, and they say, 'Ed, how can we help bring God's will to those less fortunate?' And I say, 'Share. Share the blessings that God bestowed on you. Give of yourself to the Church, and the Church will glorify God in your name.' I will tell you now, those who sit on their checkbooks and hoard their money in their bank accounts, those people do not witness for our God. You must give! Write that check today. Fill out that direct transfer form the children handed you at the entrance. Fill it out and sign your name if you want to go to Heaven, and send it to the business office."

Yonker kept talking. Jack yawned and closed his eyes. If only he could curl up in his chair . . .

A finger jabbed him in the ribs. His eyes snapped open. Next to him, Audrey was listening to Ed. Her lips barely moved. "Stay awake."

Jack sighed and stared at Yonker walking around onstage. For a while, he imagined what would happen if he turned into a lynx. People would run around, and he would growl and scare them. Then he wondered what Yonker would look like with a mustache.

Finally, people came through the aisles, passing some sort of platter around. Kaldar dropped a folded stack of bills held together with a small clip on it, and Jack gave it to some older lady standing in the aisle. The old lady made big eyes at the clip and took the platter away.

Then there was more annoying preaching: blah-blah-blah, we are so good, blah-blah-blah, God wants us to have money, then Yonker went offstage to the back while the choir sang some more, and Paul came to get them. Audrey hugged Jack and told him to be a really good boy and that she would see him soon.

Paul took them to the back of the church, all the way to

the service entrance. A van waited for them. Paul opened the van door. Two other kids sat in the backseat, a dark-headed girl and a tall, lanky-looking kid with freckles and red hair.

"Get in," Paul said.

George pondered the van.

"We're going to camp," Paul said patiently. "That's all we're doing."

"Climb in already." Jack pushed George a little.

"Don't shove me."

"Move so I don't have to."

They climbed into the van and bickered for the next fifteen minutes, until Paul told them that he would turn the van around and that, so help him God, making Ed happy wasn't worth this. They both decided that would be a good time to shut up and rode the rest of the way in silence. The van crept up a narrow road, angling away from the main streets.

"Now this is going to feel a little weird," Paul said. "There is nothing to be scared of. Just the pressure in the air here is different."

"Why?" George asked.

"Subterranean gas," Paul said. "It comes out through the cracks in the road. Take a deep breath and try to relax, okay?"

The van came to a stop. Paul stepped out and opened the side door. "Melanie and Robert, out. And you, too."

Jack climbed out of the van. Melanie took his hand. "Don't worry; it feels funny the first time."

Jack rolled his eyes. George and the red-haired kid were trying to come up with some sort of arrangement that didn't involve their holding hands. Finally, the tall kid put his hand on George's forearm.

"Let's go." Melanie stepped into the boundary. "If you feel bad, you tell me, and we'll go slowly."

Jack took a step.

The pressure of the boundary ground on him. Magic ripped through Jack, thudding in his blood, saturating his muscles. Scents flooded his nose. He felt strong again.

Slowly, step by step, Melanie led him through the boundary to the Edge on the other side. Behind them, the city still teemed with life and the noise of cars, but before them wilderness stretched. Scraggly woods sheathed hills, growing denser in the distance. A lonely road led over them into the distance, where a mountain range jutted out of the hills. He hadn't seen those kinds of mountains when Kaldar drove them around the city. Hills, sure. Mountains, no.

Melanie smiled at him. "You made it."

George yanked his arm out of the red-haired kid's grip.

"You okay?" Paul asked.

That's right, I'm not supposed to know what just happened, Jack recalled. "Yeah," he said. "Where is the city?"

"It's complicated. Come on, boys, get into the van. The camp's straight ahead up that mountain. That's where you'll be staying tonight."

The road took them over the hills, all the way up the spine of a mountain bristling with pines. They climbed and climbed, the van creaking, until finally they conquered the apex and rolled to a wooden arch marking the entrance. Beyond the arch, wooden buildings waited, all simple rectangles sitting side by side in two rows, and at the end of the row a large structure rose. Jack had expected a church, like an old Edge church they had seen a thousand times in their small Edge town of East Laporte. This church looked more like a barn, complete with heavy double doors. A man with a rifle stood at the entrance.

Paul steered the van to the arch, stopped to talk to some girl sitting on the side, and drove on, to one of the smaller buildings.

"This is your place for the night," Paul said. "Lillian will make sure that you guys get sheets and toothbrushes and all that issued to you. Okay? It's just you two in the room, since you guys are all jumpy, so you can lock the door at night."

"Why do they get a separate room?" the tall kid from the back asked.

"Because I said so," Paul said. "Anyway, go on, you two."

Paul wasn't a bad guy, Jack decided, once the van pulled away. He just had a lousy boss. The way Jack looked at it, you should know who you were working for. They worked for Kaldar, who was a cheat, a thief, and a gambler, but he was honest with them about it. George swung the door open, and they went inside. The room was small, barely any room between two beds. About fifteen minutes later, a young girl with freckles on her nose brought their sheets, toothbrushes, some towels, and two paper bags. She told them that food was served in the cafeteria, but they'd missed dinner, so they'd have to get dry rations. She smiled at George a lot.

Jack's paper bag contained another turkey sandwich, some bars made out of grain and seeds, and an apple. Jack ate the sandwich and left the bar alone. He wasn't a bird, and he wouldn't be eating any seeds.

They locked the door and settled in their beds to wait for sunset.

Two hours later, the sun finally rolled past the horizon. George sat up in his bunk and pulled a plastic bag out of the pocket of his hoodie. Inside, a small furry body lay still.

"Should've gone with the squirrel," Jack said quietly.

"Rat is better. They can get into tighter spaces."

"Yeah, but people see a rat, they try to kill it. They see a squirrel and go, 'Oh, how cute, look at its fluffy tail!'"

"It's dark. Nobody will see it." George closed his eyes.

"George?"

"Mmm?"

"What's the point of this church?"

"That's how Yonker makes money." George shrugged.

"Yes, I get that part. But what do people who go to his church get out of it?"

George furrowed his eyebrows. "People are scared to die. Most religions say that there is life after death, that only your body dies, but your essence, your soul, keeps living. Yonker tells them that if they give him money, their soul will go to a good place."

"Is Yonker a god?"

"Of course not."

"So how can he control where the soul goes?"

"He doesn't," George answered.

"So he lies."

"Yes."

"Why do people believe him?"

"Because most people are decent, Jack. They don't want to think that someone would stand up like that in front of a crowd and lie just to get their money. They want to believe that they're doing something good when they go to church."

"Do you believe in gods?"

George sighed. "I believe you have to be a good person. Whatever you do, good or bad, it will come back to you."

It made sense, Jack decided.

"Look, not all churches are like Yonker's church," George said. "Some of them are good; some of them are bad. You have to decide for yourself if you want to go and which god you want to worship or not. It's up to you not to be a sucker. Life gets really hard sometimes. You don't remember when mom died, but I do. I cried, and Grandmere told me that Mom was in heaven, in a beautiful garden, where she was happy and safe. It helped. Anyway, we'll talk about this later."

George touched the rat. A faint pulse of magic sparked from his finger to the dark fur. The little rodent rolled to its feet and sat unnaturally still.

"Ready?" George glanced at him.

Jack took a deep breath, clearing his mind. He had to commit every word George said to memory. Kaldar had a recorder, but both he and Audrey worried that the boys would be searched, so in the end they decided not to risk bringing it. Now he was the recorder. All those memorization drills William made him do would finally pay off. "Ready."

George stared into space. The rat scurried to the door, squeezed out through the narrow gap between the lower edge and the floor, and vanished from view.

"Log houses on the right, one, two, three, four, five," George said, his voice a low monotone. Jack focused, committing each word to memory. "Identical houses on the left. Six, seven. The houses end in a wide space. Cafeteria on the left. Guardhouse on the right. Three people are playing cards. The one on the left is upset because he can't remember the poker combinations. He's accusing the others of cheating him. Two more people are in their bunks. Five guards total. There is a gun rack with rifles. Pathway from the wide space leading northwest. Trees. More trees. The path is maybe two hundred elbows in length. Large building."

George fell silent. Jack waited.

"I'm at the ward. The Night plan won't work. These wards are really old, at least as rooted in as ours were on the house in the Edge. You probably can get through in the lynx form, but none of us in human form can penetrate this. Going back into the camp now."

So much for stealing the gadget.

"I'm at the church. The inside is large, one, two, three . . . twenty-five rows, in two sections in the middle of the floor. A lot of open space on the sides and before the stage. Another guard in the front row, carrying a rifle. He's reading a book. The pulpit is empty. There is magical residue. Hallway to the right." George's face jerked.

"A cat. Damn it."

"Did you get eaten?" Jack murmured, and cursed inwardly. George was so deep in trance he wouldn't hear.

"I'm hiding under a mop bucket. He broke my neck. Hurt like hell."

For the next ten minutes, they sat quietly.

"Okay, he went away." George winced. "Two rooms. One on the right has another guard. He's drinking coffee. The door on the left is fitted tight. I'll have to backtrack and chew through the wall."

Jack growled to himself. The longer George stayed in the trance, the harder it was to bring him back.

"This is a really thick wall," George said. "It will be a while."

Curse it.

Footsteps. Jack tensed. Closer, closer. Someone knocked on the door.

Go away.

The knocking persisted.

Jack padded to the door, dropped down, and sampled the draft floating under. The freckled girl from before.

He got up and opened the door half an inch. "Hey. How's it hanging?"

She blinked. "Umm, is your brother here?"

Jack braced the door with his foot. If George started mumbling, their lives would get complicated fast. "He's sleeping."

The girl licked her lower lip nervously. "Maybe you could wake him up."

"He's tired. I'm tired, too."

"I'm sure he wouldn't mind if you woke him up for me."

The way she stood, determined, one foot forward, meant she wouldn't go away on her own. He had to say something mean now, or they'd be stuck here with the door half-opened, and George could start talking any moment. Jack rummaged in his brain.

"He has a girlfriend. And she's prettier than you."

The freckled girl took a step back. "You know what? Fuck you."

"Fuck you back. Bye now." Jack shut the door and latched it. *Phew.*

An hour passed. Another. This was taking too long.

Finally, George announced, "Okay, I'm through. The room is empty except for the table. On the table there is a square glass case. I see it now. It's a low-grade Karuman emotional amplifier, level three, standard cloak-chain model, known as the Eyes of Karuman. There is a book in my luggage on automatics; it should have a picture. This item was used by a cult, and it's been banned in the realms for at least a hundred years. It doesn't just influence emotions; it cooks your brain until you become a fanatic. Judging by the mineral crust on the lower edges of the disks, this thing has been used a lot. You need to tell Kaldar and Audrey that when the device is active, the people likely think Yonker is a prophet and will defend him with their lives. But the effect is short-lived, so he has to continuously use it to keep the congregation together. The use of the device induces euphoria, and some research suggests that the congregation will exhibit dependent tendencies."

"English, George," Jack muttered.

". . . meaning they are addicted to the way the Eyes of Karuman makes them feel."

Great. Crazy addicted religious people.

"The device consists of two golden disks two inches in diameter. Each disk has a dark blue stone, probably sapphire, pillow cut, an inch and a half in diameter. There are five glyphs on each disk, radiating from the stone out. From the top going clockwise, glyph for air, glyph for mind . . ." George launched into a detailed description of the parts.

Jack memorized it all. Finally, George took a deep breath. "Okay. Bring me back now."

Jack grabbed his shoulder and shook him. "Wake up."

Nothing. Fear shot through Jack. It was all right. He still had a backup. He had water.

"Wake up!"

No response. Crap.

Jack grabbed the bottle of water, pulled the lid off, and dumped it on George's head.

"Anytime," George said.

Curse it.

Jack slapped him. Nothing. Another slap. Nothing. Panic swelled in him.

"It's not working," George said.

"No shit." Jack paced back and forth, like a caged tiger. "Don't panic."

"I'm not panicking." He didn't know why he kept talking. It was not like George could see him or hear him.

"Try burning me."

"With what, George? We have no matches." With each second, the gulf between his brother's mind and his body grew wider. They should've thought about this. They should've brought something, a lighter, matches, something.

"No wait. We don't have any matches. I forgot. Jack, you have to hurt me."

"You're crazy."

"I know it sounds nuts, but it works. You have to do it, because if you don't, I'll be stuck in this rat. Pain, Jack. Severe pain. My body needs to send me a signal that it's fighting for its life, or it will just go to sleep. You could try breaking my fingers. That works sometimes—"

Screw it. Jack grasped George's neck into an armlock and squeezed, hurting but avoiding the jugular. If he put pressure on it, George would pass out. Three seconds, and George gasped for breath. Jack kept squeezing. George's face turned purple. Jack hauled him up. George made no effort to resist. He just hung there like a cloth doll. Jack kept squeezing. He couldn't remember how long it took to choke a man to death. Of all the things, how could he, with his perfect memory, forget that one? Was it three minutes? Two? He tightened his hold.

Please, George. Please.

George's hands clawed his arm. Jack let go, and his brother crashed to the floor and sucked in a long, hoarse breath.

"Are you back?"

George curled on the floor, gasping, trying to breathe.

Jack yanked him up. "Are you back?!"

"Yes," George croaked. "Let go."

Jack dropped him, and George fell, smashing his head on the bed frame. "Ow."

Jack crouched on the bed. He had almost squeezed the life out of his brother. A little longer, and, one way or another, George would have been dead. Jack realized he was cold. His face was drenched in sweat. In his head, he was holding George's dead body.

It was over. It was done and over, and everything was well. Everything was fine.

George grinned at him from the floor. His face was red,

and a dark swollen line marked his neck. Jack held out his hand, his brother grasped it, and Jack pulled him to his feet.

George rubbed his neck. "Shit, this hurts. Your turn."

Jack rolled back off his bed and pulled off his clothes. "The freckled girl came to see you."

"Oh, what did she want?"

"She wanted to talk to you."

George grinned and winced. "Ow. My whole face hurts now. What the hell did you do?"

"Just a standard choke hold." Jack took a deep breath and let the Wild off its chain. The world crashed down around him. Pain tore through his muscles, grasped his bones, and twisted them in their sockets. His body whipped the floor, thrashing and kicking, lost in a confusion of agony and magic. He felt himself stretch into the distance, impossibly far, then he was back. Jack rolled to his feet. George was looking down on him from the bed.

"You have four hours. At five, the sun begins to rise, and there is light."

Jack bared his fangs, panting. Four hours would be plenty.

George opened the door, peered outside, and shut it. "The freckled girl," he breathed. "She's outside."

It had been like two hours. She couldn't have waited there for two hours, could she? Everyone in this place was crazy.

"I'll go first," George said.

Jack crawled under the bed to hide and squinted so his eyes wouldn't give him away. George swung the door open and stepped out. "Greetings."

Greetings? George, you dumb-ass.

"Hey there," the girl said. "Your bother said you were sleeping."

"I was." George's voice slipped into his Cursed Prince tone, calm, measured, with a touch of a blueblood accent. "He said you came by a long time ago. Did you wait here this whole time?"

"I took a walk."

Bullshit.

"I don't blame you. The moon is so beautiful tonight."
George looked up. The moonlight spilled from the sky, bathing him, and George's yellow hair seemed to shimmer, almost white. The freckled girl stared at him, googly-eyed. Jack rolled his eyes.

"You must be tired," George said. "Why don't we sit down? I think I saw a bench somewhere."

"There are a whole bunch of benches in front of that building."

"That's wonderful!" George's voice pulsed with joy, as if she'd given him a present. Jack would have grimaced if he could. "You know this camp so well."

"My mom works in the cafeteria. I'm stuck here for the whole summer. There is nobody to talk to except the Bibleheads and the runaway kids, and all of them are assholes. It's so boring."

"Not anymore, I hope." George smiled.

"No, I guess not."

They turned right and walked away.

"So tell me about yourself," George's voice floated on the draft. "What's your name?"

"Lisa."

"That's a lovely name. What do you like to do?"

"I like to read. I read about vampires a lot . . ."

Jack sprang from under the bed and dashed into the woods. The tree trunks and branches blurred. He ran and ran, as if he had wings. In that moment, with the moon rising over the treetops, the forest was his for the taking. He was the king of everything he saw.

Three hours later, when he crawled back into the room, having recited everything George had told him into Kaldar's recorder, George was already in his bed. George waited until he shifted back into his human body.

"How did it go?"

"It's done." He had met Kaldar and Audrey near the Edge boundary and recited everything George told him into a recorder.

"Good."

"How did it go with the freckled girl?"

"She thinks I'm a vampire."

Jack snickered and fell asleep.

"**WHAT** do you think?" Gaston held up two disks made of pale brown plaster.

Audrey examined the disks. The three of them had worked on the fake disks for the last two hours. Jack's recount only confirmed what they already suspected—stealing the Eyes of Karuman out of the camp was too risky. The wards guarding it had been rooted too deeply into the soil, and even assuming they did somehow break through the magic defenses, the camp was filled with children and armed guards. If anything went wrong during the heist, the chances of a child's being hurt in the confusion were too great. Even Kaldar wouldn't risk it. They had to go with the Day plan—replacing the real Eyes of Karuman with a fake copy—and hope they got out of the camp alive.

Forging the stones for the Eyes had been easy; George had recognized them as the Weird's pillow cut, which was just another name for the antique cushion cut, halfway between an oval and a square with sixty-four facets. Both she and Kaldar had handled enough gems in their lifetimes to reproduce the stones of the correct cut and size. Two thousand dollars at a specialized glass shop got them two chunks of glass that looked close enough to pass a cursory inspection. The disks were harder. For one, they had glyphs, and while Gaston was a wizard with clay and brush, the glyphs proved tricky.

The disks resembled what Jack described; he was very thorough, but that didn't change the fact that all they had to go on was a description and a picture in a book. In the picture, the disks were squares and the stones were green.

"So?" Gaston asked.

"They have to look like gold," Audrey told him. Next to her, Ling watched them with her small black eyes. She and Jack's cat had made friends finally. The cat was off hunting in the woods, but instead of going with him, Ling stuck to Audrey like glue, almost as if the little beast sensed her anxiety.

"They will, once I magic them up."

The bushes parted, and Kaldar made his way into the clearing. "Got it." He handed her a thick gold chain. Audrey held it up to the picture.

"Close enough," Gaston said. "Once I put this together, it will look like the real thing."

"I've been breaking my head about how we'll make this switch." Audrey pointed to the diagram on the piece of paper, which she'd drawn after listening to Jack's recording. "I'm guessing he goes into the room, puts the device on, does the service, goes back, and takes the device off. The guards likely watch him the whole time."

"So we hit him before or after the service," Kaldar said.

"After won't work," Audrey said. "You saw him, he goes off to the back. It has to be before, when he is doing his hug and handshake bit."

Kaldar nodded. "Not only that, but if we let him mind-rape the congregation, and he realizes we're up to something, they will tear us to pieces. Also, I don't know about you, but I'm not eager to sit there and let him magic me into thinking he's the new messiah."

Hitting Ed before the service was risky, they both knew it. The device was his most prized possession. He knew its weight and feel like the back of his hand. If he realized that something had gone wrong, there would be hell to pay.

But they were in too deep to back out now. They needed Ed Yonker's gadget to get the invitation from Magdalene, and they needed the invitation to get into de Braose's impregnable castle and steal back the bracelet diffusers. It felt like tumbling down the stairs—once started, they couldn't stop, and each step sent them deeper and deeper into danger.

"I can distract Yonker," Audrey said. "But stealing the device isn't my thing."

"I've got it covered," Kaldar said.

Really. "So what, you're a pickpocket, too?"

Kaldar paused, as if considering something. "Check your left pocket."

Oh no. No, he didn't. She thrust her fingers into the pocket of her jeans. They found empty space and fabric. Her grandmother's cross was gone. The cross was everything. It was a reminder of the only stable time in her life; it was a symbol of her finally saying, "Enough." She could lose everything, but as long as she kept that cross, she would be okay.

Audrey held out her hand. "Give it back."

"Don't be mad."

"Give it back right now, Kaldar."

Ling let out an angry raccoon noise, halfway between hiss and growl.

Kaldar swiped his fingers over her palm. The cross lay on her hand.

"When did you steal it?"

"This time?"

That bastard. "Did you take it more than once?"

"He steals it about twice a day," Gaston said. "Then he puts it back. It's not personal. He does the same to everybody in the family—" He saw her face and clamped his mouth shut.

She faced Kaldar. "Never take it again, or we're through."

Kaldar raised his hands. "I promise."

"I'm dead serious. You take it again, and I walk."

"I understand."

She turned away and went around the wyvern, away from the two of them.

"Audrey . . ." Kaldar called.

She kept walking, away, into the woods, until she was far enough not to see the blue bulk of the dragon. A tree stub jutted out of the soil. She sat on it. She felt so angry, she couldn't even put it into words.

Ling ran out of the bushes, sat before her on hind paws, and dropped a dead cicada on her lap.

"Thank you," Audrey told her, brushing the insect off her jeans. "But you better eat it."

Ling scratched at her knee. Audrey opened her arms, and the raccoon jumped into her lap. She petted Ling's soft fur.

The light sound of a twig snapping underfoot came from behind her. Ling hissed and jumped down. Kaldar circled the stump and knelt in front of her. "I'm sorry."

"Why did you take it?" she asked.

"I don't know. I wanted something of yours."

"There must be trust between partners. You broke it. When I worked with my brother and my father, I always had to guard my things. Any slip-up, and they would take what was mine and laugh in my face when called on it because I wasn't good enough to catch them in the act."

"That's not why I did it." Kaldar took her hand. "I'm sorry, Audrey. Please smile at me."

She shook her head. "No. Let me alone."

"Audrey, seriously, what do you want me to do? You ran away like a child."

She squeezed the words out through clenched teeth. "I walked away so I wouldn't have to deal with you."

Kaldar stood up, his hands held out. "Well, I'm here anyway. Why don't you just be a big girl and deal with me. What are you afraid of—"

She punched him. She did it right, turning with the punch, hitting him in the precise corner of his jaw. Kaldar's eyes rolled back in his head, and he went down like a log.

Audrey studied his prone body for a long moment. Her hand hurt. She should just leave him here in the woods. But she wasn't mad anymore—all her ire had gone out with that punch. She nudged him with the tip of her shoe.

"Get up."

Slowly, Kaldar's eyes opened. He sat up and rubbed his jaw. "Good hit."

"You deserved it."

A gray ball of fur dashed from the undergrowth, all but flying. Ling charged Kaldar. Her sharp teeth closed on his arm. Kaldar cursed in surprise, and the raccoon darted into the safety of the bushes. Ling the Raccoon Vigilante.

"What the hell?" Kaldar stared at the bite marks on his forearm.

"Don't expect mercy from Ling the Merciless." Audrey reached for him. He grasped her hand, and she pulled him up. "We better disinfect this."

He shook his head. "How did you manage to train her like that?"

"Little bit of food and petting." Audrey stepped over a fallen branch. "She is like a cat: she only does what she already wants to do. Something really bad happened to Ling when she was very young. When I found her, she was covered in blood. The vet said something bit her. I wasn't even sure she would survive. She did, but she is a terrible coward. She's scared of dogs, so she coughs when she smells them. She is scared of strangers, so when she smells or sees one coming, she will run and hide somewhere close to me. I'm surprised she'd gathered enough courage to bite you."

"She must've thought you were in danger," Kaldar said.

She wasn't wrong. The theft of the cross hurt, but it hurt most because Kaldar had done it. She had thought that all of her inner warnings to herself and all of her careful reasoning would keep her out of trouble, but she had been wrong. She'd wanted to trust him, and a small, naive part of her desperately wanted him to be better than he pretended to be. *This is the precursor of things to come,* she told herself. *Learn from this. He treated you as a mark once; he will treat you like that always.*

Kaldar looked at her. "Does this cross have something to do with why you stopped stealing?"

"The cross is mine, Kaldar. Everything else belonged to our family together. My clothes, my toys, all that stuff could be sold if we needed money or left behind if we had to leave in a hurry. I learned not to get attached to any of it. They were just things. Things changed hands a lot: I stole them from their owners and gave them to Dad, and Dad would sell them. Later, Alex would try to steal my take from me and sell whatever I stole to buy drugs. But the cross was only mine. Even my idiot father understood that. And then a violent man hurt me and took it from me, and I couldn't do anything about it. I felt so helpless. Angry, scared, and helpless. It was like he violated something deep inside me. That was when I realized what it feels like to have something you cherish stolen. So I don't do that anymore."

Guilt nipped at her. *Except when my father goads me into it.* Well, she would set it right.

"So if I were to take something other than the cross . . ."

"I will set your hair on fire, Kaldar. You'll be bald."

Kaldar got up. "You wouldn't."

"Try me."

They walked back to the clearing. "Friends again?" Kaldar asked.

"Partners," she said.

"You don't want to be friends with me, Audrey?" A seductive note crept into his voice. He said "Audrey" the way a man might say the name of a woman he had just made love to.

"I prefer partners." She raised her chin and winked at him. "Let's keep it professional."

"Isn't it too late for that?"

"Don't we have a heist to plan?"

Kaldar sighed in mock surrender. "Yes, love."

Audrey let the "love" go that time. He had to have some small consolation after being knocked out.

She was in too deep. If she wasn't careful, she'd find herself waking up next to him, then she would be in for a hell of a heartbreak.

At their approach, Gaston hoisted himself up into the wyvern's cabin and stuck his head out. "Is it safe to come out?"

"It's safe," Kaldar told him. "Audrey just explained to me that taking her things without permission is not allowed. Since I've never had anything taken away from me, I apologized."

Gaston hopped back onto the ground.

"They'll be taking us in a bus," Kaldar said. Yonker had told them as much when they agreed to the camp visit.

"Then they will walk us across one by one. Audrey is right—if things go sour, I'll need you close. I'll plant the tracker on the bus. Don't take any chances, and don't follow too closely. I don't want one of Yonker's goons shooting you."

"Can do," Gaston said.

A faint buzz spread through the air. Kaldar and Gaston looked up. A metal insect plunged down from the sky and landed on the ground between them. Gaston picked it up, extracted a narrow sliver of crystal, and pulled a gadget from one of the trunks. Shaped like a bronze flower bud, thrusting from a stack encrusted with tiny specks of crystal, the flower terminated in four delicate metal roots bent outward to provide a sturdy base.

"News from the Mirror," Kaldar said.

Gaston pushed the crystals in a complex sequence. The flower bud opened, revealing pale petals in its center made of some strange material, paper-thin, but with a metallic sheen. Gaston set the crystal in the middle of the flower.

Magic ignited inside the crystal and shot out in four streams to the ends of the petals. An image appeared above the crystal, floating in thin air. An average-looking man in nondescript clothes from the Weird looked at them.

"Erwin." Gaston's thick eyebrows crept up.

"The woman in the shot is not a member of the Hand," Erwin said. "Her name is Helena d'Amry, Marquise of Amry and Tuanin. She is a Hound of the Golden Throne. Spider is her uncle. Full file to follow. Be careful, Kaldar."

"Shit," Gaston said.

"What does that mean?" Audrey looked to Kaldar.

"The Hand protects the Dukedom of Louisiana, which is a colony of the Empire of Gaul. The Hounds protect the throne of the Empire. They answer directly to the Emperor," Kaldar said.

"Who is Spider?"

"He's the man I want to kill," Kaldar said.

A piece of paper replaced Erwin's image, covered with weird characters.

"What does it say?" Audrey tugged on Kaldar's arm.

"It says that Helena likes skinning people alive," Gaston answered. "Also says that the guy who threw that head at you is named Sebastian. He is her right-hand man. His kill count is at forty."

"Fourteen?"

"No. Forty."

Oh God.

"This changes nothing." Kaldar swiped the buckets. "We stick to the plan. Right now, we'll concentrate on getting the invitation and feeding the wyvern. We may have to take off in a hurry." He headed down the path to the stream as if he couldn't get away from the two of them fast enough.

"IT isn't really true," Gaston said quietly.

Audrey looked at him.

"What Kaldar said about nothing being taken away from him. It isn't true." Gaston sat down on the crate and checked the disks with the chain attached. "Kaldar has two brothers. Well, he had two brothers, Richard and Erian, but Erian was a lot younger than them and had a different mother, so they were never close. Their father was the head of our family. Their mother left. The family likes to pretend she died, but she didn't. She left all of them, ran off into the Broken. The Mire is a tough place to live. People try to get out any way they can."

Being left by your own parent as a child . . . Her mother had checked out on her emotionally more than once, but at least she didn't leave.

"Then a rival family killed their father. Richard was sixteen, and Kaldar was fourteen. Erian was nine, I think. Aunt Murid, their father's sister, took them in. She was tough. She'd escaped into the Weird when she was young and fought in the Dukedom of Louisiana's army for years, until they found her out, and she had to escape again and come home. Murid was hard. I used to be really scared of her when I was little. Anyway, she raised Richard and Kaldar as her own.

Richard was kind of already an adult, I guess. He's very serious. Smartest man I know. Kaldar was always like he is now, funny, hehe-haha, oh look, I stole your money out from under your nose. The family didn't starve because he and Cerise, his cousin, they hustled and sold things in the Broken. Don't ever haggle with him. It's a bad idea. Anyway, so Cerise and Kaldar did whatever they could to keep all of us fed. Kaldar always tried to impress Aunt Murid. He barely remembers his real mom, so she was as close to one as he ever had. Then Spider brought the Hand to the Mire, kidnapped Cerise's parents, and it all went to shit."

This Spider got around. "What did he want?"

"Everything," Gaston said. "Most of all, he wanted the Box. It's complicated. Just think of it as a really powerful weapon. We couldn't use it, but we couldn't let the Louisianans have it, either. The Hand declared war on us. Spider tracked my family down. My dad is a half thoas—that's why I look the way I look—and we always lived apart from the main house. I was supposed to stand watch. I left because of a stupid errand. Spider got into our house and cut off my mother's leg. Chopped it off at the knee with a meat cleaver."

"Oh, my God!" The tiny hairs on the back of her neck rose. "That's horrific."

"The Hand plays for keeps," Gaston said. "Anyway, we fought them and won, but in the final battle, Aunt Murid died. Kaldar watched it happen and didn't get to her in time. He killed the Hand freak that murdered her. Ask him sometime, he'll show you the scars on his arms. But it was too late."

Oh, Kaldar.

Gaston bit his lower lip. "He's not right. Watching Murid die broke something inside him. He still pretends that everything is cool. You can't tell by looking at him because he acts normal, but the rudder on his boat is stuck. He enlisted in the Mirror, supposedly because he wants to make sure what's left of the family is well taken care of, but that's not the reason. He wants revenge on the Hand, and he doesn't care what happens to him or how he gets it. He will kill them any chance he gets."

"Gaston," she said gently, "I know that you care for your uncle, but Kaldar, he's a grifter. He isn't a killer."

Gaston blinked. "We hold to the Old Ways in our family."

"What does that mean?"

"Kaldar's uncle, the head of our family, has a nickname."

"Aha."

"It's Death."

"I'm sorry?"

"They call him Death," Gaston said. "Because when his sword comes out, people die. We train as swordsmen as soon as we can hold a sword and not fall over. We learn to stretch our flash out onto our swords and use it in fights. Kaldar isn't as good as Grampa Ramiar. He isn't as good as Cerise. Technically, he isn't as good as Richard, his older brother, because Richard flashes white and Kaldar flashes blue. But aside from them, Kaldar has never met anyone he couldn't beat."

"Aha." Tall tales must've run in the family.

"He's killed dozens of people," Gaston insisted. "Probably over a hundred."

"I'm sure he did, Gaston." Sure as the night is light. She couldn't picture Kaldar with a sword. A crowbar, maybe. A gun. But not a sword. "And you are supposed to keep him from killing more?"

"I wasn't even supposed to come. I'm not officially an agent yet, but Cerise talked her husband, William—he's my guardian—into it. I'm supposed to keep an eye on Kaldar, in case he snaps. So he knows all about things being taken away from him. He just won't admit it."

"Gaston, if Kaldar doesn't care if he lives or dies, how are you supposed to keep him safe?"

He shook his head. His face gained a lost expression. Suddenly, he seemed so young, just a kid really, about Jack's age. "I don't know. But I have to try. Most of my family acts like I don't exist anymore. My dad banished me because of what happened to my mom. Kaldar always talks to me. He comes to all of my annual trials. He's my favorite uncle. I don't have many left anymore."

"I will help you," Audrey said. It came out as a complete surprise, but she didn't regret it. "If he loses his head, I will help you hold him back."

Gaston raised his huge hand, stained with the Mirror's clay. "Deal?"

She grasped his fingers and shook. "Deal."

KARMASH pondered the woman. She had small brown eyes and hair of an odd shade, unnatural bright red. Given that she hung upside down, her feet caught by a rope at the ankles, her hair dripped down from her head like a mop. For mid-thirties, she wasn't roughly used, he reflected.

They'd grabbed her off the street, as she left Magdalene Moonflower's building in the Broken, and brought her here, to the abandoned building in the Edge that Karmash had designated as their temporary base. Only he and Mura had managed to cross the boundary into the magicless world. Soma and Cotier had been too altered.

Karmash winced at the memory. Entering the Broken was always painful for him. A few months ago, he wouldn't have even contemplated it, but times changed.

The woman made a tiny noise, like a frightened cat.

Karmash pulled up a filthy chair and sat on it, so their faces were level. "You work for Magdalene Moonflower."

"Please let me down. I didn't do anything. Please let me down . . ."

"Shhh." Karmash put his finger on her lips.

She closed her mouth.

"Let me explain a few things," he said. "I'm a member of the Hand. I'm a spy for the Dukedom of Louisiana in the Weird. That tells you that I don't care about your life. That also tells you that I'm magically enhanced enough to crush your skull with a squeeze of my fingers. Make a note of that; we'll come back to that point later."

She stared at him in terrified silence.

"I was very successful as a spy. I made a nice name for myself. Then, twenty months ago, my officer became a cripple. Some Edgers severed his spine, you see. The Hand chose to view my performance in that affair as less than satisfactory. I lost my assignment, my prestige, and my paycheck. I have expensive tastes, and I hate to compromise on luxury. Now I have a new assignment, a very prestigious assignment with a famous officer. But I'm very new in this crew. You understand how that is, right?"

The woman nodded frantically. Nodding looked odd when performed upside down.

"What I really need to be is her second-in-command. That's the position I'm trained for, and I'm best at it. Unfortunately, this officer already has a second, and he doesn't want to step down. Now my new officer gave me this assignment. This is my chance to prove myself. If I do well, my place in the crew will be assured. If I fail, my career is finished. I tell you all of this so you will understand how important it is for me to succeed. Do you understand?"

The woman nodded again.

"Good. Let's go back to that point I asked you to remember. I don't care about your life. It has no value to me. I don't really want to torture you—it's a bother—but I will. I can cut you, I can burn you, I can pull out your nails, I can slice open your stomach and pour salt on the wound. I can yank out your teeth, I can sodomize you with jagged glass . . ."

The woman began to whimper.

"Shh." Karmash held up his hand. "Let me finish. My point is, I don't really feel like doing any of it. If you tell me what I want to know, I'm perfectly fine with letting you go, provided you disappear for a week or two, until my business is concluded. So now we know where we stand. Let's try this again. Do you work for Magdalene Moonflower?"

"Yes." The woman said.

"Did a dark-haired man and a red-haired woman come to see her in the last five days?"

"Yes."

Karmash smiled. He would deliver Kaldar Mar to Helena on a silver platter. It would cement his position and shake Sebastian from his comfortable perch.

"Where are these people now?"

"I don't know," the woman said.

Karmash frowned.

The woman's words came in a rush. "All I know is that Magdalene made some sort of deal with them. Something that has to do with Ed Yonker."

"Who is this Ed Yonker?"

"He is a preacher."

"A priest?"

"Yes, like that. He has a place in the Edge, a big wooden church in a camp. That's where he does his magic. That's where your man must be. I can show you where it is. It's not far. It's north of here."

"What's your name?"

"Jennifer."

"You did very well, Jennifer. I will cut you down now, and you will show us this church."

"And then I can go?" she asked, her eyes full of tears.

Funny how, in desperate times, people will believe anything. "Yes. And then you can go."

TWELVE

THE Wooden Cathedral was large and full to the brim. The mass of people should have made Audrey feel safer. The best place for a thief to hide was in a crowd, especially a crowd like this: well dressed, nicely groomed, seemingly law-abiding, and above reproach. Except that the gathering put out a strained, odd vibe. From the moment the Church of the Blessed people had ushered them into the bus, which had taken them to the Edge, the congregation was unsettled. Now, as they took their seats on the uncomfortable benches of the Wooden Cathedral, their agitation had reached the boiling point.

The church had only one center aisle, and Audrey had an aisle seat. People passed her, walking to their own seats, and their anxiety rolled off them like sweat. They spoke to each other, but no lasting conversations sprung up. Their faces were haggard, their eyes haunted. They fidgeted impatiently in their expensive suits and pricey dresses, grasping at their seats, searching with their stares the front of the church, where a lonely pulpit sprouted from a raised stage. Like a crowd of starving beggars who'd heard a rumor that someone was about to give out bread, the congregation waited, gripped by nervous tension.

She glanced at Kaldar, sitting on her left. His face seemed carefree, but his eyes, cold and alert, searched the crowd, evaluating it.

Armed guards waited by the door and near the pulpit. Nobody seemed to pay them any mind, as if being in the presence of men with rifles was the most natural thing in the world. Seth, their handler, explained to them that the guards are there because they had been seeing mountain lions in the area. The explanation seemed half-baked, but the guards made an effort to be cordial. They smiled, opened doors, waved at people. Most of the congregation, probably Yonker's regulars, didn't care, and if the few newcomers had any second thoughts, they kept their doubts to themselves.

Hell, if what George's book said was true, the people probably didn't see the rifles, as if the guards weren't even there. According to what they'd read, the gadget was designed by the Cult of Karuman specifically to convince its followers that Karuman's priests were avatars of their god. Followers of Karuman willingly sacrificed themselves to their deity; sometimes entire families burned themselves alive. The cult was now outlawed. How Ed Yonker had gotten ahold of a hundred-year-old relic was anyone's guess, but nothing good had come from it.

With each passing minute, the tension in the church grew thicker and thicker, electrified with anticipation and hysteria.

Audrey kept scanning the crowd, looking for the boys. They'd both heard a slight thud when the bus took off— Gaston landing on the roof—so he was here somewhere, but neither George nor Jack were anywhere to be seen.

She glanced back to the stage. Ed had spared no expense. The pulpit was rich mahogany. A heavy purple fabric embroidered with a golden cross draped the edge of the stage. Above it, pictures hung suspended from the ceiling in frames, all showing Yonker with various world leaders. She seriously doubted that there was a single un-Photoshopped image in the bunch.

"Is this your first time?" In the row in front of her, a young girl with bleached blond hair had turned halfway to her.

"Yes, it is!" Audrey tried to sound excited.

"I come here all the time. I'm a Blessed Maiden."

"What's that?"

"I help Preacher Ed connect with God." The girl nodded sagely. "He uses my body as a vessel."

Oh, Ed, you swine. "Are there many Blessed Maidens, or are you the only one?"

"There are eight of us." The girl smiled, her eyes innocent on the young face. "Don't worry, if Preacher Ed finds you worthy, you may be called to serve, too."

Yes, I'll slice his throat first. "That's nice."

The girl turned away. Audrey hugged her shoulders, crushing the fabric of the new yellow suit she'd bought for the occasion. It was just as expensive as the pink one, twice as ridiculous, and it bared so much of her breasts, she could cause a small riot. None of it made her feel better. She had a distinct feeling that their scheme wouldn't go well.

Her thoughts kept returning to the wyvern and Ling the Merciless and the little cat. Gaston had wanted to cage them, but she told him not to do it. If something happened . . . well, at least Ling wouldn't starve to death locked in a cage.

Kaldar's warm arms closed around her. He pulled her closer, leaning toward her ear, and kissed her neck, his lips hot, his touch reassuring. His whisper sounded in her ear, meant for her alone. "I have two magic bombs, and my sword is hidden in my jacket. I can carve my way through all of them. Nobody here will stop us. It will go smooth as silk. I promise."

Again with swords. "How will your sword stop a bullet?" she whispered.

"I'll show you. Relax, Audrey. You're the most beautiful thing I've ever seen. I want you so badly, I can taste it."

She pulled back from him and saw his eyes, laughing at her. "In this yellow suit?"

"I love the yellow suit," he told her. "I love your face, your eyes, your breasts, your ass, I love it all."

Impossible man. "We're about to get killed, and you're fantasizing about my ass?"

"I can't help it."

"You're insane," she whispered. Her tension evaporated into the air.

"The boys," he whispered back.

George and Jack, scrubbed clean and dressed in identical plain white T-shirts and sweatpants, came down the aisle, led by Paul. George looked calm. Jack's eyes were huge and wild. The crowd's mood was probably wreaking havoc on his nerves.

"Boys!" Audrey rose and waved.

Paul stared at her cleavage for a long second, then pushed the boys forward.

"There you are." Audrey made a big show of hugging first George, then Jack, whispering the same thing into their ears, "Get ready to run."

The kids sat next to Kaldar. Paul turned away.

"Aren't you staying for the sermon?" Audrey asked.

"No. I have some errands." Paul headed up the aisle. Other camp staffers were leaving as well. A couple of moments, and the church doors began to close behind them. Audrey watched the light between them shrink with a sinking feeling.

The doors clanged closed. They were locked in.

FROM his position at the root of a large pine, Karmash peered at the men with guns shutting the church doors. The camp sat on the side of a hill, and from his vantage point, Karmash had an excellent view of the entire place. He'd observed both Kaldar Mar and the red-haired woman enter the church and had released an enhanced message bird the moment Karmash had seen Kaldar's face.

The priest had a small but solid compound. Karmash personally counted twelve guards, quite a force. Two went inside the church, two remained by the church doors, and the rest filed into a log house on the far left. None of them would present a problem.

Cotier scuttled down the pine trunk, descending from the branches like a lizard, with his head down. Muscular, quick, the scout was an odd creature even by the Hand's standards: brown and green pigments swirled within his skin, and as he paused on the trunk, his face mimicked its colors and rough brown pattern. His voice came out as a low, slightly sibilant whisper. "What are they doing?"

"It appears they're locking them in."

"That's not good."

"Thank you for stating the obvious." He had no idea what the Edgers were doing, but whatever it was, it required armed guards and barred doors. In Karmash's experience, that was never a good combination for the party that was being locked in.

"Should we do something?"

Helena was really too permissive with her crew. Agents under his command never questioned his decisions in such a manner. Karmash weighed the choices at hand. The real question was what would piss Helena off more, acting against her orders or losing Kaldar Mar to some Edger insanity.

Nobody bothered to question the winners. If he delivered Kaldar Mar, all would be forgiven. He might even be commended for taking the initiative.

The two guards took position by the doors, brandishing their rifles.

If he screwed this up, there would be no coming back.

Karmash gritted his teeth. He couldn't take a chance on losing Kaldar. That would be unforgivable, and Helena wasn't known for her mercy.

He shrugged off his camouflage cloak. Mura stepped out from behind a tree trunk, her orange skin bright against the greenery despite camouflage paint. Karmash nearly winced. True, as a slayer, Mura was never meant to be used in a forest setting, but her skin was almost fluorescent. She would've never made the cut in Spider's crew. Helena's standards clearly differed.

To the left, Soma emerged from the underbrush and crouched. Thick, monstrous muscle sheathed the hunter's frame. His hair dripped down his back in long blond rolls, matching the crest of fur running down his spine. The hunter raked the forest floor with his enormous claws. His gaze bored into the two guards below.

"Soma," Karmash called.

The hunter didn't answer.

"Soma!"

The man slowly turned his head and peered at Karmash with pale eyes. His face showed no expression; it was like looking at a wolf.

"Do not kill the male. Helena needs him alive. Do you understand me?"

Soma didn't answer.

"Do you understand?"

Soma glanced at Cotier. The scout gave him an understanding look. Fury boiled inside Karmash.

"Don't look at him. Answer me!"

"He can't," Cotier said. "He gave up his power of speech for the glory of Gaul. He understands."

Karmash growled under his breath.

"Would you like me to take out the guards?" Cotier asked.

"No." Karmash started toward the camp.

THE choir filed onstage, their faces rapt, lit up with inner joy. Their voices blended into one. "Hallelujah. Hallelujah. Hallelujah . . ."

The side door opened, and Yonker walked into the aisle. He wore a black business suit. A crimson Superman-like cape perched on his shoulders, held in place by a gold cloak chain. Her gaze fastened on the chain. The Eyes of Karuman. They hadn't gotten the emitter exactly right, but they were close, very close.

The crowd gasped.

Yonker raised his arms.

Nobody laughed. Nobody called him out or ridiculed his outfit. An older woman in the back row began to weep. The man in front of them rocked back and forth, mumbling, "Thank you, Jesus. Thank you, Jesus."

Dear Lord, what sort of madhouse is this?

Yonker began his procession down the aisle. People reached out, crawling over each other to touch his hands. Fifteen feet.

How exactly would Kaldar pull this off in plain view? She had to shield them from the rest of the audience somehow.

Twelve feet.

Six.

Audrey hopped off her seat, putting an extra bounce into it. Her breasts went up and down in the satin cage of her bra, and Yonker stared down her cleavage. She held out her hands, smiling her big smile, tears glistening in her eyes. Yonker held out his hands, and she hugged him, sliding her hand under his cape to grab his ass. Ed's eyes widened, and he pulled her closer.

"Excuse me." Kaldar rose. His arms covered hers and he gently untangled her from Yonker's chest. "My wife is getting too much into the spirit."

"That's fine." Yonker waved his hand magnanimously and went on to the podium, his chain intact.

That hug lasted barely five seconds. Not nearly enough time to exchange the chain. The realization sank in like a heavy stone to the pit of her stomach. They had failed.

KARMASH strode to the house on the left, where the murmur of voices announced the presence of people. The three operatives followed him.

"Where are you going?" Cotier murmured, a step behind.

"We need sword meat."

"There is only one Edger man and one woman."

Karmash was getting tired of this constant opposition. "You haven't fought the Mars. I have. We'll need a shield of bodies between us. Trust me on this."

The door loomed in front of him. He punched it open and walked into the room. Eight men stared at him. He noted rifles on the walls. As he'd surmised, they were the rest of the priest's guards.

Karmash reached into his pocket and dropped a handful of gold coins on the table. A small ransom. A quiet sound fluttered through the room as six men simultaneously sucked in their breath.

"I'm hunting a man," Karmash said. "He's in your church trying to kill your priest. I need this man alive. Help me apprehend him, and this gold is yours."

AUDREY landed in her seat and leaned over to Kaldar. "What's the plan, C again?"

Kaldar slipped his arm around her, pulling her closer, possessive, and toyed with her hair. "No need for Plan C. I've got it."

"What?"

He eased his jacket open, squeezing the lining with his hand, and she glimpsed the outline of the chain in the secret pocket. "How . . . When?"

"Trade secret, love." He smiled at her.

Damn it, but the man is smooth. She leaned over and kissed the corner of his mouth.

"Careful now," he murmured.

Ed Yonker climbed to the pulpit and raised his hands. "Brothers and sisters!"

The crowd stared at him, rapt.

"Listen to me and heed my words."

The crowd stared. Someone cleared their throat.

"Today I bring you the Blessed Light!"

The crowd watched him. Yonker frowned. Alarm squirmed through Audrey. Something must have usually happened during this part of the service, and it was clearly not happening. George leaned to Kaldar and whispered urgently. Kaldar leaned toward her. "The gems are supposed to emit light when hit with magic."

"I don't suppose you can do emotion-manipulation magic?" she whispered.

"No."

Audrey eased her feet out of her spiked heels.

Yonker touched the chain. His face turned bright red with fury.

A man jumped up on the right. Slicked-back hair, pale, where had she see him before? The recognition popped like a soap bubble in her head: Magdalene's receptionist, Adam, with the weird haircut. He'd pulled his hair back off his face, and it had thrown her for a minute.

The pale man pointed at them. "They stole it! They took it!"

Magdalene had double-crossed them.

"Kill them!" Yonker bellowed.

"Cover your ears!" Kaldar hurled something toward the pulpit. Audrey clamped her hands over her ears.

The guards yanked their rifles off their shoulders.

A brilliant white light exploded between the benches and the stage, followed by a clap of thunder that punched through her hands straight into her eardrums. The church shook. The pictures danced and crashed to the floor.

A dozen people screamed at once. Men and women jumped from their seats, pushing each other out of the way in a rush to get out, concealing them temporarily from the guards. Audrey jumped to her feet and pushed her way into the aisle, trying to brace against the crowd so the boys could exit. Jack somersaulted over her head and landed in the center aisle, his eyes on fire with glowing amber. George ran along the bench like a tightrope walker. Jack grabbed her right arm, George took her left, and they pulled her to the doors. Kaldar brought up the rear.

The white light turned orange as the photographs and the purple brocade at the altar caught fire. The choir fled. Yonker didn't move. He simply stood there, bewildered, looking at the flames.

A bench collapsed in the other row, knocking a knot of bodies to the ground. The closest guard was closing in, clubbing people streaming to the doors with the butt of his rifle. A long, slender blade flashed in Kaldar's hand.

He does have a sword. Audrey blinked.

The guard took aim, almost point-blank. Kaldar sliced, someone howled, and the flood of people hid them from her view.

The crowd crashed against the church doors. They held. People smashed into Audrey, pushing her forward into the writing mass of bodies clawing at the door. *We'll get crushed,* flashed through her head.

A loud yell, savage and inhuman, overtook the desperate cries of the crowd. The doors parted, and for a moment Audrey saw a giant man, silhouetted against the light, enormous muscles bulging on his arms. He leaped aside, and people spilled out of the church, into the sunlight.

"Go!" Audrey pushed the boys forward. "Go, go, go."

The press of the crowd carried them outside. They burst into the open, running past two men with rifles. A guard on the right, a big thick man with a short beard, cursed. "Thin the crowd! Thin the crowd, or we'll lose him."

The man next to him raised his rifle and fired into the crowd. A dark-haired man dropped to the ground. On the other side of the church, another gunshot popped. A man screamed.

They were shooting at their own congregation.

The bearded guard raised his rifle.

Oh no, no you don't, you sick bastard.

Audrey sprinted and hit him, ramming him hard with her shoulder. The man went down. Jack landed on top of him with a guttural snarl, ripped the rifle from the guard's hands, and smashed the butt into the man's head. The other guard stumbled back, jerking his weapon up.

George's eyes ignited with white. Tiny streaks of white flash, bright like lightning, rolled from his hands.

The guard dropped the rifle and took off.

People still ran from the church. Kaldar and Gaston were nowhere in sight.

The kids were looking at her. They had to get a car. Audrey whirled, looking around. Yonker's Jeep Cherokee was parked on the side of the church. "Jack, grab that rifle and follow me!" She sprinted to the Jeep, her bare feet barely touching the ground.

THE exit beckoned Kaldar, a glowing rectangle of light. He walked up the aisle, light on his feet. Behind him, two men writhed in pain. Farther still, behind the low wall of fire, Yonker screamed curses from the pulpit.

A peculiar calm claimed Kaldar, the smooth serenity that always came to him in battle. His family was old, rooted in a half-forgotten time when wars had pushed elite warriors of the old Weird kingdoms into the pit of hell that was the Mire. Their blood flowed in his veins. His uncle was a man of the Old Ways—his sword was death on the battlefield. Cerise was one, too. His brother Richard was one as well. And so was he.

The blade had been a part of Kaldar's education since he could stand on his own two feet. He didn't like to kill unless he had no choice. Not even Murid's death had changed that. But he was raised to find peace within the slaughter, and that peace sustained him now.

A bullet whistled by Kaldar's ear. On the left, a young man, barely old enough to hold a rifle, tried to reload his weapon with shaking hands. Kaldar ducked and threw a knife. The blade sank into the wall next to the guard's head. The boy dropped the rifle.

"Run!" Kaldar called.

The guard scrambled outside.

"You!" Yonker snapped out of his daze and screamed like a stuck bull. "Stop him!"

A man lunged at Kaldar from the right. Large, muscular, but sadly too slow. Kaldar rolled his blade over the man's left thigh. Blood gushed. Kaldar leaned away from the man's punch and sliced the other thigh. The man croaked something and went down like a log. Kaldar skirted him and kept walking. Three guards burst through the doors, ran down the aisle, saw him, and halted. The blond man on the left looked at the two bodies behind him. "Holy shit."

"Shoot him!" Yonker howled from behind the flames. "Shoot his ass!"

Kaldar looked at their faces. "Let me pass, and you will live."

"He said to take him alive," the man on the left said.

"Fuck that." The older of the men jerked his rifle up.

Kaldar flashed. The magic flared from him in a blue sheath, shielding him. The guard's bullet ricocheted and bit into the wall.

Kaldar ran forward.

As one, the guards fired.

"HOLD on!" Audrey stomped on the gas. The Jeep roared and jumped over the threshold into the church. She saw Kaldar in the aisle, three armed men opposing him, and slammed on her brakes. Kaldar's face was so relaxed, she barely recognized him. The Jeep skidded to a stop.

The guards fired. A glowing blue wall surrounded Kaldar. The bullets impacted on it with weak ripples and bounced off. The light imploded, sucked back into Kaldar's blade.

Kaldar struck. Light, graceful like a dancer, he cleaved the first guard's arm. It fell off. Kaldar kept moving, so sickeningly fast, she had no chance to be shocked. He spun, moving as if his joints were fluid, sliced the second man's chest, his blade going through the muscle and bone like a hot knife through butter, swept past him, and thrust his blade backward, into the small of the third guard's back.

The three men dropped.

Kaldar turned toward her and smiled. It wasn't his usual smug smile. His face was at once sad and at peace. Audrey wasn't sure who this man was, but she knew she hadn't met him before.

The corners of Kaldar's mouth drooped, and the smile turned into a scream. "Get out! Get out now!"

"Kids, out!"

They scrambled out of the car. She shoved her door open. A large metal dart smashed into the hood and shivered, stuck upright, its end glowing. Audrey grabbed the rifle and dived out of the vehicle. Behind her, the car exploded in a flash of white magic. The explosion punched the inside of her head, and her skull rang like a gong being struck. Suddenly, everything was quiet.

The world swam.

Move, move, move. To stay in one place was to die. Audrey scrambled away, blindly. Someone caught her and carried her off. Pain bathed her legs. It hurt to breathe. The haze dropped from her eyes. She realized that she sat propped against Kaldar's body, his arm around her. He had grasped an arrow sticking out of her thigh and was pulling it out.

She couldn't feel her legs.

The two boys crouched next to her. Everyone was looking at the door.

A giant man with pale hair stood in the church's doorway. She'd seen him before, peering at them over the blond blueblood's shoulder as the wyvern carried them off. Karmash, she remembered.

The giant stared at them. A dark-haired man crawled over the top edge of the doorway and moved up the wall onto the ceiling like a fly. A woman crossed the threshold. Her long, tattered cloak fluttered about her. Her hood was down, and the exposed skin of her face was a bright, unnatural orange. Her hands held twin narrow swords.

A third man stalked through the church entrance. Or at least he might have been a man at some point. This creature looked more like a beast. Massive, slabbed with heavy muscle, he crouched in the doorway, his huge claws digging into the wood.

The Hand had found them. Kaldar's lips moved, but she heard nothing. George nodded, his pale face smudged with dirt.

On the ceiling, the lizard guy had crawled all the way over and paused, directly above them. His skin turned pale brown, matching the wood beams. Jesus Christ.

Karmash pointed at them.

The freak on the ceiling let go and swung down, hanging as if his feet had suckers.

"Now!" Kaldar barked. She didn't hear him, but she read his lips.

The lizard man's hands glowed. She blinked and realized his fingers held darts, the same kind that had pierced the hood of the Cherokee.

The darts rained on them and dimmed behind a glowing white translucent shield. George's eyes bled white lightning. It spilled from him in long, twisted ribbons and fed the semicircle. Ripples pounded the flash shield. The floor around them shuddered. George clenched his fists.

It's possible to die from expending too much magic, George's voice said from the recesses of her memory.

The darts kept pounding the shield.

George, kind, quiet, calm George. She looked at him and knew he would rather die than stop shielding them.

Her hands were full of something. She was still holding the rifle. She checked the magazine. One shot left.

The lizard freak couldn't shield and hurl the dart at the same time.

"Drop it!" she yelled, hoping her voice held. "Drop the shield!"

Kaldar looked at her. Understanding sparked in his eyes. He yelled something.

George shook his head. Blood spilled out from the corner of his mouth.

Kaldar's voice snapped into a rigid mask. He was biting off words.

George took a deep breath.

This was it. One shot. She made it, or they died.

The shield vanished. Audrey fired.

The lizard man's head exploded in a wet blossom of blood and pale chunks.

The last dart fell straight at her. Small price to pay . . .

Kaldar lunged. His sword slashed in a wide arc, its edge shining bright blue. The two pieces of the dart fell harmlessly on the floor.

Suddenly, sound exploded in Audrey's head, as if someone had the volume turned up all the way and had just pressed the unmute button.

"Mar!" Karmash roared. "Face me!"

Something smashed into him from behind. Karmash flew forward, rolled over, and jumped to his feet.

In the doorway, Gaston landed on the carpet. His black

hair spilled over his shoulder like a mane. His eyes flared silver, reflecting the flames. Muscles bulged on his exposed shoulders. He looked demonic, like some prehistoric monster.

Karmash hesitated, unsure.

"The Mar family says hello," Gaston growled.

The giant roared and charged. Gaston leaped, catching Karmash head-on. They collided and rolled down the aisle.

The orange woman slipped out of her cloak. Chain mail covered her body from neck to mid thigh. She dashed toward them, leaping over the overturned broken benches.

"I believe this is my dance." Kaldar flicked his sword and lunged forward, blue magic flaring about him in a flash shield. They collided. Steel rang against steel, and Kaldar and the woman danced across the ruined church like two whirlwinds.

The beast man stared at Karmash and Gaston, locked in battle, then looked at Kaldar and the orange woman. His gaze fastened on her and the kids. A predatory focus claimed his face. *Oh shit.*

"Run!" Audrey tried to get up, but her legs were still numb. "Run!"

"No." George shook his head. He was bleeding from his nose and his mouth.

Jack just stood there. He looked so young and lost. In shock, Audrey realized.

The beast man charged toward them.

"Run! Save your brother, you idiot!"

George thrust his hands out. Magic pulsed from him. The nearest corpse in the aisle jumped to its feet and clamped onto the beast man, trying to rip him apart. Another corpse joined the first. The third and fourth followed. They clawed at him, gouging the skin, ripping at his hair.

He ripped one dead guard off and hurled him aside. The body flew across the church and crashed against the wall.

"George, I order you to go! Do you hear me! Go!"

George's hands shook with strain.

The second corpse fell into the aisle, torn to pieces. The beast man kept coming.

Twenty yards.

The third corpse fell apart under the savage blows of the massive claws.

Fifteen.

The last body flew, knocked aside. George pulled a dagger from his belt.

The beast man tensed, gathering himself for the final leap.

An inhuman howl ripped from Jack's lips, a terrible mix of anguish, pain, mourning, sorrow, and rage. The scream built on itself, pounding at her, growing louder and louder. The horrible sound clawed at her ears, pierced her chest, and crushed her heart, squeezing pure panic from it. At the far end, Gaston and Karmash paused. Kaldar and the orange woman lowered their blades, their faces shocked.

Magic burst out of Jack. Audrey couldn't see it, but she felt its touch. It burned her for the briefest of moments, but in that instant she stared straight into its wild, savage face, as if the primordial forest full of man-eaters yawned and swallowed her into its black maw studded with cruel fangs. Fear gripped her, and she cried out.

Jack's scream vanished, cut off in mid-note. The thing that used to be Jack, the terrible wild thing, grinned, its fangs bared in maniacal glee. It pulled two daggers from its waist and sliced the beast man. The Hand's agent moved to counter, but he was too slow. The Jack thing carved a chunk of flesh off his side and laughed.

George landed next to her. "It will be okay," he whispered.

"What's happening?"

"Jack is rending. Changelings do this sometimes so they don't become unhinged. It will be okay."

Blood sprayed from the beast man. The thing that was Jack laughed and laughed.

"Just don't move. He won't kill you if you don't move," George said.

In the aisle, Gaston and Karmash ripped into each other, throwing pews around with superhuman strength. Three

minutes later, Kaldar sliced the orange woman in half. The
top of her slid one way and the bottom the other, but Audrey
no longer had any emotion left to spare. Kaldar walked
over to them and sat next to her. His arms closed around
her. He held her, and together they watched Jack stab the
lifeless stump of the beast man's body. He carved it again
and again, hurling the bloody chunks of muscle like it was
play sand.

The feeling slowly returned to her legs. Kaldar said
something about a temporary paralytic agent, but she
couldn't concentrate enough to pay attention.

At some point, Gaston joined them. He was bloody and
bruised, and his arm stuck out at an odd angle, but the fingers of his left hand had a death grip on the pale hair of
Karmash's head. He sat next to them, cradling it like a
watermelon. They watched Jack together.

The fire had died down to nothing. The coals turned cold.
Ed Yonker had long since gone.

Jack swayed and sat down, his gore-covered arms limp.
George stood up, walked over to him on shaking legs, and
hugged him. Jack looked at his brother's face, looked back
at the ruin of the corpse in front of him, and began to cry.

THEY found a Chevy van in the deserted camp. Kaldar
drove. Gaston sat next to him in the passenger seat. Kaldar
had forced Gaston's dislocated shoulder back into its socket,
and now the boy held Karmash's head with both hands.
Audrey cradled Jack. He had stopped crying, but he still
looked like death.

They were bloody, bruised, battered. Everyone hurt.

"This is what it's like to fight the Hand," Kaldar said.
His voice held no mirth.

The boys didn't say anything.

"Tomorrow, I will buy two tickets," Kaldar said. "We'll
put you on a plane in the Broken. You will land in a large
airport, then another plane will take you to a smaller airport
not too far from where you grew up. You will enter the Edge

there, find your grandmother, and wait with her until Declan comes to get you."

"No," George said. His voice creaked like an unoiled door. "We'll finish it."

"Jack?" Kaldar asked.

"We'll finish it," Jack said with quiet savagery.

"Okay," Kaldar said.

"Okay?" Audrey asked. "Okay? Help me out, Kaldar, which part of this is okay? Are we in the same car? Are you seeing what I'm seeing?"

"We're all alive and mostly uninjured," Kaldar said.

"We are putting them on that goddamned plane tomorrow."

"We won't go," George said.

Jack reached over and patted her hand.

"Yes, you will. This is no place for children. This is not a kid's fight. We survived today by the skin of our teeth."

"You don't have to be here, either," George said softly.

"Yes, I do. I helped make this mess. I have to fix it."

"We do, too," Jack said. "We help."

"They fought like adults," Kaldar said. "I'm treating them as adults. Adults understand the price and make their own decisions."

Audrey closed her eyes. "You are all insane."

"They are," Gaston said. "I'm good."

"You are holding a decapitated head in your lap!"

"What are you going to do with it?" Kaldar asked.

Gaston shrugged and winced, rubbing his shoulder. "I thought I'd pack it into some preservatives and take it with us."

"Why?" Audrey asked. *Dear Jesus, why would he want to keep the head?*

"I'm going to send it to my parents as a present. It won't make my mom's leg grow back, but it might make them feel better." Gaston patted Karmash's hair. "He isn't Spider, but he was his top dog."

Kaldar raised his hand, and Gaston high-fived him.

"Thank you for the flash, George," Kaldar said. "That was a hell of a shield."

George smiled through the grime on his face.

"That's right," Gaston said. "That flash was killer. And Jack, you totally kicked ass. Saved all of us, probably."

Jack sat up straighter.

"Yes. Sorry you had to go through that, but the timing couldn't have been better," Kaldar said. "You guys took out two of the Hand's operatives and helped to kill another two, including a veteran underofficer. There are Mirror agents, trained fighting personnel, who'd give their right arms to be you right now. I think there is a price on that head, actually, Gaston."

"That's fine, but I think Dad and Mom would rather have the head."

Audrey covered her face. They were just making things worse now. She had seen more violence tonight than she had ever witnessed in her entire life. Then the rusty scent hit her nostrils, and she realized her hands were bloody and she had just smeared the gore all over her face. She should feel something more. She should be sick and throwing up on the side of the road. Or be in shock and turn into a catatonic vegetable. Instead, she felt nothing. Just dullness and fear. She was so scared. It was over, and she was still scared.

"You will feel better soon, love," Kaldar said, as if reading her thoughts. "I'm so sorry. And I meant to tell you: that was a one-in-a-thousand shot."

She raised her hand. "Don't."

"It was awesome," George confirmed.

"It really was," Jack said. "His head exploded."

Something inside her broke. Tears swelled in her eyes and fell onto her bloody, tattered skirt. She breathed a little easier, as if some of the pressure inside had leaked out of her soul through the tears.

"Chocolate helps," Jack said. "We should get some chocolate for Audrey. And for me."

"We can do that," Kaldar said.

"What was that back there, seven men, Uncle?" Gaston asked.

"Six. The last was a woman."

"How did you do it?" George asked. "Swords don't sever people in half."

"I stretch my flash across my blade," Kaldar said. "Makes the edge magically sharp. You've never seen Cerise do it?"

"No."

"Ask her to show you sometime. She flashes white. She can slice through two-inch steel with one cut."

"We should wash up somewhere," Gaston said. "If we get pulled over, this will be difficult to explain."

"First, we have to visit Magdalene," Kaldar said. "She landed us in this mess."

Yes. Magdalene. That fucking snake. If it weren't for her, they would've walked out of that church, and none of this horror would've happened. "Yes," Audrey squeezed through her teeth. "Let's visit Magdalene."

"We could clean up first," George murmured.

"Oh no. No, we're going just like this," Audrey said. The dullness inside her broke apart and melted into anger. "I want her to see what a double cross really looks like."

WHEN Audrey was angry, doors didn't just unlock, Kaldar discovered. They flew open, and, sometimes, when the blast was hard enough, they fell off their hinges. The effect of a heavy door crashing down like thunder on the marble tile would've startled anyone.

Magdalene jerked. She didn't cringe; she just jerked toward them, like an alarmed cobra, with her hood flaring open.

Gaston hurled Adam at her. They'd found him hiding in one of the side rooms under a desk. The receptionist flew a few feet, slid across the marble, hit the couch, and lay still, pretending to be unconscious.

The air in the room suddenly grew heavy. Magdalene's face seemed to glow, as if shimmering ribbons of light slid under her skin.

"You don't want to do this," she said, her voice quiet but somehow reaching deeply into his mind. Her eyes, luminescent with crystalline aquamarine, peered into him. "Let's all calm down."

Fascinating eyes, Kaldar decided. She was screwing with his mind. He really ought to kill her.

Somewhere far away, Audrey said, "Gaston, give me Adam's gun."

Gunshots barked in unison, one after another, marble shattered, and suddenly the room returned to normal, and Magdalene clutched at her leg. Her hand came away red.

"Next one will go in your stomach," Audrey said.

"You stupid piece of shit," Magdalene spat.

Audrey raised the gun. "One more word, and I will shoot you again, then pistol-whip your face until it looks like hamburger."

"Go ahead! Shoot me, you stupid bitch." Magdalene fell into the nearest chair. "Shoot me!"

Kaldar reached into his jacket and pulled out the Eyes of Karuman. Magdalene's gaze fastened on it.

"George."

The boy walked over to him.

"How do I use this?" Hopefully George would catch on to his bluff, and the next thing out of his mouth wouldn't be, "I already told you that you can't use them because you don't have the right magic."

"It shouldn't be too hard," George said. "Of course, we could accidentally fry her mind."

Magdalene went pale.

Smart kid. "We'll just have to take that risk. Most women, when faced with five angry, blood-smeared people who forced their way into their rooms, would take a moment to consider their position. Obviously, this one is too foolish." Kaldar raised the emitter. "Look into the light, Magdalene."

"Fine." Magdalene slouched in her chair. "What do you want?"

"We had the emitter. Why expose us?"

She sighed. "Because I want Yonker dead. Those merchant pig fuckers actually forbade—forbade!—us to settle it. I can't even put a price on his head because it would be 'bad for business.' I've been wanting to kill him for three years now. And then you morons came along. If you took Yonker's gadget, and he found out, one of two things would happen. Either you killed him or he killed you, in which case the Mirror would come knocking on his door, looking for revenge. Either way, he'd stop breathing in the end, and I'd win. But now you fucked it all up."

"You're an evil woman," George said.

"What do you know of evil, you stupid puppy?" Magdalene turned her gaze on him. "You think this is evil? Give me two weeks with Yonker's toy, and I could make you rape your own mother, and you'd enjoy it."

"Kaldar, if you kill her, please don't shoot her in the head," George said, his face cold, as if carved from a glacier. "Raising a body with a shattered brain requires more magic, and I think we can use her corpse to make sure her relatives will get run out of town."

Now that's interesting. Kaldar studied George. He had had no idea the kid had that kind of calculated cruelty in him. He was willing to bet it wasn't genuine, but it was hellishly convincing.

"You can't do that," she sneered.

"I can," George told her. "That's what I do. Would you like me to stab Adam through the heart and demonstrate?"

"No!" Adam squirmed behind the couch. "Mother!"

Everyone had a lever. Kaldar laughed. "And the little Moonflower opens his big mouth. It's over, Magdalene."

Magdalene's face drooped in defeat.

"The invitation," Kaldar ordered.

"In the black box in the safe," she said.

Audrey handed the gun to Gaston, crossed the room to the steel door, and put her hand against it. Green magic shimmered around her. The locks clicked open.

"I have it," Audrey said.

"What are you going to do now?" Magdalene glared at Kaldar.

"Now we walk away."

"What?"

He shrugged. "What's the point of killing you? I may have to use you again."

She actually shook with rage. "If you ever come here again . . ."

"If I ever do, you will welcome me in a civil manner and do whatever is requested of you," Kaldar let the crisp tones of Adrianglian high society slip into his voice. "You will not warn de Braose. You will not seek revenge. Or the Mirror will replace you with someone more agreeable. I could slit your throat right now, kill your son, bury your bodies in an unmarked grave, and tomorrow a new soothsayer would walk through these doors and take your place. Your people won't care who they work for as long as their bills are paid."

Magdalene stared at him, mute.

"Let me put things in perspective for you: I can level this entire building with a single blast of my flash. I could've simply ordered you to hand the invitation over, but I've chosen to play by the rules out of respect. You broke the rules, Magdalene. You tried to engineer the death of a Mirror agent and a blueblood peer. That's an act of war against Adrianglia. True, we're on the other side of the continent, but we have a long reach. Think about that for a moment."

Magdalene Moonflower turned as white as the marble floor she was standing on.

"Consider it a learning experience. Next time I won't be in the mood to give you a lesson." Kaldar turned and walked out.

They had reached the parking lot before George said, "Kaldar?"

"Mhhm?"

"You're not really a blueblood or a peer of the realm."

"True." He popped open the vehicle's door.

"Also, you can't flash hard enough to level the building," Jack said.

"True again."

"So you lied?" George asked.

"Of course he lied, George," Audrey said.

Kaldar grinned. "But Magdalene doesn't know that, does she? Now pile into the car. Quickly now. We have less than twenty hours to get to Morell de Braose's castle and make ourselves presentable. The rest of the Hand can't be far behind."

The kids and Gaston climbed into the backseat.

"What if she warns de Braose?" George asked.

"And be the laughingstock of the entire western Edge, while risking the Mirror's wrath?" Kaldar shook his head. "I don't think so."

"Just out of curiosity, how are you planning on getting in?" Audrey asked, sliding into the front passenger seat. "To get into the auction, we need three things: an invitation, a pedigree, and money. We have the invitation, and we can fake the money, but you can't just show up and claim to be a blueblood noble. Morell will smell a fake in an instant."

"I've got it covered." Kaldar steered the car out of the parking lot.

She heaved a sigh. "Next you'll be claiming you're a lost heir to a blueblood fortune."

"I don't need to claim anything." He grinned. "I have the two wards of the Marshal of the Southern Provinces in the backseat."

In the rearview mirror, the two boys blinked like two baby owls.

"Do you boys still remember your etiquette lessons?"

George recovered first. "We'll manage."

THE were times in life when nothing was better than a hot, soapy shower, Audrey reflected, stepping out of the shower onto a soft white towel. After the meeting with Magdalene, it was decided that it was best to take off immediately, and so all of them, bloody and exhausted, piled into the wyvern's cabin. Three hours later, the wyvern touched down in the Edge near the small town of Valley View in southern Oregon. Ling and the nameless cat were released into the night to forage for themselves, the wyvern was watered, and everybody agreed that they desperately needed hot showers and beds.

It was determined that of all of them, Kaldar had somehow ended up being the least bloody, so he cleaned his face, got two suites at the Holiday Inn Express, and snuck the rest of them in through the side entrance. The men took one suite, she took the other.

It was almost eleven in the evening now, and Audrey had finally washed all of the nastiness out of her hair. She couldn't smell the blood anymore, only the cocoa butter from the body wash and lilac from the shampoo. Audrey scrubbed her face with a white towel and examined it. No red. Good. She wrapped one towel around herself, put the other over her wet hair, twisted it, flipped the end over, and came out of the bathroom with a towel turban on her head.

"It's amazing how every woman knows how to do that."

Kaldar sat on the edge of her bed. Well, well. Someone had been hiding lock-picking skills. Or, more likely, he had just asked for an extra keycard for her room and kept one.

The shower had turned his hair nearly black, and it framed his clean face in casual disarray. He hadn't bothered to shave his stubble, and he looked like a rogue, a highwayman who had somehow ended up wearing a white T-shirt and a pair of blue jeans.

A very sexy highwayman.

In her imagination, Audrey walked over to him. He gave her one of those wicked looks and stole her towel, sliding it off her to the floor. Kaldar ran his clever hands up her hips, over her sides, to her breasts. Audrey leaned back, letting him caress her. It felt so good. He rose and pulled off his T-shirt, baring a muscled torso. She wound her arms around him. He hugged her to him, his arms strong, his skin so hot it was nearly burning. His lips trailed the line of her pulse on her neck. The memory of the day faded from her head. The visions of blood and gore fled.

That would be nice, wouldn't it? Yes, it would. She wanted to forget the ugliness and feel like she was still alive and safe. But then the morning would come, and all of that passion would have to be paid for.

She pointed at the door. "Out!"

"Audrey," he purred.

"Out. I will let you back in when I'm dressed."

He didn't move.

Audrey crossed her arms over her chest. "Kaldar. Agent, pickpocket, rapist . . ."

"Oh, for Gods' sakes, woman." He got up and stalked out the door. She locked the dead bolt, pulled on sweatpants and an oversized T-shirt, and unlocked the door. He was still in the hallway.

"May I come in now?"

"Yes."

He rolled his eyes and went inside. Audrey locked the door.

Kaldar examined her outfit. She wore plain black sweatpants and a T-shirt with a big black cat on it.

"When did you get these?"

She snorted. "I didn't spend all of the money on those two suits. I also bought T-shirts, sweatpants, bras, panties . . ."

"White lacy panties?" he inquired. His voice was like velvet. She could've sworn there was magic in it, not the magic of the Edge or the Weird but some sort of male magic, the kind that made you fall asleep cuddled up with a big smile on your face.

"Was there something you wanted to talk to me about?"

Kaldar looked at the ceiling. "I came to ask you why."

"Mmmm?"

"I want you, Audrey. I want you so badly, you are my first thought in the morning and my last at night."

Oh, he is smooth.

Kaldar moved around her, maintaining the distance, stalking. He moved like a sword fighter: strong, sure, but graceful. Funny how she had never noticed it before.

"You kiss me like you want me, too. You thought about it. You pictured us together, making love."

She smiled at him. *Kaldar, you slick bandit, you.*

"We're both adults, we want each other, and there is nothing stopping us. Why aren't we together?"

Audrey kept her smile firmly in place.

Kaldar paused. He was looking at her, at once loving, admiring, possessive, and yearning. She'd been hit with a few come-hither stares in her time, but this one left them all in the dust.

"Do you think I'd hurt you, Audrey? Are you afraid it won't be good, and you won't like it, because I promise you, you will."

Kaldar, a man of low self-esteem, unassuming and humble.

"Help me out," he said.

"I don't think we should talk about this. I think you should go back to your room."

"Why?"

"Because it will make things between us tense and difficult."

"Things between us are already tense and difficult." Kaldar planted himself between the bed and the door. "I'm not leaving."

"You really want an answer?" Nothing good would come of it.

"Yes," Kaldar said. "I do."

"Okay. When I was little, my grandmother gave me this advice. She said, 'Audrey, if you meet a man who is smooth, who says all the right things and knows all the tricks to make a woman happy, you've got to ask yourself how he got that way.'"

"I don't understand," Kaldar said.

"How old are you?"

"What does that have to do with anything?"

Audrey put her hands on her hips. "You wanted this conversation, silver-tongue."

"Thirty-two."

"You have nine years on me, Kaldar. I bet most of your friends are married. They're probably family men. Some of them have kids, others are thinking about it. Many probably bought their first houses a few years back. Why aren't you married, Kaldar?"

He gave her an odd one-shouldered shrug. "Maybe I was waiting for the right girl."

"Please." For some reason, she felt like crying, which was completely stupid. "With your looks and your skills, I bet you've met plenty of girls. The right girl came and went, Kaldar. Probably more than once."

"I'm confused. So you want us to be married, is that it?"

She actually had to fight the tears back. It took all of her skill to keep her expression pleasant. At least she hoped it was. "Don't be silly. I can't marry you. I don't even know you. You change faces the way most people wear socks, every day a new pair. A charming rogue, an arrogant businessman, a caring uncle, a slick thief . . . You pull them off and on at will. I don't even know if I've glimpsed the real you in this masquerade. Ask me what the real Kaldar is like. What does he want, what does he need, what sort of man is he, and I can't tell you. Do you even know which one of these roles is the real you?"

He remained silent.

"Before I take a man into my bed, I need to know him. I want to trust him and like him. You are the sexiest man I've ever met. Without a doubt. The best pickpocket. The best swordsman. And you're a genius conman. You'd run circles around the best grifters I know. My father would have no chance. You'd get him to sign over his house for a snowball in January."

"So that's it," he said quietly. "You think I'm conning you, Audrey?"

"No. I know you are conning me." Audrey shrugged. "Kaldar, you stole my cross. You treated me like a mark. You have no respect for me."

"I stole it because I am obsessed with you." Emotion vibrated in his voice. "I wanted something of yours because that was all I could get."

"I'm sure." Audrey sighed. "You're not the first grifter

who tried to charm my panties off. I've seen all the tricks, I've heard all of the sweet words. I grew up with a father who was really good at manipulating women. I've seen my dad's friends 'handle' their wives. It's not that we wouldn't have fun, Kaldar. We would. And before today, I probably would have taken you up on your offer. But we almost died today. It made me realize that I deserve some happiness. And now I don't want just fun."

"What do you want, then?"

"I want honesty and loyalty, and I want to give loyalty and love in return. For once in my life, I want to be able to trust someone without having to double-check, and keep an eye on him, and worry if he's lying to me. I still want to have fun, but I want to be loved, Kaldar. Really loved. Life is too short, and I want to experience that before I die. I don't think that's the kind of fun you had in mind when you walked in here. And there is nothing wrong with that. We just want different things, and if we get together, it will be a disaster."

"You're a mind reader now?"

He actually sounded angry. *He is angry. Really? Fine. I can be angry, too.*

"Sure. I'll read your mind. It's not that difficult. All of your thoughts about me and all of your fantasies end with you between my legs and me crying out and having the best orgasm of my life, then telling you about it. You've never thought past that point, but if you had, in your head the next morning we would get up like nothing had ever happened. It wouldn't be awkward. Nothing would've changed. We'd go on with our scheme, have a lot of great sex, and if we somehow survived, when it came time to part, you'd give me a pat on the ass, and I would stand there, sad and watching you as you fly away on your wyvern to greater adventures and other women. Out of sight, out of mind. If you ever happened to be in this part of the country, you'd look me up for a quickie because you'd know that your superloving has forever spoiled me, and no other man would ever be good enough to replace you. And twenty years from now, you would still be in the exact same place you are now, having the time of your life, grifting for the glory of Adrianglia and for your vengeance, while I waited patiently for a chance to see you. No, thank you."

Kaldar stared at her. He had no expression on his face.

She leaned forward, rocking on her toes to stand a little closer to his face. "You will break my heart, Kaldar. We both know it. And now, since we have everything out in the open, how about we forget we had this conversation? You go back to your room, and tomorrow, we'll flirt and laugh and act like nothing happened."

He just stood there.

"Fine. You want it the other way, we can do that, too. Tell me I'm wrong. Tell me that's not what you've imagined, and, for once in your life, don't lie."

Kaldar leaned forward, his eyes dark. "I imagined that you might want to have a little bit of fun before you went back to wasting your life. You have the brains, the talent, and the looks, and you use all that to take dirty pictures of adulterers and flirt with insurance cheats. Is that really it, Audrey? Is that who you aspire to be?"

She recoiled.

"You're right," Kaldar said. "When it's over, I *will* fly off on a wyvern, and you will go back to your dull existence, suppressing everything that makes you you. I may not be married or trustworthy, but what I do matters, and I'm good at it."

"What I do matters, too!"

"To whom? Anyone can do your job, Audrey. Of course, you are the best at it. You have so much talent and experience, you have no competition. You're playing with marked cards at a table full of blind players. Is that it? Are you afraid of competition? Afraid to try to see how good you really are? Because I've never seen better."

"You can leave now."

"Oh, I'm going. Don't worry. Think about what I said, Audrey. You were born to steal, to grift, and to outwit people who need to be stopped. But you insist on withering your soul instead. You say you want honesty. Try being honest with yourself. Why did you break into the Pyramid of Ptah? Why, when I came to you with this possibly fatal proposition to fight the Hand and the Edge barons, did it take you less than ten minutes to take me up on it?"

He turned and walked out of the room.

The door clicked closed.

Audrey flung herself on the bed. It had to be said. Of course it had to be said. If anything, it was a wonder both of them had stayed in the room as long as they had. Most conmen ran when called on it, and neither she nor Kaldar were an exception to that rule. Audrey stared at the door. She wanted it to burst open. She wanted him to charge into the room, grab her, kiss her, and tell her he loved her. It was such a stupid little-girl fantasy, and yet she sat there, desperate, and stared at the door.

She was right. Everything she had said was perfectly valid. Everything he had said was perfectly valid, too. She had known the safest thing would have been to walk away from this adventure the first chance she got. And when she had climbed the mountain slope to Gnome's house, hyperaware of Kaldar behind her, that possibility had entered her head. But she had stayed. She had stayed because it was right, she had stayed because every twist and every challenge sent the excitement of anticipation through her. She had stayed because she cared what would happen to Gaston, Jack, and George. And she had stayed because being near Kaldar made her dream.

Audrey didn't know what she would do when it was all over. She couldn't go back to the Broken. In a twisted way, all her fears had come true: Kaldar had destroyed her life, and up until tonight, she had blissfully helped him dismantle it brick by brick.

Half an hour later, she knew he wouldn't be coming. She cried quietly until she was too exhausted to sob. Then she washed her face with cold water to keep it from being puffy and red in the morning, turned off the lights, and climbed into her bed.

The night shadows claimed the room. She usually welcomed darkness, but tonight it felt sinister. She lay for a long minute, torn between the fear of darkness and the irrational worry that if she stepped down to turn on the lights, something would grab her ankle.

This was ridiculous.

She got out of bed, turned on the lights, went to the next suite, and knocked on the door. The door swung open, and Gaston grinned at her.

"Can I borrow a knife?"

"A peel-an-apple knife or a serious knife?"

"A serious knife."

He stepped into the room and handed her a long wavy dagger with a silvery blade. "Is anything wrong?"

"No." *I'm just afraid to go to sleep by myself.* "I just realized that I have no weapon."

Understanding sparked in his eyes. "Have you seen my uncle? I thought he was with you."

"He came by but left a while ago. Thank you for the dagger."

"No problem."

She went back into her room, locked the door, put the dagger on the night table next to the bed, turned off the lights, and lay down. If any of the Hand's freaks decided to hide under her bed, she would turn it into mincemeat.

KALDAR leaned on the rail of a long balcony wrapping the third floor of the hotel. Below him, a landscaped courtyard tried to tempt him with a small pool. Mmm. A swim wouldn't be unwelcome right about now. A paved walkway wound around it and stretched on toward some small river winding its way between green shores. A full moon hung above all of it, like a pale coin in the dark sky. In the moonlight, the river's water glistened like volcanic glass.

Regret filled him, and when he looked at the moon's face, it seemed mournful to him.

He had blown it with Audrey. He said things he should've kept to himself if he entertained any hope of ever being with her. What he had said was the truth, but it would change nothing. When they were done, she would return to her life in the Broken and persist in slowly wasting away. He truly had never seen anyone better, and it brought him nearly physical pain to think she would waste it all. He sighed, hoping to exhale his frustration into the night.

Careful footsteps came from the stairwell. A moment, and Gaston leaned on the rail next to him. "Here you are, Uncle. I was worried."

"I'm touched," Kaldar replied out of habit, but his voice sounded devoid of mirth even to him.

Gaston's eyes caught the moonlight and reflected it in bright silver. He gathered himself, his gaze fixed on the pale disk as if wanting to reach for it. The thoas always had a thing for the moon.

"Does it speak to you?" Kaldar asked.

"No. But there is something about it. It's this beautiful thing you can never reach. No matter what you do, you'll never touch it. You can only look and imagine what it would be like to hold it." Gaston turned and looked at him. "Something's bothering you, Uncle."

"How old was your father when he had you? Twenty-eight?"

"Twenty-nine."

"And you're the youngest of the three."

Gaston nodded.

"I've been thinking," Kaldar said. "Before the Hand decimated the family, we had seven men within five years of my age. None of them were unmarried."

Gaston frowned at the moon. "No, except for Richard."

Yes, Richard. Bringing up his older brother's marriage was like worrying an old scab—it had healed over, but it still hurt. Richard's wife had left him, as their mother had left their father a decade before. Richard had never recovered. Come to think of it, neither had he.

Kaldar had arranged that marriage. He'd arranged most marriages within the family. Love was one thing. Getting two swamp clans to settle on the dowry and terms was another. At the time, he had no misgivings. Richard and Meline seemed perfect for each other. Both serious, both focused. In retrospect, they had been too alike.

"It's Memaw's fault," Gaston said. "She nags everyone into marriage. I remember my older brother complaining. The moment he turned twenty, she started after him with the guilt. 'Oh, I will die soon and won't get to see you have the little ones. If only you'd find yourself a nice girl, I could go to the funeral pyre happy.' She's like an ere-vaurg—once she gets her teeth into you, she won't let go until you give up."

"She never brought it up with me."

"Strange. You always had the prettiest girls." Gaston grinned. "Maybe she was scared, Uncle. If we had Kaldar number two and Kaldar number three around, nothing would stay put. You'd set something down and whoosh, it would be gone, and nobody would know what had happened to it."

Kaldar looked at the river. He had to give Audrey that one. Nobody had ever expected him to settle down. Not even his own family. He didn't inspire the family-man kind of confidence.

Thinking back, he remembered faces and names, men he used to know in the Mire. Men who were his friends. One by one, he'd stop seeing them around, and a year or two later, he'd find out they were married. They'd run into each other, they'd introduce their wives and watch him with more diligence than needed. He could imagine the conversation around the dinner table. Wives had little use for him—he was liable to get their husbands into trouble, and his former friends weren't too keen on letting him talk to their women too much.

Marriage was a trap. The moment the man said the words "I do" at the altar, he surrendered his freedom. He was no longer free to pursue other women. Staying out past the appointed hour required his wife's permission. Getting drunk with his friends resulted in a fight when he got home. He'd have to report where he went, when he would be back, who he would be with, and why he would choose to do something else rather than stay home and pick out fabric for new drapes. A married man was no longer carefree. He was a provider, a husband, and a father. His castle was no longer his. He was permitted to live there on someone else's terms. He already had Nancy Virai telling him where to go and what to do there. That was as much supervision as he cared to accept.

"Is Audrey doing okay?" Gaston asked.

"She's fine."

"Oh good. She came by asking for a knife. I think she's scared to sleep by herself."

"It's a harder thing for her than it is for us," Kaldar said. "George deals with death every day. He's come to terms with it. Jack has killed things in the woods since he could walk. He has a simple way of looking at it. You and I are from the Mire. Audrey has had very little experience with brutality. It wasn't a part of her life." And the last time she experienced it, it scarred her. She didn't seem like she was falling apart, but Audrey was an excellent actress.

Genius conman. Yes, there was the pot calling the kettle black.

There were nights when he was afraid to go to sleep by himself as well. He'd planned on making it easier on both of them tonight, but even the best of plans occasionally came crashing down.

"She's funny," Gaston said.

Kaldar looked at him.

"And pretty. And she doesn't buy any of the bullshit you're selling."

"I think it's time for you to go to bed."

Gaston grinned, his eyes shining. "Whatever you say, Uncle."

He started toward the stairway and turned, walking backward. "If you had a kid, would he be my cousin once or twice removed?"

"Keep walking."

Gaston laughed. A moment later, a quick staccato of footsteps announced his going down the stairs.

Kaldar looked back to the moon. It stared back at him,

beautiful and indifferent. The moon was the same every-where, here over some small river in the Broken or back in the Mire, hanging over the dark cypresses, serenaded by ere-vaurgs. He used to look at it like this from the balcony of the old Mar house. Thanks to the Hand, the family home lay abandoned now. None of them could ever return to it.

He missed the Mire but less than he'd expected. The family had built a new house on the edge of the Red Swamps in Adrianglia. The Red Swamps differed from the Mire, but it felt like home. He'd built his own house too, not too far from the family's, on the edge of a quiet river. It wasn't grand—the Mirror's pay wouldn't buy him a palace, and since the builder had wanted cash, the purchase had wiped out his accounts—but it was large and comfortable, and in the late afternoon, when the sun shone through the living-room windows, the polished floor and wooden walls seemed to glow.

He hadn't gotten around to putting furniture in it, except for a rocking chair on the porch. But he did own a house. At least that part she was wrong about.

Kaldar closed his eyes and pictured a woman in his kitchen. She laughed, turned, and he realized she was Audrey.

He couldn't have Audrey. He'd have to think up a differ-ent fantasy.

Audrey smiled at him from his kitchen.

They were perfectly in tune. Birds of a feather. She understood him. Oh yes, she understood him too well. She knew exactly how things would play out between them, and she had decided against it. And she was right. One hundred percent right. He was a scoundrel, and he would use her. Both of them would have the time of their lives while they did. But in the end, he wouldn't be caught, and she refused to try.

It was said that there was honor among thieves; there wasn't. But there was honor between him and Audrey. Well, aside from the theft of the cross, which she had taken rather badly. She could've led him on, she could've seduced him

into her bed—not that it would have taken much. He'd climb
a mountain to taste her again, and then, when he was comfortable and happy, she could've tried to trap him with guilt.
Most men got married because they were comfortable where
they were, and breaking free was too hard and too unpleas-
ant. She didn't go that route. No, she told him up front that
he wasn't good enough for her.

And why exactly was that? He was good at what he did.
The best thief, she'd said. The best swordsman, the sexiest
man she'd ever met. The genius conman. Genius. She told
him he was better than her father, for crying out loud. It
wasn't often a woman said something like that.

It wasn't like he couldn't provide for her. Not that he ever
intended to marry, but if he did, his wife wouldn't want for
anything. He was a Mar, after all. Mars took care of their
families.

Besides, if he ever did bring Audrey to his house, she
wouldn't stay home and bake pies. She would insist on going
with him. Now that would be an unbeatable pairing. The
things they could accomplish together . . . It was almost too
tempting to contemplate. Not only did Audrey understand
his schemes, but she could change direction on the fly. She
had no trouble improvising under pressure, and say what
you wanted about her aversion to violence, when push came
to shove, she'd blow an enemy's brains out. In their world,
there would be no unlocked doors. It would be so much fun.

Kaldar pushed himself back from the rail. Unfortunately,
their cooperation would end after they retrieved the diffuser
bracelets. That was, after all, the goal of the whole exercise.
Where would she go after this was over? Her old job and
identity in the Broken were burned. She'd have to start fresh.
And do it quietly, too. If they pulled this off, Helena d'Amry
would make it her mission in life to hunt them down . . .

Kaldar froze.

His mind painted an image of Audrey, funny, beautiful
Audrey, dead, hanging off a tree limb. Or worse, sliced to
pieces. Or skinned alive. The anxiety punched him right in
the gut with an icy fist. The Hand would kill Audrey. They

would murder her. She was hellishly smart and slick, but the Hand simply had too many resources, and Audrey knew next to nothing about them.

Kaldar paced along the balcony. She would die. No more bright smiles. No more laughter. No more sly winks and wide-open eyes.

He lived in a bitter cold place, a deep darkness where he plotted revenge on the Hand for all their wrongs, past and future. Audrey was like a ray of sunshine in the middle of his night. She had lifted him out of the dark hole he had dug for himself into a place where he laughed, and his mirth and humor were genuine as long as she stayed around.

The Hand would crush that light.

He could live in a world where Audrey existed, even if it was far away from him. He was never fond of the idea of suffering nobly; still, he could resign himself to living without her if he knew that she was happy somewhere. The Hand would not take her from him. They had taken two-thirds of his family, they had killed Murid, and he would be damned if he let them butcher Audrey while he cowered in the shadows like a frightened dog with his tail between his legs.

He loved Audrey. The realization came to him, plain and simple. He would give anything to keep her safe. The only way to do that would be to know where she was at all times. If he had to marry her to keep her safe, he would marry her. He would be respectful and responsible and all the other things that turned his stomach. If he knew she would wake up next to him, safe and happy, it would be worth it.

Kaldar stopped pacing. It was decided, then. He would marry Audrey.

He just had to convince her to see things from his point of view.

THE church sat abandoned, its doors flung wide open. Helena marched through them, the rest of her team moving quietly behind her, afraid to make a sound. Inside, overturned benches and shattered wood greeted her. The sickening, cloying stench of decomposition hit her nostrils. A stage and a pulpit at the far end of the structure still smoked weakly, their wood charred to blackness. A twisted thing of jagged metal and melted rubber lay on its side on the right—one of the Broken's vehicles, destroyed beyond recognition. The acrid, bitter reek of Cotier's explosive darts emanated from it, and from another spot, farther to the left.

Her eyes picked out a dart lying on the floor. Another. Another. At least a dozen darts lay in a circle around a wet spot on the floor. A single dart packed enough charge to explode an average-size carriage.

Helena's gaze slid up. Cotier's body hung from the rafters, upside down. A large hole gaped in the crown of his head. A matching smaller hole pierced the back of his head near the neck. He must've seen the shot coming and curled up to avoid it. The bullet caught him in the back of the skull, scrambled his brain, and exploded out of his forehead. In the next hours, the brain matter and blood had dripped out of him onto the floor.

Helena looked down on the floor. Twelve, thirteen, fourteen darts. Any physical barrier would've been demolished. Only magic could withstand an assault of such magnitude. Someone in Kaldar Mar's party could create a blisteringly potent flash shield.

Helena turned. A leg with telltale orange skin stuck out from behind a clump of benches. She approached. An orange body lay in two pieces, cleanly severed at a diagonal and peppered with dead flies, poisoned by the Mura's toxic blood. The sword stroke—if that's what this was—cleaved her from left shoulder, through the ribs, through the heart, through the stomach, and through the right side of her ribs. The cut was perfectly clean, the severed bones flat. Karmash had mentioned that the Mars possessed an ancient art of sword fighting, but this was beyond her experience. Swords didn't do this.

Behind her, a foot scraped on the ground. She turned. Sebastian bowed his head. "You should see this, my lady."

She followed him to a break between the benches. A shapeless mass of flesh sat in the stretch of open floor, hidden from her view by the demolished vehicle. It resembled a pile of meat that had been shredded and dumped in a heap. Emily, her tracker, knelt by it, sampling the air.

"What is this?"

"I believe it's Soma, my lady." Sebastian bowed his head.

"Did they put him through a meat grinder?"

"This was done by one person," Emily said. "A boy."

Helena knelt by her. "What makes you think this?"

"Only one scent with the body. Young scent. Male. And also this." Emily pointed at the floor. Two bloody shoe prints clearly visible. Sebastian put his foot next to them. The shoe print was an inch and a half shorter than his foot.

Helena rose and saw a giant headless body slumped against the far wall. A wrought-iron inch-wide beam protruded from his chest. It took her a moment to recognize it as one of the church's candelabras.

Her magic whipped around her in a furious frenzy. Sebastian and Emily backed away. Helena whirled, her cloak flaring around her, and strode out of the church.

Sebastian trailed her.

"One man, a woman, and a boy against four operatives." Helena bit off words with diamond-cut precision. "Why are they still alive? Why don't I have Kaldar's head?"

"I don't know, my lady."

Four operatives. Each a veteran, each an expert in death. Taken out by an Edge rat. Shame gripped her. When Spider had spoken of the Mars, his face was ice, and his eyes boiled with fury. Now she understood why.

A vehicle climbed up the narrow road and entered the camp.

Sebastian growled under his breath.

The doors opened. Three men stepped out, two older, one young and bruised, followed by an older blond woman.

The larger of the older men clamped his hand on the younger male and half led, half dragged, him forward.

The blond woman and the smaller of the older men

walked up to them. The man spoke. "We represent the local Edge families."

"I'm Helena d'Amry."

"You are the Hand," the woman said.

"Yes." Helena didn't feel the need to correct her. The Edgers knew the Hand and feared it.

"You are looking for a man and a red-haired woman," the woman said.

"Yes."

"We don't like problems," the smaller of the older men said. "We want the violence to end. There has been too much upheaval lately. Things must go back to normal."

Ah. "Help me, and I swear on the throne of Gaul, I will leave in peace."

The larger of the men pulled the younger closer. "This is Adam. He will tell you everything you want to know."

THIRTEEN

THE continental breakfast buffet ran from six until eight thirty. When Audrey finally awoke, the clock by the bed said 8:09, and so she dragged herself downstairs to find the trays of bagels and doughnuts mostly picked over. She loaded her paper plate with fruit, snagged a yogurt and a cup of orange juice, and went upstairs to check on the boys.

She paused by the door. Kaldar would be inside. Her throat constricted. Audrey stepped away from the door and walked down the hallway, trying to calm herself. Last night she'd lain in bed, thinking of Kaldar. He'd gotten deep under her skin. She'd thought about the wicked look in his eyes. She'd thought about his smile. She had imagined him touching her. She'd entertained improbable scenarios, where Kaldar decided to fall madly in love with her, and they went off on wild adventures. In her fantasies, they made love in the house where they lived together. It had gone on and on. All attempts of not thinking about Kaldar had led back to Kaldar.

Audrey reached the end of the hallway and leaned with her back against the wall, holding her plate and her drink.

One moment, she wished she hadn't told him no; the next moment, she'd reasoned that it was the right thing to do, the best thing for them both. Would it be awkward now? Would he be angry, hurt? Would he act like nothing happened? The only way to find out would be to open that door.

Knowing Kaldar, it could only go two ways from here. Either he cut his losses, or he would try even harder.

She couldn't stand here forever.

Audrey made her way back to the suite. Her hands full, she banged her toes against the door. The door swung open, and Audrey almost dropped her plate.

A trim man stood in the doorway. He was clean-shaven, meticulously groomed, but still distinctly masculine. His short hair, the color of dark brown sugar, was brushed back from his face. His long sideburns, shaped with surgical precision, made his face appear more narrow. He wore black leather pants of complex construction, with ornate Weird stitching and a wide-sleeved white shirt, with an embroidered high-necked collar. A vest clasped his narrow waist and wide chest, swirls and elaborate flourishes of pale gray leather over black. His hands, with perfectly clean, trimmed nails, were bare. He wore no jewelry except for a single silver earring.

"Good morning, my lady," he said. His smooth, cultured voice exuded quiet competence.

It was Kaldar. Somehow, it was Kaldar.

"Would you care to come in, my lady?" The new Kaldar stepped aside, holding the door with a slight bow.

She stepped inside on autopilot. He shut the door behind her.

"Your hair," she said.

"It was too dark before," he said, his brown eyes solemn. "People tend to notice the extremes: hair color that's too dark or too light stands out. By the nature of my role, I shouldn't draw attention to myself."

He'd cut at least three inches off too, trimming his wild mess into a structured, functional haircut.

She landed in a chair. Gaston was packing their bags. He wore dark brown leather, from his head to the toes of his tall boots. His hair had been brushed until it shone and braided away from his face. He put a wide-brimmed leather hat on his head and grinned.

"You look like a highwayman."

"He's our groom," Kaldar said. "He's meant to look menacing."

Gaston raised his eyebrows and bared his teeth. "Grrr."

Audrey laughed and picked at her fruit.

The boys emerged from the back room, both scrubbed clean. George wore a white shirt, pants of a deep green color, tucked into gray boots, and a gray jacket, which was almost leather armor, with accents of matching green. His blond hair all but glowed, framing his face like a curtain. A blue-blood prince from head to toe.

Jack wore darker brown pants and a reinforced leather vest with brass-colored accents over a beige shirt. The vest sported a raised leather collar shielding his neck. Jack's reddish brown mop of hair had somehow been coaxed into a perfectly slick bowl shape over his eyebrows that was completely wrong for his face. He looked about as happy as a boy who had just gotten himself a mouthful of overcooked spinach. Audrey choked on a piece of honeydew melon. "Jack, who did this to your hair?"

George drew himself up. "It's a very popular hairstyle right now."

"I'm sure. Do you like it?"

Jack shook his head.

"Go wet your head and bring me some hair gel. I'm going to play with your hair."

A moment later, she had a bottle of hair gel and a brush and a wet-haired Jack, who sat cross-legged in front of her chair. She worked the gel into Jack's hair and began to spike it, shaping it into a calculated mess.

"The trick is to own it," she told Jack. "If you're confident, everyone else will buy it."

"So what's the plan?" Gaston asked.

"George and Jack are themselves. I'm their tutor." Kaldar turned to the boys. "My name is Olivier Brossard. I've been your tutor for two years. Declan hired me, and your sister Rose has the utmost confidence in me. Gaston, you're Magnus, our groom."

"And Audrey?" Jack asked.

Kaldar grimaced. "Unfortunately, there is no appropriate way to include Audrey in our party. Adolescent male blue-bloods don't typically travel in the company of a woman, unless she's a blood relative. Audrey, you don't have the knowledge necessary to pull off the guise of a blueblood."

"We could dress her up as a man," Jack said.

Audrey smiled. "You're so sweet, Jack. Thank you for thinking of me. But even if we somehow managed to hide my chest, there is no way to disguise my face."

"I concur," Kaldar said. "You are too pretty and too feminine. Even if I glue a false beard on you, you would look like a woman with a false beard and not a man."

That one casual word, "pretty," made her heart speed up a bit. The way he said it, so matter-of-factly, just made the impact stronger. She'd fallen harder for Kaldar than she had thought. *Well, what's done is done.*

He was talking to her. "Would you mind staying in the cabin when we land? Magnus will stay with you to keep an eye on things, and we'll sneak you into our rooms at night."

"That will be fine." Audrey critically examined Jack's head. His hair stood on end, not completely spiky but not completely curling, either. He looked like he could kick some butt. "I don't mind hiding in the cabin."

She glanced at Kaldar, trying to gauge his emotions. But Kaldar was gone. Only Olivier Brossard looked back at her, with a calm, sardonic expression.

THE wyvern circled the mountain, obeying the gentle suggestions of Kaldar's long fingers touching the console levers. The huge beast turned and swept into the open. Next to Kaldar, Audrey leaned to the windshield. The California of the Broken was a desert in some parts, she reflected. The California of the Weird was all mountains, lakes, and lush greenery.

In the cabin behind them, the boys completed final preparations: the right weapons, the right gear. A quiet argument had broken out between Gaston and Jack over the choice of a dagger, with George acting as a referee.

Far ahead on the mountaintop, cushioned with the fluffy foliage of the Weird's old forests, a castle thrust to the sky. Tall, majestic turrets and flanking towers of white stone covered by conical roofs of bright turquoise green stretched upward, connected by a textured curtain wall. In the middle of the courtyard the keep towered, six enormous stories of carved stone, touched here and there with green and gold. The six pinnacles on top of the keep proudly bore long standards of turquoise and gold.

"It's like a fairy tale," Audrey said.

"How many people do you think died carrying that stone up the mountain, my lady?" Kaldar asked casually. He had refused to let go of the Olivier persona, sinking into it completely, with his mannerisms and voice matching his new looks.

"Dozens," she guessed.

"At the very least."

The great beast banked, and they saw the front of the castle. Its rampart, the forward wall, was three stories high and colored the same bright turquoise as the flags and the roof. Long gold shapes marked the turquoise. Audrey raised the binoculars to her eyes. Dragons. The gold shapes were dragons, carved by a master sculptor and positioned crawling on the walls. More dragons fought a valiant battle on the keep, and yet another long, serpentine creature wound itself around the corner tower.

"Wow." No expense spared. "Are you sure this is a good idea?"

Kaldar arched his eyebrow. "All of my ideas are good ideas, my lady."

"I can think of a couple that weren't."

A hint of his wicked grin touched his lips. "You are surely mistaken, my lady. I'm never wrong. Once I thought that I might have been . . ." His voice trailed off. He stared at the field below them, where several wyverns rested, each with a tent by it.

"Kaldar?"

"I know that wyvern." He spun to her. "I need you to go back into the cabin. There is a large wicker trunk near the back wall. It has a tulip on the clasp. There is a green gown in there. Put it on and style your hair."

"Why?"

"Audrey, if you don't do what I ask, I will kiss you until you do."

Oh, really? "I will slap you until you turn purple."

"I'm prepared for the consequences of our kissing," he said. "Are you?"

Good point. "Jackass."

She got up off the chair and climbed back into the cabin.

"Have George fix your hair!" he called.

"Shut up!"

THE cabin shook as the wyvern touched down. Kaldar surveyed his crew. The boys looked the picture of aristocratic finery. Gaston oozed menace.

"We'll do fine. Just be yourselves, and we'll have this in the bag. Morell de Braose will likely test you; don't be eager, but don't avoid it, either. It's to be expected. Now is the time to pull out all of those etiquette lessons you complained about. Treat me as you would a trusted teacher. If you're not sure how to handle something, come and get me. It will be expected of you to seek my guidance. Yes?"

"Yes, Mother." Jack rolled his eyes.

Kaldar reached over and thumped him on the back of his head. "Yes, who?"

"Yes, Olivier." Jack grinned.

"We have company," Gaston growled.

Kaldar turned to the windshield. Three riders approached. Two hulking men wearing bonded chain mail, lighter than steel but just as good at stopping a sword slash: veekings. Each carried an axe on his back and wore a solid, heavy sword at his waist.

The third man hung back, riding with natural ease, as if he were sitting on a couch in his living room. He wore leather and a rete—an odd hybrid of a jungle hat and a standard traveler's hat, one side bent up and boasting a merlin feather. The dark barrel of a long-range rifle protruded over his shoulder. He rode with one leg up on the saddle, and another rifle with a shorter, wider barrel rested on his knee.

"Who's the musketeer?" Audrey murmured from behind him.

"That's a Texas sharpshooter. See that short barrel? When he primes it, it splits on the sides and spits out a ball filled with shrapnel and charged with magic. It's like lashing three or four grenades together and tossing them into a crowd."

"And the Vikings?"

"They aren't Vikings. They are the veekings. They're pagan, they own Canada, and they live to kill. You're looking at thirteen hundred years of martial tradition, forged by a religion that tells you if you die in battle, your afterlife will be glorious. Their blades are magically augmented. They're a problem in a fight, especially if there is more than one."

Kaldar turned and lost his train of thought.

He had forgotten about the green dress. A beautiful moss green, the gown hugged Audrey, sliding over her curves like water. Elegant, pleated at the bottom, the dress was cinched by a length of pleated fabric that wrapped around Audrey's waist, sliding diagonally from right to left, supporting her breasts, twisting at the neckline, and flaring up to clasp her left shoulder. She'd curled her hair and lifted the golden red mass up and away from her face, leaving her neck bare. She looked . . .

She looked . . .

"Earth to Kaldar," Audrey hissed.

A knock sounded throughout the cabin.

"Hide in the tulip trunk, love," he whispered.

She moved toward the back of the cabin, melting into the shadows. A moment later, the latch on the trunk's lid closed.

Kaldar nodded. Gaston swung the door open and leveled a short-range repeating crossbow at the closest veeking. The seven-and-a-half-foot-tall man sized Gaston up. Gaston bared his teeth.

"Invitation," the giant man said.

Kaldar passed the rolled-up scroll over. The veeking looked at it for a moment. "Who should we announce?"

"You shouldn't," Kaldar said. "But when your master asks, you should quietly tell him that George and Jack Camarine are here, requesting a short respite from their journey. They're accompanied by Master Olivier Brossard, their tutor, and a groom."

The veeking peered at them. "Morell de Braose extends his hospitality. You are welcome to the main keep. A kareta will be sent for you and your belongings."

"Splendid," Kaldar said.

Five minutes later, a kareta drew up parallel with the wyvern. Sleek and aerodynamic, the vehicle resembled a small bullet train, with its ornate sides painted bright turquoise. The door swung open, and the operator, a slight dark-haired woman, stepped out. The back and side doors popped open, rising up like the wings of an insect, revealing eight comfortable seats inside and a space for the baggage, segregated by a folding wall.

Gaston proceeded to load their trunks, making sure the tulip trunk went in to the side with plenty of room. Kaldar paused by the kareta with a slight bow. George emerged from the cabin, looking slightly inconvenienced, and proceeded into the vehicle. Jack followed. The younger boy had the most priceless expression on his face: halfway between boredom and apathy. Perfect.

"Secure the wyvern," Kaldar told Gaston. "Be sure to join us before dinner. I have some instructions."

Gaston inclined his head.

Kaldar took his seat by the exit. The doors descended, the driver climbed into the front, separated from them by a sliding panel of metal mesh, and the kareta was off.

Kaldar cleared his throat. A moment later, the folding wall slid aside soundlessly, and Audrey took a seat next to him. He reached over and carefully adjusted her hair, sliding a large ornate barrette into it.

She looked at him.

"Transmitter," he mouthed, and tapped the small square of silver clasping the edge of his ear.

The kareta carried them over the bridge, under two barbicans, and into the bailey. The doors opened. Kaldar stepped out and extended his hand, with a bow. Audrey put her fingers into his and carefully exited. The driver blinked.

"Thank you for the ride, Master Brossard."

"My pleasure, my lady."

The boys emerged.

"This is the place?" George raised his eyebrows.

Jack shrugged. "I've seen better."

"Manners, children." Kaldar held out a quarter crown to the driver. The woman decided to stop puzzling over Audrey's sudden materialization and took the money.

A man emerged from the double doors of the keep. Impeccably dressed, old, and grizzled, he paused before them and bowed. Precisely the kind of butler an old blue-blood family would hire, Kaldar reflected. Morell de Braose was very concerned with appearances.

The butler straightened. "My lords, my lady. Please follow me."

HE had lost his mind, Audrey decided, moving next to Kaldar at a leisurely pace as they followed the old man through a corridor. The polished green granite floor shone like a mirror. The wall alcoves displayed statues and paintings. She had no time to look closely at them, but she bet they were originals.

She barely had enough Weird knowledge to pass on the street without drawing attention to herself. Navigating the Weird's crème of society was way beyond her comfort zone. No doubt Kaldar had another brilliant and idiotic plan, and she couldn't even ask him about it because they would be overheard.

She wanted to push him into one of those little alcoves and punch him. Not that it would do any good, since he was apparently a lethal weapon in disguise.

They entered a vast hall. The floor was white marble, the walls tastefully decorated with living plants in white vases.

Here and there, clumps of ornate furniture provided little sitting areas. Two dozen people occupied the room. At the far left, a group of young men, obviously bluebloods or hoping to be mistaken for them, discussed something with great passion. A few feet farther, a beautiful dark-haired woman listened to a young man reading her something from a book. The young man wore glasses and peppered his reading with significant pauses. More to the right, a man and a woman in their forties played some sort of board game. Two other men, one blond and one dark-haired, nursed wineglasses. The dark-haired man turned toward them. A slight change came over his face, his features somehow growing sharper. He stared at them with unnerving predatory focus, as if he were imagining breaking their necks. It was like looking into the eyes of a wolf in the forest.

Good Lord.

The man held Kaldar's gaze. Kaldar smiled at him.

The man turned away.

Audrey exhaled.

"What a handsome, friendly fellow," Kaldar murmured.

Handsome, yes—if you liked menacing and dark; friendly, no.

On the far right, seated on a congenial grouping of plush chairs, three women discussed something with frequent gasps. Right, the younger men and the loud women were window dressing. The real players occupied the center of the room. Those four looked like cutthroats.

The boys smoothly moved to the left, migrating toward the group of younger men. Kaldar led her to the left as well, and murmured, "Please go to that dark-haired woman next to the kid with the book and tell her, 'Aunt Murid sends her regards.'"

AUDREY let go off Kaldar's hand and started across the floor. Jack turned to see where she was going. Ice shot through him. At the far wall, next to some man with a book, stood Cerise.

His gaze swept the room, and he saw William giving him a death stare from the castles-and-knights board game spread out on the table.

George saw Cerise too and stopped dead in his tracks.

Kaldar turned, hiding the left side of his body, and gently pushed him forward with his left hand. "Keep moving."

Jack found his words. "But that's—"

"Keep moving."

"We're dead," George said. "We're so dead."

They continued to drift.

DO I curtsy or do I not curtsy? Do I bow?

She would murder Kaldar for this.

On the right, a younger woman joined the giggling gaspers on the chairs with a short curtsy. Okay. Curtsy it is.

Audrey put on a bright smile and curtsied before the dark-haired woman. "My lady?"

The woman glanced at her. "Yes?"

"Aunt Murid sends her regards."

The woman stared at her. Her gaze slid up. She saw Kaldar, and her eyes went as wide as saucers.

Recover, Audrey willed silently. *Recover, because I don't know what to do next.*

The woman snapped out of her shocked silence. "Ah! So she finally sent word. What are you doing out of bed? Are you feeling better?"

"Yes, my lady."

"You look feverish. Would you excuse us for a moment, Francis?"

The young man blinked, pushing his glasses back up the bridge of his nose. "But, my lady, the poem isn't quite finished . . ."

"We'll finish it later. This is my traveling companion, and she has been laid up since our landing. I suspect she shouldn't have gotten out of bed."

"Perhaps I could be of assistance." The young man was grasping at straws. "My studies in the . . ."

"Thank you, Francis, but the sickness is of a feminine nature," the woman said.

"Oh."

"Excuse us." The woman grasped Audrey's hand. She had a grip like a steel vise. "Let us get some air."

The woman headed for the open doors leading to a balcony. Audrey sped up, trying to keep pace with her. They emerged onto the balcony and continued walking. The balcony protruded far out over the yard, and the woman continued to move until they had reached the ornate white railing. At the railing, she thrust her hand into her sleeve and pulled out a small metal device that looked like a bulb. Audrey had seen one before—it was a miniature version of the one Kaldar had used to read the dispatch from the Mirror. The woman sat it on the railing and squeezed. The device opened with a light click. Inside, a small glass flower bloomed, its petals opaque. The woman looked at it. Gradually, the petals turned transparent.

She leaned over to Audrey and whispered, her voice furious. "What are you doing?"

"Sneaking in," Audrey whispered back.

"Shhh," the woman said. "Not you."

The barrette in Audrey's hair buzzed softly. *My job,* Kaldar's voice whispered.

"Why are the children here?"

"Long story."

"You dragged the boys into de Braose's castle. Are you insane?"

"Yes," Audrey told her. "He is."

"Such lack of faith," Kaldar murmured.

"If anything happens to the children, I'm going to kill you. If I don't kill you, William will."

"Empty threats, cousin. You wouldn't want to make the lovely woman next to you a widow, would you?"

Oh, my God. He did not just say that.

The woman's eyes got even wider. "You married him?"

"No!"

"Not yet," Kaldar murmured. *"Got to go."*

The buzzing died.

The woman stared at her.

"He's joking," Audrey said.

The woman nodded with a patient smile. "Kaldar's like my brother. I've known him all my life. I'm twenty-eight, and I've never heard him say that he would marry a woman. He views marriage the same way religious men view sacrilege."

"I'm not marrying him." Maybe if she grabbed the dark-haired woman and shook her, she'd get her point across. "He's insane."

"Wait until Memaw hears of this. She will have an aneurysm from the shock."

"I'm not marrying Kaldar!"

"Shhh! This dampener only works on quiet voices. How long have you known him?"

"Nine days."

"Have you slept with him?"

"No!" What kind of a question was that?

The woman slapped her hand to her face. "Oh Gods. He *is* going to marry you."

"Are all of your family insane?" Audrey told her. "Or just the two of you?"

The woman sighed. "My name is Cerise."

Cerise, Kaldar's cousin, Cerise? The cut-a-steel-beam-like-butter Cerise? The Cerise with the husband who was a changeling like Jack? What was his name . . .

"Call me Candra, Lady of In," Cerise said. "And here comes my husband."

The dark-haired man with the predatory stare walked through the doors. His eyes flared with the same lethal fire she had seen in Jack's irises just before he had lost his mind in the church.

Audrey took a step back.

The man closed the distance between them. His face was terrible with fury. He looked like he was about to lose it.

"I know, darling," Cerise said. "I know. I'm sure he has a reason for bringing the children into this."

"No, he doesn't," the man growled.

William! That was his name.

"He usually—"

"No. I don't care. I'll kill him, and we can write his excuse on his tombstone."

"You can't," Cerise said. "He's getting married."

The man turned to Audrey. "To you? You don't look stupid . . ."

"I'm not marrying him," she said.

"See?" William turned to Cerise. "She doesn't care."

"I care," Cerise said. "This isn't the time or the place for this. For now we're going to be civil. This is . . . What's your name?"

"Audrey."

"Nice to meet you, Audrey. For now, Audrey will be Lisetta, and she is my friend. She was sick when we disembarked. We don't know Kaldar, and we don't know the boys."

William growled.

"Your eyes are on fire." Cerise swiped the flower dampener off the rail. It snapped shut.

William pulled a small box out of his pocket and put contact lenses into his eyes. "This changes nothing. Come nightfall, I'll have his guts."

"If we live that long." Cerise smiled and put one hand on his elbow. "Please, William. For me?"

William's face softened. He took Cerise's hand and kissed her fingers. He looked at Cerise as if the entire world didn't exist. That look set off a gnawing ache inside Audrey, an ache that she realized was envy.

Cerise smiled at him and put her other hand on Audrey's forearm. "And we're on."

They headed back to the doors.

"Are you familiar with the Weird at all?" Cerise asked.

"Not enough."

"That's all right," Cerise said. "Just stay close to us. If we get in trouble, we'll kill everything."

Somehow, Audrey didn't find that reassuring.

* * *

THE children were natural and relaxed. They chatted with the younger men, George being polite, Jack dropping a laconic "yes" or "no" here and there with that arrogantly bored expression.

He had been incredibly lucky, Kaldar realized. After kicking him in the gut, Fortune had finally presented him with a gift. And in the nick of time, too. Getting into this gathering without the boys would've been very difficult, if not impossible.

The ornate double doors swung open, and Morell de Braose entered, shadowed by the butler. Gnome's photograph didn't lie. The man was trim, with a cultivated tan and a body honed by constant targeted exercise, and he wore a Weird doublet, a deceptively streamlined but elaborate affair of pale blue, as if he were born to it. A precise blond beard framed his jaw. He walked in with a wide smile, a tiger who was everyone's best friend. Until he got hungry, that is.

"My lords, my ladies. Welcome! Welcome to my humble abode. I and my staff are at your service. They tell me there are refreshments in the other room. Personally, I think we should take advantage of this beneficial fact before they disappear."

A few polite laughs fluttered through the gathering, and people began to move through the doors. Morell nodded and smiled as they passed. Kaldar drifted closer, and Morell's gaze fixed on him. "Master Brossard. A moment?"

"Of course."

Kaldar lingered.

George glanced in his direction. Kaldar nodded, almost imperceptibly, and the brothers moved with the flow. Morell had noticed it and no doubt filed it away.

A moment later, Cerise and Audrey fluttered by, engaged in some sort of deep conversation. Audrey looked delectable. William brought up the rear, his face dark, looking like he wanted to strangle something. Or rather someone.

"A menacing fellow," Kaldar murmured.

"He's a saltlicker," Morell said. "Born and bred in southern Louisiana. You know what they say about the families on the south coast of the Dukedom."

"Hot food, hot women, hot temper." Kaldar permitted himself a narrow smile.

"Indeed."

The last of the guests passed through the door.

"Will you walk with me?" Morell asked.

"It would be my pleasure, my lord."

They strolled through the doors and down another hallway. Arches punctured the left wall, showcasing the ground and castle battlements far below. A pair of veeking warriors emerged from the doors behind them and followed, maintaining a short distance.

"So you are employed by Duke Camarine?" Morell asked. The robber baron's demeanor was perfectly pleasant. And if the conversation stumbled, Kaldar had no doubt Morell's demeanor would remain pleasant as the two veekings hacked him to small bits at the baron's feet.

Obvious subterfuge wouldn't work. The invitation they took from Magdalene had been numbered; he had to operate on the assumption that Morell had checked the invitation and knew it belonged to Magdalene Moonflower. Trying to project an air of innocence would get them killed.

Underneath all that good cheer and polish, Morell was a ruthless sonovabitch. He understood calculated cruelty and consummate professionalism. He would reject innocence, but he would accept a kindred soul.

"I'm employed by the duke's son," Kaldar corrected.

"Ah! I see. The Marshal of the Adrianglian Southern Provinces. And the children are his wards?"

"Yes."

"And you are on a holiday, you say?"

"Indeed, my young lords wished to tour the 'other' coast."

Morell chuckled. "I recall being their age. The world was full of adventure! California holds such excitement for a young man: there are corsairs on the coast, highwaymen on the roads, great magic beasts in the mountains. There are even reports of serpents in our modest lakes. So what are you doing visiting an old bore like me?"

Speak softly . . . "I must confess to mixing business with pleasure, my lord. As much as I seek to entertain and enrich the minds of my charges, I must heed the commands of their guardians. News of your auctions has spread widely, even to southern Adrianglia."

Morell frowned. "I had no idea the Marshal was interested in art."

"The Marshal displays only a passing interest, my lord. His wife, however, is most intrigued by the stories of your magnificent collections."

Morell's eyebrows crept up. "Mhm."

"A man of the Marshal's stature may not always find it prudent to admit curiosity in acquiring art outside his realm." Translation: the Marshal can't be seen buying stolen property on the black market. "Yet he dotes on his wife, who is a woman of a refined taste."

"I see. And you assist him."

Kaldar bowed lightly. "I simply do as my master bids. What kind of servant would I be if I couldn't accomplish a task my lord set before me?"

Morell nodded. "I commend you on your devotion. The invitation you presented to me was issued to Magdalene Moonflower. She hates me. I had sent it in jest to aggravate her."

And the conversation moved to a narrow bridge over the river of molten lava. "How shortsighted of her," Kaldar said.

"I've made some inquiries. It appears Magdalene had some mishaps and chose to, shall we say, retire instead of being run out of town."

"That's unfortunate."

"Indeed." Morell grinned. "Apparently her offices had been broken into in a very quick manner. Her guards were incapacitated, and she herself has been shot. A clean shot too, very professional. No major damage, but shocking to the system, of course."

"Of course."

"You are a very efficient man, Master Brossard."

"I'm simply a tutor."

"I'm sure you are. The kind of tutor one sends out with two children into the wilderness of California, where most travel in a company of a dozen armed men."

"Our party does contain a groom," Kaldar said.

Morell laughed. "I believe we'll get on splendidly, Master Brossard. Please enjoy the refreshments."

FOURTEEN

THE refreshments consisted of tiny pieces of things on toast. As they walked to their seats, Audrey stole one from the nearest platter and nibbled on it. Some sort of fish? She and Cerise sat on the chairs. William positioned himself behind them like some grim sentry.

The square room spread before them. Elaborate carvings decorated the walls, cut out of soft, pale stone and sealed with some sort of finish that made them shine. A large silk rug sheathed the floor of brown tile. Three enormous chandeliers dripped crystals in complex cascades, but instead of bulbs, the crystals themselves glowed with gentle radiance. Chairs set against the walls, in groupings of three or four together. A mahogany table in the middle, carved with the Weird's swirls and flourishes, supported a multitude of trays. Servants in pastel turquoise uniforms circulated through the room, carrying additional platters. Armed men stood by the doorways: the giant veekings, all over seven feet in height, all muscled like bulls, all watching the crowd like wolves looking for an injured sheep. Not one cracked a smile. It was as if Morell had kidnapped the University of Nebraska's defensive line, put them through Marine Corps boot camp, and given them huge knives to hack people to bits with. To make matters worse, the Texas sharpshooters with their musketeer hats occupied a balcony above. One stray movement, and she'd be down with a bullet in her brain. On the plus side, she would probably never feel death coming.

Cerise leaned toward her. "How are you feeling?"

"Better, thank you."

Morell de Braose drifted over to them. He held himself straight, not arrogant, perhaps even friendly, but firm, like a magnanimous king of all he surveyed. The eyes didn't lie, though. In unguarded moments, his irises were cold. He would kill in an instant with no remorse.

"How is your traveling companion?" Morell asked.

"I'm afraid she's putting on a brave front for my sake." Cerise reached over and affectionately squeezed her hand. William gave de Braose an ugly stare. Morell smiled. "Let me know if there is anything I can do to ease your stay. My staff are at your disposal."

"You are too kind." Cerise smiled at him.

A servant appeared in the doorway, carrying an ornate box, and made a beeline for Morell.

Morell moved on. His stride tightened. He was walking somewhere with a purpose.

Both she and Cerise watched him.

Morell stopped before George, who nursed a cup of weak wine. "My lord."

"Baron."

They both bowed.

In the corner, Jack tensed.

"I understand you have a most unusual magic talent." Morell raised his voice. The gathering instantly focused on him.

"My dear baron, you give me too much credit," George answered.

They must've put them through an etiquette steel wringer in the Weird. Broken teenagers didn't radiate cold dignity like that. But then, George and Jack both were one of a kind. It was more important to George especially, Audrey reflected. George didn't want to be viewed as an Edge rat. "I wonder if you would deign to entertain our guests with a small demonstration? I myself have never witnessed necromancy in action."

It was a test, Audrey realized. Kaldar had passed his evaluation, but Morell still wanted to be sure he wasn't being conned.

The servant opened the box. Audrey rose to see. Three small dead birds lay inside, their blue feathers dull. Above the room on the right balcony a Texas sharpshooter sighted George through the scope of his rifle.

"I do hope you didn't take these lives for mere entertainment," George said.

"No, this was the result of an unfortunate accident, I'm afraid," Morell said.

George surveyed the birds. "Beautiful plumage. Are these a common bird to California?"

George was screwing with him. It was a dangerous game to play.

"Yes."

Come on, George. Come on.

"Do they sing?"

"I have no idea." Morell still had his smile, but his patience was wearing thin.

The tension in the room grew so tight, it was difficult to breathe.

George stared straight at Morell. "Let's find out."

He passed his hand over the birds.

A second passed. Another.

Morell's smile gained a predatory edge.

The three birds spread their wings and shot into the air, chirping a trilling melody. Someone cried out in surprise.

Jack glanced at Kaldar, a question in his eyes. Kaldar nodded.

Jack took a step back, gathering himself into a tight ball, and jumped five feet in the air. His hand closed about one of the birds. He landed, petted the bird, and opened his hand. The bird took to the air. An amber fire rolled over Jack's irises. "Sorry. Reflex."

George rolled his eyes with a mock sigh and glanced at Morell. "Are you satisfied, my lord?"

"Completely."

The birds circled the room once and shot out into the hallway and through the nearest arch to the blue skies and freedom.

A good time for a private conversation. Audrey gasped and sagged, slightly limp on her chair.

Cerise grasped her hand. "Lisetta, Lisetta, are you all right?"

Morell cleared the distance between them.

"I feel sick." Audrey pressed her hand to her mouth. "I'm so sorry."

"Too much excitement," Cerise said.

Morell knelt by her. "How can I help?"

"Is there a place we could move to? Somewhere private with good ventilation?"

"The atrium." Morell rose. "Delaver, escort Lady Candra and her companion to the atrium, please. Make sure their needs are tended to."

FIVE minutes later, they were seated in the atrium. Perched on top of a slender corner tower, the atrium occupied a huge round room with enormous arched windows. An artificial waterfall spilled from the opening in the wall, spreading through the creek bed, gently curving through the room. Fat orange-and-white fish floated above the gray pebbles forming the creek's bottom. Here and there, exotic plants spread their green leaves from thigh-high flower beds bordered with stone. Garlands of vines wound along the walls, scattered with delicate cream blossoms. The air smelled of flowers.

Audrey took a place on a white love seat with a soft blue cushion. Cerise settled on a chair next to her, slipping the flower gadget under the nearest shrub. William had remained in the dining room, and the guard sent by Morell stationed himself at the doorway, far enough for their voices not to carry.

A servant appeared as if by magic, deposited an ice-frosted pitcher of lemonade and two glasses on a table in front of them, and bent double, waiting.

"Thank you, we'll serve ourselves. You may go," Cerise told him.

The servant departed.

Cerise watched him go. "Notice how he moves? A trained martial artist. Most of Morell's staff are very fit. In a household of this size, you'd see some variation: someone will be fat, someone will be small, but no, most of his look like they spend hours at the gym."

Audrey gave her a cautious glance.

"Don't worry, the dampener is active. Even if they're listening in by magical means, as long as we don't raise our voices, they will hear nothing except quiet murmurs."

A blue bird flew in through the window and perched on the stone border.

"About time, George."

"It's a big castle," George's soft voice came from the point above the bird.

Cerise poured two glasses of lemonade. "You had specific instructions from William. All you had to do was stay out of trouble until we came back. What are you doing with Kaldar?"

She slipped a small packet from her sleeve and gently tapped it above the first glass. Granules of white powder fell into the lemonade. Cerise watched them float to the bottom and moved the glass to Audrey. "No poison."

"We decided the best course of action would be to remove ourselves from the house," George said.

"Ah."

"We stowed away on Kaldar's wyvern. He didn't know we were there until we arrived in California."

"And this was your brilliant plan to stay out of trouble?"

"It seemed like a good idea at the time."

"Which part?" Cerise asked. "The part where you put yourself on a collision course with the Hand, or the part where you complicate a Mirror agent's life to the point of compromising his mission?"

The bird didn't answer.

"Or maybe it's the part where your brother-in-law loses his head and tries to bring charges against my cousin for kidnapping you two?"

"Declan wouldn't do that," George said, but he sounded hesitant.

"I expected this from Jack," Cerise said. "He gets tunnel vision, although it's a stretch even for him. But you know better."

The bird began cleaning under its wing.

Cerise sighed. "Do Declan and Rose know where you are?"

"I imagine they do by now."

"How?"

"Lark was supposed to tell them."

"So you even managed to drag my sister into this mess." Cerise shook her head. "Jack seems calmer. Did he rend?"

"Yes."

"Was it bad?"

"Not at all."

"It was awful," Audrey said. "It went on forever, and he cried at the end."

Cerise sighed. "This conversation isn't over. I'm not covering for you with Rose, either."

"Understood," George said.

"Keep the bird here, please. I'll tap it if we need you." Cerise turned to Audrey, stuck her bottom lip out, and blew the air out of her mouth. "Hi."

"Hi."

"One day, I will have children with William. This is what I have to look forward to."

"Scary," Audrey supplied.

Cerise smiled, sharp. "I can't wait."

Audrey's earlier suspicions were confirmed. All Mars were insane.

Cerise sipped a tiny bit of her lemonade. "Jack really cried?"

"Yes."

"Would you mind telling me the whole story from the beginning?"

Fifteen minutes later, Cerise had drained most of her lemonade. "The boys kicked ass. There will be hell to pay at home, but Declan and Rose will be proud. And honestly, George is what, fourteen? Most of my family had their first taste of blood by that point."

Violent psychotic swamp people. Yep, that's where Kaldar came from. It explains volumes.

"And Kaldar, that scheme with the preacher, that's just priceless. The man is brilliant. He knows it, which makes him insufferable, but he's still brilliant. I would've never thought of that."

The subject of Kaldar had to be avoided at all costs. Audrey leaned forward. "What are you and William doing here?"

"Did you see the boy with glasses?"

"The one who follows you around like a puppy?"

"Yes." Cerise sighed. "Francis. He makes these paintings. Elaborate, ornate paintings. They make you dizzy if you look at them too long. And if you look at them under a certain magic illumination, you will see interesting things, like the complete blueprints of strategic buildings. The Ducal Palace, for example. The Castle Ordono, which is an Adrianglian stronghold on the northern Louisianan border. He has a photographic memory, and once he looks at something, he remembers it. He thinks the blueprint gimmick will make his paintings special."

They were special, all right. "How did he get access to all those blueprints?"

"When his talents were discovered, the Adrianglian military idiots in their infinite wisdom thought he'd make a good spy, so they started shoving complex blueprints at him and training him to reproduce them. He is doing exactly what they trained him to do, except, you see, he doesn't want to be an engineer or a spy; he wants to be an artist. So he ran away. We tracked him down to Morell, who will be auctioning one of his paintings. Francis thinks people are buying his blueprint paintings because they are art. He doesn't realize they are buying his blueprints to use them for their own purposes. William and I have to extract him and take him back."

"What will happen to him?"

"They will confine him. They won't kill him, but they will put him in a controlled environment, probably in Lona-ret. It's a military building, very beautiful, like a resort. Except with tall walls, magically capable guards, and handlers who make sure the guests don't leave. He is not ill or mentally deficient. Francis knows he is committing treason. He was warned before, and he is aware that someone may use his art for nefarious purposes; but he's so arrogant that he scoffs at that idea. He's convinced that his work's artistic value trumps all those silly little national-security rules. He just doesn't care. He's lucky he's talented, or they would jail his scrawny ass in some dungeon and forget he was ever born." Cerise leaned forward. "The Mirror's agents aren't permitted to discuss the nature of their missions with each other. The Mirror provided us with an invitation, and we arrived here. William is a Louisianan smuggler and a jealous thug. I'm minor nobility and a delicate flower in need of rescuing. Francis is a romantic. He filled in the blanks very quickly. We had no idea Kaldar would wind up here. We must coordinate things now."

No kidding.

"You are still thinking of marrying him, right?"

What is it with the two of them and marriage? "Cerise, he is joking. Besides, I wouldn't marry him if he paid me."

"Why not?"

"Because Kaldar isn't the marrying kind. He's the have-fun-with kind."

Cerise frowned. "You have to admit, he is a great agent."

"Yes. He's clever and capable, and he gets the job done."

Cerise glanced at her. "And he is quick on his feet."

"Yes."

"And handsome."

"Well, of course he's handsome. He's a great thief. He also did that sword thing your family does and killed one of the Hand's swordswomen, I guess you'd call them. None of it makes him a good candidate for marriage. He has wandering eyes and wandering hands." And he lies. Constantly and with great skill.

"He was always very good with the blade. He's a good provider," Cerise said.

Funny how she completely ignored that wandering eyes bit. Audrey hid a smile.

"Family is really big with our clan. In the swamp, you can't count on anyone but family. Kaldar was our matchmaker. He arranged most of the unions for the family."

Well, that explained volumes. She'd asked him about his friends' being married. Of course he knew his friends were married. He had probably married his relatives to them. And she had rubbed his nose in the fact that he hadn't tied the knot himself. That explained his sudden urge to marry.

"So you wouldn't have to worry," Cerise continued. "Kaldar knows all about what's required to start a solid household."

She was actually talking Kaldar up to her. Audrey almost laughed. Cerise loved her cousin. But her matchmaking was as subtle as a bulldozer. "I wish you would stop trying to hook me up with your cousin."

"I'm not very good at it, am I?" Cerise grimaced. "Kaldar is a son of a bitch. He steals, he brews wild schemes, and he drives my husband crazy, on purpose, because it amuses him. But Kaldar is also kind and brave and loyal. It's hard to get close to him, but those who do gain a friend for life. I love him like a brother. He always watched out for me. And you should know that when we passed him and Morell, he looked at you as if you walked on water."

Audrey drew back.

A shadow came over Cerise's face. She looked away, at the window and the clouds in the distant sky. "My family has suffered enough. Kaldar has suffered enough. I just want him to be happy. Give him a chance. If it doesn't work out, you can always find me and punch me in the face afterward."

THE dinner was served in the grand dining room. Kaldar decided that he didn't much care for castles, especially that one. The dining room, with its vast walls, ornate arches decorated by an elaborate red-and-gold border, and carved white columns, was beautiful. Majestic even. But it felt cold and impersonal. He always preferred the happy chaos of the Mar kitchen, where space was in short supply, and everyone talked while they ate.

He was seated near the end of the table, with George to his left and Jack straight across from him. A lanky young man with glasses occupied the seat on his right. According to George, the man's name was Francis, he was a traitor to Adrianglia, and at the first opportunity, William and Cerise would grab him and drag him back to the loving embrace of the realm.

The dinner consisted of five small courses. Francis wasn't eating much of it. He picked at his food, rolling the tiny tomatoes with his fork, and cast sad glances at Cerise, seated across the table four people down to their left.

Cerise looked lovely. Her gown was dyed in a distinctive sunset pattern, popular in the Weird last year: almost plum red at the off-the-shoulder sleeves and pleated, turned-down collar that left most of her cleavage exposed, the fabric flared into red as it clasped her breasts, brightened to near orange at the waist, then spilled in a glorious cascade of pleated blush, a shade too provocative to be called pink. It was a good choice. The gown was slightly out of season. It took time for the dress styles to filter from the North to the South. A saltlicker's wife wouldn't have access to the latest fashions. Red signaled sensuality, and Francis was eating it up.

Next to Cerise, Audrey turned toward him. For a moment, Kaldar forgot where he was.

Francis sighed next to him. The sound snapped Kaldar out of his reverie.

"A beautiful lady," Kaldar said confidentially.

"She is." Francis sent a look of sad longing in Cerise's direction.

"I believe she is married," Kaldar said.

"To a brute." Francis glanced at William, seated across from Cerise. "A saltlicker smuggler, which is just another name for a pirate. He made his money robbing other ships, stole a fortune, and married her. Her family is noble but poor. He practically bought her. Can you imagine?"

George cleared his throat carefully. "You don't say."

"Trust me, the man is a savage. He treats her like a slave."

"Perhaps you should be more careful with the display of your affections," Kaldar suggested. "Saltlickers are known for their temper."

"He can't do anything to me." Francis pushed his glasses up the bridge of his nose. "I'm the baron's guest. She's chained to that monster. A woman so refined, so delicate, should be shielded from the rigors of the world, so they don't bruise her. She is completely helpless, you see . . ."

Jack choked on his food and made some coughing noises that sounded suspiciously like feline laughter.

"Did I say something funny?" Francis peered at him.

"Not at all," Kaldar said. "Please continue."

"She should be free to make her own choices."

"And are you determined to liberate her?" Kaldar asked.

"Indeed I am."

"You have a noble heart," George said.

Francis preened. "Any man of honor in my place would do the same."

The naive idiot. Cerise was playing a dangerous game. Francis could do something rash, then William would kill him. "Perhaps you would listen to the advice of an older and jaded man?"

"Of course."

"In my experience, despite what outer appearances may indicate, married couples are much more alike than people realize. Take care, my friend. Tread softly."

"I thank you for your counsel." Francis raised his chin. "But I have nothing to fear."

Young moron.

The last of the dessert had been finished. The double doors opened, revealing a wide ballroom. Morell was doing this party by the book: they were permitted to mingle, treated to a dinner, and now, predictably, they would be given the opportunity to dance under the watchful eyes of the Texas sharpshooter's magically augmented rifles.

Kaldar rose. "My young lords, it is time to dance."

Jack rolled his eyes. "Do I have to?"

"I'm afraid so, master."

Jack sighed and made his way to the ballroom. George followed him.

"Youth is wasted on the young . . ." Kaldar mused, but Francis's gaze was fixed on Cerise.

"Excuse me," he muttered, and trotted over to her.

And so he was left to his own devices. Kaldar started toward the ballroom.

He positioned himself near the wall and watched the gathering. Music rolled through the disguised loudspeakers on the walls. The rhythm was brisk and familiar. The dancers were making a hash of it on the floor: some tried to dance according to the Weird's customs; others were attempting a Broken waltz. George was whisked away almost instantly by a young girl with too much mascara and a prom gown that put her square into Broken territory rather than that of the Weird. As soon as the dance ended, another candidate, this one at least three years older, stepped up to claim his attention.

Morell wanted a court. He wanted a taste of the upper-crust life—blueblood or those who reached their status by merit, he didn't particularly care. He had a beautiful castle, but the means by which he'd obtained it would get him barred from most polite gatherings across realms. So he made his own court. He invited his neighbors, robbers, added a few attractive young people with ambitions and an eye toward climbing the social ladder, and lured the lords and ladies of the Weird and movers and shakers of the Broken with promises of fine art that couldn't be bought anywhere else. Now they sized each other up, and Morell watched the culture clash with great amusement.

There was an odd mix of extravagance and ironic self-awareness in the entire affair. For a man who liked to watch other people, the ballroom was paradise. Kaldar couldn't recall the last time he was so entertained.

Morell watched his guests as well, moving from one group to the next until he finally reached him. Kaldar bowed. The baron inclined his head. A moment later, George was released by his latest dance partner and approached them.

"You don't dance, Master Brossard?" Morell asked.

"I'm afraid it's not one of my better skills."

"Nonsense," George said. "You're an excellent dancer, Olivier."

What the hell is the kid up to? "Most of the gathering is above my station," Kaldar said.

"What about that lady in green?" George made a barely perceptible nod toward Audrey. "Didn't we escort her on our way in? She was looking for her mistress . . ."

"She was barely on her feet. I doubt she is capable of dancing."

"Oh, come on, Brossard." Morell grinned at him. "You should dance. In fact, I insist that you enjoy yourself. And the lady in green seems like a perfect candidate. She is a companion to a lady from the South. They are born to dance. I know for a fact that dance classes are a mandatory part of their education."

Kaldar sighed. It kept him from grinding his teeth. Morell wasn't testing him. He was testing Audrey. "Very well."

He circled the floor, stopped before Audrey, and bowed. "A dance, my lady?"

She would never accept. His brain feverishly tried to find some sort of explanation to deflect Morell's suspicions.

A hand touched his. He glanced up and saw Audrey smiling. "Master Brossard, is it? I would be delighted."

He straightened and led her to the floor. "You were supposed to shoot me down."

"You think I can't dance?"

He stepped into position, waiting for the music to start. "We have to dance a Weird dance with Morell watching, because dancing is supposed to be part of your education."

"Lucky for you, it was. I took lessons from an Edger who taught me Weird dances. I can tango, too."

"Lucky for me?"

"You put me into this mess. I would've been perfectly happy just sneaking into the castle."

"And being shot. Try to keep up."

"I told you, I took lessons. As long as you don't start doing the cajun stomp, we'll be fine."

"Cajun stomp?"

"You heard me, swamper. And keep your hands to yourself."

He would have to have a talk with Cerise about how much she was telling Audrey about the Mire and him.

The music shot from the speakers, a solo by a melodious male voice followed by an aggressive rhythm and a fast melody, spiced with splashes of exotic sound. Morell, you bastard. It was a hell of a dance.

Kaldar shifted his position, pulling her to him, her back to his chest, his hands on her arms. Other dancers had started, and he was giving her a moment to watch them. "This is the aliya. We go fast, then we go slow, circling each other. Watch the other couples and follow my lead, and we'll be fine. Ready?"

"Bring it."

He launched them across the floor. She followed him, obeying the cues of his body, light on her feet and graceful. They parted, they came together, aggressive, passionate, and he realized that she knew the dance and was brilliant at it.

They flew across the floor again, fast, then stopped for another pass.

He paused as she circled him, one hand up, the other bent.

"Marry me," he said.

"No."

He spun her, pulling her to him, and they circled each other again. "I'll buy you a house."

"Not interested."

The music sped up, and they glided across the floor. "I love you."

"No, you don't."

"Yes, I do. Dip coming in three, two . . ."

She leaned back, parallel to the floor. He barely had to hold her. Kaldar ran his hand two inches above her body and lifted her into position. The temptation to touch her almost made him lose all sense. "I'll be a good husband."

"Lies."

"I'll be monogamous."

"Ha! Maybe I won't."

"Being with anyone else would be slumming."

"For you or me?"

"Both."

She gripped his shoulder, mimicking the other couples. He pulled her closer by her waist. In his head, they were naked.

"I made fun of you. You decided that you should marry to keep up with your family."

He spun her about, and they were off again.

"If you have to marry, I'm cute and I have nice boobs, so I would do."

"Audrey," he growled.

"No thanks."

The final notes tore out. Kaldar dropped to his knees before her. "You, me, and cute kids down the road."

She smiled and said, her lips still stretched in a smile, "Forget it."

He had to get her alone. He was so aroused, he could barely stand it. If he could only talk to her, he would convince her to say yes.

"Meet me in the north hallway in ten."

"Maybe I will, and maybe I won't."

He got up and bowed. She curtsied.

Around them, people applauded.

"Thank you, Master Brossard." Audrey gave him a charming smile.

"The pleasure is mine."

She turned and went toward Cerise, fanning herself.

Morell, George, and Jack were staring at him.

"You lied," Morell announced when he returned to his spot. "You are an excellent dancer, indeed."

"The lady is divine. Sadly, she's still feeling under the weather."

Across the room, Audrey was gently pressing a handkerchief to her face and pretending to be winded.

"I think she likes you. Don't let her get away." Morell moved on. Audrey passed by. Now they were both in the clear.

Nine minutes later, he slipped away, passing the guards, into the north hallway. Nobody paid him any mind. He'd watched people come and go all day. As long as he didn't leave the northern wing of the castle, he wouldn't get shot.

Kaldar sank into one of the shadowy alcoves. *Where is she?*

A minute passed. Another. Time slowed, barely moving like chilled honey.

Is she not coming? Will I have to go after her?

A familiar, curvy figure slipped into the hallway. He peeled himself from the wall, grasped her hand, and pulled her to him, pinning her between the wall and himself. They stared at each other for a pressurized electric second, the air between them saturated with desire. He'd wanted her for so long, it seemed like eternity.

She was smiling at him, that delicious, hot, irresistible Audrey smile. She wanted him, too.

All thoughts of talking fled from Kaldar's head. He kissed her smile, tasting her lips, so sweet and pliant. He kissed her because he had to. He couldn't help it. She tasted of wine and apples and that enchanting indescribable feminine spice that drove all reason from his head.

Her mouth parted, inviting him, and the tip of her tongue licked his. The taste of Audrey exploded in his mouth. Finally.

Kaldar pulled her toward him, his hands sliding over the firm, supple curve of her ass, and drank her in. Audrey gasped into his mouth. He pressed against her and let his tongue explore, teasing, taking, daring her to do something about it. Her left arm slid around his neck, accepting his challenge. Her right hand slipped down, along his chest, lower, to the bulge in his pants, caressing him, her skin soft and warm. Her fingers brushed against him. His body tightened in response, straining, begging for her touch. He couldn't get any harder. She ran her hand over his shaft and stroked him, propelling him right to the edge, to the desperate place where nothing but Audrey mattered. He wanted her more than anything in his life.

They needed privacy. The dark rectangle of a door loomed on the right. She kissed him again, and he blindly found the door handle. Locked. Magic stung his hand, and suddenly the handle turned. He opened the door, and they slipped inside, intertwined. He locked the door one-handed, afraid to let go of her, and hoisted her onto the desk.

FEW people recognized the moment they fell in love. Audrey had no idea when it happened. She knew only that touching Kaldar, being with him, feeling his lips on hers, was the most important thing. Somehow, between their fight and this second, she had fallen in love with him, and when he kissed her, it felt like pure heaven.

She kissed his face, his jaw, his lips, caressing him. All of the good solid reasons she should push him away and stop seemed so stupid and small compared to what she saw in his eyes. There wasn't even a word for it. Admiration? Affection? Desire? Bliss? Love. That had to be it.

Kaldar brushed the seam on her side, found the clasps, then her breasts were free. He bent his head down and kissed her neck, his hands caressing her body, his roughened thumbs sliding over her nipples, sending tiny shocks of bliss through her. Audrey arched her back. Every stroke of his hands, every touch, every heated press of his lips against her skin, felt overpowering, as if her senses had suddenly sharpened. The air grew hot. Pressure built inside her, squeezing her everywhere.

She reached for his vest and worked the clasp open. He shrugged it off and yanked off his shirt. As he pulled the fabric over his head, she unbuckled his belt and slipped her hand inside, pulling his shaft free. He groaned, his body tight, the muscles on his chest and stomach hard, strained bulges.

He was beautiful.

Audrey stroked him again, running her hand up and down his hard shaft, and he slipped his hand under her skirt, up her thigh. He pulled off her panties. His fingers dipped into her, right into the center of the aching pressure.

Oh God. She almost cried out, and he kissed her. "Shh, love. Shh."

He slid his fingers higher and touched the sensitive mound just above her ache. A thrilling jolt shot through her, so intense she jerked back, then immediately leaned into him, eager for more. He kissed her neck, sending small shivers down her spine. His fingers made small, slippery circles, sliding, hot, clever, touching just right. Pleasure spiked inside her, the pressure rolling, concentrating down, toward that spot and his hands, each touch bringing the rush of euphoria closer, as if it spiraled down. Her breath was coming in short, rapid gasps. The tension built and built. She felt as if she were flying, her brain flooded by bliss and Kaldar.

The pressure came together into a single tight knot. She couldn't stand it any longer. It peaked, and a wave of exquisite, intense pleasure swept through her, quick and followed by spasms.

He thrust into her, his shaft a hot hardness inside her. She locked her legs behind him. They moved in a steady rhythm. She kissed him, winding herself around his body, echoing every thrust, feeling every movement he made inside her. A steady ache began to build in her again, that same insistent, exhilarating pressure.

Someone tried the door handle. She clamped her hand

on Kaldar's mouth. They froze. If they got busted, she would say . . . *To hell with it.* She didn't care.

On the other side of the door, a woman made an irritated "Hmm" noise. Kaldar pulled out of her—she'd almost gasped in frustration—and moved across the carpet to the door.

Another "Hmm."

The sound of retreating steps seeped through the door. *Yes!*

Audrey slid off the desk. Her gown had to go. She wanted to feel him, all of him, without too many annoying layers of fabric between the two of them. Audrey pulled the dress off and dropped it to the floor.

Kaldar crossed the distance between them. She turned her back to him. His hands closed about her, cupping her breasts.

"I want you," she whispered.

"Marry me," he told her.

"No." He just kept asking and asking. What if he kept asking for the rest of her life? What then? "Why does it have to be marriage?"

"Because I want to be with you forever, and that's the only way I can prove it. I want to stand there in front of everyone and promise to love you. It's a promise you can't break."

His hand slipped down on her thigh, pushing her legs wider. He thrust into her, sliding in, harder and harder, in a possessive rapid rhythm. She braced her hands against the desk. He wrapped one arm around her waist, clamping her to him, his fingers hot on her skin. His right hand slipped down, over her hip, over her stomach . . . She tensed in anticipation. His fingers found that same sensitive spot, stroking her back to the edge, where the bliss waited. She pushed against the desk.

The pressure inside her crested.

Kaldar released her waist and leaned back, thrusting fast, deep, hard.

Joy drowned her, radiating through her in waves. They came and came, flooding her, overloading her senses. She felt weightless, exhausted, and happy.

He shuddered behind her. A second later, he pulled her up and wrapped his arms around her. She sagged against him, so thoroughly tired and completely content. She didn't want to move. She didn't want to speak. She just wanted to stand there, wrapped in him.

He kissed her cheek.

She was so happy.

Footsteps sounded down the hallway. Probably one of the Texas sharpshooters—the boot had a heel by the sound of it.

They couldn't stay like that forever. Sooner rather than later, someone in the ballroom would notice they were gone. No matter how much she loved being held like that, they had to clean up, get dressed, and go on with their plan before their absence drew enough attention to put them all in danger. Audrey gently pushed at Kaldar's arms, and he let go.

A bottle of water stood on the desk. Audrey swiped it, wet a handkerchief, and wiped her breasts, her waist, and then her thighs. She smelled like Kaldar. She wished she could curl up just like that, with his scent on her, and fall asleep while he held her.

She tossed the handkerchief to Kaldar.

"I told you you would like it."

"You are so humble." She brushed a quick kiss on his lips and pulled on her gown.

"Wedding at the end of the month, then?"

She pulled the clasp out of her hair and shifted it back into a decent hairstyle. She wanted the wedding. She wanted him whichever way she could get him. "Maybe."

"Is that a yes?"

"I'll think about it." She was in love with Kaldar. She knew it. Their sex wasn't just sex—it was making love. The way he looked at her made her shiver. But something inside her kept her from saying yes. It wasn't pride. Fear, she realized. She was afraid that if she told him yes, he would lose interest.

He wanted to marry her. "For men like you, 'marriage' sounds a lot like 'sentenced to forced labor in the mines.'"

"I never wanted to marry anyone before," he said. "When two people marry, they surrender a small part of themselves. They become more like each other. I never met a woman who was better than me at things I take pride in, and I never wanted to be like them. I always knew that whoever I was with was temporary. There was always a new woman around the corner. I've seen marriages shatter. Twice. My mother left, then Richard's wife. It almost broke my brother."

"So how do I know that you won't move on and leave me broken?"

"Because you are the one. You are better than me in some things, and I am better than you in others." He drew her into his arms. "I don't mind being a bit like you. I hope you don't mind being a bit like me."

He said exactly what she would have said if he had asked her why she wanted him.

Another set of footsteps echoed through the hallway. Kaldar glanced at the door.

If someone burst through that door and killed him, her life would be over. The realization rocked her, and she looked away.

"Audrey." He turned her to him.

She couldn't keep stringing him along. It wasn't fair.

He was dead serious. His eyes searched her face. He was terrified that she would shoot him down. He hid it, but she knew his face so well by now. It was the face of a man she loved, and his eyes could no longer keep a secret from her.

"Different entrances," he said. "We can't go back into the ballroom together."

"Of course I will marry you, you fool," Audrey told him.

KALDAR slipped through the arched entrance into the ballroom. Morell seemed preoccupied with some older man. A few moments later, Audrey arrived. She didn't look ruffled or disheveled. She certainly didn't seem like she had just had scorching sex. As far as he could tell, their disappear-

ance and return had gone unnoticed by anyone except for
Cerise, who was observing him with a very concerned look.

Audrey had said yes. The elation filled him, and he had
to maintain an iron grip on his face to keep from grinning.

The butler strode through the double doors and cleared
his throat. "The Marquise of Amry and Tuanin, Peer of the
Realm, Veteran of the Ten-Month War, Recipient of the
Gaulish Shield, Bearer of the Triple Seal of the Golden
Throne, Defender of the Gaulish Empire of Third Rank,
Captain Helena d'Amry. And associates."

Shit.

A servant deposited the invitation into Morell's hand.
The baron glanced at it. "I see Kaleb Green will not be joining our auction this time around."

The butler stepped aside, and Helena strode into the ballroom. She wore the midnight blue uniform of the Gaulish
Empire. Her green eyes searched the crowd unerringly and
found Kaldar.

Helena d'Amry smiled.

GEORGE closed his eyes. Kaldar paced back and forth.
He'd been trying to raise Audrey via the transmitter, but she
didn't respond. George and his birds were his only hope. He
stopped and peered out of the open window. Their quarters
were luxurious and tightly guarded. Their windows presented a beautiful panorama of the mountains, and below
them was a thousand-foot drop straight to the distant woods
below.

•   "I'm there." George opened his eyes.

"Is Audrey there?"

"Yes."

"Tell her to activate the barrette."

"She says she doesn't have it. It must've fallen out. During the dancing."

No, she'd had it during the dancing. It must've been during their other dancing. He recalled her raising her hair. He
couldn't remember the barrette being there. Kaldar almost

slapped himself. Such a simple thing, and they had both missed it.

"Tell her we have to take the diffusers tonight."

George whispered and turned to him. "She says you are crazy."

"Tell her the auction is tomorrow. If we bid, Helena will outbid us, and we never intended to bid in the first place anyway. We have to retrieve them tonight."

George whispered and paused.

"She says what do you think will happen when Morell discovers that they are gone? All the wyverns are grounded, and the giant men with very sharp swords will mince us into tiny pieces."

"Tell her I had a replacement made. We substitute the replacement for the real thing." He'd had the Mirror make the replicas before he had ever set out for California. They were real gold, just like the bracelets themselves.

"She says we did that once, and let her think, oh, it didn't go very well, did it?"

"Tell her we have no choice. Tomorrow it will be all over."

"You suck. Do you even know where the vault is?"

"Yes, I do. It's in the northern turret on top of the keep. I looked at it from the balcony. It's full of guards, it's warded, and if the castle were to fall, its contents could be quickly moved by landing a wyvern on the roof next to it."

George looked at him. "She is walking around the room mumbling to herself."

"Tell her to mumble faster; we're short on time."

"Ummm, I'm not going to do that," George said.

George frowned. "She says when?"

"Half an hour. And tell Cerise to give Audrey her claws. I know she packed some."

KALDAR stood by the window. The Mirror's night suit clung to his frame, turning him all but invisible in the darkness. He checked the pack on his back. Secure. The claws came next: thick solid bands of steel and leather, laced with veins of wires, they clasped his palms, extending up his arms to wrap around his shoulders. His shins sported the second pair. A small coin powered each claw. He pressed the coins one by one. They flashed silver, sending thin currents of magic through the wires.

"What are those?" Jack asked.

"Climbing claws."

Kaldar pressed his hand to the side of the window. Barbs shot out from the claws, biting into the stone. He hung on it with his full weight, testing. It held. He pulled his hand away, and the claw automatically retracted the blades.

"Make sure the door stays locked," he whispered.

The boys nodded.

"If someone knocks, don't open it. Let them break it down if they have to. If it comes to that, send a bird to William and Cerise for help. George, keep a bird on me at all times. If I die, go to William right away."

"Understood," George said.

Kaldar leaned out the window. Audrey was in Cerise's room, two windows to the right. Below him, the sheer drop yawned. No guts, no glory.

He climbed onto the windowsill and planted his right-hand claw on the wall. The blades clicked. He pressed his right shin against the stone. Claws pierced the wall. Climbing was never his favorite. In fact, heights weren't his favorite altogether. Swimming, that he could do.

Kaldar exhaled and stepped off the window.

The claws held.

He planted his left shin, then his left claw, and began crawling up the wall, slowly, like some sort of insect. His heart hammered against his ribs. He knew not to look down, but he didn't have to. In his mind, his claws failed. He slid down the wall, hopelessly scrambling to find purchase and failing. The wall ended, and he plummeted down, turning in the air as he fell, and smashed down on the sharp rocks below with a wet thud.

Sometimes, an overactive imagination was a curse.

A shadow crawled out of the window to the right and began making its way to him. Audrey.

Kaldar hung in place, waiting for her.

She drew even with him, her eyes thrilled, and whispered. "This is fun! The Mirror has all the best toys."

"You're scared to fly on a wyvern, but this is fun?"

"When I'm on the wyvern, it's out of my hands. I can't do anything about crashing. I can control this." She leaned closer. "Are you okay? You're looking green."

"Bet me something that we can make it up this wall."

She detached her right claw and fished a coin out of her pocket. "I bet you this coin we can't make it."

"You brought money on the heist?"

"It's small and easy to bet in case we get in trouble."

He really did love this woman. He swiped the coin and slid it under the collar of his suit next to his skin. The familiar surge of magic burst through him, snapped to Audrey, and returned to him. Kaldar began climbing.

"So how does this betting thing work, anyway?" Audrey asked, climbing next to him.

"It has to be physically possible. If it's something continuous like this or walking through a minefield, it works best if I hold the object I'm betting on. If it's a bet on other people, it works about a third of the time, and I don't have to hold anything."

Her eyes gained a sly glint. "So did you bet I would marry you?"

"No."

"Why not?"

Because it wouldn't have been real. "Didn't need it."

"You are an arrogant ass."

He grinned. "You love it."

Above them, the keep tower loomed. Shaped like a huge rectangle, the top of the tower had no roof. A textured parapet—a low stone wall interrupted by rectangular slits through which castle defenders would fire arrows at the attackers—encircled the tower's top, protruding about a foot out over the main tower wall, like the rail of a balcony. Once they crawled over it, they would be out in the open, plainly visible to anyone who was at the top of the tower.

"Are there guards up there?" Audrey whispered.

"Yes."

"Do you have a plan?"

"I always have a plan," he told her.

"Would you mind letting me in on it?"

"We create a diversion, you open all the doors, we swap the replica for the real bracelets, escape unharmed, and have hot sex."

"Good plan."

They reached the parapet protruding at the top of the tower. Below them, the keep wall plunged way down, to the cliff and certain death.

George's bird landed on Kaldar's shoulder, opened its beak, closed it, opened it again. One, two, three, four, five.

Kaldar held up his hand to Audrey. Five guards.

Audrey nodded.

He mouthed, *"Wait here."*

She nodded again.

Kaldar crawled sideways, moving crab-like along the wall, just under the archer slits of the parapet. If anyone looked over the wall and down, his goose would be cooked. *You wanted this excitement,* he reminded himself. *You wanted to fight the Hand. You volunteered, and you're living your dream.*

He kept moving along the wall until he was almost sixty yards away from Audrey. He barely saw her, a dark spot clinging to the wall to his left. Far enough.

Kaldar sank his right claw into the parapet and pulled himself up. For a torturous moment his legs hung above the sheer drop without any purchase, then his claws caught the wall again. Kaldar carefully raised himself high enough to glance through the closest archer gap.

The top of the tower was flat. In the center of the flat roof squatted a wide, rectangular, stone structure, its entrance guarded by a massive door. *Hello, Morell's vault.* Two veeking warriors stood guard by the door. To the left, a Texas sharpshooter slumped against the wall, half-asleep, his feathered hat edged over his eyes, a grass stalk in his teeth. To the right, at the end of the roof, another veeking and a sharpshooter played cards.

Kaldar pulled the cord of his backpack and slipped his hand inside. His fingers brushed a metal carapace. He pulled it out. The spy spider, one of the Mirror's better-known gadgets. Slightly larger than a dinner plate, the spider rested inert, its eight segmented legs securely clutched to its metal thorax. He slid the panel on its back open and turned the timer dial to five minutes and set the mode to rapid surveillance. The spider's gears whirred softly. Kaldar slid the panel closed and positioned the spider on the edge of the parapet. The second spider followed, but this time he set the delay to an hour and fastened the spider to the wall, just below the parapet. It would be invisible from above.

Kaldar crawled left, moving until he was hanging above Audrey, and motioned up. She climbed next to him. They waited at the edge of the parapet, peeking through the archer gaps.

Kaldar raised a small spyglass to his left eye.

The first spider stirred. Long, segmented legs shivered. It crawled over the parapet, slowly, one metal leg after the other.

One moment, the sharpshooter was asleep, the next a gun barked in his hand. The bullet hit the spider's carapace in a flash of pale green—the spider's flash shield. The spy unit snapped into evade mode and dashed across the balcony, zigzagging wildly. The sharpshooter fired again, swore, and chased after the spider. A moment later, the two veekings took off after him.

Kaldar heaved himself over the parapet, pulled Audrey up, and they dashed to the door and pressed against it. Green magic slid from Audrey's hands and sank into the door. She bit her lip.

Excited shouts came from the other end of the balcony.

"Hurry, love," he whispered.

"The lock's heavy," she ground out. Sweat broke on her forehead.

The sounds of footsteps and muffled conversation carried to them. The veekings were returning. The door clicked open. Audrey slipped inside. Kaldar ran in after her, shut the door—three locks; no wonder it took her a second—and locked it from the inside. They pressed against the door, barely breathing.

Nothing.

No heavy breathing, no testing of the locks, nothing. They were in.

In front of them, a short hallway led to a large vault door. Kaldar tapped the bird and pointed toward the vault. The bird took off to scout the way, then returned to perch on his arm.

It didn't seem alarmed. If he worked with George again, they would have to establish some sort of signal system. Wings open—the way is clear. Wings closed—run for your life. Or something like that.

They started down the corridor. The vault lay at the very end, a huge round door, thick and heavy. Audrey knelt by it. "Five locks. This is the most I've ever seen. This will take time."

He sat by her. "Anything I can do to help?"

"No. The more I can do by hand, the easier it is. Lifting a two-inch tumbler by magic is like trying to carry a hundred-pound rock." Audrey extracted a leather bundle from her pack and opened it. Thin metal lock-picking tools lay inside. The tools and the bundle looked suspiciously familiar.

Kaldar peered at the tools. "Where did you get this?"

"In your bags. You've been holding out."

Heh.

"They are mine now." She stuck the tip of her tongue out at him. "Stealers, keepers."

He reached into his pocket and pulled out her hair band with a pale metal flower on it.

"Kaldar! I've been looking for it everywhere."

She reached for it, and he yanked it back. "Stealers, keepers."

Audrey shook her head and probed the first lock with a narrow picklock. "There is a lock-picking competition in St. Louis. No electronics, no magnifying glasses, nothing but your fingers. I always wanted to enter. My dad never let me." She slid the second picklock into the lock next to the first.

"You'd kill it," he told her.

She grinned.

"So why not enter after you left the family?"

"I don't know. I guess subconsciously I always knew I'd go back to the life of crime. I didn't need that kind of visibility." Audrey frowned. "Now that's interesting. De Braose is left-handed, isn't he?"

"Yes."

She held her hand to the keyhole. A thin tendril of magic slipped from it, licked the inside of the keyhole, and vanished. "Hey, baby, can you move a bit?"

He rose and backed away.

"More. More. Keep going. Okay, that's probably good." Audrey stepped close to the door, standing on the right of the lock. Her long elegant fingers clasped the picklocks and twisted.

Razor-thin blades shot out of the floor and the wall, slicing the space where he'd stood a moment ago. On the left, a wide circular blade severed the air less than six inches from Audrey before vanishing into the wall. If she had stood on the left of the keyhole, as a right-handed person would, he would be cradling the bloody pieces of her body.

"Morell is a fun guy," Audrey said. "One down, four to go.

TWENTY minutes later, the fourth lock was down. Audrey stretched on the floor. The cold stones felt good under her back. The previous lock resisted the pick. She had to use her magic, and the five minutes of straining and gritting her teeth against the pain it took to open it had sapped her dry. The pain receded now, slowly. It was so nice not to hurt anymore.

"Are you okay?" Kaldar asked.

"Mhhm. I just need a small break. Do we have time?"

"Thirty minutes."

Audrey sighed.

"I can take the last one," Kaldar said.

"No, let me do it. Equal division of labor: you pickpocket, I open locks." She closed her eyes. "What will happen once we get out of here? Out of the castle, I mean?"

"Well, we'll take the boys back. Hopefully, Declan will be understanding. Then I will take you to meet my family. You will be expected to eat too much and carry on conversations with people whose names you probably won't remember right away."

His lips touched hers. He kissed her, and she smiled into the kiss.

"My grandmother will want to pry your entire story out of you. You have to be careful with Memaw. She is very good with sharp objects. Like swords."

"Is there anyone in your family who isn't a deadly swordsman?"

"My stepsister Catherine. She knits with superhuman speed and poisons people."

Audrey laughed. "The Mar family: everyone you see can kill you."

"Something like that. Then we'll go to my house."

Her eyes snapped open. "You have a house?"

He nodded. "You'll like it."

Audrey rolled to her feet. "Well, I better get on with opening the lock then."

"What is it with you and houses?" Kaldar asked.

"We moved a lot when I was little," she said, examining the last lock. "I lost count of how many places we lived. We never owned any of them. I want a place of our own. Okay, you might have to help me with this. I need an extra hand."

They fiddled with the lock for almost ten minutes. Finally, it clicked. The vault door swung open with a whisper. Lights flared inside one by one, weak but revealing enough to illuminate a long, rectangular room. Gold coins lay here and there, piled in casual heaps. Priceless art hung on the walls, under thick glass. Gadgets and statues from both worlds stood, each on its own pedestal, backlit by colored lamps. To the right, a huge ruby sat under glass, like a drop of blood-colored ice.

"Best date ever," Audrey whispered.

Kaldar clicked a small wheel on his spyglass and surveyed the room through it. No additional defenses. He clicked the wheel again.

"Nothing. Either Morell is using something the Mirror had no knowledge of, or he didn't bother putting heavy internal alarm systems inside the vault. Shall we take a chance?"

Audrey nodded. "You take me to such interesting places, Master Mar."

"I strive to please."

Audrey held her breath. They stepped forward in unison. Nothing.

She exhaled.

"Twelve minutes," Kaldar said, checking his watch. "We need to move."

It took them almost ten minutes to find the diffusers. They waited in the same wooden box Audrey had originally stolen. She opened it and stared at the twin bracelets. The source of all her problems. Dread washed over her in a cold wave.

Kaldar pulled out the fakes from his backpack.

"This is it," she said. "This is what my brother and Gnome died for."

He crouched by her.

"I wish I could rewind time and go back to when my father asked me to take this job. I wish I had told him no."

"Then we would have never met." He pulled her to him and kissed her.

"I wish it was done," Audrey said softly. "I wish we were free and clear. I have this awful feeling that something will go wrong." Apprehension had churned in her stomach ever since Helena d'Amry walked into that ballroom. Her instincts warned Audrey that things wouldn't go as planned, and she'd learned long ago to trust her intuition. It had saved her more than once from being caught, and now it was screaming at her to get out. But they were in, and until the auction concluded tomorrow, they couldn't leave.

"I know," Kaldar told her. "I have it, too. We'll be fine." Audrey looked at the diffusers. An irrational urge to smash them swelled in her.

"Come on," Kaldar said. "Let's replace them and be done. We have ten minutes till the spider makes the guards run around again."

They swapped the bracelets, put the box back on its pedestal, and left the vault.

MORNING came far too quickly for Audrey's taste. Last night, after Kaldar kissed her, both of them hanging on the sheer wall, she climbed back to her room, changed her clothes, and got into bed.

And then she stayed awake. She rolled on her side, on her stomach, on her side again. She flipped the pillow until both sides of it were too hot to sleep on.

She finally fell asleep and woke up at the first light, tired and groggy. Cerise had lent her a gown, a complicated twisted affair of blue that took forever to put on, but at least the skirt was wide enough that she could run in it, and the pleats hid the dagger Gaston had given her.

They just had to get through today. Just get through.

A servant brought a breakfast tray. She forced herself to eat some of the fruit and a small piece of some sweet pastry. Low blood sugar was bad in their business.

A knock sounded through the door leading to Cerise's quarters.

"Come in!"

Cerise stepped into her room carrying an odd collection of buckles and belts, attached to an oblong metal disk. About four inches wide and six inches long, the disk bore the complex ornamentation of the Weird that usually meant there were high-magic gears inside.

"What's this for?"

"An emergency escape harness." Cerise handed her the harness. "Think of it as a parachute. Kaldar has this too, more than one. They come standard issue on most missions. You never know when you have to dive off a mountain cliff. If you put your night suit on, we can fit it over it, then pick a good dress to hide it."

On autopilot, Audrey ran her hands along the belts, checking them for weak spots. "Why did you decide to work for the Mirror?"

Cerise sat next to her on the bed. "About two years ago, my family was in trouble. William made a deal with the Mirror: they would give us asylum in Adrianglia. In return, he has to work for them for ten years. He's a changeling who's been trained as a soldier. The work is good for him. It lets him practice all the skills he already has." Cerise sighed. "And if something happened to him while he was working off his debt to the Mirror, I would never forgive myself. I don't want him to die because of my family. So I go with him. That way, there are two of us, and we watch each other's back."

"What happens if William stops working for the Mirror before ten years are up?" Audrey asked.

"He won't. He gave his word. But if he ever did, our family would lose its asylum."

"And Kaldar?"

"Kaldar has no similar agreements with the Mirror," Cerise said. "He does it because he wants revenge. And because, if something happened to William, his work and mine would give the Mirror an additional incentive to keep protecting our family."

Nothing in the world was free. Audrey looked at the harness.

"Look, it's not that bad." Cerise grinned at her. "I enjoy it. As long as we follow the orders and deliver the results, they treat us like heroes. Come on, it's time to get dressed."

* * *

HALF an hour later, a guard knocked on her door. The auction was about to begin. She and Cerise followed William and the guard through the hallway to a large room Audrey promptly dubbed "Blue Hall."

The Blue Hall had five exits, the one through which they had entered and two in each of the side walls. All the walls were painted a bright, happy blue. Two guards decorated each entrance, looking like they meant business. Two additional guards stood at the end of the room, where an auctioneer's block rose, facing rows of white chairs upholstered with blue, with an aisle between them. A throne-like chair stood to the block's left, facing the audience. No doubt that was where Morell would sit. As they were led to their seats, Audrey craned her neck and spotted the boys in the third row, watched over by Gaston in black leather, with the kind of scowl that made people cringe. Farther toward the auctioneer's podium, Kaldar was talking to Morell. They seemed relaxed, their postures telegraphing calm nerves. Morell was smiling. The robber baron seemed to genuinely like Kaldar.

Like him or not, Morell would kill Kaldar all the same. She'd counted twelve guards in the Blue Hall alone. She wasn't the only one looking, either. All around her, bodyguards scanned the room, ushering their employers to their seats.

Cerise took her seat—the third chair in the row. Audrey paused, expecting William to follow, but he shook his head. "Get in."

"But shouldn't you sit together?"

"You'll sit between us," William said. "We can better protect you that way."

Audrey sat next to Cerise. Kaldar's cousin squeezed her hand, and whispered, "Stay close to me."

A moment later, Francis landed in the chair in front of Cerise, turned, and hit her with a melodramatic stare.

Helena d'Amry strode through the door. Tall, elegant,

she seemed to project aristocratic haughtiness and refinement. People moved out of her way. Men bowed. Women gave her the evil eye and shriveled the moment her slit-pupiled eyes glanced at them.

The tattooed man who'd thrown Gnome's head at Audrey followed Helena, barely a step behind. Sebastian, Audrey remembered. Fear squirmed through her in a cold, nauseating wave. She tensed and forced herself to look past him at the rest of Helena's crew. Four more people rounded out Helena's party: a bald man, hard and sharp, naked to the waist and carrying a sword; a large woman with a mane of red hair, who could probably pick up any person in the room and hurl them into a wall; a cloaked figure who could be either female or male; and another man who moved with a jerky gait. He looked hungry, and he surveyed the people in front of him like they were meat.

Helena walked by her and slowed. Bright emerald eyes took her measure. The stare promised death. Audrey stared back.

The blueblood bitch arched her eyebrows and moved on, and Audrey found herself face-to-face with Sebastian. She looked into his eyes and saw a completely different kind of threat. He inclined his head in a mocking bow and kissed the air.

It took everything she had to keep her expression calm.

The man smiled, showing her a mouthful of fangs, and followed Helena like a loyal dog. They sat two rows ahead. The bald man took a chair behind them.

Audrey took a deep breath, forced a smile, and tried to pretend she was safe and carefree.

"IS there a particular item your mistress is interested in?" Morell asked.

Kaldar smiled. "The painting, *Nature's Cathedral*." He'd taken a good look at it in the vault while Audrey had tinkered with the box. He saw her now, sitting next to Cerise. William and Cerise would look after her. He had to look after the boys. As long as all of them minded their p's and q's, they would get out of here alive.

"Ah! One of Francis's pieces. I believe I could make your life significantly easier—"

A commotion broke out at the door. A moment later, the veekings parted, and a man in a complicated pleated tunic and a pleated kilt that marked him as West Egyptian marched into the room. Muscular, he moved like a panther, stalking and graceful. A gold band sat on his short black hair, encircling his forehead, bright against skin the color of hazelnut. His face, all sharp angles and hard lines, radiated arrogance, and his eyes, completely black, promised no quarter. His tunic and his kilt were of deep emerald green.

Behind him five men moved into the room. Dressed in black, of identical height, all dark, all athletic, all with an obvious military bearing. The man in green clapped, and the five warriors snapped into a half-moon formation behind him.

Green, gold, and black. Bast colors.

The butler banged a staff at the door. "Prince Abubakar of West Egypt."

The Claws of Bast. Fucking shit.

How did they even find them?

A servant ran up to Morell's side and handed him an invitation. Morell glanced at it. "I see Jennifer Lowe won't be attending, either. Apparently, she surrendered her invitation to the prince. His lips curved in a smile. "I seem to be in the company of all sorts of new friends. How interesting. I do hope we will all get along."

AUDREY fanned herself with the booklet listing the items for auction. They had been in the Blue Hall for over an hour. Francis's painting came and went. Kaldar and Cerise had gotten into a serious bidding war over it for appearance's sake. Kaldar won, and now Cerise pretended to pout. Morell gazed on all of it from his throne, enjoying every second.

"Lot twenty-seven," the thin woman who served as the auctioneer announced. "The Bracelets of Kul."

A guard brought out the familiar wooden box.

"Bidding will start at . . ."

"Ten thousand Gaulish crowns," Helena d'Amry announced.

"Fifteen thousand," Prince Abubakar called out.

Audrey clutched her booklet. She'd pegged him for a Claw as soon as he walked through the door. The Egyptians had made the damn things. If he won the auction, he would know immediately that the bracelets were counterfeit.

Heads turned.

"Fifteen thousand once," the auctioneer began.

"Twenty," Helena said.

"Thirty," the Egyptian answered.

"Thirty-five."

"Fifty."

"Fifty-five."

"Sixty."

"Sixty-five."

"Eighty thousand," the Egyptian announced.

Helena paused. "Eighty-five."

"A hundred."

Helena bowed her head. "We accept defeat."

In the row in front, Kaldar leaned toward the boys. Audrey grasped Cerise's hand tightly.

"Sold, to Prince Abubakar!"

Cerise reached into her wide cream skirt. Next to her, William leaned back, half turned in his seat.

The Egyptian motioned with his hand. The Claw of Bast sitting closest to the aisle rose, held out a leather bag, and emptied its contents on the floor. Slender gold bars scattered onto the blue carpet. Ten ten-thousand bricks of gold.

Jesus.

"I will take the item now!" Prince Abubakar declared.

The auctioneer glanced at Morell.

Say no, Audrey willed silently. Say no.

Morell nodded.

"As Your Highness wishes."

The guard carried the box down the aisle.

The Claw of Bast picked up the box, turned, bowing, and delivered it to Abubakar. The prince rose and picked up one of the bracelets. "It's a forgery!"

"I assure you the item is genuine," Morell said. "It's been tested."

The prince hurled the bracelet at Morell. The baron snapped it out of the air. His eyes widened.

"It's a fake!" Abubakar roared.

The Claws of Bast surged to their feet.

The prince pointed at Helena. "You! It was you!"

Helena grinned, displaying even, sharp teeth. "Be careful, sirrah." Around her, the Hounds rose. The red mane on the tall woman rose like the hackles of a pissed-off dog.

People shifted away from them.

"Calm down," Morell roared. "Stay in your seats, please."

The prince clenched his fist.

"There is—"

In the aisle, the Claw of Bast jerked. His clothing tore open in a blur, and an enormous black panther leaped across the rows of seats and knocked the redheaded woman off her feet.

"—no need to panic!"

The panther's massive mouth grasped the woman's neck. Blood gushed, and her head drooped, limp.

People fled. Bodyguards screamed, pushing their charges out the door.

The Claws of Bast surged forward.

Helena's eyes spilled white lightning.

Sebastian lunged at the panther. A curved knife flashed. Blood sprayed.

William jumped to his feet, reached over the row of chairs, and yanked Francis out of his seat like he was a child. Audrey shot out of her chair. William plowed into the aisle, knocking people out of the way, dragging Francis. Audrey dashed after him.

Helena's hair stirred, as if caught by a phantom wind.

The floor underneath them shuddered. White lightning whipped from her in three spinning balls. The Claws of Bast dodged. One of them ran straight into William. The Egyptian hissed like a mad cat. William opened his mouth and snarled, a raw primal lupine promise of violence and blood. The Claw jerked back, surprised. William half dragged, half carried, Francis out the side door.

Audrey caught a glimpse of Jack's reddish hair and saw Kaldar—he was pushing the boys out through an entrance to the left.

"Keep moving," Cerise barked behind her.

A hand shoved her out into a hallway.

"What are you doing?" Francis cried out. "Let go!"

"Shut up!" William strode down the hallway, pulling him along effortlessly. "This way. The outside scents are stronger here."

They turned the corner.

"I've had enough of your brutality!" Francis dug his heels in. William didn't even notice.

Behind them, a door burst open. Guards spilled into the hallway.

Another door blocked their exit.

"I demand you let me go!"

William dropped him and hammered a kick into the door. It held.

"Reinforced," William said.

"Let me!" Audrey pushed forward to the door. Her magic streamed from her. She felt the lock—a complex key tumbler . . . and two bars across the door, one at the top, one at the bottom. Two heavy bars. Damn it. "I'll need a few seconds."

The guards sighted them.

William whirled, metal spikes in his hands. He tossed two to Cerise and thrust two into the wall to the left, one high, one at the ground.

"Wait, we can explain!" Francis said. "We're guests!"

Cerise jabbed her spikes into the right wall at the same heights as William's.

"They don't care," William told him.

The guards opened fire. A hail of charged bullets filled the hallway. The spikes flashed. A pale shield of blue magic flared between them, searing the bullets in mid-flight.

The key tumbler clicked open. Her magic focused on the top bar, trying to slide it back. Audrey strained. The bar rattled in its cradle. *Heavy. Move. Move.*

"How are you doing, Audrey?" Cerise asked.

"Need . . . a few . . . seconds . . ."

The guards abandoned their guns. The veekings trotted forward, blades out.

"Honey?" William asked.

"I thought you'd never ask." Cerise stepped forward, past the spikes.

"Lady Candra! Where are you going?" Francis lunged after her.

William gripped his shoulder and shoved him back. "Stay back, you fool."

The top bar slid back. Audrey exhaled and pushed her magic down, to the bottom. It grasped the bottom bar, tugging. It felt like she was trying to lift a car.

Cerise reached into her skirt and withdrew a slender blade.

The veekings pondered her for a moment—she looked absurd in her beautiful beige gown—and resumed their assault.

Cerise leaned forward. The pointed shoe on her right foot rubbed the ground.

"Help her!" Francis gripped William's arm. "If you don't, at least let me!"

A spark of white light slid along the edge of the blade.

The first veeking was a mere five feet away.

Cerise struck.

She moved so fast, she blurred. Cut, cut, cut, and Cerise halted, like a dancer in mid-move, her sword dripping blood.

The front four veekings didn't scream. They just fell. The one on the left lingered. His head slid off the stump of his neck and tumbled to the floor. His body dropped to its knees.

The guards halted. Francis closed his mouth with a click.

"Audrey?" Cerise asked without turning.

"One lock left."

The remaining veekings charged. Cerise cut, fast, precise, silent.

The bar slid back. Audrey gasped and bent in half, pain blossoming in the pit of her stomach. Too much magic, too fast. By the time she managed to straighten up again, the bodies of the veekings filled the hallway. Cerise wiped her blade on the skirt of her gown.

William yanked the door open, grabbed Francis with one hand and Audrey with the other, and pulled them through. They marched onto the castle ramparts into the sunshine. Cerise walked behind them, her face tranquil and slightly sad, as if she had just spent a day in prayer.

William leaned his head back and howled. The long high-pitched note of his wolf song rolled through the castle, eerie in the daylight.

A door burst open in the tower to the right, and Kaldar, Gaston, and the boys tumbled out into the sunlight onto a small balcony. Jack's hands and face were bloody, and he was grinning like a maniac. George's rapier dripped with red, as did Kaldar's sword. He saw them and saluted, a big grin on his face.

William yanked off his jacket. A harness was strapped around his chest and waist.

"What is this?" Francis finally found his voice. "Who are you people?"

Cerise shrugged off her dress, revealing a tight black suit and the emergency harness she wore underneath. Audrey pulled off her own gown. At the other balcony, Kaldar, Gaston, and the kids shed their clothes.

William pulled his jacket apart, yanking another harness out of the lining, and slapped it on Francis, hooking it to his own with a short rope.

"Audrey, you're with me." Cerise motioned to her, attached the short rope to her harness, and checked her buckles and straps.

Shouts came from inside the castle.

Gaston jumped off the balcony. Twin streams of blue unfolded from his harness, snapping into fabric wings. Behind him Jack followed, tethered to Gaston with a short rope. They glided down to the trees.

William kissed Cerise, grasped Francis, hurled him over the parapet, and jumped after him. The young man screamed. The two men plunged down, then their wings opened.

Cerise held out her hand. "Come on. We'll do it together."

Kaldar screamed out a warning.

Audrey turned. A huge clawed shape fell at them from the sky. Audrey caught a flash of furry hide, massive claws, a dark cavernous mouth on the serpentine neck, and a single rider on the beast's back.

Cerise spun, but it was too late. The creature's claws smashed into Kaldar's cousin. The impact knocked her off the wall. For a moment, Audrey saw Cerise falling as if in slow motion, her dark hair flaring about her, her mouth open in surprise and anger, and then she vanished behind the parapet. The world snapped back to its normal pace. The rope attaching Audrey to Cerise yanked and pulled Audrey toward the edge after Cerise. Before she could escape, the rider dropped off the beast, severing the rope with a cut of his knife.

Sebastian.

Audrey backed away from the edge. He came toward her, his eyes fixed on her face with predatory glee. Helena emerged from the door leading back into the castle. Blood stained her uniform.

On the other balcony, Kaldar cut the rope between him and George and pushed the boy into the open air.

"Go!" Audrey screamed at him. "Go!"

She sprinted to the edge. Helena and Sebastian dashed to intercept.

The railing loomed before her. Almost safe.

Helena's kick smashed into her. The impact spun her around, and Audrey crashed to the stone floor. A hand grasped her neck. Sebastian yanked her up.

Her throat closed, blocked by pain.

Suddenly, she couldn't breathe. Audrey tried to kick, but her feet found only air.

The world swam.

"A trade," she heard Helena's cold voice saying. "Your life for hers."

No, she wanted to yell, but her throat refused to obey. *No, you idiot!*

Through the watery haze in her eyes she saw Kaldar a few feet away. His face was so calm.

"A good trade," he said.

"No!" she yelled, but the word came out as a weak croak.

Kaldar took off his harness, dropped it on the ground, and raised his hands to the back of his head.

"Let her go," Helena said.

The pressure ground her throat.

"Sebastian! Let her go."

Sebastian hurled her over the balcony railing. She fell, plummeting downward. The trees rushed at her. Her wings snapped open, but the ground came too fast. Audrey crashed into a tree. The branches snapped under her as she fell from limb to limb, her wings a torn shroud around her, and then the ground punched her, and all was still.

Audrey staggered to her feet. Her knees shook. A piercing, sharp pain fractured her ribs.

Far above, the castle jutted out of the mountain. When they had approached the castle for the first time, their wyvern had landed to the north of it. Judging by the sun, she had landed to the west. Getting to the wyvern was her only hope.

She had to get moving. She had to find the boys and Gaston, and then she had to rescue Kaldar.

Audrey wiped the blood from her face and started walking north.

FIFTEEN

KALDAR sat in a chair. Belts restrained his arms and legs. No matter how hard he tried, he couldn't move an inch.

The room was dimly lit, but he could see Helena d'Amry with perfect clarity. She approached him with a syringe in her hand. Cold wet gauze touched his arm, then he felt the prick of the needle and watched the syringe fill with red.

"You lost the diffusers," he said.

"It stopped being about the diffusers the moment I found out you were involved." Helena examined the syringe and squirted a little of his blood into a long test tube.

Why? The question was on the tip of his tongue, but he wouldn't ask it. She would enjoy it too much.

Helena opened a vial, rolled the top of it along the rim of the test tube, allowing a few granules of pale powder to fall into the blood, and shook the test tube carefully. She turned to the table, set the tube into a wooden holder, and sat by him, leaning her arms on the back of the chair.

"My mother is a fool," Helena said. "She has no head for business or for service. She doesn't pursue a science or an art. She simply is, and my father believes the world is better for it. I never liked either of them. But I always looked up to my uncle."

"Spider," Kaldar said.

Helena nodded. "He's a great man. He taught me the meaning of dedication. Discipline. Honor. He didn't wish me to become a member of the Hand. In fact, he black-listed me." She smiled. "He said it was a difficult life. He wanted me to pursue other paths. I tried, but not very hard.

Since he wouldn't let me join the Hand, I crossed the ocean and became a Hound instead."

"Why bother?"

"Because it's my calling. A life should be lived to benefit others, not for the selfish pursuit of pleasures granted to one by an accident of birth. Being born into a bloodline carries certain responsibilities. We all have a duty to our name and to our country."

"Admirable," Kaldar said. "Do you usually tell this to yourself before or after you slaughter helpless people?"

"I'm a Hound of the Golden Throne. I don't slaughter the helpless. They are below my pay grade. My opponents are usually highly skilled."

"Like Alex Callahan, the master of combat, who was so high he could barely recall his own name?"

"A necessary casualty. He was human trash, and, once in a while, the trash has to be taken out. Are you truly in love with his sister?"

"Yes."

"Do you think she loves you back?"

"Yes."

"What about your cousin? She loves you too, no?"

He didn't answer.

"Sadly, she got away. Had I known she was in the castle, things would've gone differently."

"What is it you want?" Kaldar had finally had it.

"My uncle is confined to a wheelchair. I'd like to help him out of it."

"Your uncle is a fucking bastard who tortures defenseless women and murders children. He deserves everything that he got."

Helena smiled again. Her voice was pleasant, almost happy. "My uncle is a peer of the realm. And you are a worthless maggot not fit to be crushed under his shoe."

Kaldar bared his teeth at her. "When I get out of here, I'll kill him and mail you his head."

"I've read your grandfather's journal," Helena said. "I know all about the Box he invented. It's a wondrous device, isn't it? So powerful that as long as there is a drop of life left in a body, it will regenerate it."

"The Box was burned," he told her, unable to keep the happiness out of his voice. "I was there." They had burned it to keep Spider away from it forever. He had no regrets over its loss.

"Your grandfather was a very clever man," Helena said. "We've scrutinized his diary. We've read every letter. Sadly, we can't replicate the Box. But while we studied it, we noticed an interesting detail. While he speaks of the pig and the calf and your dear cousin, all of whom he stuffed into the Box as an experiment, he points out that they all had something in common. He made all of them drink a disgusting concoction he called earache tea. You drank it too, didn't you, Kaldar?"

"No." He remembered that vile brew like it was yesterday. He had hated it, and he'd had to drink it for about two months straight because the adults had made him do it.

She shook her head. "Yes, you did. You must ask yourself why your grandfather would torture you so. After all, the tea had only one purpose—to prepare you for the Box. The diary named several test subjects: a, b, c, d, and e. One could assume that animals were the first few, but you see, your grandfather also lists a certain schedule in his mad ramblings. The schedule has five names: Richard, Kaldar, Marissa, Ellie, and Cerise. Five names. Five test subjects."

No.

Helena grinned at him. "Now, your cousin received the lion's share of the dosage, but you did get a trip to the Box, Kaldar. I bet you heal faster than normal. You're healthier. You probably never broke a bone in your life."

He hadn't, but that didn't prove anything.

"When my uncle consumed your grandfather's heart, his blood changed," Helena said. "Oh, wait. You didn't know that? Yes, Spider killed Vernard. Your grandfather was a complete monster by then, but Spider succeeded in killing him. Spider's blood is no longer the same. There is a certain new component to it. It helps him heal. Very, very slowly.

In time, he believes he might be able to walk again. Sadly, he'll be an old man by then. Whatever that component is, he needs more of it."

"There is no more," Kaldar told her grimly.

Helena reached over to the test tube and lifted it. The blood within it had turned indigo. "There is. You're carrying it in your blood. Spider's blood turns pale blue, but yours . . ." She shook the tube. "Look at that. You are full of useful blood."

The woman was insane. "Why not take me back to Louisiana, then?"

"And risk the Hand taking you away to interrogate you? They may even trade you for one of their agents in the Mirror's dungeons after they wring everything out of you." She put the test tube back. "No, I'm going to drain you dry right here. I will harvest your flesh, your skin, your bones. I will convert your body into a tonic that Spider will drink every morning. My uncle will walk again, Kaldar. You won't enjoy the final hours of your life, but have no fear. Your body will be put to good use. You will support a man far greater than yourself."

"Fuck you."

She ignored him, walked to the door, and stuck her head out. "Bring the blood bags."

KEEP walking, Audrey told herself, climbing down the mountain. Just keep walking.

In her mind, Kaldar dropped his harness to the ground. "A good trade."

No. No, it was a lousy trade, a sucker's trade. It was unacceptable.

A bird landed in front of her. It was small and blue. "Finally!" George's voice sounded strained. "I found you!"

"George!" She almost sobbed. "Helena has Kaldar!"

"I know. We're not far. Hold on, Jack's coming to get you!"

Fifteen minutes later, when a lynx bounded through the woods, she dropped to her knees and hugged him.

Thirty minutes later, they walked out into a clearing. Their wyvern sat on one side. A different wyvern rested on the other. Between the two huge beasts, William bandaged Cerise's shoulder. Francis lay on the ground, tied like a pig.

George saw her and slumped on the grass, closing his eyes. He looked exhausted. The blue bird that rode on her shoulder dropped like a stone.

"Helena has Kaldar." Audrey strode to Cerise. "I need you to help me."

"We can't," Cerise said.

"What?"

"The Mirror broke our communication ban," Cerise said. "All agents in the Democracy of California have been ordered back to Adrianglia. The Hand is recalling its people as well."

"We made too much noise," William said. His face was grim. "The fight was too loud, too public, and there were too many witnesses. Adrianglia and the Dukedom are trying to avoid open war."

"He's your *cousin*."

Cerise's face jerked with pain. Tears swelled in her eyes. "And I love him," she said. "But we have a direct order."

"But Kaldar!"

"Kaldar is an agent of the Mirror," William said. "He knew the risks."

"It's an order, Audrey," Cerise said. "Not a suggestion. If William and I stay here, the Mirror will decommission us when we return. We'll be tried for treason. Our family will lose its asylum, and the Dukedom of Louisiana will have an excuse for an open conflict with Adrianglia. If Kaldar were here, he would tell you exactly what I am telling you now. We're soldiers in this war. Soldiers don't get to pick which orders they follow."

It sank in. They couldn't help her. They wanted to, but they couldn't.

"When are you leaving?" she asked, her voice hoarse.

William tied off the bandage. "Now."

* * *

THE wyvern was a distant speck in the blue sky. Audrey shielded her eyes with her hand and looked at it. It seemed like a dream. A painful, terrible dream.

Kaldar, his eyes, his smile, the way he kissed her . . . She had lost him. She hadn't realized how much she had wanted him until he was gone, and there was this gaping painful hole inside her. It hurt. She felt so hollow.

They could've been so happy. Why, why did it have to end like this? Why couldn't they have gotten away?

Audrey closed her eyes and willed herself to wake up. She wanted to wake up, open her eyes, and see the wyvern's cabin above her, then see him lean over her with that wicked smirk on his lips . . .

Please. Please, I'll do anything. Just let me wake up and let him be there. I'm begging you, God. Please.

Next to her, Gaston cleared his throat.

She wasn't waking up. This was real.

Audrey opened her eyes. Gaston's gaze searched her face.

"Are you leaving, too?" she asked.

"The dispatch said 'all agents.' I am not an agent. Not yet."

"Why did she want him? Why trade me for him?"

"Intelligence." Gaston shrugged. "They'll probably torture him . . . Eh, sorry. They must be on the way to Louisiana by now."

"No," George said hoarsely.

"George?" Audrey walked over and knelt by him.

George opened his eyes. His face looked haggard and paler than usual. "They are keeping him in a ruin. There." He raised his hand and pointed right. "Over that mountain. She has him tied to a chair. They are hooking him up to a machine to drain his blood. I have a bird on him."

"So he's alive?" If Kaldar was alive, she would get him out of there. Whatever it took.

"For now."

"How many people does she have?" Gaston asked.

"Six."

Six Hounds, and they had Gaston, her, and two kids, one of whom was worn to his limit and the other only twelve years old.

Audrey looked at Gaston. "How many can you take?"

"One," he said. "Maybe two."

She was no fighter. It only took one kick from Helena, and she was down. Audrey thought for a minute.

She was no fighter, but she was a very good thief. And a very good grifter. The beginnings of a plan began to form in Audrey's head. "Gaston, can you make sure the wyvern will be ready to take off in a hurry?"

"I'm not leaving Kaldar there to rot," Gaston snarled.

"We are not leaving him." Audrey held George's hand. "Listen to me," she said softly. "I don't want you to drain yourself dry. If it comes to that, you drop that bird, do you understand me?"

George nodded. "It will be fine," he said. "It's just far. It's harder to maintain the connection over such a long distance. I just need to rest."

Audrey got to her feet. "How far are we from de Braose's castle?"

"It's down the road," Gaston said. "Half an hour."

"I need new clothes." Audrey stared at her torn, bloody suit. "On the other hand, no. I'm perfect just as I am."

WHEN walking into the lair of the dragon after robbing his hoard, the least you could do is hold your head high, Audrey reflected, as the two veekings led her into the bailey of de Braose's castle. Morell's guard force had suffered losses. Every man she saw was either bruised, bloody, smeared with soot, or all three.

A cloud of smoke spilled from the third-story window of the keep in a black, oily pillar. The sound of gunfire came from somewhere to the left.

Morell de Braose emerged from the doors, carrying a sword in his hand. Black smears and blood spatter marred his blue doublet. All of his polished veneer had slid off him. Only the robber baron remained, ruthless, cold, and infuriated to the brink.

He could just kill her. She wouldn't put it past him to run her through with that sword and leave her to bleed out on the ground.

His gaze fastened on her. "This is an interesting development. Tell me why I shouldn't kill you?"

"Helena d'Amry murdered my brother. I knew she would show up here, so I came here to kill her. I failed."

"Why should I care?"

"Because Helena humiliated you. She ruined the reputation of your auction. It will be a long time before people will visit you again."

Morell grimaced. "You aren't endearing yourself to me."

"The only way to restore your reputation is to punish the party responsible and make that punishment so brutal, nobody else dares to besmirch your reputation."

"Helena is on her way to Louisiana," he snarled.

"She is less than six miles away, in a castle ruin, over that mountain." Audrey pointed to the green mountain range.

Morell grasped her face and pulled her closer, looking into her eyes. "If you're lying, tell me now. You have no idea how painful the things I'll do to you will be if I am disappointed. I'm extremely pissed off, and I will get very creative."

Her heart squeezed itself into a painful, fear-filled ball. But she wanted Kaldar more. This was her only chance to get him back.

Audrey stared back at Morell. "Over that mountain. A ruin of dark stone with four towers, one broken, three still standing. She has six people with her. When you kill her, tell her Lisetta says hello."

Morell pushed her aside. "Lock her up. And get the wyvern ready."

A veeking grasped her shoulder and dragged her down to a guardhouse. He pulled her through a large room to the back, where barred cells waited, and threw her into one. Audrey crashed against the wall. The veeking slid the door shut with a metallic clang, locked it, and walked out.

Through the open doors, she saw men run back and forth. People shouted. Then all became quiet.

She sat on the stone floor and waited.

A man cried out, a sharp, pain-filled sound, and a veeking fell to the ground in the doorway. Gaston stepped over the body and grinned.

"They are gone."

Audrey concentrated, and the lock on her cell clicked open. "Let's go get him."

KALDAR closed his eyes. He was tired of watching his blood drip out of him.

It was over. He couldn't talk his way out of this. He couldn't pry his hands free. Nobody was coming to save him. He was done.

They had moved him to the bed, and now he faced the wall instead of the door. He would die alone, staring at the blank wall.

It didn't matter, really. He'd done his job: Gaston had the emitters. He would be able to protect them, and he would deliver them to the Mirror. The boys survived. They were safe. And Audrey . . . Audrey was alive.

He let himself slip away, into his mind, in a place knitted of memories and wishful thinking, where he and Audrey lived happily ever after. In that place, he took her to his house. They made love. They sat outside in the evening, watching the fireflies dance over the water of the lake. They drank sweet wine and laughed. He was happy in that place. He wanted to stay there and let reality fade.

He would just go to sleep, Kaldar told himself. Eventually, he'd lose enough blood to pass out. Until then, what little time he had left, he'd spend with her.

The door burst open. Someone had come to change the blood bag again. Two men rolled into the room. One was

Killian, Helena's hunter. The other was Gaston. They grappled on the floor, trying to outmuscle each other.

It's a hallucination.

Audrey dashed through the door, a dagger in her hand.

Killian's mouth gaped like the unhinging jaws of a snake. Gaston clamped him down. Audrey dropped by them and stabbed the hunter in the neck again and again, blood spraying from a wavy dagger in her hand.

Behind them, people screamed and roared. The sound of gunfire and the clashing of steel filled the room.

Killian's head dropped to the side. Audrey rose, bloody, and dashed to his bed. "Are you alive?"

"How are you, love?"

"Great! I'm marvelous." She sliced open his restraints and held up a coin in front of him. "Bet me you'll survive, love."

Heh. Funny. "I bet you I can get through this alive."

The coin pressed into his hand. Magic shot through him in a welcome surge, and he realized it was real.

"Audrey, are you fucking out of your mind? What the hell are you doing here?"

"Saving you. Grab him."

Gaston heaved him over his shoulder. The tube attached to Kaldar's arm jerked the needle in his vein. He swore.

Audrey pulled the needle from his arm and yanked one of his grenades off her belt. She squeezed the grenade and rolled it to the wall. Gaston crouched behind the bed.

The wall exploded with a sound like thunder. Dust filled the air. Kaldar coughed and felt himself lifted. Gaston ducked through the new opening in the wall and took off running. Slung over Gaston's shoulder, Kaldar saw Audrey emerge through the rubble. She ran after him, the ruin dark behind her, the moon rising over it.

He was being rescued. It finally sank in. She had come to save him.

Gaston jumped. Kaldar saw the ground end and realized they were sailing off a cliff. They plummeted down and crashed into the wyvern's cabin. His exhausted body screamed in pain. Audrey landed next to him. He had never been so happy in his entire life.

Wind fanned his face as the wyvern banked. The cabin began to close.

The wyvern careened. Boxes and trunks rolled across the cabin floor onto them.

"Jack!" Gaston roared. "Watch where you're driving!"

Gaston scrambled to his feet and lunged into the front of the cabin.

The dragon righted itself.

"You are marrying me after this," Audrey told him.

Kaldar laughed.

"Don't give me that smirk. There is no way I went through all this just for some roll in the hay. I want a dress, and a big party, the whole thing."

"Of course I will marry you, you fool," he told her.

She bent down and kissed him, her face wet. He tasted tears. "I love you," she told him.

Kaldar strained and managed to put his arm around her.

"I love you, too."

EPILOGUE

THE wyvern landed on the front lawn. Through the windshield of the cabin, George could see every detail of Camarine Manor, including Declan and Rose standing side by side on the landing of the stone stairway leading to the front door.

They did not look happy.

"Courage." Kaldar clamped his hand on George's shoulder and rocked, unsteady on his feet. The loss of blood had been severe. Kaldar was walking, but not very well.

In the seat next to him, Jack swallowed.

George wished he were anywhere else. Then he wished he could fast-forward the day to after he had been given the chewing-out. Neither scenario seemed likely.

Gaston opened the door of the cabin.

Kaldar stepped out. Audrey followed.

"Come on." Gaston nodded at the door.

It was his turn.

George forced himself to rise and exit the cabin. Jack followed him, carrying his little cat. Kaldar waited for them by the cabin's door.

Both Declan and Rose looked eerily calm.

"Go on," Kaldar prompted.

George started walking across the lawn. He felt a most childish urge to hold someone's hand.

"We're dead," Jack murmured next to him.

"You say that a lot," George said.

"This time it's for sure."

"Hopefully not," Kaldar said behind them, striding next to Audrey.

"Why are you worried?" George asked.

"Would you be worried if you had kidnapped the wards of the Marshal of the Southern Provinces and nearly gotten them killed?"

"They don't seem that scary," Audrey said, looking at Declan and Rose.

"Looks can be deceiving," Kaldar murmured.

Declan and Rose were waiting. Lorimor, the house master, stood behind them with a worried look on his face.

George walked across the lawn. His legs felt heavy, as if filled with lead. He and Jack climbed the stairway, step by step. Suddenly, the steps were over.

George raised his head and looked at Declan. "My lord."

Declan stared at Jack. "When I said you needed additional supervision, I meant I would get you a valet."

Jack blinked.

"Watch my lips." Declan pointed to his mouth. "You will never be sent to Hawk's. You don't have to run away from home to escape. However, in the near future, you will wish you had been sent to Hawk's."

"You are grounded until you forget what color the sky is," Rose said.

"We're giving you to Lorimor," Declan said. "You will be doing laundry. You will be peeling potatoes. The pool needs replastering."

Laughter bubbled up from somewhere deep inside George. He tried to hold it in, but it was like trying to block a flood. It kept coming out in snorts and stifled giggles.

"Like I beat you," Declan growled. "Like I chained you in the dungeon or something. You ran away. On a Mirror agent's wyvern! What the devil is wrong with the two of you?"

"We are so sorry, Master Mar," Rose said. "We hope they weren't too much trouble."

"Not at all," Kaldar answered with a straight face.

"What's this?" Rose asked, looking at the cat in Jack's arms.

"This is my cat. I rescued him." Jack tensed the way he did before a fight.

Gods, George prayed silently. *Please, no fight. Please, no fight.*

"If you want him inside, you will be responsible for cleaning his fur off the furniture," Rose said.

Jack gazed at her, stumbled forward, and Rose hugged him.

"We love you," she told him. "I love you. It will be okay, Jack. It will all work out."

"We'll talk more later," Declan said, his voice no longer indignant. "Nancy Virai is inside in the study. She's waiting to speak to all of you."

They went inside and sat in the chairs by the study. Kaldar and Audrey went in first.

Rose sat next to George and hugged him and Jack. "I love you."

"I love you, too," he heard himself say. Jack sniffed.

His sister looked at him. "Please stop giving me gray hair. Take a couple of weeks off. Just for me."

"THE diffusers." Kaldar placed a wicker box on the surface of the heavy mahogany table.

Nancy Virai opened the box, reviewed the two diffusers cushioned in a piece of white cloth, and looked at them from behind the desk. He scrutinized her face. He'd sent a preliminary dispatch to the Mirror's office when they had crossed into Adrianglia, outlining the events that had occurred. He hid nothing. Experience had taught him that with Lady Virai, honesty was the best policy.

Lady Virai's face was unreadable.

Her gaze shifted to Audrey.

"This is my fiancée," Kaldar said. "Audrey Callahan. She is a victim of circumstance . . ."

"Kaldar," Lady Virai said. "Shut up."

He clamped his mouth shut.

The two women looked at each other.

"You've been exposed to the secrets of the Mirror," Lady Virai said. "You understand that there is no way back."

"I do," Audrey said.

"You will work for me. On a conditional basis for the first six months, with promotion to full agent if you don't screw up."

Kaldar quietly exhaled.

"And if I say no?"

"I wasn't asking," Lady Virai said, "You will find that 'no' is not a word I find acceptable."

"Can we have two weeks for our honeymoon?" Kaldar asked.

"Yes. Given that she risked her life against seven Hounds to save you—I can't imagine why—I would say two weeks of holiday are acceptable. And Kaldar, next time, do try to do your job without dragging children into it. You may go. And send George in."

THE door opened. George tensed.

Audrey emerged, her eyes huge on her face. "She's the scariest woman I've ever seen."

Kaldar followed. "Your turn."

George rose and walked through the door.

Nancy Virai sat behind the desk. She had eyes like a predatory bird: when she looked at him, a vision of deadly talons aimed at his heart flashed in his head.

George carefully closed the door, approached the desk, and stopped, his hands at his sides.

"Sit."

He sat in the chair.

"People who work for me are trained killers. Once in a while, an exception is made for those with a special talent, like Audrey. This isn't a business for tender hearts."

"I can be a killer," he told her.

"It's not a natural state of being for you."

"It's what I want," he told her.

Lady Virai leaned forward. "Why?"

"Because I believe someone must protect the country from the Hand. That someone might as well be me."

"Very articulate. Try again."

George opened his mouth, and the ugly truth spilled out. "Because I'm tired of always being seen as a second-class citizen. I would rather work for you and be the best agent you've ever had than fight a hopeless battle to prove myself to people who will always see me only as an Edger."

She pondered him for a moment, then pushed a piece of paper to him across the desk. "These are your goals for this school year. You will receive one just like it every year. Fail to meet them, and our relationship is over."

George scanned the list. Several subjects, with examinations and scores required. Necromancy testing.

"Your summers belong to me." Lady Virai leaned back. "If you agree, your childhood is over. Do we have a deal?"

He didn't hesitate for a second. "Yes."

"You are dismissed."

George rose. At the door he paused. "What about my brother?"

"All in good time," Lady Virai said. "Don't worry. The realm won't run out of enemies while the two of you grow up."

THE air smelled of ripened grapes. Sunshine warmed Spider's hands and face. He tilted his head to the sky, rolling his wheelchair to the stone rail of the balcony. He loved it here. Below him, rows and rows of grapevines crossed the green hills. He used to walk there, between the rows of vines.

It felt like an eternity ago.

Footsteps echoed behind him, uneven. Someone was limping.

Spider turned.

Helena emerged into the sunlight, dragging her left foot. A blue bruise claimed most of her neck. Her beautiful hair was a tangled mess caked with blood.

His heart clenched. He still remembered her when she

was small, a serious, solemn child. She had laughed so rarely, each giggle was a gift.

"How badly are you hurt?" he asked.

"I will heal."

She knelt by his wheelchair. Her eyes were luminescent. "I have a gift for you, Uncle."

Behind her, Sebastian moved into the light and set a steel box on the ground. Helena flipped open the lid. Inside, bags of blood lay buried in the ice.

"The blood of Kaldar Mar," Helena said. "I'm sorry. That's all I could get." She bowed her head.

He patted her hair. "Thank you. Thank you, child."

I will walk the hills again. I will run through them. And then I will settle my debts.

THE house perched on the green lawn next to a lovely lake. It looked beautiful. Audrey smiled.

Kaldar hugged her, and she leaned against him. "So this is it?"

"Mhm. I bought it for a steal. The merchant who had commissioned it backed out at the last minute, leaving the builder with the bill."

He swept her off her feet and started toward the house. He was still weak and swayed a little as he carried her over the threshold, but she said nothing. It was important.

Kaldar set her down inside. The walls and floor were golden, and as the sunlight spilled through the huge windows, the place seemed to glow. Ling the Merciless snuck in behind them and slunk through the house, her claws clicking on the floor. "You have no furniture."

"I had to buy the place with cash. It wiped me out. Besides, I was never here long enough to need any furniture. Until now."

"We don't need much," she told him. "A table, two chairs, and a bed. With both of us working, we'll get it set up in no time."

"Come, sit on the porch with me," he said.

They went out the back door and sat on the wooden porch, guarded by a wooden rail. He put his arm around her. Audrey snuggled against him.

"I thought I had lost you," she murmured. "Are you going to be all noble and chastise me for coming to rescue you?"

"Hell no! I'm bloody thrilled to be alive."

Ling padded out onto the porch and sniffed the air. She paused, poised for a long moment, and trotted down to the water.

"I believe she approves of my glorious palace," Kaldar said.

Audrey wound her arms around him. "I think we'll be very happy here."

"We will. The best thing: no neighbors. Well, except for my family, but they are five miles down."

"So nobody could see us?"

"No."

She grinned at him. "Hey. Do you want to make out?"

Kaldar gave her the wicked grin that made him unbearably handsome. "Do you really need to ask?"

She pulled him to her, and they landed on the boards. He kissed her, and Audrey melted into the kiss.

"You make me feel so wonderful," she said.

He squeezed her to him. "Did I ever tell you that you are like sunshine in the middle of the night?"

Audrey shook her head. Being with Kaldar felt so good. *If this is a dream, then please, God, let me keep dreaming.* "I hope you know you are caught, Kaldar Mar," she whispered.

"You have it wrong," he told her. "I caught you."

They kissed and made love on bare porch boards. Later, they drank sweet berry wine and ate sandwiches out of their picnic basket, watching the water lap gently at the shore in front of their home.

COMING JUNE 2012 FROM ACE BOOKS

GUNMETAL MAGIC

A NOVEL IN THE WORLD OF KATE DANIELS
BY ILONA ANDREWS

Some people have everything figured out—Andrea Nash is not one of those people. After being kicked out of the Order of Knights of Merciful Aid, Andrea's whole existence is in shambles. All she can do is try to put herself back together, something made easier by working for Cutting Edge, a small investigative firm owned by her best friend, Kate Daniels.

When several shapeshifters working for Raphael Medrano—the male alpha of Clan Bouda and Andrea's former lover—die unexpectedly at a dig site, Andrea is assigned to investigate . . . and must work with Raphael. As her search for the killer leads her into the secret underbelly of supernatural Atlanta, Andrea knows that dealing with her feelings for Raphael might have to take a backseat to saving the world . . .

ABOUT THE AUTHORS

Ilona Andrews is the pseudonym for a husband-and-wife writing team. Ilona is a native-born Russian, and Andrew is a former communications sergeant in the U.S. Army. Contrary to popular belief, Andrew was never an intelligence officer with a license to kill, and Ilona was never the mysterious Russian spy who seduced him. They met in college, in English Composition 101, where Ilona got a better grade. (Andrew is still sore about that.) Together, Andrew and Ilona are the coauthors of the *New York Times* bestselling Kate Daniels urban-fantasy series and the romantic urban-fantasy novels of the Edge. They currently reside in Austin, Texas, with their two children and numerous pets. For sample chapters, news, and more, visit www.ilona-andrews.com.